IN MARCY'S
SHADOW

A NOVEL BY
Larry Weill

NORTH COUNTRY BOOKS, INC.
UTICA, NEW YORK

ISBN-10 1-59531-052-5
ISBN-13 978-1-59531-052-1

Design by Zach Steffen & Rob Igoe, Jr.

Library of Congress Cataloging-in-Publication Data

Names: Weill, Larry, author.
Title: In Marcy's shadow : a novel / by Larry Weill.
Description: Utica, New York : North Country Books, Inc., [2017]
Identifiers: LCCN 2017016899| ISBN 9781595310521 (acid-free paper) | ISBN
    1595310525 (acid-free paper)
Subjects: LCSH: New York (State)--Adirondack Mountains
    Region--History--Fiction. | Coins, American--History--Fiction. | Treasure
    troves--Fiction. | GSAFD: Adventure fiction. | Historical fiction.
Classification: LCC PS3623.E43225 I5 2017 | DDC 813/.6--dc23
LC record available at https://lccn.loc.gov/2017016899

North Country Books, Inc.
220 Lafayette Street
Utica, New York 13502
www.northcountrybooks.com

Contents

This book is dedicated to the men and women of our armed forces who protect our nation and our liberty, here and around the world. You are a continuous reminder that the independence we enjoy as a free nation comes with a cost, which you bear voluntarily and without reservation. We all owe you our heartfelt thanks for a debt that can never be repaid.

ACKNOWLEDGEMENTS

There are a great many people who collaborated in the research and development of this manuscript, and I owe all of them my heartfelt thanks. The entire staff of the Frank Stewart Room at the Rowan University Library in New Jersey was incredibly helpful in guiding me through their massive collection of the early American Mint records collected by Frank Stewart. They worked with me every step of the way as we searched their archives for material used throughout this story. Angela Stewart was also invaluable in her efforts in guiding me through thousands of historical documents in the development of this plot.

The staff of the American Philosophical Society was equally supportive, and worked with me for an entire week to extract information from the books and microfiche collections of the APS Research Library. Earl Spanner, Iren Snavely, and Valerie Lutz spent countless hours with me in their Philadelphia headquarters, helping to locate and reproduce copies of records and manuscripts that were central to the story of the main characters, Robert Patterson and his son, Robert M. Patterson. Without their assistance and expertise, this story could not have been written.

Karie Diethorn, chief curator, Independence National Park, provided information about the area around Independence Hall and the area surrounding the American Philosophical Society and the original Mint building.

George Cannon, town supervisor of the township of Newcomb, New York, provided many valuable insights into the history of the area surrounding the now-deserted mining community of Adirondac, New York, including details about the construction of the blast furnace and the operations of the mine in the 1800s. He also supplied a complete set of technical illustrations outlining the physical dimensions and structural attributes of the furnace that were critical to the storyline of this book. His ability to recall his experiences as a resident of Adirondac while supporting the National Lead Company mining operations also brought unique insights into this work.

Many thanks go to Anne V. Wolff for translating English passages into French text.

I would also like to applaud the Open Air Institute for their stellar work in helping to acquire lands of historical and ecological value in and around the Adirondack Park. Their acquisitions in the Tahawus Tract have served to preserve and maintain the McIntyre blast furnace, as well as the McNaughton House, which is so important to our national history.

Additional thanks go out to my two personal editors, Bruno Petrauskas and my daughter, Kelly Weill, for their countless hours of proofreading and editing my innumerable typographical and grammatical mishaps. Without their detailed and meticulous reviews, this work could not have come to fruition, and I am forever in their debt.

Last but not least, I'd like to thank Rob Igoe, Jr., and Zach Steffen of North Country Books, Inc., for their tireless efforts to move my manuscripts from simple drafts through to final products. Their pride and professionalism in their work is a source of constant inspiration to me, for which they have earned my eternal gratitude.

FOREWORD

Items of great value and mystery have always sparked the imagination of adventurers, regardless of time or place. For centuries, indeed for millennia, men and women have risked everything to chase after treasures, real or fabled, to the very ends of the earth. The thrill of the find and the fame that goes with it may even outweigh the monetary reward in the minds of many seekers. This story is based upon the fictional account of such a venture—the search for a lost cache of silver that represents the rarest of rare U.S. coins.

By the start of the year 1804, the U.S. Mint was already shutting down production of the silver dollar. The large, heavy coin was worth more overseas for the value of the silver itself, and thus was being exported and melted for recasting. Rather than continue to support the unfavorable flow of dollars overseas, President Jefferson decided to terminate the mintage of the dollars entirely. Thus, in 1804, the only silver dollars minted carried the previous year's date, as the 1803 die was used for about 19,570 dollar coins. This practice was considered normal in that era, although the mint had already been directed to cease the use of outdated coin dies some years earlier. Accordingly, no dollar coins struck in 1804 ever carried that date.

Anyone who has ever collected coins, regardless of their level of expertise, knows that the story does not end there. In fact, some years later, in 1834, President Jackson ordered a small number of sets of U.S. coins to be presented as gifts to Asian dignitaries and heads of state in exchange for advantageous trading conditions. One of the coins destined to be part of this set was to be the last silver dollar ever struck, which (according to the official records) was the 1804 coin. This, of course, created a dilemma for the director of the Mint, who had no silver dollars of that vintage to offer.

With that specification in mind, staff at the Mint rolled up their sleeves and produced an "original" 1804 die, and used it to produce a very limited number (about seven) of the 1804 silver dollars. These were either gifted to the selected VIPs, or returned (often via circuitous and mysterious routes) to the U.S. Mint. A few additional coins of the 1804 vintage were struck later, in the 1850s, under more dubious conditions; these "unauthorized re-strikes" were recalled by the Mint, although not all of them were successfully confiscated. Some of these specimens, often called "Type II or Type III" coins, did survive, and today carry as much value as some of the "original" Type I variants.

Regardless of the version, there is no coin in the world that is shrouded in more mystery and fable than the 1804 silver dollar. Dozens of tales exist, describing shipments of these coins that were placed onboard sailing vessels to the Orient, or other points of romantic interest around the world. In each of these stories, a disaster or some kind, whether natural or manmade, is to blame for the demise of the ship, leaving the coins to wallow in the sands of a foreign shore, awaiting discovery.

However, each and every one of these stories has since been discounted. A plethora of investigations, thorough in scope and exhaustive in breadth, have served to indicate that there was never an original strike of the 1804 silver dollar, and that the only genuine examples known today are those that were recreated in the Mint in the 1830s, plus those examples struck later, in the 1850s, under more duplicitous circumstances. As a result, the fifteen coins that survive today bearing the 1804 inscription are valued at amounts that truly boggle the mind. The more recent examples have sold at auctions, where the final price tag has exceeded $4 million.

With such an extreme premium placed on a piece of silver that weighs less than an ounce, there is little doubt why the coin is so famous and is so often counterfeited. Numerous examples of "overstrikes" have turned up over the years, where a skilled metallurgist has replaced the '3' in an 1803 dollar with a '4,' and thus created a temporary buzz of excitement. However, regardless of how skilled the craftsman, a detailed inspection by an experienced numismatist has always resulted in the exposure of the counterfeit specimen.

The story that follows is a fictitious accounting of the 1804 dollar, detailing its exciting voyage through time. Starting with the story of the esteemed Robert Patterson, the fourth director of the U.S. Mint under President Jefferson, it spins the tale of mystery as the "forbidden coins" are hidden, discovered, and then concealed once again in a location that would remain a secret for five generations. Considered an embarrassment by those in charge of the U.S. Mint, they were sealed away forever in a location that was believed to be beyond compromise.

From the nineteenth century, this story "fast forwards" to a modern cast of characters. Chris, Sean, and their band of friends are "everyday people" who have accomplished some amazing feats in their young lives. Fresh off an adventure that netted over six million dollars in gold bullion and resulted in the discovery of a new Adirondack cave, they are sucked rapidly into a plot with seemingly unsolvable clues.

This is a mystery that pulls us back to the earliest days of our country and to the birth of our federal Mint. It challenges our characters with codes and ciphers that have evaded decryption for centuries and puts them in the path of a cunning adversary who will use any tricks at his disposal to throw them off track. It is the story of investigation and intrigue, woven into the history and lore of the Adirondacks.

Before proceeding with this story, I feel a strong need to offer a few disclaimers for historical and moral reasons. First of all, while many characters in this book are genuine historic figures, the events described in this text are purely fictional. It is true that Robert Patterson and his son, Robert M. Patterson, were both early directors of the United States Mint. They had much in common, from their duties and interests to their respective careers in academia and public service. They were both highly esteemed men who contributed greatly to multiple disciplines, including math, science, and philosophy. However, the details of this saga, including their thoughts and actions in relation to their official functions in the Mint, have been completely invented to fit the plot of this story. This part of their story, as told through these pages, is purely the fabrication of the author.

Additionally, this text employs a number of Adirondack settings, including several of historic significance. These were selected due to my own personal love of the Adirondacks and my sentiments towards the lands and landmarks contained therein. However, the incidents in this book that occur within these locations are purely fictional and should not be construed to represent actual events. There is no treasure hidden in any of the structures or locations described within this text, nor should this be used as a suggestion of such a cache. The historical landmarks that serve as the setting for this text must be preserved forever, safe in their environs for future generations of Americans to experience.

With this in mind, I'd like to welcome the reader to prepare for a unique Adirondack adventure. This is a voyage of the imagination that starts in the city of Philadelphia over two hundred years ago and reaches its climax in a North Country ghost town that resides in the very shadow of Mount Marcy. This story will carry you back in time, as well as ahead into the future. You will look at parts of the Adirondacks as you have never done before. And hopefully, it will open your eyes to some of the wonderful places and historical landmarks that fill our "Blue Line" countryside with reminders of our storied past.

And now, welcome to the year 1804. Please enjoy the voyage.

PART I

THE MYTH OF 1804

CHAPTER 1

March 26, 1804 – U.S. Mint, Philadelphia, PA

Hiram Perry sensed the flash of the cane whipping through the air a split second before he felt the searing impact on his skin. It was a lightning strike delivered with incredible speed, given without warning or provocation. Hiram, a small man with mild manners and delicate limbs, fell backwards under the assault.

"I told ye to have this lot o' coins finished before we struck the bell for supper, and ye haven't put your mind to the job. Ye are a slacker, with no mind fer the job. I ought to take this cane to ye but good, and learn ye the lesson ye deserve!"

The words were delivered at full volume and close range by the foreman of the U.S. Mint, Nathaniel Grainger. A bull of a man, with thick muscles and a craggy expression, Grainger ruled his employees by force and intimidation. His shaggy red hair fell in a dense mop across his brow and down the back of his neck, lending more to his wild and untamed appearance. His very presence in a room was enough to silence the workers and send them into a fear-induced spree of frenetic productivity. The flask of whiskey he'd consumed since the noon meal served to further boost the volume of his voice.

"I'm…I'm sorry, Mr. Grainger, but the press jammed early on today, and we had problems with the dollar dies," said Hiram, looking fearfully at his boss. "It took me over an hour to get the first twenty silver dollars pressed, and even that was tough until Amos found the problem in the gearing. But we're moving much quicker now, and I promise you we'll reach our quota by nightfall."

"Damn right ye will," shouted Grainger, leaning over the much smaller man, forcing him back against the machinery table. "Or I'll give ye another smack on yer other side that will make the first one look like a peck on the cheek. Now GIT MOVING!" And with that, Grainger turned on his heel and stormed off to the hallway that led to the storeroom.

Hiram's hands shook as he turned his attention back to the press table, where blank coins, called planchets, stood stacked in rows while waiting to be pressed into silver dollars. The official policy of the U.S. Mint in Philadelphia did not include physical abuse of any sort. In fact, these early federal employees were all hired for their solid reputations and abilities to work long hours with little thought of the creature comforts. Their fifteen-hour workdays were spent, for the most part, in silence as they went about their duties. Yet they all lived in fear of the man who knew just how far he could go without incurring the attention of the Mint director, Elias Boudinot, or the other higher officers of the facility.

To be named as an employee of the Mint was an honor for the men who worked inside these buildings. It was one of the very first federal complexes in Philadelphia outside of Independence Hall. Located at the intersection of Seventh and Filbert Streets, the site was acquired by John Rittenhouse, the first director of the Mint. The original building located there had been a whiskey distillery, which was demolished to make room for the construction of the three-building Mint complex. Groundbreaking commenced in July, 1792, and work progressed rapidly. By September of that same year, the building was ready for outfitting with coining machinery. Full operations followed shortly thereafter.

Life inside the Mint was a dreary affair, with harsh work conditions and insufficient lighting. None of the men who were actually engaged in the physical production of the coins displayed any emotions as they went about their tasks of rolling the gold and silver into sheets of uniform thickness, punching out the round planchets, and stamping them into coins of various denominations. The press was a screw-type device that was handled by a pair of workers, putting pressure on the planchets with an engraved die until the coin was formed. It was slow, tedious work, and the coins were stamped individually, one at a time, in a never-ending parade of repetitive motion.

In back of the press stood Amos Parson, a journeyman laborer who was employed to help with the routine operations of the shop, plus the lesser-skilled tasks of general maintenance. He was known for having a temper of his own, although his youth and lack of seniority served to hold his emotions in check most of the time. Still, he hated the foreman as much as anyone and swore that he would someday, if given the chance, put him in his place. It was a thought he entertained often, emboldened by his own consumption of alcohol on the job. For a lad of twenty-two, he drank often, and in volume. There were many times that he consumed a pint of rum before noon, and his temper became even worse after his imbibing.

"I'd like to have that bastard alone in the assay room for five minutes," growled Amos, his face reddened with anger. "Just five minutes. I'd take that cane of his and turn his backside into bloodied flesh." His face quivered with emotion, as his hands grasped the handle of the screw press.

"Rest easy, son," countered Hiram. "It's not worth it. He's the foreman, and he's our boss. He's pretty fair, and he's never bothered anyone when he's sober and the job's getting done. It's just his way."

As Hiram spoke, he tenderly massaged the outside of his arm, where Grainger's cane had left an ugly, oozing welt. It was an unpleasant reminder of the foreman's meanness, and it further served to infuriate his younger colleague. Amos could feel the blood coursing through his veins as he watched his friend suffer in silence.

"Well, you might feel OK with his ravings and beatings, but I don't have to," retorted Amos. "Just let that old cuss try that on me, just once, and I'll show him!"

"Come on, lad, let's get back to work," replied Hiram in a calm voice.

"We'll get these blanks stamped out, and then we'll get the rest of the sheets rolled out for tomorrow's run before we knock off. It'll all be well, lad. It'll all be well."

As Hiram spoke, he placed another blank planchet into the screw press and took hold of an extended arm of the machinery. It was a large, sinister-looking device, with two long lever arms designed to provide the tremendous torque that was required to stamp a blank circle of silver into a United States silver dollar. It required a pair of men to operate the machine, and Hiram had been working with Amos on this particular press for over a month. Some of the larger rolling and cutting machines relied on horses to exert the shear amount of brute force needed for the job.

With Hiram pushing on one of the lever arms and Amos on the other, they began their endless circling, watching as the two sides of the die pressed into the coin and stamped the familiar pattern into the metal. It took about twelve rotations of the lever arms to fully impress the front and back designs into each coin, although Hiram no longer needed to count the rotations. He had enough years on the job to feel when the dies had reached the required point of pressure.

Hiram was about ready to back off and reverse the direction of the rotations, although he sensed that Amos was still moving in the original direction.

"Hey, that's enough," said Hiram, motioning to the cylindrical stamping die in the middle of the machine. "That one's finished. Now let's back her up!"

Amos, though, seemed lost in his own world. His mind was still seething over the endless tirades of the foreman, and he scarcely heard the directions given by his coworker. He pictured Grainger's face close to his, the screaming, the belittling, and the bullying. Although he was not as big a man as Grainger, he had the youthful strength and energy that came from his upbringing on a farm. That energy surged through his body as he pushed against the press with all his might, oblivious to all else. Teeth gritting and muscles bulging, he was still leaning into the equipment with everything he had.

Hiram was opening his mouth to repeat his command when he heard the ominous sound of the distressed die shatter. It wasn't loud enough to attract attention beyond the pressing room. But to the trained ear, it was a distinctive sound that signaled the irreparable fracture of the stamping die.

The sharp crack of the steel interrupted Amos' rage, and he turned to Hiram with a quizzical expression. "What was that?" he asked, cocking his head toward the main screw shaft. "That die can't be more than a week old. We changed that one out early last week, didn't we?"

"Yes, Amos, we did at that. But you overtorqued the turn bar to the point where the die caps were pressing steel-on-steel. I tried to stop you, but you were deaf to my voice. Let's open her up and take a look. Maybe Arthur can reforge the steel, if the damage isn't too bad."

After reversing the turns on the press and removing the deeply stamped silver dollar, Hiram carefully removed the apparatus holding the coin die in place. He and Amos carried the heavy piece up the dark and narrow flight of stairs to the administrative office, where Arthur Snyder maintained his work bench. Arthur was the chief die forger, and the most experienced man in the Mint on die repair and preservation. He had worked on Colonial coinage for twenty years prior to becoming a Mint employee, and he knew his business inside and out.

Snyder scowled as he leaned over the damaged die, his head tilted over an eyepiece for greater magnification. He turned the die around in his hands and adjusted the position of the lantern that was hooked to a beam over his desk. For a good three minutes, he said nothing, just rotated the die to view it from all angles. Then, he placed the cylinder on his desk and removed his spectacles. His eyes were deeply set and bloodshot, making him appear even older than his seventy-one years indicated.

"I'd say that this one is fractured beyond the point of further use," said Snyder, rubbing his hand over the length of his thick grey beard. "It's got a pressure crack that runs across the entire surface of the obverse pattern, and it is so deep that it will split in half as soon as it's put back on this press. But the rest of it looks pretty new, so whoever cranked this last must have really put their back into it."

Hiram decided to sidestep the issue, since he didn't want to put his assistant on report for negligence. "Could we get a replacement for it in time to get back in production within the next hour? We've got a deadline to meet before day's end, and we can't afford to lose much more time."

Snyder looked up at the two mean wearily, then raised himself slowly from his chair. He came around to the front of his desk and put his hand on Hiram's shoulder.

"I'm afraid, young man, that this puts us into a bit of a spot. You see, it isn't nearly as easy as that. Please allow me to explain. When we created the 1803 dies, we made enough of them to last throughout the entire calendar year, with a possible overlap into the beginning of 1804. Then we were in the process of cutting a full order of 1804 dies, but we got an order from the President to scrap the whole batch."

Hiram looked at Snyder with a mixture of surprise and irritation. "Scrap the whole batch? What are we suppose to cut the new coins with? Our teeth? We need either a replacement '03 die, or one of the new '04 dies, and we need it NOW."

"And I'm telling you that you can't have another '03, because there aren't any more to be had," said Snyder. "You've just ripped apart the last of the casts. I'm not blaming you, son. But there isn't much I can do to help you either."

Hiram seemed to wilt inside his shoes as he listened to the chief coiner. He knew from his official record that there were supposed to be twenty thousand of the dollar coins stamped and ready for the banks before production was halted. So far, only slightly more than sixteen thousand had been completed. Somehow, he had to find a way to finish the job, or he would incur the wrath of Nathan Grainger. It was not a pretty alternative.

"Arthur, good sir, I need your help," pleaded Hiram. "Officially, it is 1804, and we've been using the 1803 dies all along. But it's March now, and our formal directive states that we're supposed to stamp the actual year onto the coin. That means we're supposed to be using the 1804 die anyway. Isn't that right?"

"Well, that's partially correct," replied Snyder. "But Jefferson's executive directive stated that we were to cease coinage of all dollar coins, since most of them are ending up overseas anyway. So yes, we were supposed to produce twenty thousand dollar coins this year. But I've been ordered to finish the whole lot of them without spending additional funding on any new dies, because they are too expensive to cut for a coin that's being eliminated anyway. That's why we've stuck with the 1803 dies as long as we have."

"I beg of you, sir, please allow me the use of the new die, just to complete the final run," implored Hiram. "It won't take more than another couple days, and we'll return it to your shop in pristine condition. I'll personally oversee every turn of the screw press myself. Please!"

Snyder looked at the desperate eyes and harried expression on Hiram Perry's face, and he understood. As a youngster, he had worked for his share of cruel and unbending task masters who would think nothing of beating an employee for the simplest oversight. He knew that those men working for Grainger lived in fear, and he felt compassion for Hiram's angst.

"I'll tell you what," said Snyder. "I'm not going to give you the 1804 master die, but I do have one production copy that I cut just before we received Jefferson's edict. I've got it locked away in the safe. If you'll promise to take extra special care of it and return it directly to me by the end of the month, I'll allow you to use it. I'll just clear it with the director, and he'll smooth things over with Grainger. OK?"

"Thank you," said Hiram, letting out a relieved gasp. "Thank you! You have no idea how much you're helping me."

"Oh, I think I might have a pretty good idea," chuckled the old-timer as he opened the safe. "Just remember me when your missus bakes up an extra loaf of that wonderful cornbread, OK? I've dreamed about that since last summer."

"You've got yourself a deal," said Hiram, picking up the new die and moving toward the doorway. "And Amos and I have got a lot of work ahead of us. Let's go, son."

Hiram and Amos descended the flight of stairs more by feel than by sight. It was lit by a single tallow candle, which barely illuminated the middle of the staircase. They then proceeded down the hallway and back into the press room, where Amos immediately began setting the new die into the immense press.

As Amos aligned the die with the center press post, Hiram moved over to the day record book and recorded the change out of the equipment. This was not an official log book; the legal record books were maintained in the administration office, and then transferred to the Treasury Building. However, this ledger, which was maintained by the pressman of the day, served to record the smaller events that transpired from shift to shift. Most of these notations were of little interest to the director and officers of the Mint, although they were always available at a later date if such details were needed. Generally, each day record book would last for about three months before it was filled, after which Grainger replaced it with a new one. Grainger himself stored the old books, although no one knew where, as they were seldom ever reviewed once filled.

In his characteristically small but flowing handwriting, Hiram recorded the event: "Monday, March 26, 1804: Last of 1803 dies is damaged beyond repair. Replacing with new cut die to complete production. Count 16,950." He then stepped back over to the press and inspected Amos' work.

Amos, meanwhile, had inserted a blank planchet into the die, and had independently operated the lever arm to create the first coin of the new batch. "How's that look?" asked the young assistant, holding up the new dollar.

The large silver piece reflected the light from the overhead lantern as Hiram flipped the coin over to view the front and back sides, noting the sharp detail and the evenly milled edges. "That's fine, lad. You do nice work," he murmured quietly.

"Do you think anyone will be bothered that we had to use the 1804 die to finish the lot?" asked Amos, as he placed a carton on the side table to hold the inventory of the evening's press work. "After all, you heard what Mr. Snyder said; we were supposed to finish the allotment of 1804 dollars with the same 1803 die, by orders of the president."

"Don't worry, lad," replied Hiram. "They'll all go on the same Treasury Department production report, which is the only official record of what we do here in the Mint. This log book is just an unofficial accounting of our shift work, so no one will know the difference. Unless Thomas Jefferson himself ends up with a piece, he'll never know what happened. And to tell you the truth, I doubt that he cares. Now, let's get to work here and get this press moving! With the evening shift pitching in, we should be able to get back on schedule before the end of the day."

With Amos and Hiram working feverishly until the early evening, and another crew taking over until the eight o'clock bell, they were able to produce enough coins to appease the ever-angry supervisor. And, true to his word, Hiram personally ensured that the quota on the dollar coins was achieved by the scheduled deadline. He was aided by the fact that the requirement to actually stamp the full 20,000 was reduced by a small percentage, and the 1804 production requirement was reduced to 19,570.

Hiram's final entry into the day record was simple. It read, "Completed 1804 allotment of one-dollar denomination coins on March 28, 1804, at 2:35 PM. Returning die to Mr. Snyder's vault for permanent storage. Commencing production of half-dollar coins at 3:10 PM. Ongoing use of same die as last week. Light wear, high quality impressions."

Then, without giving it another thought, the staff of the coin Press Room resumed their work, unaware that they had created one of the greatest fortunes and mysteries in American history.

The argument escalated in volume between the two men, each making his remarks more vociferously than the other. Henry Voight and Silas Montegard were both high-ranking officers of the Mint, tasked with oversight of the production and distribution from the federal facility. Voight was the chief coiner, while Montegard was the operations manager. With the exception of the Director, they were the two highest paid employees of the Mint.

As they fought, their voices echoed from the storeroom and along the roughly carved passageway. Only the basement setting of the debate kept the shouting from reverberating throughout the rest of the building. Between them rested a moderate-sized strongbox, filled approximately two-thirds of the way to capacity with newly minted silver coins.

"And who, in God's name, authorized the use of the 1804 die for these dollars?" demanded Voight. "I gave strict instructions for that cast to remain in storage and never see the light of day!" Henry Voight had been at the Mint since it opened in 1792, and he was as authoritative a figure as could be imagined. His jaw jutted forward, and he looked down his nose at the shorter, yet stockier metallurgy expert.

"I don't know, and to tell you the truth, I don't care. We had an order to fill and we filled it," countered Montegard. "Our production request was for almost 20,000 pieces, so that's what the boys in the press room made. And I don't care whether they used a die that said 1803, 1804, or 1215," his last comment being a sarcastic reference to the year the Magna Carta was signed.

The remark infuriated Voight, who considered this the last straw in their tenuous relationship. His facial features quivered as he moved his face directly in front of his colleague's, so closely that their noses were almost in contact with one another. He could feel Montegard's moist breath on his face as he uttered his barely controlled response.

"Well then, you, my good fellow, may have the pleasure of informing the director himself that we have selectively ignored President Jefferson's directive. And the consequences for your actions shall fall on your shoulders, and your shoulders alone. Now good day, and good riddance!" Voight finished his diatribe and turned abruptly for the door. He wasted no time striding through the doorway and into the stairwell back to his office. The debate was over.

The meeting between Silas Montegard and Director Elias Boudinot never took place. Boudinot, the third appointee to fill the role of director of the U.S. Mint, was a meticulous man with a keen eye for details. His knowledge of the science of metallurgy and machinery was superb, but he excelled in his job due to his unparalleled accounting habits. He went "by the book," and tracked every ounce of metal that passed through the refinery. However, it appeared his tenure in the position would be limited, as the rumors were already flying that he would be stepping down from the job within the next year.

With this in mind, Montegard prudently decided to segregate the 1804 dollars into a separate bin placed at the bottom of the distribution stockpile, and then to rotate them monthly so they were always in the "reserve stock" supply. By doing this, he could effectively hide them in plain view until the director was gone. He was still unsure what he would do at that point, although he felt certain that his new boss would be more lenient on this transgression that his current one.

As it happened, Montegard's plan was effective. The dollars that weren't supposed to exist were never discovered by Elias Boudinot. Within a year, he left the Mint and retired to a newly-built home in New Jersey, where he pursued numerous interests including religion, education, and human rights. His successor to the job, Robert Patterson, would not arrive on the scene until early in 1806, and there was little face-to-face turnover between the two men. Even if there had been an extended period of time when Boudinot could have tutored Patterson on the nuances of the job, he still couldn't have informed him of the 1804 dollars, as he didn't know of their existence. Accordingly, they remained buried in the recesses of the storage room, part of an inventory that became less relevant as the monthly mintage figures expanded.

Montegard himself was erased from the scene within the next year. In the summer of 1805, an outbreak of yellow fever (which had closed the Mint on several occasions) struck suddenly and severely. Montegard was smitten with the virus, which was accompanied by a high fever and chills. Just as his doctor thought he was entering recovery, he relapsed into a more severe phase of the disease and became jaundiced from liver dam-age. He held out for another few weeks, too ill to move from his bed, and he died at the end of the month of August without ever revealing his secret about the hidden cache in the basement of the Mint. It was never mentioned again, and the memory of the 1804 silver dollars soon faded to black.

CHAPTER 2

January, 1807 – U.S. Mint, Philadelphia, PA

Robert Patterson mopped a silk handkerchief across his sweaty brow and sank into a sturdy wooden chair. He was fatigued from the week-long exercise of inventorying the Mint's three buildings, a job he had wanted to tackle before ever assuming the directorship. It was a dirty, time-consuming task that involved digging through countless drawers, boxes, and storage rooms. Some of these eternally-dark corners of the facility had accumulated records and other materials for over fifteen years without ever seeing the light of day.

Patterson had decided that he could not effectively manage the facility without knowing what materials were maintained in every room on the site. He could have delegated this task to a subordinate officer, as much of it was routine categorizing and recording. However, he decided to perform the work himself, with the assistance of Ben Gardner, who was a clerk to the treasurer, plus one additional laborer.

The three men had spent the previous hour working their way through a dank storage area below the main coinage press rooms. The laborer had removed crate after crate from the stacks of materials, most of which contained die-making hardware in various states of disrepair. A separate corner of the room held boxes with small denomination coins, which had been counted and stored in rolls. These coins, which were still maintained on the books of the treasury, had served as a form of reserve in the earlier days of the Mint. However, they were no longer used for any purpose and had been largely forgotten by the current staff of the facility.

"Make a note of the contents, Ben, and then let's get this stuff out of our cellar and into circulation," said Robert Patterson to the clerk. "No need to be holding anything down here anymore. We're not a bank, you know."

Ben nodded as he made a notation on a sheaf of papers. Thorough and meticulous, he felt embarrassed that there wasn't an existing inventory of the Mint on hand. That was supposedly one of his duties, along with maintaining the financial records for the Treasury Department. Yet, his new boss hadn't made reference to this, nor had he criticized anything that had transpired prior to his directorship. In fact, even though Patterson only served in his role as director on a part-time basis, he seemed to have a better grasp on the daily operations of the Mint than most of his full-time officers.

Robert Patterson had served in a number of capacities prior to assuming his current role in Philadelphia. A former soldier and instructor, he was an intellectual who was well educated in mathematics and the natural sciences. He went on to become a professor of mathematics at the University of Pennsylvania, where he later served as vice provost until stepping down in 1813. It was during the height of his prominence as a professor at the university that President Jefferson asked him to become the director of the U.S. Mint in Philadelphia. Jefferson assured him that his duties would be part-time and would not encumber his academic work at the college.

Patterson was also involved in countless other pursuits, such as philosophy, physics, and astronomy. He corresponded often with President Jefferson, not only on matters of the Mint, but also about science, mathematics, history, and more. He was a highly respected man of his day, and his works appeared in a variety of publications. He also served as president of the American Philosophical Society, an organization founded by Benjamin Franklin for the advancement of study within the disciplines of the sciences and humanities.

Turning their attention back to the stack of boxes, Patterson and Gardner watched as the laborer grappled with the last box in the pile. It was the bottom crate in the stack, with a lid that had been nailed over the solid wood siding. It was extremely heavy, and it required the clerk's assistance to move it into the beam of the lantern.

As the director and the clerk watched, the laborer applied a beveled crowbar to the sides of the lid. One by one, he slowly pried the nails from the top of the crate until the cover fell to the side, exposing the contents of the box. Inside were row upon row of silver dollar coins, stacked fifty to a pile, filling the bulk of the container. They looked brand new, which was not surprising since they almost certainly had never entered circulation.

"Hmmm, now this is unusual," said Gardner, leaning over for a better view. "We've never kept this many dollar coins reserved for anything, even when we used this place to store currency for the treasury. There must be a story behind this somewhere."

Patterson quietly looked on from the other side of the storeroom. He remained expressionless as he bowed his head thoughtfully. "Let's get Henry Voight down here." Then, turning to the laborer, he said "James, would you please run up to Mr. Voight's office and see if he could stop down for a moment? Perhaps he could enlighten us as to why these have been left here."

The laborer quickly departed to retrieve the chief coiner of the Mint. As he exited the room, Patterson turned his attention back to the silver dollars in the box.

"These look as though they came off the press this morning," said Patterson, holding up a coin at eye level for inspection. "There's no doubt they were stored here immediately after being struck. But why?"

"I have no idea, sir," replied Gardner. "Perhaps they were defective for some reason, and they were scheduled for melting and recasting."

"No, that couldn't be the case," reasoned Patterson. "If they'd been defective, they'd have been immediately surveyed, and then impounded into the refining and smelting building. Anyway, look at this strike; it's absolutely perfect. I'm not an expert on this yet, but if I had to venture a guess, I'd say that this coin was struck on a brand new die. There's not a sign of wear anywhere. It's flawless."

"Then why, sir, do you think this box has been abandoned in this manner? Are you thinking that perhaps it was hidden for some reason, or just stored and forgotten?"

"I'm not sure of anything," replied Patterson. "I'm only guessing that whoever put them here did so for a reason and then probably forgot about them. Either they were scheduled for a shipment that was cancelled, or someone simply didn't want them to be found."

Patterson's thought process was interrupted by the sounds of footsteps approaching through the dim subterranean light. The laborer entered the wooden doorframe, followed by the tall figure of the chief coiner.

"Hello, Henry," said Patterson, smiling warmly at his highest subordinate officer. "I trust you are well today."

"Yes, sir, Mr. Patterson, I am. And now, what can I do for you today?"

Patterson motioned downward with his arm as he spoke. "It appears we have a bit of a mystery on our hands," he began. "We were finishing our inventory of the coinage reserve and storage room when we came across this container. It's a single crate with between twenty-five hundred and three thousand silver dollars, all apparently coined within the last few years. We have no theories as to why they were placed here and never sent into circulation, and we thought that perhaps you might have some information to enlighten us."

The distinguished coining and engraving expert knelt down beside the box and lifted a number of samples from the interior. One by one, he held them up to the lamplight, turning them around to observe the details and die marks. He examined at least a half dozen coins in this manner, all performed in cathedral silence as the other men stood and watched. Finally, he stood and straightened to his full height, massaging his lower back as he did. He did not look pleased.

"Gentlemen, I'm afraid that what we have here is the last legacy of Mr. Silas Montegard," said Voight, his voice sounding tired. "May he rest in peace."

"Please do explain," said Patterson, looking a bit confused. "Are you saying that Silas intentionally placed these coins here in a sealed box prior to his death?"

"Yes, Mr. Patterson, that is exactly what I am saying," said Voight, his voice becoming more focused and authoritative. "You see, before he passed away, Mr. Montegard and I had a rather contentious exchange on this very subject. I hadn't known that he had permitted this strike to occur. I'm assuming that you noticed the 1804 dates on these coins, correct?"

"No, Henry, I'm sorry, but I overlooked that detail in my brief examination. Please explain the implications of that particular date."

"Well, my sir, we were placed in quite the situation that year," explained Voight. "We were given a quota of about twenty thousand silver dollar coins to place into circulation, among the other silver and copper pieces. And yet the president also decreed that the last year of dollar coins should be 1803, with none struck in 1804 or beyond. Mr. Boudinot decided that we would meet the quota by using the 1803 dies, but only until the last die had irreparably broken. At that point, we would claim that we had reached our quota, regardless of whether we had attained the twenty thousand limit or not."

"So I take it that your dies expired before the quota was reached?" queried Patterson.

"That is correct. However, the story didn't end there. The pressman went directly to Mr. Snyder, our die forger, and obtained the only new 1804 die that was cast from the original mold. He didn't tell another soul; he just minted enough dollars to meet the original quota, and then returned the die to Snyder. All this happened with Montegard's tacit approval. It was almost as though they had worked out a deal in advance, regardless of the adverse circumstances."

"But from the sound of it, the pressman did nothing wrong," stated Patterson. "The errors in judgment were made at Snyder's level and above."

"Yes sir," replied Voight, clearly wishing to keep the discussion objective. "Mr. Snyder shouldn't have permitted the die to be used, as he knew of the executive order. And Mr. Montegard knew of the restriction as well, yet he permitted the activity to proceed in order to supply the stated number of dollar pieces to the Mint without producing additional 1803 dies."

Patterson looked down at the coins again, evaluating the ramifications of their discovery at this late date. Then he looked back at Voight and fixed him with a steady gaze. "And you are certain that this is the origin of these coins? You are one hundred percent certain that these were the dollars struck in 1804 using the new die?"

"Yes, I am," replied Voight, "as sure as I am that my own name is Henry Voight, your humble servant."

Patterson stared at the man for another moment, observing his every movement and intonation. Then, he placed his hand on Voight's shoulder and smiled. "Thank you, sir. You have helped us to clear away the mist of the unknown from this riddle. We can now settle on the most logical and practical solution to this problem, which appears to be very minor indeed."

"Thank you, sir," said Voight, relieved that his role in this inquisition appeared to be over. "Please let me know if I can be of further assistance."

"I most certainly will, Henry," replied Patterson. "You may return to your work now."

The elderly gentleman nodded to his employer, then turned and left the room. Patterson smiled again and then shifted his gaze back toward the other two men, signaling his readiness to recommence their inventory. However, despite his carefree mannerism, he realized that he was in a bit of a predicament. His Mint had a large supply of coins on hand that were struck against the President's orders. He couldn't release them into circulation, since the 1804 date was clearly stamped on the front of each piece for all to see. And he feared melting them, because they had already been included on the 1804 Treasury Department production record, and there were no additional 1803 dies with which to restrike the coins. It was, indeed, a problem with very few solutions. In fact, Patterson could think of only one way out.

Robert Patterson was a soldier-citizen cast from the old-school mold. An early student of the military sciences, he served as an instructor in the pre-Revolutionary era to ready the American forces for the coming war with the armies of England. He was firmly indoctrinated in the ideals of responsibility and accountability, and he held himself in strict adherence to these principles. The United States Mint was under his command, and his alone. Regardless of who had been in charge when the dollar coins were struck, it was now his watch. Once they discovered those coins, he naturally assumed responsibility for all that had transpired. It was his turn to lead, and he would correct all prior mistakes. He thanked his lucky stars that he had the financial wherewithal to achieve it.

Although not rich, Patterson had accumulated some degree of wealth, and he had acquired properties and other commercial interests across the region. And so, when confronted with this dilemma, Robert Patterson quickly decided on a solution that would bring closure to the event. Over the course of the following few weeks, he liquidated a few of his holdings and collected the resulting sums in the form of ten dollar gold pieces, called "American Eagles." He stored these coins in his own private vault inside the Mint until he had a collection of over 260 pieces. He then used these coins, in even exchange, to trade for the silver dollars they had found in the storage locker that January afternoon.

Patterson completed this transaction with the cooperation and concurrence of the Mint's treasurer and clerk, each confirming that the values balanced exactly. In doing so, he fully believed that he was merely exchanging one form of currency for another, and in the process hiding the ambitious and yet erroneous undertakings of the previous Mint administration. It was a noble deed performed for the highest motives. And yet, on that one afternoon in the fall of 1807, Robert Patterson became an unknowing accomplice in the greatest mystery of United States coinage when he purchased the entire inventory of the famous 1804 silver dollar. Over the next two centuries, it would become the most valuable and coveted coin in the world, with an auction price of several million dollars. It would have been a great investment, had he lived to see the day.

Following his purchase of the dollars, Patterson moved them into his personal vault, which was also located in the cellar of the Mint building. It was a space similar to the rest of the basement – dark, dank, with a pervasive odor of both mold and machinery oil. The room had no lighting of its own, relying on hand-carried lanterns for illumination. Patterson held the only key to this chamber, although the night watchman had a master key that would permit access to every space in the facility.

Once the unique silver dollars were off the official books, they became even more of a problem for the practical-minded director. They were paid for in full and were now his property. However, he could not use them for his own expenditures, as they could never be released into circulation. Patterson also considered them a potential source of embarrassment, a scandal, of sorts, that he did not create, and yet for which he assumed personal responsibility.

Within a month's time, Patterson decided to seal the box in its original condition. Before doing so, he drafted a note, which he would place on top of the coins. It was a short, simple letter that was to serve as an explanation of the coins' origins, in case they were discovered after his death. However, he was uncertain to whom he should address the correspondence. He felt the need to draft a letter of apology to his president, Thomas Jefferson, to whom he directly reported on all matters of the Mint. However, he also supposed that Jefferson would no longer be in office at the time when this letter would be read.

Patterson decided to draft the document to address a dual audience. He would offer it as an explanation to Jefferson, if he was still in office (and interested at all), as well as to the executor of his own estate, since the coins were now his property. In either case, the letter would serve as an explanation and an apology and would be sealed forever with the load of silver.

Patterson was thoughtful and introspective as he penned the note, his quill pen moving deliberately across the sheet of paper. He worked slowly, selecting his words with individual care, as though he realized the historical significance of the text. His words read as follows:

Tuesday, September 22, 1807

To my President, and to my Executor,
The contents of this parcel are the result of an error committed by the United States Mint. These coins exist only through a lack of commitment to accuracy and direction by myself, your humble servant. Had I to conduct these matters of the U.S. Mint coinage anew, I would have served in this capacity with stronger oversight and increased devotion to detail of task. For this, I profess my extraordinary sorrow. May it please you to be advised that I have made personal compensation for this silver from my own personal assets, and that the United States Government has suffered no loss from my poor judgment. I remain your loyal and obedient servant.

Robert Patterson
Director, United States Mint

After completing the letter to his satisfaction, Patterson placed the sheet on top of the coins and fitted the solid wooden lid onto the top of the crate. Above his head, the single oil lantern swung slowly from side to side, casting a swaying shadow across the floor. He sat on a low wooden chair, half crouched beside the sturdy wooden Mint box. On the floor next to the container sat a small pile of square iron nails, rough in appearance yet superior in their holding ability. Patterson hammered the first nail into place, repeatedly pounding the nail head down until it was completely buried in the wooden surface. Then, he picked up the next and hammered it into the other side of the lid until the nail head was obscured from view. He continued this process, burying nail after nail into the box, when in fact the first two would have sufficed to hold the top in place. It was obvious that this regimen was not intended to secure the lid for temporary storage. In fact, whoever would eventually open this parcel would have to do so by destroying the box with either a large crowbar or a sledgehammer.

Patterson was alone as he entombed the silver coins in the cellar of the Mint building that afternoon. It was a very physical task, as the wood was strong and the nails were roughly shaped. He noticed that his shirt was damp with sweat, his breath heavy and labored as he finished striking the last nail in place.

As he sat back on his seat to inspect his work, his eyes took in the other contents of the room, which held his own personal effects. Numerous boxes were stacked in piles, holding a variety of belongings including his notebooks and ledgers, correspondence with other educators and men of science, and even a few instruments for performing navigational and surveying procedures. Each box was labeled clearly on the side panels: "Property of Robert Patterson, Director, U.S. Mint."

Using extreme force, Patterson edged the heavy box against the outer wall of the vault, where he stacked a number of other crates on top of it to form a new pile. He wasn't overly concerned that anyone would steal this box, since it was in a locked room, and no one really cared what was stored in the cellar anyway. Patterson had seen multiple storage sites where his predecessors, dating back to the first Mint director, David Rittenhouse, had deposited items that had never been moved. He left these in place, in case they were ever reclaimed by their original owners.

Finally, after completing his labors, Patterson stepped outside of the vault and replaced the heavy lock on the door latch. Once the hasp had snapped into place, he gave it a quick tug to ensure that it was secure. Then he wiped the sweat from his brow and brushed his hands together to remove the dust from the cellar floor. It was a somewhat symbolic act, for just as he brushed away the dust and debris from the store room, so did he clear his mind of the sealed box containing the silver dollars. The coins had reached their terminal resting place for the remainder of their tenure in the Mint. The box was never again touched by human hands until it was removed from the building almost two decades later.

Robert Patterson lived to serve another seventeen years in office, filling the director's position until the middle of 1824. He also continued in his duties as vice-provost of the University of Pennsylvania, president of the American Philosophical Society, and later as the founder of the Franklin Institute of Philadelphia. However, his role in this story had reached its conclusion. Patterson died quietly on July 22, 1824, having been relieved by Samuel Moore as director of the United States Mint. His death marked the end of a truly remarkable life, which was well chronicled and uniquely accomplished.

Before his death, Patterson knew he had to take care of one last personal matter. He had to find a way to dispose of the 1804 dollars in such a way that they could remain hidden forever, even though he no longer possessed the strength of body to do so himself. All others who knew of their existence had predeceased him. Henry Voight had died of natural causes almost ten years earlier. The treasurer and the clerk had also passed away, one due to a farming accident, the other succumbing to the scourge of yellow fever. The two pressmen, Hiram Perry and Amos Parson, were told that the dollars had been melted back into silver for recasting, so they were likewise uninformed.

On his deathbed, Robert Patterson turned to the one man he knew he could trust to preserve the family honor. The man he selected to keep the faith and do the right thing was his very own flesh and blood, his son Robert Maskell (M.) Patterson. In subdued tones, his voice attenuated by age and disease, the elderly Patterson passed along the incredible story of the case in the vault and why it meant so much to him and to the family. The son listened, nodding his understanding at his father's thoughts and advice. He made mental notes of the placement of the cache in the cellar crypt. And all the while, his mind whirled with ideas of how best to carry out his father's wishes.

"Of course, Father, please do not give it another thought," Robert M. said to his father. "I will carry out your intentions, and this box with all its contents will remain unseen for eternity."

"Thank you, Son. Thank you," repeated Patterson, over and over again. His hands trembled as he grasped those of his son, gratefully, as the last ounce of strength seeped from his body. "Thank you. Thank…" and then his eyes closed forever.

Robert M. Patterson, son, devoted student, teacher, and protégé of his father, bowed his head until it rested on the hand of his parent, and he wept. In his sorrow, he vowed to keep his promise to preserve the secret forever.

He was a good man, and he almost lived up to his end of the deal.

CHAPTER 3

1824-1850 – The Myth Lives On

Robert M. Patterson didn't just follow his father's footsteps; he walked inside them every step of the way. Born in 1787 to Robert Patterson and his wife, Amy Hunter Ewing, he quickly distinguished himself as a budding scholar. By the time he reached the tender age of 14, he had already devised an ingenious cipher code which he used to write a letter to President Jefferson. The president was unable to crack this code, and neither were other cryptographers for over two hundred years. He would go on to use this code repeatedly for providing secrecy to his most sensitive documents. He possessed an unquenchable thirst for knowledge, and was an avid student of the physical sciences like his father. He supplemented his initial college education with additional years of schooling in France, where he furthered his studies of the natural sciences. His strongest interests were astronomy and astrophysics, in which he published several scientific papers at a very early age.

Robert M. Patterson's similarities to his father did not end with his interests. He became a professor of mathematics and chemistry at the University of Pennsylvania and served in that capacity while his father was still filling the role of vice-provost. Likewise, he was nominated for membership in the American Philosophical Society and was later elected to the position of vice president of that organization. Most striking of all was his appointment to serve as the sixth director of the United States Mint. The comparisons are many, with the son following the career of the father at every turn. However, many of these events had not yet transpired at the time of his father's death.

Although Robert M. Patterson had been told of the crate with the 1804 dollars by his dying father in 1824, it was another year before he was able to remove this container from the Mint building. Since they were Patterson's personal belongings, they were not inspected during the moving process.

The younger Patterson had the box transported to the cellar of his residence in Philadelphia, where it would lie in the dark for another quarter century. He briefly conducted his own research into the pedigree of the silver dollars, but because his father had described the contraband contents of the container, as well as his own embarrassment over their existence, Robert M. never saw the need to pursue the matter further. The box would remain hidden within the confines of his home, where the coins would eventually become forgotten altogether.

In 1835, Robert M. Patterson accepted an appointment to relieve Samuel Moore as director of the United States Mint. The position, which was offered by President Andrew Jackson, had grown significantly since the days of his father. The directorship now required the full-time attention of a competent manager with skills in business, production, metallurgy and refining, accounting, and other related fields. President Jackson recognized these attributes in Patterson and never seriously considered another candidate while making his selection.

Patterson immediately accepted the directorship offer, and in the process stepped down from his latest teaching position at the University of Virginia. His academic knowledge in the natural sciences, which extended to chemistry and metallurgy, would be called upon as he stepped into his new role at the Mint. He was also highly interested in upgrading the processes and equipment in the art of producing coins, and the timing was right for both. New ideas, such as more efficient mining techniques and the use of steam power to run the coin presses, were just being introduced to the industrialized nation, and Patterson wished to capitalize on these improvements.

In fact, it was the industrial use of technology, and not just the theoretical "ivory tower" application of theory, that had spurred Robert M. to leave the university to return to Philadelphia. He loved the world of academia, but he found himself hypnotized by the siren call of the steam engine and the new world of automated machinery. It was this, the thriving, bustling environment of the production floor, that captured his imagination and drew him to his new profession.

Patterson's new world in the Federal government also brought him in contact with a great many other industrialists, most of whom were engaged in private enterprise. Vast fortunes were to be made by those with innovative ideas and the means to put them into practice, and Patterson observed these advances with great interest.

Two of the men with whom Patterson engaged in correspondence were Archibald McIntyre and David Henderson. McIntyre was born in Scotland and brought to the United States as an infant when his family immigrated in 1773. He grew up quickly and became involved in the politics of New York State while still in his teens. He served as a member of the New York State Assembly and also as the state comptroller until 1821. Shortly thereafter he helped to found the Elba Iron and Steel Manufacturing Company in North Elba, in the heart of the Adirondack High Peaks. He was also interested in prospecting for silver, which led him to some of the most remote locations of the Adirondack region.

David Henderson was McIntyre's friend, advisor, and business partner. He was also related to McIntyre through marriage, having wed his daughter Annie. It was Henderson who, while visiting the Lake Placid region in 1826, met a Native American trapper named Lewis Elijah Benedict. Benedict presented Henderson with a large ingot of pure iron, which piqued his interests sufficiently to pay the Indian for an escorted tour to the source. Benedict led Henderson through "Indian Pass" to Tahawus, the remote location where the ingot had been mined. David Henderson immediately staked a claim on the mineral rights in the area, which was granted in time to start operations within a matter of months. And thus, in 1827, mining commenced at the "Upper Works" to produce high-grade iron from the Tahawus landscape.

At that time, most northern mining companies transported their raw ore to Lake Champlain for processing, rather than conducting on-site refining. However, the mine in Tahawus was beyond the reach of the rail system, which complicated matters considerably. McIntyre and Henderson lobbied extensively for the construction of a railroad that would lead to their site in the woods. Meanwhile, they constructed a "puddling furnace" in 1837, which would allow them to do some refining of their own ore while still in their remote location. Soon after, they commenced construction of a small blast furnace, which was replaced by an even larger version within a few short years.

It was during his early years as director that Patterson became acquainted with the men from New York and commenced corresponding with the pair. Henderson had relayed his initial (and overly-optimistic) outlook for mining silver in the Adirondack region. This was of obvious interest to Patterson, who was always searching for the closest locations from which to obtain American silver and gold. It represented a new possibility for a relatively local source, which would in turn reduce the transportation expenses enormously.

Over the next decade, Patterson became sufficiently familiar with the operations of the McIntyre mine that he decided to visit the facility to meet the principals. He had hoped to engage in a mutual exchange of ideas and information for furthering the science of refining ores. Patterson was interested in learning of advances in blast furnace technology, while McIntyre and Henderson were looking for investment capital to further modernize their facility in the Adirondack forest. It was a relationship born of mutual friendship and respect, and that affiliation blossomed with the passage of time.

Unfortunately, Patterson was never afforded the opportunity to meet David Henderson. The latter was fatally wounded in the summer of 1845, in a well-chronicled accident that occurred on an unnamed pond near the

Hudson and Opalescent rivers. The body of water was later named Calamity Pond in memory of the man who had given so much of himself to the McIntyre company. He was mourned by his family and associates alike, and a monument was later erected on the site of his death. This memorial stone, which still stands today as a tribute to his life, was sledded into the woods shortly after Patterson's first visit.

Operations continued after Henderson's death, and McIntyre decided to "go big" by investing in the most advanced equipment of the day. This included a massive blast furnace, which would take five full years to complete. Meanwhile, Patterson was maintaining a continuous exchange of ideas and information, lured by the potential of substantial loads of precious metals, including silver. He was also interested in the applied science of industrial improvement, which was a necessity to the founders of the McIntyre operation. Such were the professional factors that motivated Patterson to commence his first journey north in the summer of 1850.

In addition to his official duties as Mint director, Patterson also had a personal reason for wanting to travel. Although only sixty-three years of age, he was in declining health and no longer benefitted from the unlimited vigor he enjoyed in his youth. He experienced premonitions of an early death, and he had already given some thought into organizing his estate and preserving his legacy. The Adirondack Mountains had gained a reputation as a restorative environment for the weak and infirm, a factor that further enhanced his desire to journey away from Philadelphia and into the relatively obscure forests of the North Woods.

Unfortunately for Patterson, his first trip to the McIntyre Iron Company (as it was then known) was a logistical nightmare. The voyage took almost four days, and included lengthy sections of railway, boat travel, and horse-drawn carriage. The roads of northern New York were primitive at best, and they could be torturous if traveled at the wrong time of year. They were strewn with boulders, tree roots, and deep mud puddles that forced the passengers to hold onto the side rails for fear of their lives. The back of the coach was loaded with trunks and supplies, and it was not uncommon for the driver to have to halt the team in order to recover items that had been jolted loose and fallen off the wagon.

It was a painstaking adventure. During the winter months, the roads were iced over and could support sleds carrying heavy loads. However, such was not the case in the summer of 1850, and the passengers became pedestrians for the final leg of the trip, accompanied by a few packhorses to carry the luggage. The final destination was the settlement of Tahawus, which was the name given to the collection of houses and buildings that supported the McIntyre Iron Company.

Patterson knew that they were closing in on Tahawus quite a while before setting sight on the mining establishment. He could see the obvious signs as the woods thinned, then vanished, the trees cut to provide the charcoal fuel for the furnaces. Thousands of acres were clear cut in order to keep the furnaces running, and most of this timber was removed from the acreage bordering on the roadways and railways. It was a sad and stark reminder that there were tradeoffs for the industrial revolution sweeping the country, even here in the remotest part of the North Country.

Patterson's first meeting with Archibald McIntyre was memorable for both men, as each held the other in the highest esteem. Patterson admired McIntyre for his entrepreneurial spirit and his ability to bring modern technology into such a primitive setting. McIntyre, meanwhile, considered Patterson to be the ultimate Renaissance man, successful in government, education, science, and the humanities. He was an intellectual giant of his time, and McIntyre was ecstatic to have the pleasure of his company for the week.

As the passengers and drivers entered the small settlement of Tahawus, they observed the structures actually involved in the crushing and refining of the ore, but there was little to indicate that a full community existed here in the middle of the Adirondack wilderness. The homes of the workers were scattered, hidden amongst the trees, and the other buildings used by the employees for commerce and other functions of daily living were likewise obscured from view. Only the sounds of the iron workers toiling in the heat and the similar sounds of the masons working on the new blast furnace served notice that this was the site of a major industrial undertaking.

Patterson was met by a young company employee who led him to one of the cabins in the woods. It was a small structure at the end of a residential row of houses, yet set apart from most of the others. It had a main living quarters and an attached storage shed with its own entrance. One of the drivers carried his trunk into the building, where Patterson promptly lay down on the narrow bed. It had been a long trip with an exhausting terminal phase, and he was in serious need of rest. Within minutes, he drifted off to sleep.

Patterson had no idea how long he had been asleep when he heard the sharp rapping on the door. "Please, do come in," he called out, pulling himself to a sitting position.

The door opened, and in walked Archibald McIntyre, principal and founder of the mining company. He was a good-sized man, standing about as tall as Patterson, but with broader shoulders and decidedly more bulk. His dark hair and moustache had grayed over the years, lending an air of distinction to his face. He smiled in a most genuine manner as he extended a hand in greeting.

"And you must be my esteemed guest, Mr. Patterson," McIntyre said, shaking the Mint director's hand.

"Your assumption is correct. And you must be Mr. Archibald McIntyre?"

"Yes, yes, but please call me Archie. No one in these parts of the woods stands on formalities."

Patterson threw back his head and laughed. "Yes, we are in a bit of a remote spot here, aren't we? I believe that I left several of my vertebrae on the last few miles of road back there."

"I am most sorry about that," said McIntyre, turning serious. "Maintaining a road that is useful for transporting any kind of heavy load is almost impossible to do on a year-round basis. We can do it in the winter when the snow comes, and we can pack the ice down into a sheet. That's when the sleds take the heaviest loads in and out. But summers can be hell, especially if it's been a rainy season."

"And you are a long ways away from any navigable natural waterway or open terrain," Patterson remarked. "What's your plan for the long term?"

"That is a good question," replied McIntyre. "We've got some ideas, but they depend on finding a few wealthy investors, and more than a little bit of luck. But listen, rather than talk about that in here, let me show you around the settlement. I can give you a tour of the whole operation before supper. Have you recuperated sufficiently for that undertaking?"

"I'll be fine," nodded Patterson as he pulled his boots onto his feet. "I'd enjoy a guided tour of your operation."

It was late in the afternoon as the two men stepped out into the bright sunshine. The mountain air was filled with the sounds of productivity. The two furnaces in operation were fully engaged, with over forty men involved in feeding the fires and smelting the iron from the ore. McIntyre spent over an hour discussing the furnaces with Patterson, including the theories of operation and the practices they'd employed to increase the efficiency of the process. It was very involved, and Patterson listened with an attentive ear.

As they finished their discussion, McIntyre led them away from the noisy furnace. "Come, my friend, let me show you around the rest of our settlement. We are very proud of what we've built here in the North Country. Our town is almost completely self-sufficient, with the exception of what we cannot grow or raise ourselves."

McIntyre was about to start describing the community's school system when Patterson noticed something of interest on the side of the path. It was a finely cut and highly polished stone, approximately eight feet in length, lying on its side in a partially opened wooden crate. It had the appearance of a monument or a grave marker of a large scale, and Patterson found himself staring at the inscription carved into the rock.

It read: "This monument, erected by filial affection, to the memory of our dear father, David Henderson, who accidentally lost his life on this spot 3rd September, 1845."

McIntyre fell silent for a moment as he waited for Patterson to complete his reading. Then he spoke softly. "I'm sure you corresponded with my partner before his untimely death?"

"Yes, several times," replied Patterson, still looking down. "He seemed like a good man, highly dedicated to the advancement of the country and the development of our natural resources."

"Agreed; a good man," said McIntyre, nodding his head solemnly. "And an outstanding partner, businessman, father, and husband, not to mention my son-in-law. All of us miss him today, five years after his death, as much as if it happened only yesterday. We still observe a day of prayer on September 3 each year as a way to keep his memory intact."

"And this monument, why does is rest on the ground as it does? Is it to erect within your community in the near future?"

"No, my friend. David's family paid for most of that piece, including its transportation thus far, as a way of commemorating his life. Our plan is to sled it over the early snows into the very spot where he lost his life. It is quite a way from here, but I can assure you that almost the entire town will show up for the raising of the marker and the service that will follow. Mr. Henderson meant that much to most of us."

"Please send me notification of the memorial," said Patterson. "If I am traveling away from Philadelphia, I may try to attend."

"By all means," said McIntyre, bowing slightly in return. "I am certain that my ex-partner would be most honored that you thought so much of him to take the time from your busy schedule to pay your respects."

McIntyre then proceeded to lead his guest throughout the rest of the settlement, describing the means by which the workers and their families lived and conducted their lives in the remote mining community. They visited an area where there was a concentration of about fifteen houses, a school, a boarding house, and a small general store where the residents could purchase dry goods and other merchandise. Another pocket of buildings included several mills for sawing and grist, a granary, a tool house, and a carpenter and blacksmith shop. Several barns had been erected to house cows, cattle, and pigs. There was even a library and post office, all run by the workers of the community and their families. It was a simple life, and one without many luxuries. But the people seemed happy, and everyone knew that they could rely on the others in times of need.

As they strolled around the grounds, the men conversed on a number of subjects. Patterson was most interested in the new technologies of industrial metallurgy, with an eye towards bringing some of the ideas into practice at the Mint. McIntyre, meanwhile, was carefully probing Patterson for insights into funding, whether from the federal government or from private investors whom Patterson may have known. Each of the men knew that the other had his own interests at stake, but neither minded in the least. This was the reason behind Patterson's visit, and for McIntyre's desire to play host.

As they emerged out of the woods into a small clearing by the road, Patterson saw something that stopped him dead in his tracks. It was the outer framework of the new blast furnace that was under construction – and it was enormous. Although unable to determine its exact proportions, Patterson guessed that it measured at least thirty feet on each side, with massive stones serving as the outer walls. At least twenty men were laboring on the fledgling structure, with masons, stonecutters, and brick layers all working hand in hand to raise the height of the new structure. It would be, when finished, a marvel of construction for that era.

Patterson turned toward McIntyre, his face aglow with wonder, and merely stared in disbelief. McIntyre read the surprise on his face and laughed.

"I interpret your expression as a sign of approval?" he asked.

"I had no idea that you were undertaking a project so mammoth in scale," said Patterson. "Please, educate me in the details of this project. I am completely unfamiliar with anything so enormous."

"It would be my pleasure," beamed McIntyre, obviously thrilled by the opportunity to share his knowledge with the renowned scientist. "As you know, the science for this type of furnace has been around for many centuries. The Chinese actually invented the blast furnace several centuries before the birth of Christ. However, much has been done to increase the efficiency of such operations since that time. Unfortunately, we cannot take advantage of all these developments due to our great distance from rail transportation."

"I am aware of your logistical problems," said Patterson, nodding his concurrence.

"Yes, I would like to discuss those with you in greater depth some-time," replied McIntyre. "But on the subject of technology, some of the biggest advances have come from my old country, Scotland, within the last twenty years. It was there that the concept of heat exchange was first employed, and the escaping heat from the furnace gases was used to pre-heat the incoming air supply, which is blasted in from the bottom of the furnace. It serves to both increase the efficiency and decrease the smelting time. I'm really surprised that no one thought of the idea any earlier."

"Mr. Henderson indicated that you were using the regional water sup-ply to provide the forced air supply. How will that take place?"

"Please, step this way," said McIntyre, taking Patterson's arm in his own. "I'd like to show you what we have in mind, and how we are going to harness our existing natural resources as a free source of power."

After strolling through a forested area, the two men descended a short but steep decline and found themselves on the edge of a river. About ten men were gathered around a newly laid foundation, working the soil with shovels and pickaxes. Some of the crew was employed constructing a deep wall into the side of the bank, while others were working to expand the excavation. The amount of sheer manual labor appeared to be over-whelming, and Patterson marveled at the effort.

"How's it going today, boys?" asked McIntyre, mingling with the men and patting a few of them on the back. "Is the ground getting a little easier now that you've gotten below the tree roots?"

A man who appeared to be in charge of the work detail stepped forward to speak for the workers. "A little bit," he replied. "We're finding a lot of large rocks and boulders that fit right into the wall line, so we're using them as much as possible. No use in moving anything that we don't have to. But we're getting along OK."

"That's great news," said McIntyre. "And I wanted to let all of you know that the coach came in today and brought in a large shipment of gloves. We'll pass them out to everyone this week so that you'll have them before the cold sets in."

"Thank you," several of the men answered in unison. They appeared to be content in their work, and Patterson noted that there was a certain unspoken affection between the company owner and his employees.

Turning back towards his guest, McIntyre continued his explanation of the water-powered air supply. "As you know, the blast furnace works by forcing air through the bottom of the furnace, while the ore and fuel are fed from the top. We're preheating the air from the stack gases, and then using a pair of large waterwheels in the river here to operate a set of large bellows. These will continuously force the hot air into the base of the furnace without requiring men or beasts for power."

Patterson was highly impressed with the planning and implementation of the project. "So, as long as you have a sufficient flow of water over the wheels, you have an unlimited amount of forced air."

McIntyre nodded in concurrence. "Yes that's the theory of the operation. And based on the climate we've experienced here over the past twenty years, we don't have to worry about the water in the river. We'd have a better chance of being washed away in a flood than seeing her go dry."

McIntyre then treated Patterson to a half-hour lecture on the pending power plant, including the future locations of the wheels, the bellows, and the heat-exchange lines. He described the layout of the construction in great detail, explaining why the particular configuration had been selected and how the equipment was being shipped into the woods for final assembly and installation. It was a superbly detailed treatise on the industrial application of theory, and Patterson was awed by McIntyre's knowledge and vision.

"My good sir, you have left me overwhelmed with the sheer magnitude of your operations," he said looking directly at his host. "I do believe that there are a number of investors within the city of Philadelphia who might be interested in your company. But please, before I give further thought to that, I would like to ask you an honest question, given that you are an honest man, true to your word."

"And what is that question, I ask?"

"What are your prospects for finding a continuous and unlimited source of iron ore, and how close are you in your efforts to attract a railroad spur into your location?"

"Those are good questions indeed," murmured McIntyre, looking back at Patterson in agreement. "I must admit that the answer to your first question is much easier to find than your second. According to the state geologist, Ebenezer Emmons, we have a massive supply of some of the highest grade ore in the country. The samples he tested showed that we are well above the threshold needed to sustain our operation at a profit as long as we can maintain a viable supply of fuel for the furnaces. That's why we've gone ahead with plans for the larger blast furnace we just looked at. We've got the ore to keep us in business for years to come."

"But the railroad, which could both bring the fuel in and the processed iron out, that's not looking as promising, is it?"

"No, not at the present time," conceded McIntyre, shaking his head. "We've tried for a number of years to get a railway built or a vastly improved road put in, all to no avail. It has been the single most discouraging aspect of running this operation. I can keep the ore coming in, and I can keep the iron going out. I want this operation to succeed as badly as anyone, because I believe that our young nation needs our product to grow in size and strength. But without the railroad, it may become impossible to keep our company competitive with the southern mines."

"I understand your problems, my friend," said Patterson. "I will bring word of your plight home with me, and I will plead your case wherever I might find potential support."

"Thank you," said McIntyre, grasping his hand firmly. "That is all that

I can ask of you. And now, perhaps you would like some time to yourself before supper? I will send my assistant to call you to my house when the meal is ready."

"I appreciate that," said Patterson, thankful for the offer. "I might just stroll around the grounds for a short while to collect my thoughts, and then sort out my things."

"Very well. I will see you for supper." McIntyre smiled, and then came to a position of attention before turning on his heel and walking back to his office.

Patterson pledged to use this time wisely. As much as he wanted to wash off the dirt and grime from the voyage north, he decided to first talk to the workers who were laying out the base of the new blast furnace. They were just settling down for a late afternoon break when he walked into the clearing. A number of laborers were seated on upturned stumps, smoking rolled tobacco and pipes. Others were perched on small boulders. One of the men standing nearby, a tall fellow with a sheaf of papers in one hand, appeared to be giving directions to some of the stone cutters. Patterson assumed that he was in charge of the lot, and he approached him with an extended handshake.

"Good afternoon, good sir. If it isn't too much trouble, I'd like to ask you a few questions about this magnificent structure you are building. I trust that you are the foreman?"

"Yes sir, Mr. Patterson. I am. What can I do for you?"

Patterson was somewhat shocked that the man standing before him, a complete stranger, should call him by name. "I don't believe we've ever met, Mr...." he paused.

"VanderBrooke's my name, sir. Peter VanderBrooke. And you don't have to worry yourself with introductions. Everyone here knows who you are. Mr. McIntyre has been telling us about you for the past week. He's very excited about your visit, as are we."

"Well, I am equally honored to make your acquaintance," said Patterson, shaking the man's hand enthusiastically. "I have travelled from afar to learn of your work and the technology you are employing in your endeavor."

"Really not much to it," said VanderBrooke, turning back toward the construction. "Basically, all we are doing is replicating our previous efforts on a much grander scale."

"Indeed, a much grander scale," agreed Patterson. "Just how tall will this structure rise when complete?" he asked.

"We're not entirely sure," said VanderBrooke, wiping his brow with a handkerchief. "The base is close to thirty feet on each side, and the plans we're using specify a maximum height somewhere between fifty-five to sixty feet. A lot of that will depend on the number of stabilizer rods we build into the exterior walls of the furnace. We're still several years away from that point, so we won't know until we get there. But that's the plan right now."

"Several years away?" repeated Patterson, trying to comprehend the extent of the work.

"That's right, Mr. Patterson. We don't have a deadline presented to us by the boss, but we know from the plans that we'll be able to add, at most, ten to fifteen feet per year, including the internal brickwork. It's not easy, as thou must know."

"Of course, of course," Patterson said in a reassuring voice. "It's just that I've never seen a work of this magnitude, so I had no idea what to expect."

"It is quite grand," said the foreman, turning back to his work. "Just think; in a few short years, we'll be able to put this part of the state on the map for its productivity and role in the growth of our young country. We expect to be the largest producer of high-quality iron in the northeast. It makes a man proud thinking about that, you know?"

Patterson looked at the young man, energetic and enthusiastic about his responsibilities. His energy spilled over to his entire work crew and provided constant encouragement throughout their long days. He was a model supervisor, leading his crew to attain uncommon results. Patterson concluded that he had established a contact that might be of value in his future endeavors.

"I agree wholeheartedly," said Patterson, already considering the next step. "And I do say, Mr. VanderBrooke, that I concur completely with your thoughts on the effort put forth here in Tahawus. I must ask you, would you mind if I corresponded with you from my office in Philadelphia? I would be most interested if you would keep me apprised of your work as the furnace is constructed."

"Of course, Mr. Patterson. I would be most honored," replied VanderBrooke.

"Fine then, lad. I look forward to hearing from you on a regular basis," said Patterson, again extending his hand. "I, too, will deem it an honor to receive your correspondence. Until then, I bid you good day."

It was getting closer to the supper hour as Patterson re-entered his cabin to wash up for his upcoming meal. He found that his mind was pre-occupied with the events of the day, and with thoughts of all that had transpired to bring him north to the Adirondack Mountains. He reminisced about the milestones in his own life, and how he had come to be a federal employee for the past fifteen years, bound by the strict guidelines placed around the Mint operations. It was a far cry from the freedom of his current surroundings, this vast wilderness where the inhabitants made their own rules as they went, bound only by their creativity and passion.

After donning a clean shirt and combing his hair, Patterson extracted a leather-bound journal from his trunk and sat down to write. He had done this almost every day for the past twenty years. It wasn't really a diary per se, because it usually didn't discuss his comings and goings for the day. But he did record his thoughts on a variety of matters and often referred back to these entries when considering personal issues. Each page was dated, with a line drawn across the bottom of each day's record. His last entry was from two nights previous, written while he was sitting at a stagecoach rest stop during his voyage north.

After reviewing his previous entry, Patterson dipped a quill pen into an ink bottle and began to write:

July 11, 1850. Arrived at McIntyre Iron Company, Tahawus, NY, after a journey that seemingly jarred my nerves as well as my physical well-being. I have met Mr. Archibald McIntyre, and many of his employees, and have been thoroughly charmed by them all. The operation of the iron works consists of much difficult (and often menial) labor, which does not appear to dampen the spirits of the workers. There is an overwhelming sense of freedom that abounds here, of life on the frontier that is most liberating. It is my belief that the clearness of the air and water breeds a clarity of mind that I find most refreshing. Mr. McIntyre has availed himself to my every need, and has extended an open invitation to visit the premises whenever I desire. We spoke of his deceased partner, Mr. Henderson, and the emotions that his passing still evoke. There is a memorial marker of considerable stature that has arrived at the settlement, and this will be erected at the site of his death sometime later this year. I hope to return to witness this event. I also spent some time with Mr. VanderBrooke, the foreman of the new blast furnace that is under construction next to the Tahawus road. He is a most astute gentleman, also a master stone-cutter with an eye for precision. We exchanged thoughts and ideas on a number of subjects concerning construction and engineering. He, too, offered to correspond with me as the project advances towards completion, as my own interest in this behemoth furnace has grown since my arrival. In summary, I find the life in this location to be favorable to many other settings of more urban character, even with the hardships endured by the inhabitants. I have never met a more affable group of people.

Patterson concluded his writing and put down his pen at the same moment that a young man knocked on the outer door. Patterson stepped outside to find a lad of about eighteen, who guided him to McIntyre's log home near the edge of the settlement. He spent the next few hours with McIntyre and his wife, enjoying a meal of locally raised chicken, herbed vegetables, and oven-fresh bread. It was the equal of of the finest food put forth on a Philadelphia table, and Patterson was again amazed at the self-reliance of these people.

At the end of the evening, Patterson found his own way back across the town, stopping only to marvel once again at the foundation of the new furnace. The workers were done for the day, and the site stood deserted in the waning sunlight. The large rocks, each cut to fit in a specific location in the outer wall, cast long shadows that overlapped one another. The darkness and the solitude served to further amplify the magnitude of the project, making it appear even larger than it was. Patterson found himself entranced with the sheer size of the base, imagining how it would look when completed.

After spending some time at the site of the construction, Patterson returned to his cabin and lay down. It had been a very long day, and his earlier nap had done little to relieve his exhaustion. He briefly considered writing more in his ledger, but instead decided to retire early and get a good night's sleep. After one last visit to the outhouse, he extinguished every lamp in the room and then crawled into bed. By his own guess, it was about nine fifteen PM, and he quickly fell into a peaceful slumber.

Patterson was, by nature, a fairly sound sleeper, and he could tolerate a significant amount of sound without awakening. However, on this night he tossed and turned, rolling across the padded bed as though in distress. It was a subconscious awareness, a subtle perception of an unknown calling that brought him repeatedly out of his sleep. He opened his eyes several times throughout the night, looking around for something of substance on which he could pin his discomfort. There were voices, but not to be heard. Not while he was awake. But they were there; or were they in his dreams? He didn't know, and he kept an open ear as he dozed.

Some time later, Patterson was yanked out of a deep sleep by a sound that was positively human. It was the cry of a young child, sobbing loudly, and then abruptly ceasing. He was certain that this was real, and not part of a dream. Yet he knew that there were no other cabins nearby, and certainly no one slept in the attached storage room. The cry seemed to come from inside the room, which was quite impossible.

Patterson rose from the bed and slipped on his boots without bothering to don socks. He was dressed in only his bed clothes and a well-worn jacket, which he pulled over his chest. Carrying an oil lantern, he slipped out the front door and walked around the outside of the building, looking in the shrubs and undergrowth for signs of life. He was passing the front of the storage shed when he stopped and cocked an ear toward the darkened entrance. He heard the faint sound of movement, with a hint of a human voice in the background. It sounded distant and muffled, but it was there.

After pulling the door fully open, Patterson stepped into the shed, giving his eyes a minute to acclimate to the darkness. The dim light of the lantern barely penetrated the utter blackness of the space, and he moved it continuously to provide the best perspective as he worked his way around the room. After making a complete inspection without result, he turned to exit the enclosure when the crying resumed for a moment. It was there, somewhere in the darkness. He was certain of it.

Patterson moved into the most distant corner of the shed and peered into a wooden crate. It was empty, so he moved it out of the way. Beneath the crate was a flat board that was covered with dirt and moisture. His nose detected the strong odors of mold and mildew in the air. On one end of the board was affixed a loop of rope, fashioned into a handle. Patterson reached down and grasped the rope and pulled up, lifting the board off the ground. The left edge of the board remained in contact with the floor, and Patterson quickly deduced that it was held in place by a hinge. The right side swiveled upright, exposing an excavated room below the cabin. A crudely manufactured ladder, with unevenly spaced boards as steps, dropped vertically to a basement level below~~~~.LP.org

Patterson hesitated momentarily, knowing that he was hardly an adventure-seeker capable of defending himself against unknown threats. At sixty-three, his age and deteriorating condition had left him somewhat weakened and infirmed. However, he felt compelled to investigate what seemed to be the sound of a baby crying and render assistance if it was needed. Trusting his gut instinct, he decided to descend into the darkness.

By placing the lantern nearby and sitting on the edge of the opening, Patterson was able to swing his feet onto the ladder and secure a foothold. He then took hold of the lantern and proceeded hand over foot, rung after rung, down the ladder until he finally reached the bottom.wives

It was dark, so very dark. The smell of mold and dirt was overpowered by other, more noxious scents that were very human, the smell of bodies, of sweat, and waste. Patterson wanted to call out to find the infant in the darkness, but he couldn't find his voice. The combination of fear, awe, and intense concentration stifled his tongue, and he stood, silently, rooted in place~~~.L4L.org

The cellar appeared to be entirely man-made, although he couldn't be certain. A few reinforcement beams were visible in the dim light, but the rays of the lantern were insufficient to view anything beyond the range of a few feet. Patterson couldn't determine the dimensions of the room because he couldn't see the walls. It may have been fifty feet, or it may have been twenty. As his eyes became even more sensitized to the darkness, he began to identify a few more items around him. Some horizontal platforms, held up by rough square beams, appeared to be used for sitting or sleeping. A pile of dirty linens and quilts confirmed that this had indeed been used as living quarters.

Patterson then expanded his search of the premises, moving along a row of the improvised bunks until he had almost reached the eastern wall of the cellar. At that moment he heard another cry that sounded as though it came from directly beneath his feet. He bent down and looked underneath a bed frame and received the shock of his life. He found himself staring at five or more sets of eyes, all looking back at him in fear. Frozen in place, he realized that there were people, a lot of people, hiding behind the entire row of bunks. Each bunk served to conceal at least three or four beings, ranging in age from infant to elderly. They were all of African descent, with very dark skin and eyes that glistened with the reflection of the lantern. The universal expression across the group was fear. Total, complete, abject fear.

Patterson didn't know what to do. He didn't know who these people were, although he did harbor some strong suspicions. For the time being, he didn't feel threatened, but he did want to exit the room as quickly as possible. He also wanted to tell these people that they should not fear him, that he would do them no harm. But he didn't know whether they spoke English and would be able to understand his reassurance. He slowly rose to a standing position and brushed the dirt off his knees.

"Good evening, my friends," he said, trying to sound as nonchalant as possible, given the circumstances. "I'm sorry if I have inconvenienced you in any way. I'm simply a visitor here, and I mean you no harm. I shall leave now, and you may go back to sleep." Then, as he stepped back onto the ladder and began his climb into the shed, he called back, "Please excuse me again. I hope you have a most pleasant evening."

Patterson re-entered the shed from below and replaced the trap door in its original position. He moved the empty crate back over the door, and carried the lantern back into the cabin. Since no one had attempted to follow him out of the cellar, he deduced that the people he'd met were not being held against their will, although he still puzzled about their circumstances.

Before returning to bed, he sat at the small desk in the corner of the room and recorded his unusual experience in the journal as an addendum to the events of the day. The late-night entry was not long or complicated. It simply served as a record of what he had seen, and of the emotions that accompanied his discovery. Somehow, Patterson found that writing in his journal had a certain amount of therapeutic value, and he immediately sensed a feeling of relief after putting away the book. He then looked out the window one more time before returning to his bed, where he immediately fell fast asleep. It had, indeed, been a very unusual day.

After a visit that lasted another two days, Patterson was ready to depart for home. Although he spent many hours conversing with McIntyre over those next days, he never mentioned his experience in the cellar of the cabin. He reasoned that either the owner knew of their plight and was helping them in some way, or someone else was doing the same. He felt that he would have been out of place initiating the conversation, so he never brought up the subject. It remained a private topic between Patterson and his journal.

The last day of Patterson's visit was filled with additional discussions with McIntyre, as well as with the foreman of the blast furnace construction, Peter VanderBrooke. Their relationship was most cordial, and genuine friendships developed between the men. All were sad when the last of Patterson's parcels were loaded onto the coach for the return trip to Philadelphia.

"It has indeed been an honor to have spent these past few days in your company," said Patterson, shaking hands with McIntyre, then Vander-Brooke. "Please let me know when the arrangements are finalized for the memorial to our dearly departed Mr. Henderson. I would most like to attend the ceremony."

"Absolutely, and with pleasure," said McIntyre, returning the handshake. "You are welcome as my personal guest any time you desire."

Patterson then turned to address VanderBrooke directly. "Remember to keep me abreast of the progress on the furnace," he said, his eyes locked on the foreman. "I would enjoy following the progress of its construction."

"Yes, Mr. Patterson," said VanderBrooke as he removed a roll of papers from a heavy satchel. "Mr. McIntyre informed me of your desire to hear of its development, especially since you are considering building a similar furnace at the Mint in Philadelphia. With that in mind, I have located a duplicate set of the building plans, which you may take away with you."

As he spoke, he handed Patterson the loosely scrolled documents.

"Thank you, my good sir," said Patterson, accepting the papers. "I shall review these at my earliest opportunity. And I hope to hear well in advance of the day when I might return to witness the first load of iron produced in your magnificent furnace."

Unfortunately, Robert M. Patterson would never live to see that day.

CHAPTER 4

October 11, 1850

True to his word, Patterson returned later that fall to witness the placing of Henderson's memorial stone at Calamity Pond. He arrived without much fanfare, shortly after the first snows of the season carpeted the ground with a soft curtain of white. McIntyre, himself, was there to greet him as he stepped down from the coach, which was able to pull into the middle of the settlement now that the ground had hardened.

As he passed the site of the new blast furnace, Patterson was pleased to see that the outer walls had risen to a height of almost eight feet. Some of the bottom blocks were gigantic, weighing many tons apiece. This would be a landmark feat of construction, and Patterson found himself transfixed, as he had been earlier that summer.

"We've made some progress since your last visit," said McIntyre, standing next to the Mint director. "But that's not even a hint of what's to come. Before we're done, we'll be up over fifty feet off the ground, with enough forced air from the water-powered bellows to keep this thing roaring non-stop. It'll be a sight to see."

"What are those square plates on the outside of the wall?" asked Patterson, pointing to a pair of iron plaques held in place from inside the furnace.

"Those are the anchor plates on the tie rods," answered McIntyre, moving closer to the rock. "It's the same principle that builders use when putting up a house, only on a larger scale. As the furnace walls are built, a series of tie rods are inserted from the front wall to the back, and from the left side to the right. The rods extend through the center hole of the anchor plate, where they are fastened in place by a cotter pin, which you can see here." As he spoke, he pointed to a flat blade-like pin that was inserted into a slot in the protruding end of the rod.

"And that series of thicker, sturdier bars embedded in the middle of each side. Are they part of the same support design?" asked Patterson.

"Yes, those will connect an additional seven sets of tie rods that will run diagonally through the middle of the furnace, although obviously they will avoid exposure inside the stack, itself. This furnace has more iron stabilizing its walls than any forge I've ever seen. But without those rods, the expansion and contraction of the rock would probably destroy this thing within a decade, if not sooner. Remember, the temperatures inside the brick wall lining will exceed thirty-five hundred degrees Fahrenheit. That's a lot of heat to handle, even for something this large."

"So the rods serve to maintain the shape of the walls and prevent them from buckling in either direction once the structure is complete and the fires are lit," stated Patterson, looking to McIntyre for confirmation.

"That's about it," said McIntyre. "Without those rods, this thing would rely solely on the precision of the stone cutters and the stability of the ground around us."

"Well, it worked for the pyramids, didn't it?" asked Patterson.

"Maybe," smiled McIntyre. "But no one ever melted iron inside of a pyramid. And I'd hate to have to catch one of these boulders if it suddenly decided to topple."

Following their brief conversation, McIntyre walked Patterson to the door of the same cabin he'd occupied during his previous visit. It appeared to be reserved for the personal guests of the company president, and it was always kept spotless.

Patterson went inside to rest for a while, as he was again tired and overly fatigued. He no longer tolerated the rigors of exertion well, and he sensed that his body was deteriorating. In fact, he had already decided that he would most likely resign his position at the Mint sometime the following year, enabling him to pursue his personal interests such as traveling and writing.

The ceremony at Calamity Pond was conducted the following afternoon, following a walk of several miles to reach the site. Patterson helped to prepare the monument before the proceedings began, using a leveling instrument to ensure that the obelisk was perfectly upright and secure. The younger workers involved in the process were impressed by his energy and commitment to the task. They had no idea of the exhaustion he experienced while performing these duties.

Patterson spent most of the next day resting. He wrote several pages in his journal, devoting most of the lines to the memorial service and the blast furnace. They were the two attractions that had drawn him to return so soon after his summer visit, and his words spilled out across the pages describing these activities in great detail.

Early in the afternoon, Peter VanderBrooke stopped by his cabin to talk, and they discussed various aspects of the furnace construction. Patterson was particularly interested in hearing further details on the stabilizing rods, which fascinated him. VanderBrooke explained the theory behind the rods, including their numbers and positioning relative to the mass of the furnace walls. Patterson was intrigued, and he immediately began experimenting with theoretical ways to increase the efficiency of this system. He had an agile and inquisitive mind, and VanderBrooke was in awe of his genius.

Patterson's visit lasted only three days this time, the result of an overly busy season in Philadelphia. He made the most of his stay, however, by spending most of his waking hours with either VanderBrooke or the construction crew. He was constantly looking at the furnace, plans in hand, while making mental observations and measurements. Several times each day he would return to his cabin and record his thoughts on the large sheets displaying the furnace plans.

As he worked, Patterson kept an ear tuned towards the storage shed where he had discovered the door leading to the cellar. However, on this trip there was nothing but silence. The same was true at night; not a sound creased the absolute quiet of the dark Adirondack evening except for the crickets and the hoot of the barred owl. He considered looking inside the shed for signs of activity, but decided against investigating. From all indications, the cellar was completely unoccupied.

Having attended the memorial service and completed his discussions with VanderBrooke and the construction crew, Patterson departed Tahawus, bound for Philadelphia. It would be another two years before he would return to the mining community in the woods. By that time, he would be fully retired, having turned over the Directorship of the U.S. Mint to George Eckfeldt in July of 1851.

By the time Patterson submitted his resignation to President Fillmore, he was a very tired man. Although only sixty-four years of age, he was aware that something was robbing him of his energy and vigor. He noticed that his mind wandered aimlessly at times, and he had a hard time concentrating. Although Patterson observed these symptoms, his limited knowledge of medicine would not permit him to diagnose the underlying problem. Even his own personal physician was unable to reach a conclusion or prescribe a cure for the ailing patient.

As a result of his illness, and his general mental demeanor, Patterson found himself putting his final affairs in order over three years before his eventual death in 1854. He revised his will and ensured that all his personal matters were in order. He donated large volumes of his books and writings to the various universities where he had taught. Other documents and records he gifted to the American Philosophical Society, especially those dealing with its members and organization.

While cleaning out his cellar in his Philadelphia home, he came across the crate which held the horde of 1804 silver dollars he had hidden away so many years before. He smiled as he looked at the outer casing, which still held a label with his father's handwriting. It was a fond reminder of the man who had shaped his mind and career from such an early age. However, his smile dissolved as he considered the issue that still lingered because of these coins.

Patterson knew that the records listing the production counts had long since been forgotten, buried in the depth of the National Archives in Philadelphia. For all he knew, they may have been destroyed by one of the fires in the Treasury Department buildings before even being transferred to the Archives. And yet, he asked, "What if...?" What would happen if the Treasury Department was to discover after all these years that those dollars had been produced, and had somehow disappeared during his father's tenure in office? He had promised to his father as he lay dying on his death bed to preserve the family honor, yet he did not want to pass this debacle on to his children. Rather, he would find a hiding place outside of his home, outside of his community, where the dollars could be hidden forever without the possibility of being discovered.

This problem consumed him for many months, his mind turning the matter over repeatedly. Then, one night almost a year later, as he sat in church on a cold December evening in 1851, the solution flashed before his eyes. It was simple, accessible, and available. But he needed to take action immediately if he was going to make it work.

Patterson would make two more trips to Tahawus over the next two years, in 1852 and 1853. Between visits, he traded correspondence continuously with both McIntyre and VanderBrooke. Some of his letters now rambled a bit, deviating from the topics of metallurgy and industrial construction. VanderBrooke, in particular, was puzzled by some of the unusual questions posed in his writings. However, he always remained polite and professional in his replies, and he tried to accommodate each of Patterson's requests.

Patterson's final pilgrimage to Tahawus was in the fall of 1853. On that final visit, Patterson brought along a visitor, a young man of about eighteen or twenty, whom he introduced only as Henry. He was a most unusual lad, so quiet that Archibald McIntyre believed him to be mute. Even when introduced, he said nothing, although he apparently understood the conversation around him. Also of interest was the newcomer's physique. He was very tall for a man of his era, standing almost two full inches over six feet. Although trim in the waist, he obviously possessed enormous strength. His arms literally bulged with muscles. A great barrel chest filled out the front of his shirt, and his legs resembled a pair of tree trunks. He appeared to be half man and half bull, and the other men glanced at him curiously as he hopped down off the coach.

As McIntyre helped Patterson down from the front of the carriage, he couldn't help but notice how much his friend had aged in the past year. He was frail, and had difficulty navigating even a small uneven step. McIntyre could also see that he was not in the mood for idle chatter. He decided that any conversation could wait until the following day.

Henry easily offloaded all of Patterson's luggage, which was limited since he was only planning a short stay. The cargo included a small rein-forced clothing case, a heavy-looking wooden chest, and a few smaller items of personal effects. It all appeared weightless to Henry except for the wooden chest, which he hoisted to his shoulder with a great amount of effort. Then, they disappeared into the cabin to set up housekeeping for the night.

McIntyre bid Patterson goodnight, then retired to his own home. However, Peter VanderBrooke appeared at Patterson's door within the hour, and the two men conversed for some time. As the conversation neared its conclusion, Patterson passed a parcel to the foreman, which he opened immediately. It contained all of the engineering drawings he'd given Patterson the previous year, along with an envelope that was closed with a wax seal. The two shook hands without further discussion, and VanderBrooke turned away for home.

The moon was out in full glory that evening, a complete sphere that glowed like the sun under a cloudless sky. By midnight, it had risen to a point above the horizon where the entire settlement was bathed in a silver light that negated the need for a lantern. The lamps in each of the houses had been extinguished, and the sounds of the North Country night pre-vailed. Only a solitary pair of figures, silhouetted against the moonlight, made their way silently across the hamlet. They moved slowly and stealthily through the damp night air, not making a sound that might disturb the slumbering inhabitants. Just before vanishing into the trees, they were joined by a third person, a shadowy presence who seemed to materialize from the mist. The trio then melted into the woods for a lengthy spell, only to reappear some hours later. The original pair then retraced their steps, just as quietly although somewhat more quickly than before. Then, they disappeared once more.

The following day, McIntyre went back to find Patterson in order to invite him to supper at his house. He found the pottering ex-director placing his clothing back into his case for the return trip to Philadelphia.

"My friend, surely you are not departing already! You arrived only yesterday, and we've barely had a chance to talk. Please, I beg of you and your guest, stay another day so that we might perhaps enjoy some additional time together."

Patterson turned to face McIntyre, his eyes wistful and full of emotion. "My dear Archibald, I wish that I could. But my time here is very limited, and an extended stay is out of the question. If I am blessed with additional time before being called to meet my Lord and Savior, then perhaps I will rejoin you and your wonderful compatriots within the next year. You have truly given me much joy in the friendship that we've shared. But for now, I must go."

McIntyre realized that Patterson expected to die in the very near future. He could only accept what he had heard and bid his friend farewell.

Patterson's premonition became a reality. He passed away in July, 1854, less than ten months after leaving Tahawus for the last time. McIntyre read the obituary in an old newspaper almost a month after his passing, and silently said a prayer for the deceased.

As for Patterson, he was buried in a graveyard in the middle of Philadelphia. His family secret would be successfully shrouded for over 160 years, when it would be uncovered by technology, good fortune, and the juice of a single pomegranate.

PART II
NORTH COUNTRY GHOST TOWN

CHAPTER 5

Saturday, August 8, 2015

The figure on the shoulder of the road was tall and lean, with toned muscles that rippled with each long stride. His gait had shifted from a relaxed jogging pace into a much more vigorous run, despite the rapidly inclining hill that lay ahead. It wasn't quite a sprint, but the runner's arms and legs pumped rhythmically at an impressive rate.

With the final half mile in sight, Chris Carey, Jr., had one thought in mind: push hard until the end, and then cool down with a nice shower. It was Saturday, and the rest of the weekend was before him. His mind wandered into a different realm, and he never noticed the car pulling up behind him.

The vehicle was a tan 1966 Mercedes-Benz 250S, and although it was old, it sparkled like the day it came off the showroom floor. The owner sat in the driver's seat as he pulled up behind Chris, keeping pace with his movement. In order to remain out of view, he stayed slightly in back of the runner's peripheral vision, easing off the gas and coasting down to about eight miles per hour. Even at that pace, he noticed that the athlete in the dark blue jersey and shorts was pulling away ever so slightly. He compensated by gently nudging the gas pedal.

"Hey, what's a guy got to do to ask for some simple directions," hollered the driver out the open window. He grinned as he noticed the startled expression on his friend, keeping pace on the pavement.

"I thought you finally got GPS in that antique of yours," he yelled back, still running. "What's the matter? Can't read the owner's manual?"

The driver of the car simply laughed, pulling abreast of Chris as he neared the top of the hill. "Eat my dust, buddy. I'll see you at your house." Then he pulled away, leaving his friend to finish his route solo.

By the time Chris sprinted the final hundred yards, the driver of the vintage car had already climbed out of the front seat. Sean Riggins had been Chris' friend for close to twenty years, since the time when their desks sat next to each another in the same elementary school classroom in Utica, New York. Since that time, they had shared dates, drinks, and dares without losing touch with one another. It was a close-knit friendship that had brought their two families together over the years. There wasn't much they didn't share,

Together, Chris and Sean had been through some pretty adventurous times, although Chris considered himself to be much less the swashbuckler than his friend. Sean's eyes seemed to glow with passion whenever he read about ancient mysteries involving treasures, no matter how old or how improbable. He was also a bit of a thrill-seeker, and had talked Chris into sharing a skydiving experience. Once.

Sean pulled his car to the end of the dirt lane and into a short driveway that led to a small, white A-frame house. The canopy of trees hung low over the roof, and a thick carpet of pine needles cushioned the ground, giving the entire setting a park-like appearance. A few squirrels chased each other up a beech tree, chattering their complaints about the intrusion of the Mercedes.

Sean had barely swung his legs out of the driver's seat when Chris crested the hill and bounded the final hundred yards towards the house. Even though he had covered the last quarter mile in little more than ninety seconds, he was still breathing easily as he slowed to a walk. Sweat glistened against his skin and ran down the side of his face in tiny rivulets. It was all part of the routine; five miles of roadwork every morning, with an extended eight mile run on Saturday. At age twenty-six, he had lost none of his speed from his days playing college lacrosse. If anything, his endurance had increased since graduation, and he prided himself on his conditioning regimen.

"I figured I'd catch you somewhere along the homestretch here," said Sean, tossing his buddy a clear plastic bottle. "But I had no idea that my timing would be so perfect."

Chris looked at the container in his hands and wrinkled his nose. "Strawberry-scented water?" he asked, feigning disdain. "If you're going to bring me a fruit-flavored drink, at least have the courtesy to put some rum in it. Some people have no manners!"

"I'm sorry, Your Majesty. I'll have the courier bring a Mai Tai to your chamber immediately."

"Much too sweet," replied Chris, still acting indignant. "But why don't you come inside and have an unsweetened iced tea?"

"Deal," replied Sean, following his friend across a short walkway to the front door.

Chris pressed a sequence of buttons above an ornate brass handle, and then pushed the door open into the house. It wasn't an elaborate dwelling, with less than a thousand square feet of living space, including the loft. It was a quiet neighborhood, with very little traffic reaching the terminus of the dead-end street. Chris had shared this house with a roommate while attending college, and had never felt the need to move after completing his schooling. He now had the house to himself, which fit his busy lifestyle and unconventional schedule.

Chris looked over his shoulder at Sean with a lopsided grin as he fetched two bottles of tea from the aged refrigerator. "So tell me, what evil intentions have lured you away from your beloved golf course on a Saturday morning? Maggie's not working today?"

Sean laughed at his friend's sarcasm. He was an avid golfer who lived in a cottage that bordered a small village golf course in Little Falls, New York. His love for the game was partially responsible for his choice of girlfriends. Maggie, his current steady, had worked as a drink-cart attendant at the course for several years. It was a comfortable setting, and

Maggie willingly ignored Sean's nightly free incursions onto the course, where he practiced chip shots from his back garden.

"No, Maggie is working this morning," Sean replied matter-of-factly. "But I had business to attend to in downtown Syracuse, so I figured I'd surprise you with a visit. I can come back if you're busy."

Chris threw back his head and laughed. "Oh, please, stop. It's bad enough when my mom lays on the guilt trip. I don't need to hear it from you, too. Of course I have time. What's up?"

"Well, first of all, I wanted to know if you'd want to join me in a little excursion," said Sean, pulling out a thick sheaf of papers. He pulled a couple pages off the top of the pile and placed them on the kitchen table. "The Genesee River is up to its highest level in almost twenty years. The white-water rafting is pretty outrageous; it's a real rodeo. You want to join me next weekend for a trip through the gorge?"

"Sure, as long as my schedule is open," said Chris, rather hesitantly. "But that sounds kind of tame compared to your normal expeditions. Is that all you came to ask me about?"

"Uh, no," admitted Sean, shifting his feet awkwardly. "I guess you know me a bit too well to believe that."

Chris laughed again and looked up at his friend. "Well, you gave me a two-page advertisement for the white water rafting, and you're still holding onto another hundred pages of print. It does lead me to think that you have something else up your sleeve."

This time is was Sean's turn to laugh.

"OK, OK," he admitted, looking down at the other papers still in his hands." So I'm guilty as charged. Do I still get time to present my case, or am I sentenced to life without parole?"

"Please, counselor, approach the bench," said Chris, playing along with the game.

Sean rifled through his papers and extracted a single page. This he placed on top of the rafting advertisement, all the while maintaining his silence. Chris looked at the page in front of him and focused on the graphic. It was a single frame—a coin, centered on the page with a one-line caption. It read: "1804 silver dollar: auctioned at $5.5 million dollars in recent sale."

"Yeah, I know about this," said Chris, looking at the article briefly before tossing it aside. "Every coin collector in the country knows about the 1804 dollar. It's the granddaddy of U.S. coinage. There were only a few of them ever struck, and they're all worth millions, if you could find one. But it's believed they're all owned by the big dealers around the country, and no one else can afford them. So what's new?"

As he was speaking, Sean was rifling through the remaining papers in the stack. He nodded his head occasionally to concur with Chris' remarks.

"Probably not much," he agreed, all the while searching through his documents. "But you do have to admit, this is kind of strange," he said, pulling out a stapled packet of pages. "Just take a moment and read through that."

Chris looked at the top page of the packet, glancing first at the headline. It read, "Intrigue of 1804 dollar has many local links." It was an extract from a New York newspaper from earlier that month. Chris skimmed through the text of the article, noting the many fables associated with the storied coin.

"And what, may I ask, brought this to your attention?" asked Chris, looking at his companion. "This is hardly news either. Every few years a new story appears with the 'real scoop on the 1804 dollar.' Why is this different than anything else in the National Enquirer?"

Sean had the expression of a schoolboy who had just asked out his first date. "Because I've been doing some investigating, and I've found some good stuff. But first, did you see the mention of the Adirondacks in that article?"

"Well, no, I guess I didn't get that far down the page," admitted Chris. "Let me take another look."

Chris held the page up to catch the morning light that flooded through the kitchen window. He perused the article quickly, reading through the text that reviewed the romantic past and rumored demise of the rare dollar coins. Many of these fables had been around for decades, including the one that claimed the entire year's mintage had been destined for shipment to a U.S. port, or perhaps overseas. But the ship was somehow sunk in a storm, or captured by a band of pirates who buried the case on a deserted island.

Only when the story reached the last column did Chris suddenly get interested. At that point, certain words highlighted themselves and seemed to jump off the page.

Connections have been established between numerous sites in New York and Pennsylvania as potential burial sites for these legendary coins. Some stories have been passed down throughout the generations that Thomas Jefferson ordered Samuel Moore, Director of the Mint, to melt the coins. However, Moore instead hid them in the cellar of the Mint, where they were buried when the building was destroyed. Another plot recorded the passing of the coins from Robert Patterson, the 4th Director of the U.S. Mint, to his son, who served in the same capacity many years later. According to one account, a large crate containing thousands of the rarities was transported by the son to an undisclosed location in upstate New York that later became part of the Adirondack State Park. However, none of these stories has ever been corroborated by historical record, and most real experts on the subject discount them as romantic folklore.

From there, the article went on to discuss the latest auction prices of recent coin sales, at which point Chris' interest faded. He placed the copied article back on the wooden kitchen table and turned sideways to face Sean. One eyebrow was raised in interest as he addressed his friend. "So what's your take on all this? Has anything of substance ever been found that represents a genuine thread of evidence leading to a particular place and time?"

"Well, no, not really," admitted Sean, looking somewhat sheepish.

"But that could be a good thing, because you'd better believe that any concrete leads would have been run into the ground ages ago. It's the 'faint and wispy' clues that intrigue me."

"So I take it that you've been searching your wonderful fantasy world of virtual reality looking for clues?"

"Not really looking for clues," said Sean. "I'm just having fun looking under rocks that no one might have looked under before."

"Find any snakes?" asked Chris, as he drained the rest of his tea.

"Snakes, no. But I've found a few interesting snake holes that I'd love to explore. And to tell you the truth, I was hoping you might like to join me."

"Why certainly, I'd love to!" exclaimed Chris in an exaggerated tone of excitement. "I think it would be a great idea to leave my new business, which is only now starting to turn a profit, to go streaking around the woods looking for a crate that *supposedly* disappeared two hundred years ago, but probably never existed in the first place. Please, buddy, sign me up right away!"

Sean looked at his friend in disappointment, his eyes narrowed so that his eyebrows almost merged in a single line. "It seems to me that you were rather skeptical when I first dragged you into a search for some precious metals out in the West Canada Lakes," he chided.

Chris didn't need to be reminded of that episode in the heart of the Adirondacks. It had been a little over a year since the two had stood the state's historical society on its ear with a major find in the middle of the remote wilderness region. They had tracked down a massive hoard of gold that had been lost prior to the country's independence and brought it to the attention of the world. The amount of gold, which became known to historians as the Gordon Treasure, was unprecedented within the borders of New York State. Worth millions, it solved a mystery that had remained hidden for almost 240 years. In the process, they had also discovered a new cave system that had evaded detection for eons.

"I hope you remember that little adventure... and none of that would have happened if you hadn't decided to come along for the ride," continued

Sean. "As I recall, that netted around six million dollars in gold. Remember?"

"Sure. And a lot of good it did us! The state ended up claiming the whole thing, and we got zero out of the deal," whined Chris, faking irritation. In reality, Chris considered teaming with Sean to make the historic discovery to be one of the high points of his young life.

"What do you mean, you got 'zero out of the deal?'" asked Sean, incredulously. "You got the beautiful girl, just like the plot was supposed to go. What more can you ask for than that?"

Chris just nodded his head and laughed. "Yes, I must agree with you there. I did get the girl. I still wonder how that happened, considering that we were reintroduced when I performed a flying tackle that flattened her into a pancake back at Lost Pond."

The two friends lapsed into laughter recalling the episode. Chris had met his girlfriend, Kristi, when he and Sean were seeking out the lost cache of gold in the remote region of the Adirondack forest. She was a graduate student in geology who was attempting to find a hidden cave when their paths crossed. Even though Kristi had originally deceived Chris and Sean in order to get information about the cave, all was quickly forgiven after they discovered her following their footsteps in the woods. Chris soon found himself entranced with her good looks and confident demeanor, and a romance blossomed overnight.

After a minute of daydreaming, Chris dragged his thoughts back to the matter at hand. "So, if we assume for a minute that the 1804 silver dollars were actually struck, which is highly doubtful, what have you found that might substantiate an Adirondack connection?"

"Nothing really solid. Nothing at all. But there are some interesting documents on file that I'd like to check out," said Sean, rifling though his papers. "Unfortunately, they're scattered all over the eastern United States in one museum or another."

"Well it looks to me as though you've got copies of most of them already," quipped Chris, nodding at the thick stack of reprints.

"I do, and they're all business-related, so the photocopying fees are one hundred percent deductible."

Chris rolled his eyes in mock disbelief. "Remind me of that fact when I'm acting as your character witness in tax court."

Sean's search was finally rewarded, and he extracted a few stapled pages from the bottom of the pile. "You ever hear the name Robert Patterson?" he asked, laying the papers in front of his friend.

"No, the name doesn't ring a bell. Who is he?"

"Actually, it would be more appropriate to ask the question 'Who are *they*?'" explained Sean. "Robert Patterson and his son had the same first and last names. They lived rather distinguished lives back in the eighteenth and nineteenth centuries. As a matter of fact, the son, Robert Maskell Patterson, led a life that was almost identical to his father's, right down to his professorship at the University of Pennsylvania. It was almost eerie how their careers overlapped."

"OK," said Chris, reading through the biographical sketches. "But how does this relate to your goose chase for the silver dollars? I still fail to see the connection."

"It may be nothing at all, but there are some bits of correspondence between Patterson's office in Philadelphia and the head honchos up at the McIntyre Iron Company in Tahawus that raised my interest. I've got to admit that, after reading this story, I became intrigued with how the Adirondack version got started. It turns out that no one really knows, but rumor has it that a load of contraband coins worth a fortune somehow became hidden within what later became the Adirondack Park. So I started checking out the threads to see where they led."

Chris listened as he leafed through one reference after another, nodding his head occasionally in acknowledgement. "Wow, this guy really got around," he noted, pouring over the life story of the father. "Military instructor, university professor, director of the U.S. Mint, and president of the American Philosophical Society. Not bad for a man who arrived on our shores as a penniless immigrant."

"Yes, I saw that part about the American Philosophical Society. That looked fascinating, although I can't really profess to know what it's all about," said Sean. "Some sort of gossip club for the high-and-mighty of the day, I suppose."

"Actually, that's far from the truth," said Chris, still looking at the reports. "It was founded by Benjamin Franklin as a think tank for the brightest minds of the day, across a multitude of disciplines. It still exists today, and membership is by exclusive nomination only."

"Anyway, Robert M. Patterson, who was the son, traded a number of letters with the principals of the iron mine in Tahawus, which I thought was odd," said Sean. "I mean, what possible interest could he have had in the mundane operations of a refining outfit so far from his own locale? And why would he *ever* decide to visit there, much less bother to write?"

"According to his bio, Patterson was an expert in the field of metallurgy, as you'd expect in his line of work with the Mint," offered Chris. "Also, here was a man who was interested in just about anything that dealt with the natural sciences. So why would you think of that as being suspicious? It all adds up to me."

"Well, I agree with you that he'd have a natural interest in the scientific aspects of mining and refining," replied Sean. "But according to the research librarian at Blue Mountain Lake, Patterson was writing to other individuals at the McIntyre Iron Company who weren't involved in the mine's operations. It just got my curiosity going."

"OK, now you've got my curiosity going too," said Chris, a twinkle dancing in his eye. "The 'research librarian at Blue Mountain Lake,'… I assume you mean Debbie Santori?"

"One and the same," said Sean, smiling back at his friend.

"Oh my God," groaned Chris, thinking back to his last encounter with the museum professional. "She's such a nice lady, but I doubt she'd ever want to lay eyes on me again since I 'borrowed' those two Spanish doubloons from her collection." The reference was to a pair of gold coins that Chris had discovered hidden inside a chest in the basement of the Adirondack Museum. He had used the coins to lead them to the mother lode of the Gordon Treasure, only returning the priceless pieces later when the discovery was announced.

"Nonsense, my skeptical buddy," quipped Sean, patting him on the shoulder. "Not only did she remember you, but she credits you with uncovering two of the most famous exhibits in their inventory. If not for you, she said those gold pieces would never have seen the light of day."

"Thank goodness she's a forgiving woman," said Chris, lifting his head from his hands. "But I still doubt that she'd ever allow me to do research in her facility again without having an armed guard looking over my shoulder the entire time."

"I doubt there's any truth behind that," said Sean. "I told her that I'd like to stop by sometime and look through their collection of Patterson's correspondence. She responded by saying that, while their collection of Patterson's letters were not fully catalogued, either of us would be welcome to look through them any time we wanted. *Either* of us."

"That's nice to know," said Chris, thankful that his reputation had not been trashed by his prior escapades. "But it's not going to be easy for me to dash up to Blue Mountain Lake any time soon, especially with two new accounts starting to ramp up this month. And I doubt there's anything behind this fairy tale anyway. I mean, it sounds interesting, and maybe you'll be able to write a magazine article from your findings. But I'm afraid you're chasing after a phantom this time."

"Probably," agreed Sean. "But I like chasing phantoms. It keeps life interesting."

Chris stood up and removed a lacrosse stick from a hook on the wall. He looked thoughtful as he tossed a white lacrosse ball against the rear brick wall in the living room, scooping up the rebound and repeating the act. An avid, competitive lacrosse player in college, Chris still engaged in solitary "backstop catch" as a means of concentrating.

"So, you're really thinking of driving up to the museum and spending a day poring through everything this Patterson guy has ever written?" asked Chris, catching a low grounder.

"No, that would be impossible," replied Sean. "First of all, both the father and the son were prolific writers, and their letters are held by dozens of museums and archives around the eastern United States. The Adirondack Museum only holds a small fraction of those documents, those which were discovered when cleaning out the original Tahawus town offices, or donated by other members of the McIntyre Iron Company."

"Where are the rest of the Pattersons' papers archived?" asked Chris.

"From what I can find online, there are significant holdings of letters, manuscripts, and other works at a number of locations, including the University of Pennsylvania, the American Philosophical Society, and the Frank Stewart Room," said Sean. "To go through all of those would take years."

"The Frank Stewart Room?" repeated Chris in a questioning tone. "I don't believe I've ever heard of that."

"I can't say as I blame you," said Sean. "But it's a really interesting story. Evidently, there was an electrical supplies salesman by the name of Frank Stewart working out of Philadelphia in the late 1800s. He was pretty successful at his business, which he developed into a thriving company. As the business grew, he looked for a new home for the enterprise that would provide more space inside the burgeoning city. Among the buildings he purchased was one that was the original facility built to mint the first United States coins. It was called 'Ye Old Mint,' and it had stood on that site since its construction in 1792."

"I'm surprised that he was allowed to purchase those buildings," said Chris. "It seems to me that the government would be interested in preserving those structures as historic sites."

"Maybe today," agreed Sean. "But back then, the whole historic preservation movement really hadn't gained momentum. As a matter of fact, Stewart tried like heck to get the government to move the main Mint building to another site. His efforts were rebuked, and he ended up having the buildings torn down to build his new facility."

"And this 'Frank Stewart Room,' is that still there today?"

"Actually, the Frank Stewart Room is a special collection at Rowan

University, located across the river in southwestern New Jersey. You see, Stewart was also a historian and a collector of documents. He amassed a huge library of historical records on topics ranging from geography and government to Indian affairs. When he passed away, he willed most of this material to the university, who built a special room to house its contents. From what I hear, it's quite a place. And, among other things, it holds a number of Patterson's writings, plus countless other documents from the early days of the U.S. Mint."

"What about the version of the story of the 1804 silver dollars that were buried in the cellar of the Mint building when it was ripped down?" asked Chris. "You'd think that this Frank Stewart guy would have known about that and been looking for them."

"Apparently, nothing of that sort was found," answered Sean. "But he did come across a number of coins that had inadvertently fallen between the walls and cracks in the floor. I noticed a display of these pieces on the library's website. Stewart himself donated them to the city of Philadelphia. He was evidently quite the philanthropist."

"What are your plans then?" asked Chris. "It sounds to me like you might be biting off more than you can chew."

"Nah, not really," said Sean, leaning back in his chair and stretching his back. "I've got an appointment with the IT department down at Princeton University early next week. As long as I'm down there, I'm thinking of stopping into Rowan and checking out the Frank Stewart Room. I'm not expecting to find anything earth-shattering. But as long as I'm having fun, what the heck?"

"I'll tell you what," offered Chris. "I have a meeting with a tax accountant in Plattsburgh next week. As long as I'm that far north, I'll detour the extra hour or two and come back through Blue Mountain Lake. I'm not promising you any huge time commitment, but I will at least see if I can zero in on some of the more juicy tidbits about this Patterson fellow. I'll see if they have anything that looks promising about his communication with your beloved McIntyre Iron Company, OK?"

"Deal!" exclaimed Sean, extending a handshake to Chris. "I feel like we're back in business."

"I feel like we're chasing a red herring," said Chris, chuckling. "Mom better not find out about this. She already thinks you waste too much of my time with your shenanigans."

"Yeah, I get that feeling from her, too, ever since I talked you into that skydiving package a few years ago. Jeez, she hardly spoke to me for months after that one."

"Don't worry," laughed Chris. "She still likes you. After all, she thinks you're the one who hitched me up with Kristi. I think mom fancies her as a potential daughter-in-law."

"That's part of being a mom," agreed Sean. "Gotta get those kids married off before you can really be independent yourself!"

"So, regarding your Genesee River whitewater trip, is that still on the table, or was that just a cover to come over and spring your proposal about the 1804 dollars on me?"

"No, of course it's still on. I'd love to shoot the rapids down through the gorge. Wouldn't you?"

"Sure," replied Chris. "But with everything I have going on, I think I might have to decide 'either-or,' so you tell me: would you rather I went whitewater rafting with you, or burned a day stopping at the Adirondack Museum?"

Sean hesitated for a brief moment, his face registering an expression of pleasant surprise. "I guess I'll take a rain check on the rafting."

"OK then," said Chris, raising himself off of his seat. "I'll go through everything they've got up in Blue Mountain Lake, while you do your thing down at the Frank Stewart Room. I still think this is a major waste of time, but I can see that you're not going to get off of it until you've run out of leads."

Sean looked like a kid who had just received his entire Christmas wish list. "This is too cool, guy," he said, slapping Chris on the back. "I definitely owe you one."

Chris walked Sean back out to the dirt-packed driveway. Secretly, he hoped that Sean would give up on this crazy idea rather quickly, although he knew from experience that his friend was dogged once he got something stuck in his head. Chris only wished that he wouldn't waste too much time playing the role of the willing accomplice.

They shook hands one last time. Then, Sean climbed back into the old Mercedes and took off down the road, leaving behind only a cloud of dust.

CHAPTER 6

Sunday, August 9, 2015

Sunday was a rainy, overcast day across the entire state of New York. Chris had braved the elements to tough-out his daily five miles of road work, noting all the while the rumbling of thunder in the distance. He ignored the conditions and finished his run in below-average time, taking advantage of the cool temperature.

After a quick shower and a bottle of water, Chris locked his front door and trotted down the walkway to his Jeep. The Liberty had been a present from his father a year ago, and it still held its showroom gleam. Today, it would take him on the forty-five-minute drive to Utica, to the home where he had grown up and attended school. It was a sentimental pilgrimage that he tried to make at least twice a month, although other duties sometimes interfered with his visits.

Chris maneuvered the moss green four-wheeler up the hillside roads, not really paying much attention to the world around him. His mind was filled with a host of unrelated topics: his new consulting business, an upcoming visit with Kristi, and now the potential involvement in Sean's latest treasure-hunting scheme. He often wondered how he allowed himself to become so 'booked' that he didn't have time for himself, for the other things in life that he really enjoyed. He was still a member of a band he hadn't seen for over a month, and they were threatening to find themselves a new bass guitarist. And he hadn't indulged himself in a single cave exploration in almost a year. Spelunking was one of his favorite pastimes, and he missed the impromptu trips he took during his school years.

The Jeep slowed only enough to navigate a sharp left turn between two stone gate posts and into the Carey's hilltop retreat. Some people might have called it a mansion, although it was in fact merely an oversized farm house from the early days of the last century. Chris Carey, Sr., and his wife, Theresa, had spent a great amount of time and money restoring the big old home to its original glory, and then some. A new wing was added, but in the old style of architecture, and the entire inside of the home was gutted and rebuilt with modern conveniences. It was a beautiful dwelling, and the only home Chris, Jr., had ever known. As Chris' father's legal practice grew in Washington, D.C, he spent more and more of his time there, and he eventually acquired a townhouse in Georgetown. He also owned a boat on the Potomac River that could serve as a temporary residence. However, even though he spent so much time in the nation's capital, Theresa still lived full-time in their Utica homestead. "Too much traffic and too many politicians," she stated as her reasons for keeping her distance from the beltway.

Chris' thought process was interrupted as he drove the Jeep into the loop that crossed in front of the full-length porch. It wasn't his mother's Chevy (her all-American "MomMobile," as she fondly called it) that grabbed his attention. Instead, it was the dark sapphire-colored BMW Z4 roadster that sat in the entrance to the garage that he noticed with surprise. That was his father's personal toy, the car he took when he wasn't escorting deep-pocketed clients around the D.C. area.

Chris bounded up the stairs in his normal leaps, taking them three at a time en route to the front entrance. The heavy wooden door was open, and he quickly pulled open the screen door and went inside.

"Hello...anyone home?" he called out, instinctively heading for the kitchen.

"We're back here," called his mother, her voice coming from the back corner of the house. Although the stately residence had several sitting rooms and an extensive first-floor library with comfortable chairs and couches, the family had always used the kitchen as a gathering place to sit and talk. It was there that Chris found his mother and father, seated at the kitchen table with cups of coffee and bagels.

"Hey Dad, I had no idea you were coming into town," said Chris, leaning forward to give his father a hug.

"I didn't either, until yesterday," said Chris, Sr., winking at his son. "But I had some business to tend to in Albany that couldn't be delegated, so I called your mother and set up a hot date for dinner and a show."

"Oh my God, what has the world come to when I'm your definition of a hot date," laughed Theresa, leaning back in her chair. "You must have been breathing too many of those exhaust fumes on the drive up here."

"Hey, you're still the prettiest girl in town," her husband responded, kissing Theresa on the top of her head. "And I should know. I'm a well-known judge of beautiful girls, you know."

"Well anyway, this is a nice surprise," said Chris. "I only wish that I was sticking around a little longer. I'm putting together a presentation for a large tool manufacturing company in Syracuse on Tuesday, and then I've got to make a trip up to Plattsburgh to meet with some accountants. So life is kind of busy right now, which is a good thing, I guess."

"Wow, your schedule sounds like mine," laughed his father, shaking his head in amazement.

"Yeah, I know," said Chris, a sad smile crossing his face. "And on top of that, Sean talked me into spending a day doing research on another one of his crazy scavenger hunts. I've got to be the biggest sucker in the world to go along with him."

"Seems to me the last time you 'went along with him,' the two of you ended up in the national news," said Chris, Sr. "I had every news channel in the capital area standing in my office trying to get the scoop. None of them believed me when I told them that I knew as little about your find as they did."

"Sorry about that, Dad. Neither Sean nor I ever thought we'd see that kind of a reaction from the press. We figured it'd make the back section of the local paper, nothing more."

"So what's Sean up to this time?" asked the father. "Trying to find Al Capone's missing vault treasures? Or perhaps the final resting place of Jimmy Hoffa?"

"Nothing that easy," replied Chris, staring back with a deadpan expression. "He's trying to find a load of coins that was lost over two hundred years ago, which probably never existed in the first place."

"Two hundred years ago? Were they, perhaps, Spanish?" asked Chris, Sr.

"No, they were American. But they were silver dollars from a year when they supposedly didn't make any dollar coins. At least, none that carried that date. It's a long story," said Chris, who had helped himself to a mug of coffee.

"Ah, all now becomes clear," said his father, smiling across the table. "Are we talking about the famous 1804 silver dollar?"

"As a matter of fact, yes," answered Chris. "Are you familiar with the story?"

"I'm hardly an expert, but I do know that it's perhaps the rarest of American coins, probably worth millions by now. And I take it your buddy Sean knows a guy who knows a guy who knows where to find one, right?"

Chris, Jr. laughed at his father's humor. "No, Dad, not one. But hundreds of them. Thousands of them."

"And Sean wants you to help him find them?"

"Exactly," said Chris, Jr. "And how did you surmise that?"

"Oh come on now," said his mother, looking back at her son. "Ever since you and Sean were boys, he's always had the wanderlust spirit about him. Sometimes I think he picked the wrong field of employment. Instead of working with computers, he should have become a professional reality-show contestant."

"In what capacity has Sean requested your services in his quest to find the Holy Grail of American coins?" asked his father. "I hope you're not wasting too much time chasing around the country on this. It all sounds kind of far-fetched to me."

"It's OK," said Chris, reaching for one of his mom's homemade chocolate chip cookies. "I'm just going to be stopping in at the Adirondack
Museum to check out some correspondence between a guy named Patterson
and the owners of the McIntyre Iron Company, back in the 1850s. Sean
thinks that there are some details about Patterson's life as director of the
Mint that may have been overlooked by other researchers. I told him I'd
check it out, since I'll be up in the neighborhood next week."

"What do *you* think of Sean's idea?" asked his mom. "Does he have anything backing up his suspicions about the coins, or did he just get excited
about something he read in the paper? That's the way he is, you know."

"I think it's a little of each," said Chris. "He doesn't have anything concrete that proves the 1804 dollars exist, and almost every authoritative
investigation has concluded that they don't. But he has done some
research from a few new angles that points out some interesting activity
involving this fellow Robert Patterson, and his son, Robert M. Patterson,
who both served as directors of the mint. Overall, though, I'd have to
agree with dad's assessment that the whole idea is rather far-fetched."

"My guess is that Sean won't give up on it once he's sunk his teeth into
the idea," said Theresa.

"I agree," said Chris. "But you know, there is one thing that I believe
Sean could do that might answer the question right up front. He should
just check into the treasury archives down in Washington and see what's
on record. It seems to me that the whole accounting should be there, in
black and white, for the world to see."

Chris, Sr., rubbed his fingers on his chin, scowling in thought. "No, I
don't believe you're in the right city," he said finally. "If I recall correctly,
the Mint records are in the National Archives in Philadelphia. I remember
that because we were called in to prepare some evidence in a counterfeit-
ing case about five years ago. Also, some of the older records were burned,
as the Treasury Department caught fire several times in the early years of
the nineteenth century. But if those records still exist, I'd start in Philly."

"Thanks, Dad, but not to worry. I don't have time to get down there anyway. If Sean wants to check out the Mint records in the archives, he'll have to go there himself. I have business to attend to and bills to pay. Unfortunately for Sean, my business pays the bills, not Sean."

"Understood," said his father. "I know how that goes; your mother and I were there once, too, about thirty years ago. Anyway, if you're interested in the archives, I could do you a favor, if you'd like. We have a gentleman in Philadelphia who does some work for us from time to time. He's a professional researcher, although his expertise is more in the realm of law and government. But if you'd like, I could have him stop into the stacks of the Treasury Department records down there and make photocopies of anything interesting. If nothing else, it might help put Sean's mind to rest on the whole matter."

"Gee, Dad, that would be great!" Chris replied. "I wouldn't ask that of you ordinarily, but if he's going to be in the vicinity anyway, I agree; it could be a way to tie up the whole thing in a nice neat package. Sean would be happy, and I could avoid making my detour to Blue Mountain Lake next week."

"OK, I'll contact Ron as soon as I get back to the office. Oh, yes—his name is Ronald Greer, and he's one of the best there is in the field. So if he can't unpeel the onion, you can tell Sean that there is nothing to be found. OK?"

"OK, Dad. And thanks again."

That evening, Sean found himself speeding across the New York Thruway and down Route 87 en route to his appointed round of talks at Princeton. He had counted on arriving in New Jersey late on Sunday in order to accommodate an 8:00 am meeting with the IT coordinator. The talks would be focused on some intranet consulting work that the university had put out for bid, and Sean was confident that he could submit a winning proposal for the contract. An avowed night owl, he viewed early morning meetings with some degree of contempt. However, he had purposely scheduled the conference for that hour in order to facilitate an early arrival at his next stop, an appointment sixty miles away, in the town of Glassboro, New Jersey.

The morning meeting and presentation lasted an hour and a half, and Sean left the conference room feeling hopeful about the proposal. He slipped into the upholstered front seat of the old Mercedes and revved the engine. A firm believer in the art of electronic navigation, he plugged in the street address for the library at Rowan University and shifted the automobile into gear.

New Jersey is well-known for its rush hour traffic, and the level of congestion on this particular morning was worse than most. Even though he was past the peak of the morning drive time, it still took him close to two hours to arrive at the school, and pull into a tree-canopied parking lot across from a red brick building that was labeled as the Keith and Shirley Campbell Library.

Since it was the middle of August, the campus was relatively deserted. A few graduate students and staff strolled around the grounds, with an occasional volunteer leading prospective-student tour groups across the scenic campus. Sean strolled down the pavement and between the tall square columns into the library's main foyer. He had made an appointment with the librarian in charge of the Frank Stewart Room, Penney McPherson, who had agreed to meet him at the main circulation desk. There, he signed into the guest log book and was issued a day badge.

As he was putting the badge around his neck, the elevator opened near the front door, and a tall brunette woman emerged from inside. She wore grey slacks and a white linen shirt with a bow tied across the neckline. Her hair was pulled back into a tight bun, and her brown eyes were framed by a pair of tortoise-shell glasses. The resulting picture was that of a stereotypical professional librarian, with an authoritative command of her duties. She stepped forward and extended her hand.

"Sean Riggins, I presume?"

Sean returned the handshake, and was surprised by the firmness of her grip. "Yes, that's correct. And you must be Penney?"

"I am Penney," she replied, her eyes smiling back at her visitor. "It's nice to meet you. I'm glad you were able to call ahead with the time of your arrival. Normally, we don't open until noon or one o'clock, so it's always good to know when we need to have someone here early."

"I hope I didn't inconvenience you?" asked Sean. "I could have come later, but I wanted to have as much time as possible in your facility. I only have one day for research, so anything that I can't find today will require a separate visit."

"No, no, please!" exclaimed the librarian. "Our facility is underutilized, considering the significant historical content of our materials. Our original benefactor, Mr. Frank Stewart, was an avid collector of almost anything ancient. His donation was so extensive that we've barely scratched the surface on cataloging what's here. We have a lot of student volunteers, but even with the added help, it's still a bit of a mess. So please don't feel bad; the more visitors and researchers using our collection, the better."

"I can't thank you enough for the opportunity," said Sean, stepping into the elevator behind his host. "I'm looking for some pretty specific materials, so this might be futile. But I'm still hoping to come away with some good leads on my search."

Penney pressed the button for the third floor, and the elevator started its ascent.

"You mentioned something about the original U.S. Mint building in Philadelphia, as I recall," said Penney. "What exactly are you hoping to find?"

"I'm looking for a few things," said Sean, scanning a printed sheet of paper in his hand. "I'd like to find anything that Stewart had showing the details of the interior of the original Mint buildings, especially the larger front one that housed the administrative offices. Also, I'd like to be able to track down his family tree, especially to find out if he has any surviving relatives in the area today. Finally, I'd like to know if he maintained a diary. If he did, I'd love to see it. I know I couldn't read through the entire thing today, but I'd like to review the days and months leading up to the destruction of the Mint buildings in 1913."

The librarian nodded as she listened, then broke into a quiet laugh. "My God, you do hope to get a lot done in one day," she said, looking Sean in the eyes. "I doubt you'll cover much of that ground today, because most of the materials on the Mint are still sitting in the same boxes as when they arrived here over forty years ago. I hope you don't mind doing some of your own digging."

"Of course not," said Sean, as the doors opened to the Frank Stewart Room. His eyebrows hoisted themselves up his forehead as he gained his first glimpse of the facility. It was quite extensive, with a central research room filled with long reading tables and overhead lamps. Surrounding the central space were specially-designed storage rooms with temperature and humidity controls to maintain an optimal environment for document preservation. A number of computer stations around the room maintained the records of inventory and storage locations, replacing the card catalog systems of old. The entire setup was modern and efficient, and Sean was highly impressed.

"You'll have to sign in all over again," said Penney, retrieving another register book and a pair of forms. "Please understand that the overall Campbell Library works on one set of rules, but our Frank Stewart Room imposes additional restrictions and guidelines on what you may access and how you can use the material. It's all pretty regulated, and you'll need to sign a number of forms, including one that limits your ability to reproduce anything you see here."

"Of course," said Sean. "I will abide by any rules that govern your facility."

"Thank you for understanding. I'll need your driver's license or other official identification to copy, which I'll return to you before you leave today. Is that OK with you?"

"Certainly," said Sean, extracting his wallet from his back pocket. "But you'd better be careful making a copy of my ID. My picture has been known to damage sensitive photocopying equipment."

"That's OK," laughed Penney, glancing at his photo. "I've seen a lot worse. By the way, your request is interesting. You asked to see our materials on the layout of the original Mint buildings. I've never been asked for anything like that in my entire twenty years in this building. Now, I get two requests in the same month. It's funny how things work."

"Someone else asked for the Mint floor plan?" asked Sean, sounding somewhat surprised. "Do you recall what materials he or she looked at?"

"No, I don't, because he never stopped by. I'd say he was probably middle-aged, from the sound of his voice. As I recall, he mentioned that he might try to schedule a visit sometime in the near future. He wanted to see one of our copies of Frank Stewart's works on the Mint. Stewart wrote two books on that subject, you know."

"Yes, I saw that when I conducted my original database search on Stewart's historical writings," said Sean. "It looks like his second work, in 1924, was much more extensive than his original book. That's probably the one I wanted to see as well."

"You could do that," said Penney, "but that might not be the best use of your time. I believe that entire book might be accessible online. I'll look for you once we get inside the stacks. You might want to spend your time going through the loose collections of Frank Stewart's papers and records on the subject of the mint. Far fewer people have ever perused any of that material. You might discover some real finds in there."

"OK, I'll take your recommendation and go that route," said Sean, nodding his concurrence.

Once Sean had been completely registered and received his badge, he was directed to a stack of sturdy cardboard boxes, stacked neatly on top of one another in a corner of a side room. A student assistant, who introduced himself as Brian, was assigned to transport the boxes one at a time into the reading room for Sean's inspection.

As Sean sat down with the first carton of materials, a number of thoughts played upon his mind. First, he was shocked at the sheer mass of documents accumulated by the late Frank Stewart. Although his primary business had been electrical sales, he had developed quite the reputation as a historian, archivist, and author. The massive number of pages contained in these boxes dedicated to the U.S. Mint was astounding. But the overall size of the Frank Stewart Room, with all its various collections on government, geography, etc., was simply more than Sean could comprehend. Stewart must have owned a separate warehouse just to hold his extensive library.

Also of concern to Sean was the intent of the other person who had asked for access to the Stewart collection of mint material. Who was this individual, and what did he want with the floor plans of a building that had been demolished over one hundred years ago? Was it possible that someone else was tracking the same mystery, following the same clues, while attempting to discover the fate of the 1804 dollars? Sean thought that the chances of that were extremely remote, and he quickly banished those thoughts from his mind.

Sean worked quickly through the first box of materials, which contained hundreds of reports and bulletins detailing routine operations of the mint that were too insignificant to be of interest to the National Archives. Also present in bulk were stacks of scientific reports on refining and smelting processes, including new ideas for improvement that had been brought over from Europe. As he worked, Sean kept his eye peeled for anything that came from the era of either Robert Patterson or Robert M. Patterson. The dates that most interested him were 1803–1804, and 1835–1851, when the son was the director of the mint, But so far, he found nothing that matched these parameters.

He quickly sorted through the second, third, and fourth boxes, using the student assistant to repack the boxes after he removed the contents. Sean laughed inwardly at himself every time he looked at his hands, which were covered with special white linen gloves. Any researchers working in the collections were required to wear these protective garments, in order to prevent the oil from their hands from tainting the fragile documents.

A clock on the wall chimed dully, signaling that it was two o'clock. Two more hours before the room closed, and Sean was only through six of the fourteen cases. Even though he was tired and needed to rest his eyes, he plugged on, doggedly scanning one document after another, discarding them as quickly as possible in order to find whatever pertinent material existed.

Finally, as the hour hand on the clock crossed three, Sean began to find some files that caught his attention. The first was a rather thick folder of the names and job titles of personnel employed by the mint over the first sixty years of operations. Much of this information was already public knowledge, but Chris still asked Brian to help photocopy the pages for later use. Next came an inventory list that displayed, room-by-room, the contents of the original mint buildings from 1793 through 1810. Of particular interest to Sean were the names and descriptions of the various storage rooms and vaults throughout the complex. It appeared as though there were a great many repositories for coins and precious metals that were located below the ground floor. Sean reflected upon this fact, his thoughts wandering back to the theory of the coins being buried in the cellar.

Sean had parsed his way through about half of the tenth box, and was about to conclude his search for the day, when he came upon an old-fashioned, brown cardboard folder. It was wrapped with a string, and carried a handwritten label that had been affixed many years after the original file had been closed. In plain cursive letters, it read: "Mint records – returned by family of Robert M. Patterson, for forwarding to official Records Bureau. August 10, 1858." This was extremely interesting to Sean, since he knew that Patterson had passed away over four years earlier. The family must have found these records and believed them to be official records that belonged in the Treasury Department archives. Somehow, they had found their way to Frank Stewart, who included them with his other historical mint documents.

Without knowing what to expect, Sean untied the string and opened the portfolio, allowing the cover to fall to the table. Inside were a few very old and yellowed pages of various sizes and descriptions. The first was a ledger titled "Mint Production Record," dated January 1804. Sean's heartbeat quickened as he looked at the page. It contained a series of numerous notations, written in columns. The dates started on January 7, 1804, and ended on March 28 of the same year. From the looks of the page, it appeared to be extracted from a larger, sequential record book. The number 154 appeared on the bottom of the page, which Sean supposed was a page number. However, there were no other pages present, so Sean could not determine what the numbers in the columns meant. He assumed that they were production figures for coins of some denomination, but nothing else could be derived.

One item that did jump off the page was an asterisk next to a date and number. The annotation read, "die cracked, 3/26/1804; employed new die from Chief Coiner's Office." Sean paused and looked at that line for over a minute, trying to grasp its significance. However, without the rest of the missing record to provide details, he was lost as to its meaning.

He asked Brian for a copy of the record and then moved on to the next papers in the folder. There were a few pages of routine assay results, and a listing of silver resources that had recently been discovered in the United States for producing new coins. The very last sheet in the binder, however, took Sean's breath away. There, in front of his eyes, was a large yellowed page containing a sizeable matrix of letters. It had been written in series of rows and columns, neatly formed into a grid, with each row stacked perfectly onto the one below it.

Sean sat at the desk, transfixed by the paper in his hands. If his suspicions about this document were correct, it could be quite a find. Robert M. Patterson had been an enthusiast of ciphers and codes, and he had invented several of these programs himself. It was a well-known fact that he had exchanged letters with President Thomas Jefferson and offered Jefferson a sample of his cipher to try to break. The president had been unable to do so, even though the code was supposedly "simple enough to break without a key." Jefferson was so impressed that he wanted to designate the young Patterson's cipher as the "national code of the American military."

Within a few minutes, Brian returned with the photocopied records, along with a worksheet to account for the fee for making the reprints. He looked over Sean's shoulder at the encrypted page.

"Hmm... exactly what the heck is *that*," he asked, tilting his head sideways in confusion. "I don't believe I've ever seen anything like that before."

"It's a matrix of sorts," replied Sean. "The man who wrote this enjoyed playing around with word games, and I'm guessing that he was just having some fun when he penned this word puzzle. It's been a common source of entertainment for centuries now, you know. It's not like the folks in the 1800s could log onto their laptop computers and play interactive video games. This is all they had."

Even as Sean spoke, he knew that this document was probably meant to hide something of greater importance than a word game. However, the less the student knew, the better, so he decided to tone down his excitement at the find."

"Yeah, I guess you're right," said Brian, placing the reprints on the table. "Do you want a copy of this, too? I can still make it for you, but I'll have to add another twenty cents onto your bill."

"Sure, why not," replied Sean, nonchalantly. "I've always played the crossword puzzle in the Sunday New York Times. Maybe this will be a little more challenging."

Brian nodded his head and departed with the document, leaving Sean to pack up his notes and personal belongings. He was just taking off his protective gloves when Penney returned from one of the inner storage rooms.

"I hope your time here today has been worthwhile?" she asked.

"I think it has," he replied, stretching his body to relieve some of the tension and fatigue. "I've uncovered a few personnel records from the early days of the mint that should be of use, as well as an interesting production record from 1804 that appears to come from some other source. I only wish I could find the original document, because it's tough trying to figure out a few lines when taken out of context."

"I know exactly what you mean," said the librarian. "However, you have to remember that these documents come from a wide variety of sources. Most were received directly from Frank Stewart, but others have come from smaller donations by local families and individuals who have come across items laying in their basements or attics. Some of them are priceless. But others are worth very little, unless we could learn more about their origin."

"I also found a nice record from one of my main characters of interest, Robert M. Patterson," said Sean. "As a matter of fact, Brian is making a copy of the document for me now."

"Robert M. Patterson… Robert M. Patterson," repeated Penney, a thoughtful expression on her face. "Where have I heard that name before? And just recently. Oh yes, that other researcher who called a week or two ago was asking about the same name. I thought it sounded familiar."

"Someone else was asking about Robert M. Patterson? Are you sure?"

"Of course I'm sure," said Penney. "I had never heard the name before then, even though his papers have been part of this collection for over forty years. That's kind of ironic, I think."

"It sure is," said Sean, his mind churning the possibilities.

As he spoke, Brian returned with the copy of the cipher page. Sean thanked him for his assistance, and then turned back toward Penney. "Let me ask you a question. I'm going to put this document right back into the same folder in which I found it. Then, I'm going to place the folder into the bottom of the box, just like it was. Do you think, if I asked really nicely, you could keep this under wraps for a while?"

Penney sighed and put her hand on Sean's arm. "If you mean, could I keep it a secret, the answer is no," she said. "The whole purpose of this library is the free and open use of Frank Stewart's collection for scholarly study. Anything that is available to one person should be available to others for similar examination. Now, that being said, it would be very tough for any one researcher to determine what you've looked at. But in your case, since you've made copies of certain papers, we do keep records that show what you've deemed important enough to duplicate. In other words, you've sort of broadcast to the world what you've found, and anyone else can obtain copies of those same documents."

"That's OK, I understand," said Sean. "It's all for the scholarly pursuit of the truth, so that's all that matters." As he spoke, he rolled his eyes at himself, amazed how he could sound so convincing and altruistic while considering such a mercenary pursuit.

"That's right," said Penney, giving Sean a friendly pat on the back. "We're all fellow researchers, working relentlessly toward the discovery of truth. In a way, we're all part of the same team, regardless of who gets credit for the next major discovery. All of us involved in the process can know that without our own individual contributions, none of it would have been possible."

Sean did his best to pretend that he was a firm disciple of Penney's philosophy as he collected his driver's license back from the librarian. Maybe someday he could inform her of his actual intent, but not today. Without further commentary, he slipped his wallet back into his rear pocket, and gathered up his notebooks. The less said, the better.

"Thank you for your time and the assistance of your staff," said Sean, already poised to enter the elevator. "Your facilities and your own personal expertise have been invaluable in my research."

"We're so glad to help," replied Penny, taking his hand. "Please come back and see us again soon."

"Thank you. I very well might do that," smiled Sean. Then, he slipped into the elevator and was gone.

Chris walked back into his house after a long day in a client's office. The customer was a non-profit organization that had hired him to detect a case of suspected fraud and embezzlement from their general fund. He had spent the entire day looking at balance sheets, expenditures, and bank statements, trying to identify where and when any monies had been misappropriated. It was exhausting work, and Chris' brain felt fried.

Entering the home, he tossed his briefcase on the couch, quickly followed by his sweat-dampened necktie. As hungry as he was, all he wanted to do was collapse on the couch and nap for an hour or two. After that, he might be ready for a light meal, or perhaps a short run. The answering machine on the kitchen counter blinked a red beacon, indicating that at least one new voice message was waiting. He reached out and pressed the button to retrieve his calls.

"My fellow citizen, my name is John Samuelson, and I'm running for election to the State Senate seat in the…" That was as far as the message played before Chris hit the delete button. The next message then started.

"Hello, Chris. My name is Ron Greer. I'm an employee of your father's law firm, and he asked me to do some research for you in Philadelphia today. I have some interesting information, if you have time to talk today. Please give me a call when you get back."

The message was followed by a phone number, which Chris quickly recorded on a notepad next to his phone. As he jotted down the information, he could feel his fatigue fall away, and his natural sense of adventure injected a healthy dose of adrenaline into his weary body. He hung up the phone, then immediately dialed the number of the caller.

"This is Greer, can I help you?" came the terse voice from the other end of the line.

"Hello Ron, this is Chris Carey Jr.," said Chris. "I got your message when I returned home tonight. Do you have time to talk?"

"Of course," said the investigator. "What can I do for you?"

"First of all, Ron, thanks for calling," said Chris. "My father told me that you'd be contacting me."

"Well, I'm glad that he briefed you," said Ron. "I'd hate to do all this work and then have you hang on up on me thinking I was a telemarketer."

"I only speak with telemarketers if they are females with sexy voices," quipped Chris.

Ron laughed. "Yes, I know. My home phone gets about thirty calls a day down here in the City of Brotherly Love."

"So, Dad says you went through the U.S. Mint records in the national archives branch in Philly looking for anything interesting in the

1803–1805 production records. Find anything?"

"Well, no and yes," said Ron, hesitating in his response.

"Now there's an interesting answer to a question," said Chris, trying to picture Ron's face across the miles. "Exactly what do you mean?"

"Sometimes, as a professional researcher, you have to realize that *not* finding a document is as important as finding it. Do you understand what I'm saying?"

"Not really," replied Chris, holding the phone to his ear while gazing out the back window. "Please explain."

"Well, whenever we review records, whether official or otherwise, we not only look at data that is recorded, but also consider what is omitted as well. Sometimes we can uncover gaps in the record trail that lead us to stories of much bigger proportions."

"Ah, OK, sort of like forensic accounting," said Chris.

"Exactly!" shouted Ron, his enthusiasm showing through the phone lines. "And that's precisely what we found today."

"OK then, lay it on me," said Chris.

"Well, as you might imagine, the official records were all pretty boring," said Ron. "They listed the production figures for each denomination coin, from penny through ten dollar gold piece, for every year since the mint started production in 1792. It was all very thorough, considering that it was done without typewriter or calculator. I was really impressed by the neatness and accuracy of their records."

"Great. Now give me the juicy stuff," said Chris, cutting to the chase.

"Ah, I love a man who gets right to the point," said Ron. "The truth of the matter is that I came across two big discoveries, both of which should make you happy. I'm not even sure which one to tell you first."

"Surprise me," said Chris, barely able to contain his excitement.

"OK, I'll do my best," said Ron, building up to the delivery. "But first, you have to realize that there is more to the story here than the official record."

"What do you mean?" asked Chris.

"Well, the head archivist at the national archives branch in charge of the U.S. Mint records is an old friend of mine. His name is Jim Cardwell, and he's a pretty useful resource; he's got a photographic memory, and he can also tell you where to find almost anything in the Library of Congress. We go back a ways, and we have both worked for your father's company at one time or another. Anyway, he told me of a rather astounding contact he had with a visitor, which took place about a month ago."

"Go ahead," said Chris.

"He said he had a gentleman, a big strapping redheaded fellow, about six foot two, who came in to look at the mint production records for the years of 1803 through 1805. He said that this guy looked at all the records on file, and then broke out a record of his own."

"His own record?" parroted Chris, clearly interested.

"Yes. According to Jim, this guy had a log book, which appeared to be authentic, from the year 1804. The book showed the details of the day-to-day operations of the press room in the early mint building. It was small stuff, you know, that you'd record if you were the foreman in charge of the work shift, or something like that. It included notes, reminders, and things that passed down from one work crew to the next throughout the day. But it also included some details that you might find of interest."

"Care to share?" asked Chris.

"Well, he didn't allow Jim enough time to make a thorough examination," said Ron. "But it appeared as though it was a complete, albeit unofficial, record of the daily operations of the coining room inside the mint building. If I was to take a guess, I'd say that it was the work of a foreman, or other lower-level supervisor, who recorded daily activity for routine purposes."

"And what exactly did it say?" asked Chris. "You sound as though you have something very specific in mind."

"I do," replied Ron. "And it ties back into the part about the missing data I was telling you about a minute ago."

"Go ahead," said Chris.

"Well, there was a pair of entries in this book that were a few days apart. The first one was dated on Wednesday, March 26, 1804. It said that the last of the 1803 dies was damaged beyond repair, and that they were replacing it with a new die to complete production. It looks like they had only produced 220 coins at the time when the die cracked, which brought their total count to 16,950."

"Interesting. Go on," said Chris.

"The next notation that caught Jim's attention was dated two days later, on March 28. It stated that they completed the allotment of 1804 one-dollar coins on March 28, 1804, at 2:35 pm. It further went on to report that they returned the die to Mr. Snyder's vault for permanent storage. From there, the notes moved on to another subject."

"Who was Mr. Snyder?" asked Chris.

"According to the records, he was the chief die forger, which means that he took the master engravings and used them to produce the actual dies used in the production process. He would have had access to, if not custody over, every die in the mint."

Chris leaned against the kitchen wall and rubbed his chin, trying to piece together the notations. "So, what you're saying is that the last of the dollars coined in 1804, approximately 2,600, or something like that, were produced using a die that was dated something *other* than 1803, correct?"

"I'd really rather not get into that discussion," said Ron. "I'm a researcher, and I deal in facts. All I can tell you is what I found, and what I *didn't* find. Which leads me to the other point of interest."

"The bit about the missing evidence?" asked Chris.

"Exactly. And here's where it gets a little intriguing. There are official records on file from the very beginning of the U.S. Mint, commencing in the first year of operations in 1792. These ledgers document the production of every coin and note ever issued by the United States Government. However, there is one, and only one, page that is missing from this record."

"Let me guess: it's sometime in the spring of 1804. Perhaps March or April," ventured Chris.

"You must be a psychic," said Ron.

"Not really," replied Chris. "Since we're talking about this specific period of time, and you obviously know the intent of our search, it's only logical that you came across that hole in the record."

"It's still strange, though," said Ron. "All the official log records are there, neatly recorded and well-preserved. Right up until the last week of December 1803. Then, the next page is just gone. But there was a note page left to document the missing record. It said 'Page 154 of this record is missing. Annual coinage totals found in the yearly report do include coins produced through the first quarter of 1804." The note was dated February 11, 1808, and signed by an official of the Treasury Department."

"Do you think it could have been removed by someone who was investigating the 1804 silver dollar issue?" asked Chris.

"That's not really probable," said Ron. "I've got to admit that I looked into this whole story myself after I got home from the archives; it really caught my interest. But you've got to realize that no one really cared about the 1804 dollar back then, nor did they even know of its existence. If any of them were actually produced in 1804, they apparently never made it into circulation, or we'd have seen at least a few examples of them in collections around the country. The other few dollars bearing that date were coined much later, in the 1830s. So I'd have to say that the missing record was not taken by a treasure-hunter, but rather by someone either inside the mint, or within the Treasury Department."

"Based on the facts, I'd have to agree with you," said Chris. "I doubt we'll ever discover what happened there, since it was apparently removed from the record sometime before February of 1808. But now, I do have one more question for you."

"What's that?" asked Ron.

"Did your friend happen to get the name of the man who brought in the log book you mentioned, the one with the notes from the mint coin press room?"

"Of course," said Ron, sounding slightly insulted that he might have forgotten such an important detail. "Jim got his name off the visitor's log from the sign-in register. His name is Benjamin Grainger, although I don't have a lot more than that. He listed his address as Binghamton, New York, although he didn't record a street address or phone number. Jim said that was kind of strange as well, because visitors are supposed to fill out the complete form with all their contact information."

"Did your friend say whether he asked for a copy of the record book that this Grainger fellow brought in?"

"No," replied Ron. "But he said he did ask where he had obtained it. He said that Grainger told him it had been in the family for several generations, and that he had ancestors who had worked in the mint building."

"Oh really?" said Chris, surprise registering in his voice. "Now there's a lead that's worth following."

"Yes, I thought the same thing," said Ron. "However, I didn't take it that far. I figured I'd just look at the 1803–1805 records, and then let you develop the rest as you see fit."

"Well, thanks for your time," said Chris. "You have no idea how helpful you've been. I know we're probably not going to get to the bottom of this story, but you've sure opened a few windows and let the sun shine in."

"No need to thank me," said Ron. "Your father pays me very well for my services. Please let me know if I can be of further assistance."

After getting Ron's phone number and email address, Chris signed off and opened up the freezer. Seeing nothing worthy of consumption that could be thawed in a few minutes, he threw together a peanut butter and jelly sandwich with a few pieces of stale bread.

Sitting down at the table, Chris nibbled at the sandwich as he thought. He had too much to do already with his new business and not enough time to do it. And now, on top of his work, he had become ensnared in Sean's latest adventure, following the trail of the phantom coins. But even so, stretched as he was, he felt his interest in the matter rising. Ron Greer had introduced some intriguing facts that tweaked his imagination. There was, somewhere, a real mystery involved, with at least one other contender seeking to unravel it. Chris' natural competitive instincts were awakening, making him feel revived and energized.

Tomorrow, he would make the pilgrimage back to the Adirondack Museum in Blue Mountain Lake. The door had opened a crack, and Chris was about to jump through.

CHAPTER 7

Monday, August 10, 2015

Long before setting his alarm clock, Chris had decided that he couldn't visit the Adirondack Museum and complete his business in Plattsburgh in the same day. Both represented lengthy periods of concentration, and they were several hours apart by country highways. Despite his own internal grumblings, he adjusted his calendar to account for a two-day road trip. He would leave home early the following morning, on Tuesday, and drive up through Blue Mountain Lake to search through the museum's collection of letters and documents. Then, he'd hit the road again and spend the night in Plattsburgh, where he'd have the next day with the tax accountant's staff. It all fit into his agenda, and he made his final preparations for the trip.

Chris had already called the Adirondack Museum to tell them of his upcoming visit. Much to his surprise, his call was answered by Debbie Santori, the same research librarian who had worked with him a year earlier when he was researching the Gordon Treasure. He was also relieved to find that she harbored no outward resentment towards him for his temporary pilferage of the two gold pieces he had "borrowed" in the case.

Before turning in for the night, he logged on to his laptop and checked his email. The only news of interest was an instant message from Sean. In it, he sounded purposely cryptic, which Chris found somewhat annoying at this time of night. It read:

Sean-Riggins-IT: Greetings from the road, down around Philly. Can't wait to tell you what I found in the Frank Stewart Room. We've got leads! But apparently, we're not in the hunt alone. I've also found a little old lady I want to meet in Philadelphia, so I'm staying here an extra day. I should be home by Wednesday afternoon. Talk to you later this week. Cheers.

"We're not in the hunt alone," repeated Chris out loud. "Well now, that's very nice to know, Mister Riggins. And I don't suppose you'll let me in on the secret until the next time you blow through here."

Even though Chris knew his friend wasn't online, he tapped out a quick response to Sean's message.

chriscarey1986: Sounds great; I can't wait to hear about it, as well as your date with the little old lady. I've got some news to tell you, too, from the research dude my dad hired to check the National Archives records on the mint from 1803–1805. We can trade stories when I get back from the Adirondacks on Wednesday night. Until then, don't let the bedbugs bite.

Chris was about to sign off when he instead decided to fire off one last email. This was to his father, who would be back in Washington by now. Chris didn't want to abuse his access to his father's extensive resources, as he was fiercely independent and enjoyed fending for himself. However, in this case, he needed the services of an established investigator, and he knew of no other solution. Swallowing his pride, he opened a new email and addressed it to Chris, Sr.

Dad, would you be able to find information, including an address, on a man named Benjamin Grainger, in Binghamton, New York? All I can tell you is that he is about six foot two, with red hair, and he has an ancestor who worked in the U.S. Mint

buildings in the early 1800s. I've tried the phone directory, Facebook, and Google, but came up empty. Any chance you might be able to have someone run a check on this guy? I'll explain later, and I will pay the bill if you can come up with anything. Thanks, Dad. It was great seeing you last weekend!
Love, Chris.

The next morning was cool and overcast for mid-August. Chris looked up into the gray sky as he tossed his overnight bag into the back of the Jeep Liberty and shifted into reverse. He had chosen to skip his morning run in order to be on the road before seven thirty, since he wanted to be at the museum when it opened at ten. He stopped at a local coffee shop for a cup of extra-dark coffee before starting the drive. Chris had a habit of sticking to the local, winding roads to get almost anywhere. And while his friend, Sean, loved his GPS system, Chris preferred to navigate "by the seat of his pants." His girlfriend, Kristi, claimed that he had once stopped near a rural field and asked directions from a dairy cow. It wasn't true, of course, but it had become a standing joke between the two.

Winding his way along the bends and curves of Route 28, Chris' thoughts drifted back to Kristi. They had become so tight over the past year that sometimes Chris couldn't believe they'd met only the previous summer. Since then, she had wrapped up her master's degree at Cornell and had taken on some teaching assistant duties. She harbored thoughts of going on for her Ph.D. and then applying for a professorship at the Ivy League university, but she wasn't sure if she wanted to take some time off first. She took comfort in talking with Chris about her decisions, and the two of them spent hours exchanging their thoughts and dreams for the future.

Timing the drive perfectly, Chris pulled into the Adirondack Museum just two minutes before ten. The parking lot was still almost empty, with just a few cars and campers beginning to congregate in anticipation of the opening. At the admission desk, Chris flashed the membership card that allowed him unlimited visits to the facility for a single fee. He had purchased the membership after his last visit to the museum to show his support for the staff members who had helped him so willingly in his previous work there. It was, he figured, the least he could do.

"Thank you very much," said the receptionist, as Chris dropped a five dollar bill into the donation jar. "You should come to visit us more often. Would you like a museum map and guide for your visit today?"

"No thanks," replied Chris. "I'm just going through to the research library. I know the way."

Chris exited the back door of the entry building and walked along the sidewalk towards the large complex that housed the library and photo collections. It was a much larger facility than most people realized, since this part of the museum wasn't open to the general public. However, researchers could request access almost any time, and generally were granted permission to use the entire collection whenever the museum was open.

Debbie Santori was sitting at her desk in the back of the Lynn Boillot Art Gallery when Chris entered the spacious room. She was a short, wiry woman in her mid-thirties, who looked as though she spent a lot of time training for long-distance road runs. She wore a white skirt, with a red blouse and matching red shoes. Chris wondered if she always wore red, since this was the same color she sported at their last meeting.

"Chris, it's good to see you again," said Debbie, who seemed to launch out of her chair. "It's been so long since you've been up to see us."

"It's nice to be back," said Chris, blushing slightly from the effusive welcome. "I was hoping you'd still let me in the door, after I used a third party to return the gold coins I 'borrowed' from you last year."

Debbie took Chris' arm and tugged him back towards the front door. "Come, come, you've got to see the end result of your discovery," she said, excitedly. They backtracked into an exhibits building across the complex, where Debbie led him to a large display case. Inside were photographs of the cave where Chris, Sean, and Kristi had discovered the original hiding place of the Gordon Treasure. A map, with lines traced in blue string, followed the route of the treasure from Lake Champlain to the cave at Lost Pond, and then on to French Louie's hermitage at West Canada Lake.

"Do you recognize those?" asked Debbie, pointing out a separate display cabinet inside the main window. It was a thick, unbreakable viewing case that had been bolted to the floor of the exhibit. Inside the display space were two gleaming gold doubloons, each sparkling in the glare of the overhead lighting. An alarm system was conspicuously mounted inside the case, a testimony to the value of the coins.

"Wow, Debbie. You've really done a nice job of this. I had no idea that this exhibit was even open yet. It looks fabulous."

"It's been our most popular stop on the tour this year," said Debbie, staring into the glass. "Everyone's heard of the Gordon Treasure, and they all want to know about how we became involved in the discovery. Of course, we had to include you in the story." As she said this, she nudged Chris closer to a framed panel on the wall next to the display. Chris looked at the photograph inside the matting and flushed again. It was an image of Chris and Sean standing next to the pile of gold at West Canada Lake. It had been taken by the New York State Troopers who had helped them carry the gold from the woods after its discovery. Beneath the photo was a caption plate that read, "Chris Carey, Jr., and Sean Riggins, finders of the Gordon Treasure. Discovered on August 9, 2014, at West Canada Lake, Adirondack Park, New York."

"Oh my God," exclaimed Chris, turning towards the librarian. "You didn't have to do that."

"Of course we did," replied Debbie, resolutely. "We wouldn't be telling the whole story if we didn't show who found it and where. All our visitors would be asking anyway."

Chris, feeling slightly embarrassed by the publicity, steered his host back to the matters at hand. "So, you know what I'm looking for today, right?" he asked.

"Yes, you mentioned you're looking for correspondence between the Macintyre Iron Company and the United States Mint in Philadelphia, especially those letters penned by Robert Patterson. Correct?"

"Almost correct," said Chris, leading the way down the corridor. "The name I'm really concerned with is Robert M. Patterson, who was Robert Patterson's son. Anything in the middle part of the nineteenth century, say, around 1849–1854, is of particular interest."

"I pulled a few boxes of folders and loose letters this morning, after your call yesterday," said Debbie. "We've cataloged most of the letters from the more well-known addressees, such as the governors, the state survey office, and other elected officials. But we just get so much material that letters from the rest of the population are largely uncataloged, and to tell you the truth, probably unopened."

The two strolled casually back across the museum complex, while Debbie pointed out some of the improvements they'd made over the past year. Already, a small river of people was beginning to wind its way across the center square en route to the more popular exhibits. They re-entered the building housing the library and storage rooms and descended into a specialized area that Chris had seen before. A series of ultra-modern, climate-controlled spaces provided enough room to accommodate several research teams simultaneously.

Debbie directed Chris to a table at the end of the main reading room. There, a row of four boxes of various sizes and shapes were lined up on the far edge of the work surface. In front of Chris' seat were a few papers and a pencil, which were obviously put there for his use.

"As you may recall," said Debbie, "you must sign our disclosure agreement that says you are not to remove any documents from this library, not that you paid any attention to that in the past." She rolled her eyes in jest as she spoke.

"Hey, I didn't remove any documents last time," complained Chris. "Just a few invaluable pieces of gold!"

"I'm not listening to you," laughed Debbie. "Also, you must have our permission to make copies of anything in the collection. If you decide that you want copies, let me know, and I will produce them for you. The fee for copies is eight cents per page, and we only have a black and white printer. Are you OK with everything so far?"

"Crystal clear," said Chris, signing the forms and handing them back to Debbie.

"OK, then you're just about ready to go. Now that you've signed the paperwork, you may put away your pen, as only pencils are allowed for use in our research library. It's now 10:22 AM. You have until 4:00 pm to conduct your work. Good luck."

Debbie then walked back to her desk, leaving Chris alone in the well-lit room. However, Chris noticed that he was still being observed. Another librarian had her desk situated at the entrance end of the room and was watching him through a large pane of glass. Although she could not have heard Chris' voice had he spoken, she would be in superb position to view his every move. He also noticed a closed-circuit television monitoring camera above his head, although it did not appear to be energized. Chris waved at the lens to see if it was motion-activated, but it remained dormant despite his gesticulations.

As he pulled the first box towards himself, he realized that he probably had bitten off considerably more than he could chew with this assignment. Each box was literally stuffed with documents, loose pages, manuscripts, letters, and brochures. According to his rough estimate, he had about an hour and twenty minutes to spend on each box, assuming that he remained at his desk and didn't take any breaks. If each box contained a hundred items, that would mean he'd have to act as a human scanning machine for the rest of the day. Rather than allowing himself to be overwhelmed by the thought, he dived in, pulling the first few inches of papers from the first box.

In many ways, Chris' job mirrored the work performed by Sean the previous day. It meant moving endless piles of documents, quickly surveying each for a glimmer of pertinence before moving on to the next. Debbie had pulled aside almost all correspondence to and from the iron mine for the five-year period from 1849 through 1854, so the volume of paper was enormous. Chris thought it extraordinary that so many records and letters had been preserved so fully from over one hundred fifty years in the past.

Once Chris was able to locate the papers of Robert M. Patterson, he could focus in on a small fraction of the larger mass. Evidently, the contents of the Tahawus library, along with the personal papers of those charged with running the iron company, had been donated in a couple of large gifts by descendants of the men, and these papers had been collected by the museum. Chris quickly formed a few piles of letters and packages, which he segregated by author and year. It was a challenge, but he could think of no better way of accomplishing the task.

A few letters in the stacks had been left unopened, while others had resealed themselves over time. Chris asked the observer behind the glass for a letter opener, which he would use to tease open the envelopes which were sealed with wax or glue. It was a tedious process.

Chris discovered the point where the letters from David Henderson abruptly ceased and correlated this to his untimely death in the woods. He also located volumes of letters from Archibald McIntyre and, even more importantly, correspondence between McIntyre and Patterson. However, he noted with surprise the number of letters between Patterson and a man named Peter VanderBrooke. He had never heard that name, so he quickly jotted it down on a piece of paper and formed a new pile of documents displaying his name. It quickly outweighed the other few piles combined.

Chris began reading individual pieces of correspondence between Robert M. Patterson and Archibald McIntyre. Most of them were general questions involving the operations of the iron works and the estimates of the iron deposits in the area. A few letters from Ebenezer Emmons and the State Geological Office were present, but none of those appeared to be of interest in Chris' search. A great many of the other letters to McIntyre discussed the logistics of getting to and from the Adirondack site, including the arrangement of carriage transport and train routes.

Chris noticed a difference when he began reading through the letters between Patterson and Peter VanderBrooke. They reached a level of detail that puzzled Chris. While he knew that Patterson, like his father, was a devotee of the natural sciences, he couldn't understand why he would become so involved in the building of structures such as furnaces inside a tiny mining community so far from home. He also noticed Patterson's adamance about journeying to the Adirondacks to observe the memorial service for David Henderson in 1850, and the erection of the stone monument in the woods. It didn't make sense. Unless, of course, Robert M. Patterson was just becoming more eccentric as he entered his older years. He doubted that, but considered it as a possibility.

The next item of interest Chris saw was an oversized portfolio containing a stack of engineering drawings. The folder had a significant quantity of notes written on the inside cover, and the same handwriting appeared sporadically across the diagrams themselves. Chris suspected that they were written in Patterson's hand, so he compared them side-by-side to a letter written by Patterson prior to his first visit in 1850. The two samples matched exactly. Once again, Chris was surprised at the level of analysis apparently applied by Patterson when reviewing the designs. On top of the actual design, he had sketched in a series of alternate patterns, some of which appeared to use additional internal tie rods and anchor plates for even more support.

After completing his review of the furnace plans, Chris felt the need to rest, if even for a few minutes. He pushed his chair back and stood up, stretching his lanky frame to its full height, then flexing his arms and legs in a series of cat-like extensions. Glancing up, he was shocked to see that the clock read three fifteen. He had only forty-five minutes of reading time left with the papers.

Before he could get started again, Debbie Santori stepped into the room and walked behind the row of tables.

"Well, hey there," she said, half sitting on the back of a chair. "I've felt like stopping by to ask how things are going, but this is the first time I've seen you take your eyes off these papers. You sure do have amazing powers of concentration."

Chris had to laugh about this observation. "Actually, I'm usually fairly easy to distract," he said, smiling back in return. "But this is all pretty fascinating stuff. I love old letters and papers; even the penmanship is different from modern-day writing."

"Well, I would hope so," said Debbie. "In case you hadn't noticed, no one actually writes letters any more. We're all so attuned to our laptops and cell phones, it's no wonder we can't use a fountain pen to make pretty cursive designs. It's become a lost art, unless you're into that calligraphy stuff."

"Anyway, to answer your question, yes, it's been a very productive day," said Chris, sitting down once more to review the rest of the pertinent documents. "I've gone through almost everything I could find between Patterson, McIntyre, Henderson, and this other fellow, Peter Vander-Brooke, who I'm now convinced was the head engineer at the McIntyre furnace site. My only problem is that I think I've raised more questions than I've answered."

"Ah, yes," sighed Debbie, shaking her head in understanding. "This is the age-old dilemma faced by many professional researchers. Unfortunately, most documents of antiquity don't come annotated with the author's explanations."

"No, I don't think they do," agreed Chris, reaching for a thick brown envelope near the back of the box. "By the way, I hope you don't mind me working while we talk. I'm just trying to get through this last box before you close today. The other two boxes don't appear to have much related to my search."

"Of course I don't mind," replied Debbie. "I really should leave you alone and allow you to finish up."

"It's OK," said Chris. "I enjoy the conversation. I've been sitting here with blinders on for the past five hours, and my mind is about fried."

As he spoke, he gently used a letter opener to pry open the seal on the back of the letter in his hand.

"Wow, this one is pretty darn heavy," he said, looking down at the parcel in his hand. "There are a lot of sheets in here, but I think VanderBrooke must have used lead ink, because it feels like a brick."

The wax seal finally released from the back of the envelope, allowing Chris to pull the folded papers from inside. As he did this, a large coin rolled out of the middle and settled noisily onto the table. It seemed to take a long time to stop spinning and come to rest.

"Oh, nice!" said Chris, who appeared to be more interested in the papers than in the coin. "Hmmm, this appears to be a random assortment of letters from Robert M. Patterson to Peter VanderBrooke in the last year of Patterson's life. For some reason, VanderBrooke must have seen fit to take the entire year's worth of letters from Patterson and seal them for posterity."

"What about the coin?" asked Debbie, her eyes glued to the eagle gracing the back surface.

"It's definitely old; a 'draped bust' type dollar," said Chris, lifting his eyes to the piece. "OK, let's see what we've got here."

He picked up the coin and examined it in the light. Then, he flipped it over to get a look at the date. In clear, crisp figures, the year 1804 was stamped in silver, just beneath the bust of the Liberty figure.

Chris looked at the date in silence for a moment, and then burst into laughter. His mirth puzzled the librarian, who repeatedly asked for an explanation before Chris could catch his breath.

"OK, right!" said Chris. "I'd love to know who made this specimen, and from what?"

"Whatever do you mean?" asked Debbie, who was clearly in the dark about anything numismatic.

"I'm sorry," said Chris. "I don't mean to be rude, but this is just too funny. Let me explain."

"Please do," urged the librarian.

"The 1804 silver dollar is perhaps the rarest of all U.S. coins," began Chris. "As a matter of fact, there weren't any actually produced in 1804, or at least none that carried that mint year on the front."

"Well, if none were produced, then how could the coin be rare?" asked

Debbie. "Wouldn't non-existent be a better description?"

"Technically, yes," answered Chris. "However, there were a number of coins that were struck much later, for reasons that are too lengthy to explain right now. Fifteen of those coins survived, and today they command prices ranging into the millions."

"Are you serious?" shouted Debbie, her eyes as round as the dollar coin in front of her. "Could this be one of those examples?"

"Unfortunately not," said Chris, patting his host on the shoulder. "I'm sorry to burst your bubble, but all fifteen of the genuine 1804 dollars are owned by either wealthy collectors or the U.S. Mint itself. However, there is a regular cottage industry focused on producing counterfeit 1804 restrikes, some of which look pretty darn authentic. What you are looking at right here, I'm sure, is one of those counterfeit dollars. I'm sorry."

"I knew it had to be too good to be true," said Debbie, a crestfallen expression on her face.

"My guess is that this coin was originally an 1801 or an 1803 dollar that was altered to add the '4.' And you know, the sad part about this coin is that it probably would have been worth several thousand dollars for its actual mint year, had they not altered the date. It's in really nice shape."

"Well, what do you think we should do with it?" asked Debbie.

"I'd like to package it up and take it to a recognized authority I know back in Syracuse," said Chris. "Even though it must be a fake, I'd be interested in finding out exactly how it was created, which might even lead us to the 'when' and 'where.' Once I get an answer, I can return the coin to you, and you can return it to your collection. Heck, you might even be able to create an exhibit out of it, if we can establish an Adirondack connection with the forger."

"I'm OK with that," replied Debbie, considering the options. "As you know, our rules would typically prohibit you from removing anything from the premises. But I can draft up a quick property transport form that will give you permission to carry the piece off-site for purposes of historical analysis. I can truly say that we are not set up to perform such a review at this facility, and I trust your reputation enough to know that you will have this piece back within the allotted time period."

"I appreciate your trust and confidence, Debbie," said Chris, touched by her faith in his character.

Debbie looked back at the clock, which now read three fifty. "OK, please give me a few minutes to prepare the forms. Then we'll have to take a few close-up photos of the dollar, for our own records, just to ensure that you return the same piece. After that, you'll be good to go."

"Just to make sure that I return the same piece?" parroted Chris. "What happened to all that trust in my character?"

"This is just routine procedure," said Debbie as she strode from the room. "Rules are rules, after all. I'm sure you understand."

It was well after four by the time Chris made his final exit from the museum. He took with him a significant stack of photocopied letters, along with a plastic bag containing the newly-photographed dollar coin. He tossed all of these into a box in the back of his Jeep, not bothering to organize the stack before closing the rear door.

Chris then hopped into the front seat and pulled a well-creased map from the center console. He unfolded the large sheet across the steering wheel and considered the best possible route to get him to Plattsburgh. Distance didn't matter, since he wasn't due at his client's office until 10:00 the following morning. Additionally, Chris had a lifetime aversion for taking the most direct route between any two points, especially if it involved a major highway.

Chris was about to put the map away when he noticed a detail written in very small print. About halfway between Long Lake and the Northway, he noticed a notation for "Upper Works and Tahawus." The road he'd chosen would take him past the very community he'd just researched and the large blast furnace that was the pride of the refining community in its heyday. With little else to do and an excess of time on his hands, he decided to make the unplanned excursion and see the site for himself.

In less than an hour, Chris had almost completed his side trip to the site of the iron works. The final few miles of pavement were new, having replaced the dirt road that existed through the end of the twentieth century. Chris was amazed at the extent of the detour, which took him far off the main east-west road. After driving around endless curves and dips, he emerged at the ancient ghost village of Adirondac, home of the Adirondack Iron and Steel Company.

Parking his car at the hikers' parking lot, Chris backtracked to the furnace, where he stood looking at the historic structure in awe. It was as though a piece of history had been ripped from a book and transported into the modern era. As he gazed upon the scene, he could only wonder at the tales that this ghost of the North Country could tell. This massive furnace had the same effect on everyone who looked upon it for the first time. Its proportions were too enormous to comprehend at first sight. After walking a few laps around the base, he extracted a small camera from his jacket pocket and snapped a couple dozen photos. Then, he returned to his car to resume the trip north, leaving the behemoth rock pile to disappear in his rear view mirror.

CHAPTER 8

Tuesday, August 11, 2015

Having spent over an hour touring the site of the blast furnace at Adirondac, Chris completed the rest of the drive to Plattsburgh, where he found the larger hotels booked due to a business convention. He was eventually forced into taking a room at a small, worn-out motel on the outskirts of town. It had a flimsy door and only one working lamp to provide lighting in the dingy room. On top of that, the television received only three channels, and the entire place smelled of stale cigarette smoke.

Chris was so leery of the place that he slept in his long warm-up suit, deciding to leave his suitcase in the car in case of bedbugs. The bed was old and saggy, and he awoke with a sore back the following morning. He arose feeling like a very old man, which he tried to counter with about ten minutes of concentrated stretching exercises.

The meeting with the client turned into an all-day affair. The original purpose of the conference, which was to develop a business plan for expanding the small accounting practice in order to compete medium-sized firms, became bogged down in training and human resources issues that had not been part of the original discussion. Chris welcomed the additional tasking, but felt woefully unprepared for the unexpected turn of events. The meetings went on, hour after hour, with sessions between partners of the firm and other employees. By four thirty, Chris' eyes were bloodshot and he felt as though his head was about to explode. He couldn't have been happier when the final handshakes were exchanged and the consulting agreement was signed.

Chris pushed his way through the revolving door in the old office building and made his way to the parking lot on Court Street. He started up the Jeep and immediately pulled his way into the heavier downtown traffic, heading west until he was able to navigate onto Interstate 87, commonly called the "Northway." As much as he usually avoided large highways, he felt mentally exhausted, and he gladly fell in line with the rest of the cars heading south.

After a few minutes of mindless staring through the front windshield, Chris decided to check up on his email request of Monday night. He pulled over and called his father at his office in Washington. Even though it was now well past five thirty, he wasn't surprised to hear his dad pick up on the first ring.

"Well now, seems like I've been hearing from you quite a bit lately," said Chris, Sr., without preamble. "To what do I owe the honor now?"

"Hi, Dad," said Chris, not trying to hide the amusement in his voice. "I hope I'm not bothering you too much. I felt kind of funny sending you that request for information on the guy in Binghamton, but I couldn't think of anyplace else to turn, given the circumstances.

"No problem," replied his father. "We have unlimited agreements with at least one detective agency in each state, and several in New York. Obtaining information from the Department of Motor Vehicles and other sources is relatively easy, which leads us to lots of other databases revealing all sorts of information. You'd be surprised how much information is available if you're willing to pay the right price.

"Were you able to find out anything about Benjamin Grainger?

"As a matter of fact, we were," replied Chris Sr. "It took a few attempts, but we finally found the right man and worked his story backward from there. And I must say, while he's not a full-blown criminal, I probably wouldn't offer him a job as night watchman in a jewelry store."

"Hmm, interesting…" said Chris, his voice trailing off in thought. "So what did you find out about this guy? Maybe I could get the basic contact info first, and then we could go from there."

"Sure," said his father, rustling some papers in the background. "First of all, his full name is Benjamin Randall Grainger, and he's the third of three children in his family. He's twenty-seven years old, a fairly large guy, six foot two, with red hair and blue eyes. I have his address, phone number, an email address, and even his vehicle description and license plate number. I can send you all that information later today"

"Sure," said Chris. "The more I know, the better. What else do you have?"

"From what I can see, he's been living in his current residence for about a year. Before that, he apparently lived in Philadelphia, where his parents still reside today. He appears to have an employment history in the electronics business, where he's worked in sales for a number of retail and wholesale outlet companies. From what I can see, he was in the process of being investigated by his last employer in Philly when he suddenly decided to pull up stakes and move to the southern tier of New York. The electronics company decided not to spend the time and effort to prosecute any further and the investigation was dropped."

"What were the charges?" asked Chris.

"There was nothing official on record," said his father, "but my contact in the Police Department hinted that it was related to theft of equipment and a potential resale ring involving Grainger and at least one other employee. They were both terminated at the same time."

"Anything else?"

"Well, yes," said Chris, Sr. "Grainger had been living with a woman at the Binghamton address for a few months when there arose some domestic violence issues. Her mother called on her behalf, trying to get a restraining order placed against him. However, as long as no complaint was filed by the daughter, the local authorities had nothing to act on. So once again, no legal action was taken. From what we can see, the daughter is no longer living with Grainger, although nothing further is known about her whereabouts. Did you want our people to follow up on that?"

Chris thought for a moment before responding in the negative. "No thanks, Dad," he replied. "If we need more information on this guy, I'll come back to you later. But for the time being, I'll assume he's simply out chasing clues left behind by his grandfather or other relative. He's got every right to do that, so I'd rather just let the matter drop."

"'His grandfather or other relative...' I don't understand," said Chris, Sr.

"Your research man in Philly, Ron Greer, said that Benjamin Grainger told the archivist that he was a descendant of one of the original mint employees. That's how he apparently got his hands on the ledger book that first mentioned the crack in the last die of the 1803 dollar. That's how we got into this whole thing in the first place," explained Chris.

"I see," said his father. "I must admit that I never really talked to Ron in detail after his day in the National Archives."

"No problem, Dad. By any chance, did your investigator have time to look into Grainger's ancestry? I'm just curious what role, if any, this relative of his played in the original operations in Philadelphia."

"No, Son, we didn't look into that. They just checked out the guy's background, much the same as if he was pulled over for a traffic violation. To tell you the truth, I had an answer back from their office within an hour after our office opened on Tuesday. It was pretty quick, but not very in-depth."

"That's OK, Dad. I really appreciate everything you've done for us."

"Oh, and Chris..." his father began again, "I'd rather you didn't tell anyone that my company's investigative resources went into this effort."

"What effort?" asked Chris, feigning ignorance.

"That's my boy!" said his father, signing off the phone call.

Monday afternoon, Sean checked into a room at a moderately luxurious three-star hotel in downtown Philadelphia, which he had obtained at a bargain rate through an online discount service. Then, unable to resist the temptation, he punched in the GPS coordinates for Geno's restaurant on South 9th Street, in the "Little Italy" section of the city. Finding a parking space nearby, he strolled along the store-lined streets until he came to the neon-lit restaurant that had made its fame by perfecting the Philly cheese steak. He dined on cheese steak and cheese-covered French fries, more for the experience than for the culinary excellence.

While resting later in his hotel room, Sean went online using the room's wireless network. He then removed his notes from the Frank Stewart Room from his briefcase and scanned the pages. His goal was to find any living relatives of Frank Stewart who might still be located within driving distance of Philadelphia. This process was complicated by several factors, including the fact that Frank Stewart had been dead since 1937 and had no children. Sean reviewed website after website of ancestry information. It was a tedious process, logging in and entering each name into each website and then tracing the family names back through time to find connections. Somehow, there had to be a better way, he thought, although he had yet to discover it.

Finally, after a full ninety minutes of searching multiple databases, Sean was able to follow a thread from the 1870s all the way to the modern era. Frank Stewart, who had purchased the original mint building after it was abandoned for larger quarters, appeared to have a living descendant still residing in the Philadelphia area. The name was Rosemary Stewart, and she looked to be the great-granddaughter of Frank Stewart's brother, William B. Stewart. According to the information he could find, Rosemary was born in 1949, which would put her age at 66. To confirm his discovery, he retraced his steps, this time starting in 1879 and moving forward to the current date. The connections worked, and Sean nodded his head in satisfaction.

Next, he pulled out the white pages phone directory of the City of Philadelphia. Predictably, there were multiple columns of Stewarts. He followed the first names down the page until he came to a single listing for Rosemary Stewart, at 18 Sawgrass Lane. According to the online mapping application, her address corresponded to a street in the heart of the city. With that and the phone number, Sean's hopes skyrocketed.

Looking at the clock, he saw that it was still about 8:40, which shouldn't be too late to call a residence, even during the middle of the week. He decided to take a chance and call her immediately, using the phone in his hotel room instead of his cell phone. He figured it would make more sense, in case Rosemary had caller ID, for her to see a local number rather than his area code from upstate New York. The phone was picked up on the third ring.

"Hello," was the simple greeting from the other end. It was offered in a friendly tone of voice, and Sean pictured an older woman who would be responsive to his call.

"Rosemary, my name is Sean Riggins, and I'm in Philadelphia conducting research on the original United States Mint. I'm calling you because you're the only person I can find who, as best as I can tell, is a living descendant of Frank Stewart. Would you mind talking for a bit?"

"Oh my goodness, you have done your homework," said Rosemary, not sounding the least bit disturbed at the call. "But you probably know that I'm not directly descended from Frank Stewart, but from his brother, William, who was born three years after Frank."

"Yes, I did find that," said Sean, hesitating as he spoke. "I only hope that you don't mind the intrusion, or think that I'm looking to invade your privacy. Please, if I am bothering you, let me know and I'll end this call immediately."

"No, it's OK," said Rosemary, who sounded as though she enjoyed having someone with whom to converse. "But one other thing you should know is that I never met Frank Stewart. He died about twelve years before I was born. A gentleman called here once, perhaps around thirty years ago, and he was also conducting research. He said he wanted to talk to me about Frank's life for a book he was writing, which would have been nice. But I never heard back from him after that, and I never saw a book produced on that topic. That's too bad, because my uncle loved books of all sorts. It would have been a real tribute to a very important citizen."

"Yes, it would have been fitting," agreed Sean. "But don't worry about the prospect of Frank's contributions being forgotten. I just spent a full day at the Frank Stewart Room at Rowan University, and his entire life is commemorated inside that institution. It's a real honor to his memory."

"I know. I've been down there on a couple of occasions, and it is a wonderful addition to the school's library," said Rosemary. "I'm sure Frank would have been pleased if he could have seen it today."

Having established a nice rapport with the woman, Sean next decided to go for broke and see if she would meet with him. He was due back in New York the following evening, so it had to be now.

"Rosemary, I was wondering if you'd be willing to let me stop by tomorrow to talk with you about Frank Stewart, as well as his brother, and anything you might know about the building. Would that be possible?"

There was a bit of a pause on the other end of the line, followed by Rosemary's measured response. "Well, yes, you could stop by at around ten thirty in the morning. I work part-time in the Philadelphia school system, and I'm still on summer break. My niece might be over visiting at the same time. Is that alright with you?"

"Of course, it's fine," replied Sean. Inwardly, he smiled, knowing that the niece would only be there to ensure that Sean wasn't visiting under false pretenses. "I appreciate any time that you can give me."

"OK," said Rosemary. "I'll see you then."

The following morning, Sean checked out of his room after breakfast and threw his luggage into the trunk. The overnight rain had ceased, and a bright blue sky dominated the view overhead. If nothing else, he would have a great day for driving back to his home in Little Falls.

After failing to locate a curbside parking space, Sean pulled his car into a parking lot about a block away from his destination. He then locked his car and walked with his briefcase to the address on Sawgrass Lane. It was situated among a number of older brownstone-style buildings that had been wonderfully restored.

Sean pressed the antique-style doorbell on the left side of the darkly-stained wood door. He couldn't hear the bell ring, so he assumed that it must sound somewhere on the upper floor of the dwelling. He was about to ring the bell a second time when he heard the sound of footsteps. Shortly thereafter, the door swung open, giving Sean his first view of Rosemary Stewart. He was surprised by what he saw. For some reason, he had expected a woman who looked much older, with perhaps more gray hair. However, the woman who greeted him was tall and vibrant, and looked about ten years younger than her age. He wondered if he'd gotten the wrong address by mistake.

"Why, you're right on time," said Rosemary, as she pushed open the outer screen door. "Please, do come in."

"Thank you so much for letting me stop by," said Sean, shaking hands with the woman. "I guess we've already introduced ourselves."

"Yes," laughed Rosemary. "We can bypass that part of the conversation, although I'd love to know the reason behind your investigation. But first, please, come upstairs so we can sit down in comfort."

Sean followed Rosemary up a long flight of stairs to a sitting room in the front of the house. The room was filled with colonial furniture and houseplants, with large windows overlooking the main street. An antique harpsichord was placed against the side wall between two bookshelves filled with leather-covered volumes, giving the entire scene an air of class and sophistication.

Sean was about to compliment Rosemary on her taste in décor when a much younger woman walked into the room, stopping him in his tracks. She had the effervescent glow of youth and long, caramel-blonde hair that swished across her shoulders and down her back in flowing waves. Her skin was soft-toned and tanned, and her eyes glowed that bright blue hue that tends to make men forget what they were about to say. About 5'8", she was as tall as Sean, although she was wearing shoes with a slight heel. The rest of her athletically-trim body was clad in shorts and a halter top. Sean was hypnotized by her beauty.

"Sean, I'd like you to meet my niece, Tracey. Tracey, this is Sean Riggins, the man who called to talk about your great-uncle, Frank Stewart."

"Nice to meet you," said Tracey, her smile exposing a set of perfect white teeth. Even her smile was amazing.

"The pleasure is mine," said Sean, accepting her handshake. He wanted very much to say something witty or interesting, but he found himself tongue-tied.

"Are you in town for long, or just passing through?" Tracey asked.

"Actually, I'm leaving today," said Sean. "Your aunt was very kind to allow me to stop by on such short notice."

"Well, I'm going to do some practicing," said Tracey, motioning at a guitar that sat on a stand in the corner. "I'll be in the next room if anyone needs me."

Sean watched her exit through the doorway, and then dragged his eyes back to his host.

"She's studying music at the University of Pennsylvania," said Rosemary. "She wants to go into the performing arts. Then again, her advisor at school thinks she should try acting instead. She is rather good at it, and she has the looks to go along with the talent."

"She is a very attractive young woman," agreed Sean, trying his best to maintain a professional demeanor. If Maggie, his girlfriend, could have seen him at this moment, she probably would have had some words to say to him.

Rosemary directed Sean to an overstuffed parlor chair, before taking an identical seat across an oval wooden table from him. Meanwhile, Sean used this interlude to regain his train of thought.

"So please, tell me, exactly what is it that you hope to learn from me about Frank Stewart?" she asked. "My curiosity has been building since our conversation last night."

"Well first of all, I'm sorry if I sounded mysterious in any way," chuckled Sean, recalling their initial talk. "I found you by use of some Internet databases, and I felt funny about calling. But I'm trying to learn anything I can about Frank Stewart's activities regarding the original buildings, before he tore them down in 1907. I have so many questions, and no one appears to have any answers, including Frank's own autobiography."

"The thing you probably don't know," said Rosemary, "is just how hard he tried to have those buildings preserved—all three of them. Frank was a self-avowed historian. He didn't just collect history books; he wrote them as well. To him, it was sacrilege to tear down such historic buildings. However, he had already paid for the property, and he would have gone bankrupt had he not gone ahead with his business plan. So, when the government refused to relocate the buildings to a different site, he was left with no choice but to destroy them. Even then, he had them demolished in stages, hoping that the government would wake up to the atrocity, and step in to save whatever was left. They never did, so the country lost one of its greatest landmarks."

"That must have been hard on him," said Sean. "But I bet he came across a lot of interesting artifacts that were left over from the previous tenants as the buildings were dismantled?"

"Well, yes, as a matter of fact, I can tell you about that," said Rosemary. "Then again, I suppose most of Philadelphia knows about it as well, because he donated most of what he found after the work was completed."

"Are you talking about the coins from inside the various walls and floors in the building?" asked Sean.

"Yes, I am. The workers came across quite a few pieces that had slipped between floor boards and other crevices inside the coining rooms and vaults, enough to fill a small display case. If I'm not mistaken, it's still on display over in city hall, or in one of the city administration buildings."

"And his collection of books and other documents, did all those go to Rowan University?"

"Yes, mostly," said Rosemary. "But you know, originally, they were supposed to be donated to another recipient. Frank had first selected a local historical society to receive the entire collection of papers, letters, manuscripts, and maps. The collection was huge, almost twenty-five thousand individual items, some dating back as far as 1551. Other documents in his collection were valuable because they were one-of-a-kind, such as his copy of the minutes of the Stamp Act Congress of 1765. So you can only guess how distraught the society was when they learned that he had changed his mind and designated Glassboro State Teachers College of New Jersey to receive the whole lot."

"Yes, I read about that," said Sean. "That was the predecessor of Rowan University, right?"

"That's correct. They changed their name in 1992 to honor the donors of a massive gift to the school."

"So he gifted his entire historical library to the university, and the coins he found in the mint building to the City of Philadelphia," confirmed Sean. "Did he leave anything else behind?"

"What do you mean?" asked Rosemary, studying his face.

"Well, I guess I'm looking for two different kinds of possessions, the first being personal, such as family bibles or other records. The other items I'm looking for are any artifacts that might have been left over from the mint buildings that he *didn't* donate to the city or university. Anything left behind by this man that I could hold and examine for clues of his life and times."

As Sean spoke, Rosemary's expression changed. He could see her smile fading, being replaced by a more guarded expression. It wasn't obvious, and it wasn't intentional. However, Sean found himself instantly worried that he might have touched a raw nerve.

"Frank Stewart was a very wealthy man," said Rosemary, her eyes averting Sean's for a moment. "He and his wife Abigail had no children, no one to whom they could leave their amassed fortune. As such, yes, a lot of material goods were distributed to other family members after their deaths. Frank's brothers and sisters all received items of material and sentimental significance, I'm sure. My own father had part of a room filled with some antique instruments and furniture from Frank's house. That harpsichord is one of the surviving pieces," she said, lifting her head toward the exposed keyboard.

"Is there anything else," asked Sean, taking the direct route. "Anything you might have from Frank Stewart that is directly connected with the

Mint and its early operations?"

"I don't know...I'd have to think about it," said Rosemary, her voice trailing off as she spoke.

Sean said nothing in response. He just sat quietly and regarded her without expression, waiting for her to speak again. The stillness was lengthy. In the background, an ornate carved clock ticked on the wall, marking the seconds as they passed in silence. Finally, she looked up at Sean and stared into his eyes with a slight trace of a smile.

"Yes, I do have something here that came from the mint," admitted Rosemary, shrugging her shoulders as she spoke. "And I have a funny feeling that you knew about this all along."

In fact, Sean hadn't known of any such thing. However, he maintained his silence and simply nodded back at her, waiting for further explanation.

"Sean, I don't mind sharing this with you. But before I do, I want your assurance that you are *not* connected with the government, and that you are *not* going to file a claim on their behalf to have this taken away from me."

Sean could read the fear and mistrust in Rosemary's eyes, and he felt the need to disarm her as quickly as possible, to put her mind at ease that he was not pursuing her story for personal gain. He leaned forward and took her hand in his.

"Rosemary, I promise you, my interest in your ancestor is only from a numismatic and historical point of view," he said earnestly. "My friend and I are pursuing the story of the legendary 1804 silver dollar, which most experts believe doesn't exist. Frank Stewart was one of the few men of his time who believed that it did. I'm here because I'm trying to prove that he was right."

Rosemary's eyes lit up, and her facial expression immediately brightened. "Why didn't you say that right up front?" she asked, squeezing his hand back with enthusiasm. "I think that's a wonderful idea! And yes, I'd love to show you what I have. I don't really know whether it would help you in your efforts, but it's worth a try."

She then rose from her seat and beckoned for Sean to follow. But before leaving the room, she called to her niece. "Tracey dear, I'm going to take Sean downstairs for a few minutes. We'll be right back, OK?"

"OK," a voice called back during a lull in the guitar strumming.

Rosemary then led Sean through a door which opened to another flight of stairs, which took them down the back side of the house. It ended at a storage room on the lower level, although there was yet another staircase leading to the basement.

Once in the storage room, Rosemary opened a sliding panel door, which exposed a series of shelves. Most of these shelves were loaded with a variety of old dishes, appliances, and other household supplies. She ignored these and retrieved a small step ladder, which she placed on the extreme left side of the closet. Then, reaching up, she began to maneuver some object towards the edge of a shelf.

"Could you give me a hand please?" she grunted, pushing at the container with both hands raised over her head.

Sean approached the ladder, where he could see a shelf that was completely hidden from view. Unless a person stood at the very end of the closet, and looked up toward the ceiling from the right angle, they would never know it was there.

"That's a pretty clever way to conceal your valuables," said Sean, reaching up to take the item from Rosemary's arms. It was a very old wooden box, which was reinforced with steel bands and latched shut with a modern padlock in front.

"Yes, I know," said Rosemary. "I had it built into the closet about ten years ago. It's probably safer than a safe, because no one would ever think to look in there. In a way, it's my own personal vault, only I don't need to worry about a key."

"Whatever is inside must warrant all the security" commented Sean, trying his best to maintain a calm expression.

"I believe so," said Rosemary, "My father said his uncle told him that it was quite valuable, and that it should remain in the family. He said that the chest had originally belonged to a gentleman named John Rittenhouse.

You'll notice I've written that name down on the inside of the box. From what I hear, he used to work at the mint, too."

"Yes, he did," said Sean. "In fact, he was the first director of the U.S. Mint, back in 1792, and a renowned scientist as well. He was a very distinguished man in his day."

"I didn't realize that," said Rosemary, dusting off the top of the chest. "Anyway, there are some pretty unusual things in here, like utensils and such. But there are a couple of tiny coins, too, the likes of which I've never seen before. If that's what you're looking for, you can take as much time as you want with them."

Somehow, the adjective "tiny" didn't seem to fit in with Sean's search for silver dollars, and his spirits were dampened. However, he was still eager to view the contents of the case. Rosemary started to spin the combination dial on the front of the lock, so Sean turned his head as a courtesy. In a few moments, he heard the hasp pop open, and he looked back at the ornate antique chest.

"First of all, what do you think of this?" asked Rosemary, holding up a beautifully carved silver candlestick. It sat on a broad, octagonal base, with extensive fluting and beaded patterns along the edges. Sean had never seen anything so exquisite, and he held the specimen gently in his hands.

"This is an absolutely marvelous piece," said Sean. "I wish I knew more about this kind of thing, because I'm certain that it must be very valuable." He turned it over and noticed a crest stamped on the back. It was that of a bird, perhaps an eagle, with outstretched wings, resting on a circular ring. Sean paused and looked at the symbol for quite a while, not quite sure whether to trust his instincts. He then put the piece down without saying another word, and looked for the next item in Rosemary's hand.

This time, she removed four spoons from the case. One of them was longer than the others, with a deep scoop that resembled the ladle from a punch bowl. It, too, carried some intricate carvings on the handle, including the same eagle crest as the candlestick.

Next came a large, round serving plate, with a series of carved, fluted edges, followed by an even larger oval serving tray, with a pair of simple handles on either side. Finally, there appeared a few more spoons at the bottom of the chest, simpler in design but of substantial weight. All these items had two things in common: they were made of silver and carried the same eagle crest somewhere on the surface.

Sean's anticipation was becoming stronger with each successive exhibit. Yet, he held his tongue, deciding to see what else his host had in store for him. He didn't have long to wait, as he watched her reach down into the far corner of the box and lift out one final item. It was a small, white jewelry box of a completely contemporary design, the kind you get when you buy a necklace or bracelet from a modern-day jewelry store.

"Here are those coins I was telling you about earlier," said Rosemary, removing the lid from the box. "I stored them in here so they wouldn't be overlooked inside this big box. They're cute little things, aren't they?"

Sean took the box from Rosemary and looked inside. It contained a pair of tiny coins, each smaller in size than a modern-day dime. Even though the lighting wasn't outstanding, he could still see the clean, crisp mint stamps in the heavily tarnished metal. He was pretty certain that it was silver, although the surface had turned a deep gold, with hues of green, blue, and other shades as well. On the front was the bust of a woman, surrounded by the letters "LIB PAR OF SCIENCE & INDUSTRY." The date 1792 was displayed beneath the bust.

Rather than touch the coin itself, Sean tore a small piece of paper from his note pad and rolled it into a miniature scroll. He used this as a tool to flip the coins from front to back. The reverse side of the coin was graced by an eagle, not unlike the bird on the crest of the silverware in the chest. "UNITED STATES OF AMERICA" curved around the top border of the coin, while the words "HALF DISME" appeared on the bottom of the back.

Sean looked at the two coins in disbelief. When he was finished with his examination, he gently set the box on the table and stared at his host.

"Well, what do you think?" asked Rosemary. "Are these as valuable as my great-uncle indicated? And will this help you with any clues about

Frank Stewart's theory about the 1804 dollar?"

Sean wasn't really sure where to start. He knew he should be leaving Philadelphia shortly in order to make it back to his home at a decent hour. Yet here he was, sitting in front of history, as distant from his own investigation as it might be. He decided to spend some extra time and sacrifice his sleep later that night.

"Rosemary, these coins are worth a great deal of money, as are the other artifacts. But what's even more amazing is the story you have here, if you wish to make it known to the world."

"I'd probably rather keep it to myself, but go on," urged Rosemary. "You're really building up my level of suspense. So tell me, TELL ME! Start with the coins, please."

"OK, I'll do that," said Sean. "The coins are called 'Half Dismes ,' with each one worth one-twentieth of a dollar. They were the very first coins authorized for production in the United States. As a matter of fact, they were minted even before the first United States Mint building was completed, in a private facility authorized by George Washington himself. John Rittenhouse, whom you mentioned earlier, probably oversaw the engravers and press men who made these coins possible."

"And their worth?"

"Based on their uncirculated condition, and the fact that they have probably been sitting in a clean storage location for the past 220 years, they are definitely worth several thousand dollars apiece," said Sean. "There's no doubt about it."

"Oh come on," shouted Rosemary, not believing her ears. "Each one of these is worth thousands?"

Sean picked up the box one more time, eying each coin critically. As he gazed at the two, he spoke analytically, as though performing an on-the-spot appraisal. "Yes," he said, still looking down at the two specimens. "As a matter of fact, I will personally offer you four thousand dollars for the example on the left, and six thousand for the other coin, which appears to have sharper images on the front side. That's probably a pretty fair price, although you might want to have them professionally graded before selling them, if that's your desire."

"Ten thousand dollars for the two? I accept!" said Rosemary gleefully. "Do I get it in cash? Soon?"

The trap had been set, and Rosemary Stewart had fallen into it, head-first. It was a good thing, thought Sean, that he was an honest man, or he could have become very wealthy that day without breaking a sweat. He returned the box to the chest and took another deep breath.

"No, Rosemary, you don't get the cash today, because, in a sense, you've just been robbed, and you never even knew it."

"WHAT?" said the woman, her face clouding over in doubt and dismay. "What do you mean? What are you telling me?"

"Rosemary, I'm trying to point out a simple fact to you, that these coins do not belong here. You should have them locked in a bank vault. Because, you see, I wasn't telling you the truth about the real value of these pieces. I just wanted to see if you were susceptible to a potentially untrustworthy dealer, and I'm afraid you were."

"OK, if they're not worth several thousand dollars, what is their value?"

"The last example of a coin in this condition was sold at auction about three years ago. The gavel price was over three million dollars."

As soon as the words left Sean's lips, he knew that he shouldn't have told her in such a direct manner. Her face, which had been flush with color only moments earlier, drained to pure white, and her fingers began to quiver.

"You, you....y-y-you mean that the contents of this box could be worth over six million dollars?" she asked, trying hard not stutter.

"Probably more, because the coins are in such pristine condition. They've probably never been touched. But only an expert dealer, in conjunction with a major auction house, would be able to answer that question for sure."

"Oh dear. Oh my goodness, gracious me!" exclaimed Rosemary. "I hadn't expected anything like this. What do I do?"

"First, you lock these things up in a safe deposit box," said Sean patiently. "Then you need to decide exactly what it is that you want to do with them, whether you'd rather sell them or keep them in your possession."

"OK. I know that's good advice," agreed Rosemary.

"But there is something else here that you need to know about that is probably even more important than the value of those coins."

"The other items in the chest?" guessed Rosemary, looking back at Sean.

"You got it," replied Sean, a smile creasing his face. "I did some research on the history of the U.S. coinage before I came down here, and I read up on some interesting folklore that you, my dear lady, may have just proven to be fact."

"You're kidding?" gasped Rosemary. "How could that be?"

"George Washington authorized the first coins to be struck in July 1792, which resulted in the first batch of fifteen hundred coins ever minted under the banner of our new country. Less than ten percent of those coins still exist today, two of which are sitting in front of you as we speak."

"Go on," said Rosemary, glued to the story.

"Those were the days before we had either an official mint building or a reliable supply of silver from which to press the coins. For over two hundred years, the myth has existed that George and Martha Washington donated some of their personal silverware to create our nation's first coins. Some collectors believe this story, while others consider it to be a cute bit of folklore. Regardless, Washington's personal silver set had a characteristic shield stamped on every piece."

"No!" shouted Rosemary, staring incredulously.

"Yes," replied Sean, resolute in his belief. "Washington's personal shield was an eagle, with wings outstretched, sitting on a circular ring. I am certain that the pieces in your possession belonged to President George Washington."

Within twenty minutes, Sean was pulling his Mercedes up in front of Rosemary's townhouse, having volunteered to provide shuttle service to deliver her and her precious cargo to the bank. She had decided to make this trip immediately, upon learning the value of the treasure she'd kept unsecured in her home for so many years. After getting her mind back in gear, she briefly considered calling an agency to arrange an armed guard to accompany them to her safe deposit box. However, Sean quickly persuaded her that the extra precaution would probably raise more attention than anything, and might even reduce the chances of a safe delivery. Instead, she decided to ask Tracey to come along for the ride. "There is safety in numbers," she said resolutely. "I'd like her to join us."

Sean wasn't about to object. He had already advised Rosemary not to disclose the full nature of the trip, only to say that she needed to visit the bank and that she desired Tracey's company. He made no comment as she opened the back door and lithely climbed into the back seat, while her aunt took the passenger seat up front. They were obviously in the middle of a conversation as they got into the classic car.

"Please don't worry about it, Rosemary. I'd love to keep you company, no matter where you go. Maybe we can do lunch afterwards down at the Bourse?" Her remark was in reference to an old commodities exchange building near Independence Hall that had been converted into a large food court, with specialty stores carrying souvenirs for the crowds of tourists.

"OK, honey, we can do that," laughed Rosemary. "But I must say, I am jealous. I don't see how you maintain that sleek figure with how you eat. It must be your young metabolism."

"And daily aerobics classes," reminded Tracey, chiding her aunt. "I keep trying to get you to come along, but you never want to try."

Once they reached the bank, Sean accompanied Rosemary to the safety deposit desk, where she was escorted by a bank employee into the vault area. Tracey remained behind with Sean, and quickly struck up a conversation with him.

"So what's this all about?" she asked, her natural smile creating a pair of dimples on her cheeks that Sean thought irresistible.

"Let's just say that your aunt has a couple of items that are extremely rare and incredibly valuable. I advised her to keep them locked up in a safe deposit box, and she accepted both my advice and my offer of a ride."

"So, what are you?" asked Tracey, the smile never leaving her face. "Just a Good Samaritan who drives around giving people rides to the bank?"

Sean laughed, realizing that Tracey must have been slightly suspicious of his motives from the beginning. "No, hardly anything like that. But I am part of a team investigating an early mystery inside the U.S. Mint, and your ancestor, Frank Stewart, was quite involved in the plot. Your aunt is the only surviving relative I could locate on short notice, so here I am."

"Yes, she told me about that," said Tracey. "She also told me a little bit about what you've done for her this morning, and I must say, you really must be a pretty nice guy. Rosemary didn't want to tell me everything, but I could see by the look in her eyes that she was very pleased. You know, a lot of people in your position would try to take advantage of someone unsuspecting like my aunt Rosemary. I'd like to thank you on her behalf for being so kind and helpful. Please let me know if there is anything that I can ever do for you, OK?"

Sean hesitated for a moment, then decided to ask a question. "Actually, there is something that you might be able to do for me. Rosemary said that you are a student at the University of Pennsylvania, right?"

"Yup. I'm in my sophomore year."

"One of the main subjects of our research was a professor at your university almost two hundred years ago," said Sean. "I believe that he gifted some of his papers and books to the school's library, and those documents are part of their permanent collection today."

"That's pretty cool. I didn't know we had anything that old at our library. Everything looks so new inside," remarked Tracey.

"Anyway, since I live in Upstate New York, I'd really appreciate having someone there whom I could pay to look up documents and send me copies. Would you be interested in taking that on?"

"Sure!" said Tracey, her eyes a fiery azure blue. "I could use some spending money from time to time."

"OK then," said Sean, removing his wallet from his rear pocket. "Here is my business card. Do me a favor and send me an email whenever you have time, just so I'll have your email address. Then, I'll contact you as soon as we need the assistance."

Tracey looked at the card and noticed Sean's name next to the title of "President."

"Oh, wow! You own your own company?" she asked.

"It's no big deal," he replied, smiling back at her. "I'm really just a one-man show with an IT consulting practice."

"Well thanks again," said Tracy. "I'll send you an email when I get home tonight, and then I'll look forward to hearing from you."

Within a few minutes, Rosemary returned, although without the box. "All locked up tight," she said, as she smiled at the two. "I can rest easy now."

"We're going to have lunch now, Sean," said Tracey. "Would you like to join us?"

"Thanks, I'd really enjoy that. But I have almost six hours of driving ahead of me, and I need to be home by this evening," said Sean. "Could I take a rain check on that for some other time?"

"Of course you can," said Rosemary, answering for her niece. "If you could drop us off somewhere near the Independence Mall over on Market Street, we could catch the bus back to my house."

"It would be my pleasure," said Sean, opening the passenger door for Rosemary.

The traffic between the bank and the Independence Mall was atrocious, as always, with thousands of tourists milling around the Liberty Bell exhibit and Independence Hall. As they crept along, being passed by pedestrians on the sidewalk, Rosemary brought up a topic that had already crossed Sean's mind.

"So tell me," she began, "now that we've locked up the two coins, what do you think I should do about the rest of the antique silver left in the chest?" She wore a concerned expression as she considered the issue.

Sean just raised one corner of his mouth and shrugged noncommittally.

"No, really," continued Rosemary. "You've been so very honest and helpful. Tell me what you are thinking."

"Personally, if I was in your shoes, I'd probably consider those items as part of the historical record of our country," said Sean. "They were the personal property of our first president, and they represent a very important part of our nation's heritage. Based on that thought..." Sean let his voice fade off.

"So you think they belong in a museum?" asked Rosemary.

"If I owned them, I would probably consider that as the most logical option," nodded Sean. "However, that is your call and your call only, and I won't mention a word of this to anyone. In the end, it's you who must decide what to do."

"And the coins?" asked Rosemary. "What about the two coins? Do you think those belong in the same place?"

Sean considered this for a moment before smiling back at her. "No, I think the coins are a different matter altogether. After all, there were about fifteen hundred of them made, of which you only own two. I think those are yours to keep or sell as you see fit."

Rosemary's smile widened to encompass her entire face. "I am immensely grateful to you, Sean, for everything you've done. You have no idea how much you've changed my life in the last three hours."

"I'm only too pleased to help," said Sean. "It's been fun, too, helping to confirm a piece of American folklore about Washington's silverware. In a way, Rosemary, it is I who should be thanking you."

By now, Sean's Mercedes had finally reached the corner of Market and Ludlow Streets, where Rosemary and Tracey got out of the car. They both gave Sean big hugs, and Rosemary promised to keep him updated with her decision about the silverware. Then, they were off, lost in the crowd headed into the Bourse building.

Sean plugged in his GPS and pressed the button for "home." As the device sought to find satellites, his mind wandered over the events of the morning. So far, it had been a very good day. He had helped prove true an age-old legend and discovered at least six million dollars in rare coins, all before one o'clock.

CHAPTER 9

Wednesday, August 12, 2015

It was Wednesday night before Chris and Sean were both back at their respective houses, each having completed road trips that mixed business with intrigue. Because of Chris' forced stay at the run-down low-cost motel, he had been without Internet access for a full day by the time he arrived back in North Syracuse. Even though he felt painfully out of touch with his business and personal contacts, he still opted for a long shower and a power nap before logging onto his laptop for email. It was already past ten o'clock.

A short time later, his cell phone signaled that he had an incoming call from Sean. It wasn't much of a surprise; Chris had expected that Sean would call shortly after he arrived back home from Philly, even at this late hour.

"Hey, stranger, long time no hear," Chris answered, trying to pop open a can of diet soda with his free hand.

"Don't try to blame me for that," countered his friend. "I'm not the one who hasn't joined the modern era of satellite cell phones. You've been out of range for days now."

Chris had to laugh, for he knew Sean was right. While his high-tech junkie friend had been using a "no blackout zone" satellite phone for over a year now, Chris still preferred the basic old model he'd carried for years. It was a comfort thing, he felt, that didn't need modernizing. Besides, there were some times when he enjoyed being unreachable, and his old clunker phone gave him just the right excuse.

"Yeah, I saw that you had called a couple of times when I got into Plattsburgh this morning," said Chris. "But I've been pretty busy the entire day, without much of a break in the schedule."

"That's OK," offered Sean. "I just got home about a couple of hours ago myself. What a trip!"

"Sounds like you had a great time," said Chris. "Anything you'd like to tell me about? And what the heck was that message you sent me about some older woman?"

This time it was Sean's turn to laugh. "Sorry about that, buddy, but I wanted to tell you about a woman I found online."

"Now that sounds rather dubious," replied Chris, making fun of the clumsy way Sean had worded his last line.

"If you must know, the woman I tracked down is a living descendant of Frank Stewart... as in *the* Frank Stewart. I located her via an ancestry website, and WOW, did I find a story!"

"From the sound of things, we both had productive trips," said Chris. "My day at the museum turned up a slew of interesting artifacts relating to your search, although I'm not really sure that much of it means anything."

"I can't wait to hear about it," said Sean. "But what do you mean by 'my' search? I'd like to think that we're in this together."

"OK, OK, our search," laughed Chris. "Anyway, I got copies of a bunch of letters between Robert M. Patterson and the various principals of the iron works up in Adirondac. I must admit, some of them are pretty interesting. You can look through them when we get together again."

"Sounds like a plan," said Sean. "How about we meet this Saturday at my house? I have a few things that I want to tell you about, and I'd rather do it in person. Think you could come over in the afternoon? We could call in for pizza and maybe catch a ball game."

"OK, I can do that," said Chris.

"I've got to tell you about a couple of coins I found among the things," said Sean.

"Hmm, that sounds a lot like my day," said Chris, listening with interest.

"I don't suppose your coins were large, with 1804 stamped on the front?"

"Nope, no such luck," replied Sean. "But they were incredibly rare and worth a lot of money. The lady I was telling you about had no idea what she had. I'll fill you in more on Saturday.

"Sounds like a plan," agreed Chris.

"So tell me your story; what coins did you find, and where?"

"OK, as long as you asked," said Chris. "I found a whopper at the Adirondack Museum, and it *was* large, and it *did* have 1804 stamped on the front."

"No, really, what was it? Did you really find anything?"

"I'm telling you the truth," said Chris. "I found a one-dollar coin that was stamped 1804 on the front. It was inside an old letter from a man named Peter VanderBrooke. He was the stonecutter and mason in charge of the effort to build a massive blast furnace in Adirondac. The coin is obviously a fake, but it's fascinating anyway."

"Oh, wow," said Sean, surprised at the news. "That really is interesting. I wonder how this guy ever got hold of it all the way up in the Adirondacks."

"That's one story we'll probably never know," said Chris. "Anyway, I'm still interested in this coin, even if it is a fake. From what I've heard, even the fakes are worth a bit, if nothing else than for the effort it takes to create them. I'm going to take it down to Wes' coin shop and let him take a look at it." Wes was a local dealer with a store a few miles from Chris' house. He had gained the trust of the two friends by providing valuable advice as they searched for the Gordon treasure.

"Let me know what you find out," said Sean. "Heck, I'd like to see that coin myself, just to hold it in my hand and pretend that it's real."

"Wouldn't that be nice?" agreed Chris.

"When is Kristi getting back from her trip?" asked Sean, changing topics. Chris' girlfriend had been leading a summer geological trip to a fossil-rich area in central Pennsylvania, and she was returning soon.

"Her group is due back on Friday night, although it might be pretty late. Why do you ask?"

"I thought that as long as you and I are going to get together to compare notes, maybe we could make it a foursome. Maggie gets out of work at four o'clock on Saturday, and I don't think she's got anything planned."

"I could ask her," said Chris, thinking ahead to the weekend. "She may be busy trying to get caught up from spending a week in the field, but I think she wanted to stop by sometime over the weekend anyway. I'll ask her as soon as she gets back."

"Sounds great," said Sean. "Remember to bring along copies of everything with you, and I'll do the same. We can compare notes and see what we've got."

The following morning, Chris was up at five o'clock in order to hit the pavement for his run by five thirty. After a quick shower, he grabbed something to eat in the car on his way to a meeting with a local equipment manufacturing firm in Syracuse. Chris was working with a process engineer to increase the efficiency and output of the company and was using the experience to gain a foothold in the business. He had agreed to spend most of the next two days on site with the management team.

Over lunch hour, Chris left the plant and headed out to his Jeep. He pulled the vehicle out of the lot, heading north towards his own small community. He snaked the SUV in and out of traffic until he was able to make the turn into a small shopping plaza, which looked as though it had seen better days. A number of storefronts were vacant, with "For Rent" signs prominently displayed.

In a quiet corner of the plaza, next to an old shoe repair shop, hung a sign that read "Syracuse Coin and Gold Exchange." It was a tiny store that seldom attracted more than one or two customers at a time. A neon sign on the front window advertised the fact that "WE BUY ALL GOLD AND SILVER, IMMEDIATE CASH." In fact, the spike in gold prices and the steady profits to be had from the purchase of unwanted jewelry was the biggest source of business to the store.

Chris climbed out of the Jeep and walked around to the back of the vehicle, where he reached into a box in the back storage area and pulled out the silver dollar. He quickly looked around for an envelope or other suitable holder for the coin. However, when his search came up empty, he simply grabbed a sock from his bag and headed toward the store.

Chris pulled open the door, which jingled the small bell that hung from the top of the doorframe. There was only one customer inside the place, and she was just about to leave. A senior citizen who was cashing in a bag full of old rings and necklaces, she sounded very pleased with the transaction. "Wow, six hundred dollars?" she asked, looking with delight at the stack of hundred dollar bills. "I think I'll go back home and see if I can find some more!"

"You do that, Marilyn," said the gray-haired gentleman behind the counter. "I'll buy as much as you have. You know where to find us."

The old woman nodded one final time, and then exited the shop. The dealer, Wes Hawkins, turned around to record the transaction and drop the gold into a special holding box inside a locked safe. Chris waited patiently to begin speaking.

Wes was a very reputable dealer with a reputation for his extensive knowledge of United States coinage. An expert at grading and appraising early American coins, there was little he hadn't seen in his seventy-eight years, including over fifty years in the coin business. Many of his younger colleagues claimed that he knew so much because he had been alive when most U.S. coins were minted. However, he took their good-natured jibes in stride, and often assisted them in their own businesses. There was no doubt that Wes Hawkins had become a bit of a legend within American numismatics.

After storing the bag of jewelry, Wes turned around to face his visitor.

"Well, hello again, you old wrangler," he shouted, grabbing Chris' hand in greeting. Chris was surprised at the strength that remained in his grip. "You've been avoiding me since you became rich and famous!"

Chris smiled as he returned the handshake. "No, I'd never avoid you, Wes, you know that. But I'm now in business for myself, and I've been riding the boss pretty hard lately."

"Ha!" roared the dealer again. "Yeah, it's tough workin' for yourself, isn't it? Because when times get lean, there's no one else you can blame."

"You said it," agreed Chris.

"So what can I do for you today?" asked Wes, leaning over the counter. "You have more of those lovely Spanish doubloons to sell me? Or perhaps an engagement ring from your last love gone wrong?"

"No, nothing so dramatic," said Chris. "Only a coin I'd like to you take a look at, if you have a few minutes. It's been altered by someone, but a very long time ago. I came across it up in Blue Mountain Lake a couple days ago."

"With pleasure, lad," said Wes, turning on his magnifying lamp and adjusting the light over a special padded surface. "It seems you always come in with something special. So surprise me."

Chris reached into his pocket and pulled out the sock with the coin. Wes watched in amusement as Chris looked for the opening.

"I see we've invested in an expensive carrying case, too," said Wes, his eyes laughing as he spoke.

"Nothing but the best for my loot," retorted Chris, still fumbling with the footwear. Finally, his effort was rewarded, and he pulled the dollar coin from the toe.

"Here you are, Wes. Have a look—I think you'll find it interesting. I know it's a fake, but I'd love to know how it was made, and what your thoughts on the original mint year are."

Wes flipped the coin over to look at the front of the coin, and his eyes flew open. His expression quickly morphed through a series of emotions, from surprise, to amazement, and finally to humor.

"Ah, another 1804 dollar," he said finally, once he regained his composure. "Yup, I get these in here almost every week."

"Really?" asked Chris, a tone of disbelief in his voice.

"No, not really," replied Wes, adjusting the magnifying glass for maximum power. "But I have seen a few clever fakes at major coin shows. Some of them could probably fool a fairly experienced collector." As he spoke, he pulled on a pair of white gloves and began his examination.

"Well, I couldn't tell much about the coin when I first saw it. All I knew was that it couldn't possibly be a real coin, which is why I decided to bring it back to you."

"Oh, it's a real coin," said Wes, peering through the glass. "It's just a faked date. In a minute or two, I should be able to tell you the original number underneath the '4.'"

"How's that?" asked Chris.

"The original number underneath the '4' in 1804," repeated the dealer. "It's how ninety percent of the fake 1804 dollars were produced. Someone would either carefully remove the original number or add onto it. For example, a clever metallurgist could alter a '1' to look like a '4.' It might not look very convincing to true experts, but some gullible collectors might be taken just enough to pay a healthy price for the fake. I've seen some strange things in my time."

Chris watched Wes for a few minutes as he became more involved with his inspection, turning the coin to view it from different angles. His brow became furrowed, and he moved his eyes even closer to the glass.

"It was a pretty interesting trip up there," said Chris, making small talk about the museum just to pass the time.

"Oh yes?" replied Wes, sounding preoccupied.

"I think I read every single letter written in the nineteenth century," he continued.

"Mmm," said Wes.

"Have you ever been up to the Adirondack Museum? It's a fascinating place."

Chris' last question was met with total silence. He glanced back at Wes, trying to determine his thoughts or emotions. However, there was nothing there to gauge. The concentration on his face was total and complete, his mind clearly absorbed in the activity. At that moment, Chris thought that he could pull a rattlesnake out of a sack without the old dealer taking notice.

Rather than further distract Wes, Chris decided to take a look through the display shelves that graced the counter area. It never ceased to amaze him how much people would pay for almost any coin that was uncirculated. Some of the samples on display were quite recent, but still commanded a significant premium over face value. It crossed his mind that he should get in on the act too, by saving a few rolls of each denomination coin from successive years. He quickly gave up on the idea, realizing that he'd probably raid his own supply in search of laundry change.

Chris' thoughts were interrupted by Wes, who had looked up momentarily from his examining pad. "Where did you say you found this?" he asked, looking more than a bit puzzled.

"In an envelope in the stored archives of the Adirondack Museum," replied Chris.

"Tell me more," said Wes. "What can you tell me about the letter itself, as well as the person who originally put the coin in it?"

"OK, as best as I can tell, the envelope contained a collection of letters that were accumulated by a craftsman by the name of Peter VanderBrooke. He was in charge of some construction up in the town of Adirondac, back in the late 1840s through mid-1850s. The letter, which was never mailed, was probably sealed some time during that period."

"Interesting," said Wes, murmuring his one-word response.

"Finding anything worth telling me about?" asked Chris.

Wes simply shrugged his shoulders in return, leaving Chris to continue his tour of the shop. As he looked casually from one shelf to another, Wes stepped into the back room and returned with an old sheaf of papers. He opened the package and laid it flat on the table next to the dollar. As Chris moved closer, he noticed that many of the pages had multiple photographs depicting other dollar coins of that era, most notably those that were fakes and counterfeits. Wes continued to study the papers, turning from one page to another, then returning to the magnifying glass.

It was only when Chris began making obvious signs that he needed to leave that Wes spoke again. "Short on time, son?" he asked.

"I'm afraid so, Wes," he replied. "I'm on my customer's time clock right now, so each minute comes with a price tag."

"I understand," said Wes, stepping around in front of the counter.

"So is there anything you can tell me about when this coin was made?"

"Not yet," answered the dealer. "I've never seen one like it. I keep looking for the typical clues that would identify it as a fake. But so far, I just can't find any."

The assessment came as a jolt to Chris. "Are you saying this thing is real?" he asked, amazed at the possibility.

"No, I'm not," said Wes. "But I'm not saying it's fake either. As a matter of fact, I don't know what to say, except that it's probably the most clever reproduction I've ever seen. Do you think you might be able to leave it with me for a couple days?"

"Sure, Wes, I could do that."

"I'd be willing to take a few closeup pictures of it for you, just in case you're worrying about it disappearing," offered Wes.

"No, that's OK," said Chris. "In order to get it out of the museum, the curator required a series of detailed photos that would distinguish it from any other coin. So I think I'm covered on that end. But, if you don't mind me asking, why do you want to hang on to it?"

"Because I'm doing a show this coming weekend in Boston, and I'll be seeing an authoritative source who knows just about everything that can be said about the 1804 dollar, including the varieties of fakes. If anyone can tell us the origins of this coin and how it was produced, it would be him."

"By all means, then, please, take it along with you," agreed Chris. "I'd love to hear what he thinks. And I really appreciate your help with this, because I'd have nowhere else to turn for an opinion."

"Why of course," nodded Wes, smiling for the first time since he started his examination of the piece. "And thank *you*, sir, for never failing to make my life interesting with your amazing finds."

"Great! Well, I've got to get back to work in a hurry here, so I'll talk to you again next week," said Chris, his hand already on the doorknob.

He was halfway out the door when he was halted by the sound of Wes clearing his throat. It was an intentional calling, a loud rumbling that was meant to remind Chris of something. He looked back at Wes one last time, just in time to see the old-timer reach over the counter. As his arm achieved full extension, Chris saw the reason for his action—it was held pinched between his thumb and forefinger.

"Sorry," said Chris, cringing at his own forgetfulness. Slightly embarrassed, he stepped back inside and accepted his old sock from Wes' outstretched hand. Then he fled the store.

The following evening, Chris was lounging at home, taking a rare period of downtime from his work. The start-up had been everything he had expected, and his client list had expanded faster than his development plan anticipated. However, with the business came the workload, and he often found himself burning the candle on both ends, with late nights and early mornings becoming a common pattern.

This evening, he was stretched out on a long couch facing the flat-screen television. Propped up on one elbow, he had a beer in one hand and a bag of pretzels in front of the other. His degree of comfort was accentuated by the fact that his team, the Boston Red Sox, had a seven-run lead over the Yankees in the ninth inning.

As he moved his hand back to the pretzel bag, his cell phone vibrated, signifying an incoming call. He lifted the phone to look at the screen, waiting to decide whether to take the call. Once he saw the ID of the caller, he quickly swung his feet around to the floor and put the phone up to his ear. A wide smile bisected his face as he answered the phone.

"Hey, this is a treat," he said into the phone, not waiting for an initial greeting. "I didn't think they were letting you back into civilization before tomorrow afternoon."

The caller was Kristi, his girlfriend, companion, and soul mate for the past year. She had been incommunicado for the past week, out of cell phone range in the Appalachian Mountains of Pennsylvania. Having just received her master's degree in geology from Cornell University, she was gaining valuable classroom experience as a teaching assistant at the same institution. Chris tried to visualize her face as she spoke.

"You're right, hon, we weren't supposed to be coming out until tomorrow. But it's been pouring down there all day, and everyone got totally soaked. We found a lot of good material to bring back to the labs, so I made the executive decision to shorten the expedition by a day."

"I know about the storm," said Chris, looking out the window. "It's moved here, and the entire Mohawk Valley is getting pounded as we speak. It's not supposed to end until tomorrow morning, and then we've got another storm coming in for the weekend."

"Lovely," said Kristi, her voice interrupted by a clap of thunder.

"Oooh, that one sounded close," said Chris, listening to the rumbling over the distant connection. "Anyway, as long as you're done with your trip, do you have any plans for tomorrow? Sean wants to know if we could get together with him and Maggie for dinner."

"Is that the only reason I should come up," said Kristi, her voice pouting, "...because Sean wants me to come up for dinner?"

"No, of course not," laughed Chris. "Hopefully, you can come up tomorrow morning, and we can spend the day together first. Then, and *only* then, will I share you with Sean and Maggie."

"Promise?" asked Kristi.

"Promise," agreed Chris. "I give you my word as an eagle scout."

"Well, OK then," giggled Kristi, her voice bubbling with happiness. "How could I ever doubt that kind of commitment?"

"What time should I expect the pleasure of your presence?"

"If I can take care of my chores before bed tonight, I should be able to make it by ten tomorrow," replied Kristi, reviewing her mental schedule.

"Great," said Chris. "We'll have most of the day together, because I don't plan on getting to Sean's house before late afternoon. I think Maggie's working until around four o'clock, and she won't be over for a while after that."

"Well, it's not like she has very far to drive," said Kristi, laughing at the short commute from the golf course to Sean's house on the eleventh hole

"Besides," continued Kristi, "they can wait a few hours for us. I think we owe each other some quality time first, wouldn't you agree?"

"I'm glad to see that great minds think alike," said Chris, anticipating the visit. "Besides, I'm guessing that they can keep themselves occupied until we get there."

After signing off the call, Chris retrieved a pad of note paper. Next, he sat down at the kitchen table with his phone recorder and played back the conversation with his father. He paused the machine from time to time, making sure to record the information on Mr. Benjamin Grainger, including his home address and phone number, email address, make and model of car, and license plate number.

Chris knew that there was no immediate reason to look much further into the background of this shadowy figure. After all, he had done nothing wrong, and it was certainly within his right to spend his time and effort seeking a legendary cache of coins. However, his sixth sense was being prodded by *something*. He couldn't explain the internal alarms that sounded in his brain, and yet they were there.

Without much else to do, Chris placed the notepad on top of his other papers and prepared to turn in for the night. By now, he regretted that his thoughts had gone back to his father's investigation. Although he had been relaxed just a short time earlier, he was suddenly nervous and agitated. It was an unpleasant emotion that had no logical explanation.

Chris went to sleep picturing the red-headed Grainger over and over again in his mind. His face appeared a thousand different ways, and all of them were evil. He never settled on a final appearance, because he had never seen the man in person. Yet, somehow, he knew with certainty that their paths would cross.

CHAPTER 10

It was still raining in southern New Jersey as the red Mini Cooper pulled onto campus. The driver steered his car into the guest parking area of Rowan University and stopped at the guard shack. After receiving his parking pass, he pulled into a space reserved for visitors, and then stepped out of his car.

The driver was a solidly built man, well over six feet tall, with broad shoulders and a thick neck. He wasn't especially muscular, although he looked as though he could hold his own in a barroom brawl. However, the most prominent feature of the newcomer was his hair, which hung in a thick, bright-red mane. Even in the dreary light of the rainstorm, it seemed to reflect invisible sunlight.

Not bothering with the crosswalk, the visitor surprised a few drivers by walking directly across Mullica Hill Road without so much as a glance at the traffic. Most of the cars slowed quietly to let the pedestrian cross in safety, although one woman in a van honked her horn in anger. Without acknowledging the irate driver, he continued across the sidewalk and down the path to the Campbell Library.

Entering the building through the front door, he signed in and received a visitor's badge from the registration desk. The guard working the shift pushed a button on the phone next to his chair and spoke into the receiver.

"This is Greg, at the front desk. Would you please tell Penney that she has a visitor?" he said, looking at the ID handed to him. "Mr. Leon Garvin is here to see her."

After listening to the response from upstairs, the employee made another notation and checked off the badge number in a separate record book. "She'll be down in a minute, Mr. Garvin. Please make yourself comfortable."

Within a short period of time, the elevator whirred into motion, stopping at the ground floor. The doors opened and Penney McPherson stepped out, greeting her second researcher of the week.

"Hello, it's so nice to meet you, Leon," she said, offering a handshake. "I'm glad you could make it, since your schedule sounded so hectic."

"Thank you, ma'am," said Leon, bowing his head to the librarian. He neither smiled nor frowned, but remained tight-lipped throughout the introduction. Penney could not remember ever having been called "ma'am" on the college campus.

"I'm sorry that we didn't have longer to talk when you called to arrange your appointment," said Penney as the elevator ascended to the third floor. "Had I known more about your research topic, I could have had one of the student assistants pull out some material ahead of time."

"That's OK," said Leon. "I'm sure I'll find what I'm looking for."

"What is the focus of your search in our library today?" asked Penney, trying to get the visitor to elaborate.

"I'm interested in Frank Stewart's collection of records on the United States Mint, especially anything he had from around 1803 and 1804."

Penney's head turned quickly to look at Leon again. "Why, what a coincidence! We had another man in here just this week who was looking for the exact same materials. I believe he was researching something about silver dollars of that era, although he mentioned a lot of specifics that I don't recall."

This time it was Leon's turn to look surprised, although he masked it very quickly. "Oh really?" he replied. "Well, that doesn't surprise me. There are several people all working the same story. As a matter of fact, we're all part of the same team. If I saw the name, I'm sure I'd know who it was."

"I'll show you in the registration book, since you'll have to log in as well."

Penney led Leon through the same sign-in procedure she'd completed with Sean just four days earlier. He gave her his driver's license, which she placed in a holding box until he turned in his badge.

"Here it is," said Penney, pointing out a line that was further up the same page in the register book. "Yes, he was here just a few days ago. Sean Riggins. Are you working with him?"

"Yes, I am," replied Leon. "Most of us don't see one another very often, but we're all putting our heads together on the same project." Then, taking a longer look at the name, he spoke again. "It looks as though Sean has changed his email address since I last spoke to him. Maybe that's why I haven't been able to reach him for the past month. If you don't mind, I think I'll jot it down in my pad here so that I can still get in contact with him."

"Why of course," smiled Penney. "I'm always happy to help our scholars any way that I can."

As she spoke, an assistant called to her from the storage room, and she excused herself for a moment. As she left the room, the visitor quickly copied the entire line of information, including Sean's home address, phone number, and email address. Then he moved his notebook and papers onto a reading table to await Penney's return.

"OK, it looks like you're about ready to get busy," said Penney, stepping back into the reading room. "And since you're working the same materials as your colleague this past week, I'll give you a choice. We have fourteen boxes of material that Frank Stewart left us on the United States Mint. However, Mr. Riggins already went through the first nine or ten of those, so you might choose to bypass those if you think it would be duplicating your efforts."

Leon looked a bit uncertain as he tried to weigh the merits of starting over again. There was a veritable mountain of material in front of him, more than he could ever wade through in a single sitting. However,

Penney made the decision easier by throwing him an unexpected bonus. "If you'd like, though, I could probably give you a head start by asking Brian to show you the materials Mr. Riggins selected to copy. He's the student assistant who helped Sean on Monday, and he keeps a list of everything that we photocopy here in the Frank Stewart Collection."

"Yes, ma'am, that would be great. As a matter of fact, I'd gladly pay for a duplicate set of copies, because I won't be seeing Sean for quite a while yet. So that would be very helpful."

"Great," said Penney. "I'll have Brian get right on that for you. We'll give you a bill for your copies before you leave today."

"That's fine," said Leon, his eyes avoiding the librarian. "I do have one other favor to ask of you."

"Anything, just ask," said Penney.

"I wonder if Brian would be available to help me look through some of the boxes to point out what Sean already reviewed. It would save me a lot of time."

"Of course," said Penney. "He'll be over as soon as he makes your copies. I'll leave you to your work now, but please feel free to call me if you need any assistance."

As soon as she left, the red-haired researcher pulled out a box of papers and began aimlessly removing papers, looking through them in a random manner. He spent longer on some documents than others, but he didn't seem overly interested in anything he saw. He was relieved when the student assistant appeared with a stack of printed photocopies.

"Are you Leon Garvin?" he asked.

"That's me," said Leon.

"I guess I could have assumed that," chuckled Brian. You're the only one in here who isn't a student or librarian. Anyway, here are the items that Sean had copied on Monday. I've also made notations on each copy that shows the box number and location for each original document, just in case you want to go back and look at anything again."

"Thank you, Brian. That's a big help," said Leon, smiling for the first time that day. As he spoke, he pulled his wallet from his pocket and removed a twenty-dollar bill. "As a matter of fact, I'm sure you can help me out even more this afternoon, because I'm not much of a library person, and I'm sure that you are." He folded the bill into a tiny wad of paper and slid it across the table at the student. "For your time and effort," he said, still grinning.

"Oh, thank you, but we're not supposed to accept anything from our researchers," said Brian, looking slightly flustered. "We can accept donations for the library itself, but not for ourselves."

"Nonsense, Brian," scoffed Leon quietly. "You're going above and beyond the call of duty this afternoon, working with me and getting yourself all dusty and dirty. And for what? About seven dollars an hour? Please, take this and use it to get a beer and a sandwich tonight. It's the least I can do."

Brian was on the edge, wavering on his principles. Leon could read the internal debate taking place inside, and gave voice again.

"Really, Brian, it's quite common to tip someone who helps you. There's nothing wrong with it. And besides, I've already decided to leave a substantial donation to the library, for being so accommodating to our entire team."

After a quick look into the back room, Brian stuffed the folded note into his pocket.

"That's a good lad," said the visitor. "Now, let's get to work."

Over the course of the next two hours, Brian showed him each of the original documents that Sean had copied. Leon seemed most interested in the documents Sean had found inside the brown folder in box number ten, and he asked to see the folder.

"I remember where that was," said Brian, pulling reams of material forward in the heavy cardboard case to recover the old brown folder. "Sean seemed thrilled with some of the papers in here, especially the cipher matrix."

"Cipher matrix?" repeated Leon, looking at the assistant questioningly.

"Yeah, he said that this guy who ran the mint back then devised and used a coded matrix to keep certain things to himself. He said that this page inside the folder looked like part of that code."

After untying the string on the folder, Leon leafed slowly through the contents, reading the aged script and taking notes on his pad. At one point, he asked Brian to see if he could find any other records on file from the regime of Robert M. Patterson.

"Anything we'd have on that would probably be right inside this case," said Brian.

"Well, please do me that one favor and check one last time," said Leon. "I'll be fine while you're gone, and I really do need to make certain that I'm not leaving any information uncovered."

Brian agreed to the task and proceeded back to the facility's computer bank, leaving Leon alone in the room. As soon as he did so, Leon opened his own folder and shuffled some of his personal papers around, moving pages back and forth between it and that of the library. After a short burst of activity, he stole a glance around to make certain that no one was watching. Then, he quietly stepped across the room and slipped his plastic folder back into his book bag near the door. By the time Brian reappeared from the back room, Leon had returned to a scholarly pose in front of the last few boxes.

"Sorry, but all we have are a few mentions of Robert M. Patterson in our reference bank. Most of those are cross-references to books that are either in Stewart's own writing or in other libraries."

"That's all right," said the visitor. "I might have known that this library wouldn't have documents belonging directly to Patterson in the early days of the 1800s, but it was worth a try."

"What would you like to see next?" asked Brian, ready to open the next box in the stack.

"You know, I think I've actually got most of what I came for," said Leon, closing up his notepad. "We could spend hours searching the remainder of those other boxes, but I doubt we'd find anything else that would be of use in our pursuit. But I would like to thank you for your assistance, Brian. I cannot begin to tell you how much you've helped me out today."

As Leon prepared to check out, Penney returned to the reading room to handle the sign-out procedure. She handed him his driver's license in exchange for his library visitor's badge, which she returned to her metal box.

"Now remember, if you need anything, we're just a phone call away. Our numbers are on the paperwork we gave you and also on our brochure," Penney said.

"OK, ma'am, I'll keep that in mind," said Leon.

"Oh, and don't forget your bag," she said, reaching in back of her to retrieve the book bag he'd carried into the facility.

"I won't," said Leon. "And thanks again."

Then he was gone. Penney took the copy of the visitor's non-disclosure agreement and filed it in a desk drawer. She returned the visitor's sign-in register to the tray next to the door and neatened the desk where her guest researcher had worked. Then, satisfied that all was back to normal, she retreated to her desk in another room.

Brian finished moving the storage boxes back to their original location in a corner, near a large frame of smaller window panes. As he worked, he looked out the window and saw the red-haired visitor bound across the street towards the visitors' parking lot. As he ran, he held the book bag over his head to fend off the rain, which had increased in tempo through-out the afternoon. He unlocked the door on a red Mini Cooper and tossed the bag inside. Within a minute, the small vehicle maneuvered its way out of the lot and disappeared from sight.

The following morning was Saturday, and Chris was out of bed by six-thirty. Still feeling off-balance from his thoughts of Ben Grainger, he had decided to work off some nervous energy by setting off on one of his endurance runs, which stretched his route out to twelve miles. The long distance runs not only relieved his tension, but also gave him time to think through his more complex problems. As his feet pounded the pavement through the rolling hills of North Syracuse, his mind roamed free to consider the parts of the puzzle that had become his life. The hunt for the 1804 dollars had captured his imagination. But who was this Ben Grainger person, and why was he apparently moving on a parallel course with him and Sean? Did Grainger know about the two of them, wondered Chris? And how was he going to continue to balance this search with his increasing workload and his often-ignored personal life? He felt a stab of guilt there, considering that he tried to fit both Kristi and his mom into a tiny segment of his schedule that wasn't big enough for either. It was an impossible shell game with no good solution.

Once Chris was locked into a train of thought, he remained focused until pushed out of it by an outside force. Today, the only thing that broke his spell of concentration was the final hill leading back to his house. Until that stretch of road, he had been on autopilot, mulling items over in his mind and then reconsidering them multiple times. He surprised himself when he realized that he had completed the extended road circuit in slightly less than ninety minutes.

After a quick shower, Chris walked into the kitchen to fix himself a second breakfast. He'd gulped a protein bar before his run but had saved most of his appetite for later in the morning. Wearing only a towel, he started the coffee machine and scrambled a few eggs with sausage links. This was far beyond his normal weekday fare, when he'd settle for a bowl of cereal and a glass of juice.

Chris ate at a leisurely pace, allowing himself the pleasure of reading a spelunking magazine he'd received over a month ago. By the time he finished, he had only ten minutes to get ready for Kristie to arrive, just enough time to climb up to his bedroom loft, where he pulled on a pair of worn jeans and a faded T-shirt.

True to her word, Kristi pulled her red Chevy Cobalt into the area in front of Chris' house at nine fifty-seven. The vehicle was eight years old and needed a bit of body work. However, Kristi was dedicated to it and sometimes assigned it human-like characteristics. "She's very loyal," she claimed, referring to the vehicle affectionately as "Chloe."

Chris answered the door before she had a chance to press the buzzer.

"Hello there, my long-lost lover," he said with a grin. "Back from the wilderness already?"

Kristi responded by leaping forward and throwing her arms around his neck in a huge embrace.

"Yes, silly, and don't tell me that you're not glad to see me. I won't believe it for a minute."

"I'm a lousy liar," said Chris, returning the affectionate hug and kiss. "Besides, I don't have any other date for tonight, so you might as well come in."

"Keep that up and I won't," pouted Kristi, faking a scowl. "You're not the only game in town for a temptress like me, you know."

Chris stepped back and admired her. Dressed for the occasion, she sported a svelte-looking gray Armani sweater tunic, which she wore over a pair of black leggings. The loosely-knotted belt tied around her waist accentuated her toned, shaply body. It was enough to make any man turn for a second look.

"Wow, you look nice!" exclaimed Chris, taking her in his arms again. "I didn't think they let geologists dress like that."

"They don't," said Kristi, her smile disappearing quickly. "You have no idea how I looked when we got through with our dig on Thursday. I had mud covering ninety percent of my body. I think I'm going to throw my jeans in the trash."

"So where exactly was this place that you decided to sentence yourself and your students to exile?" asked Chris.

"It was a place called St. Clair, down in Schuykill County, Pennsylvania. There's a famous spot called the Llewellyn Formation. It's well-known for its abundant fossil record, primarily the flora such as Alethopteris ferns, which are seed ferns from the Carboniferous period."

"Of course, doctor," said Chris, with an exaggerated serious expression on his face. "The Carboniferous era."

"Will you stop it?" cried Kristi, hitting Chris on the arm. "I'm trying to tell you about my week. Maybe I *will* turn around and head back home."

"Please don't," said Chris, taking her hand in his. "I'm sorry for the sarcasm. I've had a long, tough week, too, and I guess I'm just trying to ditch the stress by taking it out on you. I promise, I won't goof anymore, OK?"

"OK," said Kristi, flashing her smile back at him. "So anyway, you want to tell me more about this latest hunt that your partner-in-crime has you wrapped up in, or would you rather keep me in suspense?"

"No, I'd be happy to fill you in," said Chris. "But why don't we do it over enchiladas down at Nicola's Cantina?"

"Ooh, now there's an idea!" said Kristi, her eyes sparkling at the suggestion. "I could have gone for some gourmet Mexican food while I was sitting out in the slop this week."

"Then hop into my chariot and allow me to escort you to the home of Syracuse's best homemade salsa."

Chris opened the car door and held it for Kristi as she stepped inside. She loved the fact that he was from the "old school," when men still opened doors for women and treated them like ladies.

As the couple backed out of the driveway and started the drive to the restaurant, Chris filled Kristi in on the activity of the past few weeks. She listened as he told her about Sean's original premise and their initial findings from the Adirondack Museum and the Frank Stewart Room. Chris didn't know everything that Sean had discovered, other than what he'd mentioned in their brief conversation, but it was enough to tweak Kristi's interest. The briefing lasted for most of the ride into the city, with Chris doing most of the talking.

"Well, I agree with you," said Kristi, finally voicing her thoughts as they approached the parking lot of the restaurant. "It's probably another wild goose chase, like many of Sean's adventures. But it does sound as though there are some puzzling issues there, almost as though someone in the past was trying to cover up something."

"That's the feeling I get, too," said Chris. "So many people have researched the mystery of the 1804 dollar that, if it ever existed, it should have been found by now. But so far, nothing's ever turned up. Maybe it just wasn't meant to be."

"If they were actually minted, and then lost at sea like one of those stories said, you'd never be able to prove it one way or another, would you?" asked Kristi, looking at Chris sympathetically.

"Nope, we wouldn't," said Chris. "And that would mean that this was all a great big waste of time. In the meantime, we might as well go inside and stuff our faces so we'll feel better."

"Deal," laughed Kristi as she jumped out of the Jeep.

The two went inside and were given a table near the back of the restaurant. Kristi, who didn't care for the extreme heat of some Mexican foods, chose roasted tomato chipotle salsa, while Chris asked for the papaya habanero salsa, which he claimed he'd previously used to remove the paint from an old car he'd fixed up back in high school. The salsas came with a basket of yellow and blue corn chips, which were baked in the restaurant's oven.

"I don't see how you can eat that stuff," said Kristi as she watched Chris swallow another mouthful of the fiery pepper sauce. "You're probably vaporizing the lining of your stomach with each bite."

"Nah," replied Chris, enjoying the sensation. "It's not hot enough unless I feel a bit of sweat breaking out on the top of my head. It's got to bite me back."

As they munched on the chips and salsa, Chris described his visit to the old mining site up in the ghost town of Adirondac. His travelogue included a summary of the history of the iron works, along with the story of its eventual downfall.

"Yes, I remember reading about that," said Kristi. "How ironic that they had to cease operations because of an unknown impurity that they couldn't remove, only to later learn that it was titanium! If only they'd been able to see into the future, they could have made enough profit to carry them through indefinitely."

Chris was about to respond when a waiter appeared with their lunch platters, and they decided to put the conversation on hold while they dug into the feast.

Finally, after satisfying their appetites, Chris pushed his plate away and folded his napkin. "So, let me ask you a question," he said, looking thoughtful.

"Sure, fire away," said Kristi.

"Based on your geological knowledge of the Adirondacks, do you think it's possible there is a vein of silver anywhere in the northern part of the park, up near the iron mine in Adirondac?"

"Oh no, not that again!" said Kristi, looking slightly incredulous. "Isn't this what got you and Sean into panning for gold a year or two ago?"

"No, seriously," said Chris. "I guess I'm not looking for an actual silver mine as much as I am the *possibility* that David Henderson and Archibald McIntyre believed one existed. I found references to it in their notes this past week."

Kristi's eyes narrowed in thought as she considered the matter. "Well, there's no telling what they might have believed back then. I guess they could have written that there was a diamond mine with thousand-carat stones right beneath the surface. But that doesn't mean it's based in reality."

"Of course," said Chris, nodding in agreement.

"Regarding the presence of a genuine vein of silver in that area, no, I'd have to say that it simply wouldn't exist. The rock stratum isn't compatible with a silver mine in the Adirondack region. My guess is that the old-timers you mentioned from the mining company up near Mount Marcy were hopeful they'd find silver because it can often be detected when refining lead ore. But in the case of the raw ore extracted from the North Country mines, no, that just never panned out. No pun intended."

Rather than pursue the topic any further, Chris decided to focus on enjoying the day with Kristi, which was a rare treat for both of them. Their busy schedules precluded an abundance of shared time, which they both regretted but were forced to accept due to the formative stages of their respective careers. Chris always felt that, when the time was right, they'd be able to establish a life together.

After spending the afternoon browsing the mall in Syracuse, Chris and Kristi hit the road for Little Falls, which was about seventy miles eastward on the New York State Thruway. Finding little traffic on the roads, Chris was able to complete the drive to Sean's house by five o'clock.

As he climbed out of the car, Chris reached into the back seat and removed a thick manila folder that was crammed with papers. It contained copies of everything substantive he had found in the museum in Blue Mountain Lake, as he knew his friend would expect a full report.

The couple knew from experience to bypass the front door. Instead, they strolled down the flagstone walkway on the right side of the cottage, expecting to find Sean practicing chip shots towards the par 3 green. As they rounded the back corner of the building, they saw the white covered golf cart parked in back of the row of shrubs behind the patio. However, instead of chipping golf balls, Sean was sitting on a reclining deck chair, his feet up on a wooden bench. Maggie was on a chair next to Sean's, her feet propped up on his thighs. Nearby, a barbeque grill was stoking itself to life, emitting faint wisps of charcoal-scented smoke.

"Wow, that smells great!" said Chris, smiling at the reclined couple. "Anything ready to eat yet?"

"Not unless you have a craving for some freshly ignited briquettes," answered Sean, looking up at the newcomers. "I just lit the coals about ten minutes ago, so we'll be able to throw the steaks on in about twenty minutes. Why don't you two take a load off your feet and have a seat. But first, there's a case of chilled Molsons in the fridge. Help yourself; you usually do."

"I don't have to be asked twice," laughed Chris, heading to the back door. He reappeared in a moment with two bottles of beer, and passed one to Kristi.

Maggie, meanwhile, rose from her seat and embraced Kristi with a hug. The two had only become acquainted within the past year through their relationships with Chris and Sean, yet they had become good friends in that short period of time. Unlike Kristi, who had attended college and then graduate school without a break, Maggie had taken a number of years off after high school, working at a variety of local jobs. She was finally looking forward to attending college the following year. As she decided on schools and majors, she relied on Kristi for advice, and the two emailed each other frequently.

Sean had anticipated discussing Chris' findings for the past week. "Why don't the two of you catch up while I pump Chris for information from the Adirondack Museum?" he suggested to Kristi and Maggie. "We've got almost an hour until dinner is ready; you think you could excuse us until then?"

Maggie looked at Kristi in silence, rolling her eyes. They both shrugged their shoulders and laughed, apparently sharing a common thought. "Of course, we wouldn't want to intrude on your secret treasure hunt," said Maggie, pretending to be slightly offended.

"Yeah, we'll just sit by ourselves and talk about girlie things," said Kristi, "like shoes, and perfume, and handbags." Maggie giggled.

"Oh, stop, or I'll have you grilling your own steaks," said Sean, turning his back on the two.

"Try it, mister, and I'll have you arrested for playing rounds of free golf every weekend," threatened Maggie.

"You wouldn't?" implored Sean.

"Try me," replied Maggie, staring back.

"OK, you win," said Sean. "But just give us an hour to talk, and you'll have our undivided attention for the rest of the night. I promise."

After winning his reprieve from the girls, Sean pulled Chris aside and set a stack of papers on the picnic table. Chris deposited his own folder on the same surface as the two sat down to talk. By prior arrangement, each of them had made a second copy of all the materials he'd gathered, making the resulting piles even taller.

"Wow, it looks like you've been busy, too," said Sean, eying the volume of documents in front of him.

"I've got to admit, I found a lot more material than I thought possible," said Chris, opening the folder. "I even found some correspondence between your main man, Robert M. Patterson, and the owners of the Iron Works up in Tahawus. Good stuff."

"Great! I can't wait to have a look," replied Sean, opening his own binder. "As for me, I discovered that a lot of the material down in the Frank Stewart Room has never been viewed, much less catalogued. I spent the whole afternoon there, and there were still four boxes of material dealing with the mint that I never got around to opening. But I did find something that is really intriguing, because it might be a missing treasury report from the early part of 1804. Also, I think I found one of Patterson's cipher codes inside the same box. I'd love to be able to find a way to get that cracked and translated into plain English. Even if it doesn't talk about anything related to the 1804 dollars, it still would be exciting to see something that he deemed worthy of encrypting over one hundred fifty years ago."

"If memory serves me correctly, his primary code was broken a few years back by a cryptologist using a high-speed computer," said Chris.

"That's right," said Sean. "I think it will be possible to use that information to break this cipher using the same formula. I'll look into it next week if I have time. Anyway, give me the *Reader's Digest* version of what you found in the museum."

"OK, I'll do my best," said Chris, organizing his notes into a few orderly stacks. "First of all, I was able to locate a lot of correspondence between the director of the mint, Robert M. Patterson, and the folks in charge up at the mine in Adirondac. He seemed to be focused on two main topics: the first was the erection of the monument to David Henderson, which is located on a trail in the middle of nowhere. The second was the construction of the massive blast furnace, which was started in 1849 and completed about five years later. Both of these endeavors must have been important to Patterson, because a lot of correspondence exists in regards to each."

"You mentioned that your dad had a professional researcher give us a head start inside the treasury records at the National Archives in Philly," said Sean, changing gears. "Did he come up with anything worth mentioning?"

"Actually, he uncovered two items of interest," nodded Chris, recalling the conversation with Ron Greer. "He came across a hole in the treasury record from the year 1804. It appears as though a page from the official record book was removed sometime before 1807, when the book was filed away at the treasury records office. It listed the issuance of coins minted in the first three months of 1804. They have the year-end summary record, but not the original month-by-month log."

"Let me guess," asked Sean, putting his fingertips to his forehead like a fortune teller. "The missing page was numbered 154 in the record book. Correct?"

Chris just stared at his friend, unable to believe what he'd just heard. "Either you have your own source inside the National Archives, or you must really be psychic," he said finally.

"Neither, my friend. It's all a simple illusion." With that, Sean pulled the copy of the page he'd found in the Frank Stewart Room from his portfolio. "This was in the last box I scanned. I was pretty sure I knew where it belonged, but you've just confirmed it for me." He handed the copy of the large ledger sheet to Chris as he spoke.

Chris examined the document wide-eyed, trying to fathom how it was misplaced, and by whom. "The mystery deepens," he said. "It's quite a coincidence that this page, which documents the production of the 1804 dollars, was separated from the rest of the record. And sometime before 1807. I wonder why?"

"It would appear to me that someone didn't want this part of the mint production record examined," said Sean, responding to the question. "Did you notice the last entry, the one dated March 26, 1804?"

Chris followed the dates down the left-most column on the page, until he located March 26. Then, he read the words that had caught Sean's attention so thoroughly in the Frank Stewart Library: "Die cracked, 3/26/1804; employed new die from Chief Coiner's Office."

"Read the next line, too," urged Sean.

"'March 28: 2,840 dollars, plus 1 assay coin.' Hmm, that sounds to me as though a couple thousand dollar coins were stuck in 1804 with a new die," speculated Chris. "But, unfortunately, we don't know what that new die looked like, or the date it carried on the obverse side."

"Very true," agreed Chris. "Those may prove to be critical bits of information if we're going to piece this together."

"I'm convinced we can still get there," said Sean. "It will just mean looking harder into resources that people haven't used yet in this investigation."

"One other thing you really should know," said Chris, looking directly into Sean's eyes. "There is someone else out there right now who apparently is looking for the same thing we are. He's already visited the archives in Philly, and according to Ron, he has possession of some mint records he obtained via 'other methods.' The archivist in the treasury records gave Ron a copy of his contact info, so we know who he is and where he lives. Oh, and by the way, he's not the type who helps little old ladies across the street."

As Chris spoke, he pulled a stapled batch of papers from his folder and slid it in front of Sean. "Meet Ben Grainger, part-time electronics salesman, part-time thief, part-time abuser of girlfriends and other women. From what I've learned, he's a real nice guy."

Sean looked at the front page of the packet, which displayed an enlarged picture of Grainger's driver's license and other personal information. The thick matte of red hair stood out above all other features. He also noticed the data on the back of the card, which indicated that the owner was six feet two inches tall and weighed 245 lbs. "Not exactly a small guy, is he?"

"Big enough to play college football, that's for sure," nodded Chris.

Sean continued to leaf through the pages of information on the mysterious stranger, noting the depth of coverage in the material. "This is fantastic," he said, admiring the compilation. "Did your dad help you acquire this info, or did you break down and hire one of those online intelligence services?"

"Uh, it was, um, yeah, you're right. I used an online service," stuttered Chris.

"I thought so," said Sean, grinning at his friend's subterfuge. "Next time you talk to your father, tell him that his boys do nice work."

"You didn't hear it from me," replied Chris, skimming through the remainder of his papers. "Regardless, this guy is out there somewhere, interested in the same endgame we're interested in. However, he appears to have a head start. If, as the curator of the archives told Ron last week, this Grainger guy had a relative who worked inside the mint, he might have possession of other documents as well. Who knows where that might lead him? We'll never know, because none of those records have ever been seen by the public."

"Lovely," said Sean, considering the new wrinkle. "Come to think of it, Penney, the librarian at the Frank Stewart Room, said that someone had called her last week to arrange a visit about the same subject. It appears that we're simply one of a crowd in the same hunt."

Chris furrowed eyebrows in thought, trying to piece together the puzzle. "Maybe the crowd isn't as large as we think," he said.

"What do you mean by that?"

"I'll hold off on answering that question for a bit, if you don't mind," said Chris.

"Sure," replied Sean, looking slightly confused by his friend's remark. "But why don't you tell me about this coin you found...the counterfeit dollar from the museum."

"There's not much to tell," said Chris, smiling at the subject. "I was going through letters with Debbie up in the reading room when a silver dollar fell out of an envelope. It was from a collection of letters from Mr.

Peter VanderBrooke, who was involved in coordinating the construction of the larger blast furnace in Adirondac. As soon as I saw it, I suspected it was a fake, simply because of the date. People have been replicating 1804 dollars since the middle of the 1800s, although none of them have ever fooled a genuine expert."

"So what did you do with the coin?" asked Sean.

"Well, like I told you the other night, I took it down to Wes' shop," explained Chris. "He asked for permission to bring it along with him to a show in Boston this weekend, where he'll meet up with a couple of experts on the subject. Believe me, if anyone can tell us where that coin was made, it's Wes. We'll have an answer by early next week."

"Sounds like an interesting story," said Sean, listening intently. "But as long as we're talking about coins, I'm afraid I've got you trumped by a country mile. Do you remember the woman I was telling you about in Philadelphia? The one who was a descendant of Frank Stewart?"

"Sure," said Chris, recalling his friend's narrative of the visit.

"Well, she showed me a wooden chest that had been left in the mint building from the very first days of its operations, which had somehow been passed down through the years from her great-uncle," began Sean. "It contained several pieces of silverware and serving pieces, along with two coins that were known as half dismes, dated 1792."

"Wow, that's going back there," said Chris, amazed. "I'll bet there aren't many examples of those floating around today."

"You're right," said Sean, smiling at the thought. "As a matter of fact, I looked them up online, and they'll probably go at auction for around three million dollars each."

"Yikes!" shouted Chris, jolted by the figure. Even Maggie and Kristi, who had been engaged in their own conversation, appeared startled to hear that number.

"So what's the connection of these half disme coins to our own search?" asked Chris.

"There really isn't any," replied Sean, his eyes still reflecting a look of anticipation. "But you'll never guess what else I found there?"

Chris looked back without responding, waiting for Sean to continue.

"The silverware and other utensils I found in the same chest were stamped with the personal crest of President George Washington."

"I don't get it," said Chris, weighing the answer. "Why would part of George Washington's silver set be diverted to an old chest in the original U.S. Mint?"

"Don't you see?" said Sean, somewhat impatiently. "Ever since the early days of U.S. coin collecting, there's been the myth that George Washington donated some of his own personal silver in order to jump start the production of America's first coins. But there was no way to prove or disprove that story *until now*. We found samples of the very first coins in the same container as Washington's silver! So, whether we find any silver dollars or not, we still have an interesting story to tell, and we may be able to claim that we solved a centuries-old fable of American numismatics."

"Well, that's interesting," said Chris, yawning as he spoke. "But it really doesn't do much for us in our current pursuit, does it?"

"You really know how to shoot a guy down, don't you?" said Sean, looking disappointed.

As Sean spoke, he stood up to remove the lid of the barbeque grill, exposing a beautiful bed of glowing coals. He then opened a chilled thermos cooler and lifted a package of steaks from the bottom, laying them across the bare grates to start cooking. On the outside portion of the surface he arranged a number of shish kabob skewers with stacks of peppers, onions, mushrooms, and tomatoes. An aromatic cloud of steam wafted about the patio.

"That smells good already," commented Maggie. "How long 'til dinner?"

"Twenty six and a half minutes," said Sean, sarcastically.

Maggie shot Sean a look of disgust, then returned to her conversation with Kristi.

"OK," said Chris, refocusing on the discussion. "So we know that someone inside the mint, and presumably in a position of power, felt the need to try to cover the mint records from 1804. We also know that there was a long lapse in suspicious activity of any sort, until Patterson's son began taking interest in a little-known iron mine in the northern part of the Adirondacks. Now we've also discovered that one of his contacts at the mine may have come up with a fake 1804 silver dollar, although how he did it and when are complete mysteries to us. It doesn't sound like we have anything to go on."

"It sounds as though you're abandoning ship, my friend. Do you want to give up on this whole idea, just when it's getting interesting?"

"I never said I was abandoning you," replied Chris, shaking his head. "I'm just wondering whether we still have viable leads to follow, or whether the clues have run their course and we call it a day."

"Personally, I'm sticking with this, at least for now," said Sean. "After all, we've made some pretty amazing finds in our first week of searching, haven't we? And I've got more to dig through down at Rowan, as well as at the APS library in Philly."

"APS... American Philosophical Society," recited Chris, recalling their earlier discussion.

"Exactly," said Sean, encouraged by Chris' renewed interest. "They've got thousands upon thousands of documents down there that no one has ever laid eyes upon. Who knows what we'll find if we happen to get lucky."

"I know what you mean," agreed Chris. "I find it amazing that some of Thomas Jefferson's papers are only now being scanned and catalogued. But when you consider the fact that each of our founding fathers had a hand in writing tens of thousands of letters and other documents, and that those documents are spread far and wide across the libraries of the world, it's no wonder we're still discovering new materials."

"Now you're talking!" said Sean, flipping the steaks on the grill. "So let's lay out our plans for the next week or two so that we can run some of these issues to ground."

"Uh, OK," said Chris, hesitating to commit to an additional outlay of time. "But I've got an even heavier workload coming up in the next two weeks, so you'll have to settle for whatever I can spare."

"That'll be enough," said Sean, agreeing to compromise. "Maybe we can meet up somewhere once your rush subsides and work together for a couple days."

"That could be fun," considered Chris. "But it won't be this week; I'm booked solid already. And guess what? It's all local, so I get to sleep in my own bed for a full week. Hooray for small wonders!"

Within another few minutes, the steaks and kabobs had grilled to perfection and were ready for consumption. Maggie had laid four ears of corn on the grill as well, which had blackened on the outside to an appealing charred state. The resulting sight and scent was mouthwatering, and everyone suddenly joined in preparations for the meal. Maggie brought drinks and condiments out from the kitchen while Kristi set the table with plastic plates and utensils. Chris and Sean set up a relay system, passing the steaks and other items from the grill to the picnic table. Within ten minutes, they were all seated and enjoying their meal.

"So, were you boys able to lay out your plan of attack?" asked Kristi, gently elbowing Chris in the ribs.

Chris flinched, leaning over into his girlfriend's side. "What plan of attack? I don't know what you're talking about," he laughed.

"You know—for finding the hidden treasure and making the world safe for democracy," she smirked.

"Nothing quite that dramatic," replied Sean. "We're just having a little fun and trying to clear up a long-standing mystery."

"Yes, Chris has told me about much of it," says Kristi. "It's actually pretty interesting, although it sounds like an impossible riddle to solve since it happened so many years ago."

"So many years ago?" mimicked Sean. "And this coming from a geologist? I thought most of the events you tracked happened a couple billion years ago."

"Oh, lighten up," said Kristi, smiling back at Sean. "Better yet, try another beer. Maybe that'll help your mood."

"Speaking of lightening up, I have a present for you," said Maggie, giving Sean a kiss. She reached over to a side table for her handbag, from which she produced a small black box. "My brother got this as a gag gift, and he didn't want it, so he gave it to me."

"And now you're passing it off on me, is that it?" laughed Sean as he pulled the lid off the box. Inside was a small black device with a cord and some additional hardware, along with a set of instructions. A separate envelope held a CD-ROM.

"What this thing?" asked Sean, examining the piece of electronics as he turned it over in his hands.

"Oh no," said Chris, covering his mouth with his hand to hide the smile. "I think I know, but I don't want to say."

"Read the top of the instruction sheet and it will tell you," said Maggie coyly.

Sean unfolded the paper and held it up to the sunlight. "GPS locator device," he read, scanning the specifications that followed. "OK, so this is a tracking device?" he asked. "Like something you'd see in a spy movie?"

"That's the idea," Chuckled Maggie, putting her hand on Sean's shoulder. "You mount it in your car, and I can read your location on my PC."

"You've got to be kidding me," laughed Sean, looking at Chris in doubt. "You expect me to put this in my car so you can follow me around all day? I don't think so."

"What are you trying to hide from me?" asked Maggie, still laughing at Sean's expression. "Afraid I'll find out about all your extracurricular activities?" Her remark was accompanied by another round of laughter from everyone except Sean.

"I'll tell you what," said Sean, placing the GPS device back into the box. "I'd like to hang onto this thing, if you don't mind. I can think of a couple of useful ways to deploy it to our advantage."

Chris looked at him questioningly, but Sean simply winked back in reply.

"I think he wants to stick it onto your car," said Kristi, looking at Maggie. "Just watch; he'll be keeping tabs on you without you knowing it."

Sean continued to look over the directions as he spoke. "Oh, wow," he said, perusing the text. "I guess the advantage of this model is that it contains its own battery power supply, so you can attach it quickly to someone's car or truck without them seeing a thing. It looks pretty handy."

"Welcome to the wonderful world of electronics," said Chris, looking over Sean's shoulder.

"Hey, I just joined that club myself," said Kristi, pulling a new cell phone out of her purse. "I finally traded in my last-generation phone for a high-tech version that relies on satellite communications."

"That must have cost you a pretty penny," said Maggie, staring at the phone."

"Yeah, it did, and the service fees are up there too," admitted Kristi. "But I got tired last week of being out of touch with the world simply because I was stuck behind a hill somewhere on a fossil dig. So now, no matter where I am, I'm just a phone call away from anyone."

The group continued their conversation for another couple hours, watching the sun drop below the trees as the day turned to night. The warmth and humidity of the evening brought out the hordes of mosquitoes that lived and bred in the waters around the golf course, so the foursome decided to move back inside.

Chris situated himself with Kristi on the overstuffed couch, while Maggie went over to Sean's computer on the desk by the front window.

"You mind if I check my email?" asked Maggie, lowering her head to the level of the monitor.

"Sure," replied Sean, who had backtracked to the kitchen for another beer. "But before you log me off, would you check my inbox quickly to see if I've received anything from a rowan.edu account? I'm expecting something from the librarian down at the Frank Stewart Room."

Maggie scanned down the list of emails in Sean's account, and called back quickly. "Nope, there's only one new email in your inbox. It's from traceylee7@yahoo.com."

"Oh, cool," called Sean enthusiastically. "Would you open that one and read it to me? I hadn't expected an answer from her so quickly."

Maggie quickly double-clicked on the email titled "Re: Follow-up from Sean." The email opened, and Maggie did a double-take. Then, still not believing her eyes, she stood there staring at the screen for a good fifteen seconds before speaking.

"Um, Mr. Riggins, would you tell me who this girl is who is 'so happy to meet you?'"

Sean trotted in from the kitchen and peered over Maggie's shoulder at the screen, cringing at the image. He had sent an email, as promised, to Tracey, the niece of Rosemary Stewart, about conducting some research for them at the University of Pennsylvania library. She had answered him using her personal yahoo email stationery, which included a photograph below her signature line. Her response was an innocently-worded bit that said: "It was such a pleasure to meet you this week. I would really love working for you!" The photograph below the name did nothing to hide her natural beauty. Her stunning features almost jumped off the screen.

"So this is what you were doing in Philadelphia?" Maggie said, half-joking, but with a serious undertone to her voice. "Maybe I should have held onto that GPS thing. I'm not sure I should trust you around this girl."

In the background, Chris looked at Kristi with an apologetic expression, and the two of them seemed to sink into the couch.

"She is simply the niece of the descendant I found of Frank Stewart, and she's a student at the University of Pennsylvania," countered Sean defensively. "Since she goes to school there anyway, I thought it would be handy to have her look up articles and other items of interest at their library, which is where a lot of Patterson's personal documents were donated."

"And you expect me to believe that," said Maggie with a grin.

"Of course," said Sean. "The *girl* you are looking at is a whopping nineteen years of age, a virtual teeny bopper. You think I'd ever even turn my head to look at a teenager?"

"OK, just as long as I know where your heart is," said Maggie, throwing her arms around Sean.

"That's actually a pretty smart move, acquiring a contact to look up documents at U of P," said Chris, joining the conversation. "I found several references to their library in my own research up in Blue Mountain Lake. It sounds as though both Pattersons bequeathed a lot of their personal libraries to that institution."

"Sounds like one guy sticking up for another," said Kristi, laughing at the remark.

With the controversy settled, the group fell back into a general banter, which lasted for another hour before Chris began making signs that it was time to depart.

"We've got over an hour's drive to get back to Syracuse, and then Kristi has an even longer trek to get home," he said, explaining his movement towards the door. "I'll give you a shout tomorrow afternoon, and we can coordinate our schedules for later next week."

"You're on," said Sean, shaking hands with his friend. Following an exchange of hugs, Chris and Kristi stepped out into the cool night air, headed for the westbound lanes of Interstate 90 that would take them home.

As they stepped up into Chris' Jeep, Kristi looked across the front seat at her date and asked a question. "So, from what you know about Sean, do you think he's interested in this Tracey woman whom we saw on the email? I didn't want to say anything while we were in there, but she's quite a knockout."

"No, of course not," answered Chris, confident in his reply. "Sean's an intelligent, loyal guy. I've known him since we used to sit next to each other and shoot spitballs at Miss Hendrow's back in English class, and he's never been the kind of guy to fool around."

"How about you?" ventured Kristi, her eyes reflecting the light of a mostly-full moon. "Do you think that you could resist the temptation of a beautiful woman if she threw herself at your feet?"

Chris laughed and took her hand in his, holding it close to his lips. "That's one question that I *can* answer with certainty. There is only one woman in my heart, and that's you." Then he added, "Please forgive me, mother," which elicited a giggle from Kristi. "And you never have to worry about that, OK?"

"OK, sweetheart," she said, hugging him tightly. "And I'm sure your mom would pardon you. She's such a sweet lady."

"That she is," agreed Chris, backing out of the driveway. "And now it's time we got you back to Syracuse so you can start your return trip to Ithaca. It's already late, and I don't want you falling asleep at the wheel."

"Well then, maybe I'd better not attempt the drive home tonight," sad Kristi, smiling back at Chris. "After all, it is getting late, and I have such a hard time driving at night."

Chris considered her response for a millisecond before extending an offer of his own. "My home is your home," he said, squeezing her hand tighter as they pulled onto the main road and drove off into the night.

CHAPTER 11

Wednesday, August 20, 2015

The first three days of the following week passed in a blur for Sean. Caught in a scheduling nightmare, he found himself trapped with a large customer account installing a new network security system for almost thirty-six hours straight. After catching a scant four hours sleep on Tuesday night, he was back on the job by seven o'clock the following morning, performing follow-up tasks and system checkout routines. By early afternoon, the strain was showing on his face, and his bloodshot eyes looked like he'd been drunk for four days.

Just as he was about to leave the client's print shop, his phone rang. He looked at the number of the incoming call, which indicated a location in central New Jersey, before saying hello.

"Hello, is this Sean Riggins?" came a familiar voice.

"Yes it is," said Sean politely. "Who is this please?"

"Sean, this is Penney McPherson, the librarian and archivist at the Frank Stewart Room."

"Hi, Penney! What an unexpected pleasure," said Sean, his face brightening visibly. "You're about the last person I was expecting to hear from today. What can I do for you?"

"I was hoping that perhaps we might be able to help each other," said Penney in a voice tinged with concern.

"What's the problem?" asked Sean. "I hope I didn't do anything wrong."

"No, no, it's nothing of the sort," said Penney, dispelling his worries.

"But in a way, it's much worse than that, and I don't know where to start."

"OK, then," said Sean, calmly. "Why don't you just tell me what the problem is and how I might be able to help."

"Well, it all started the end of last week. If you remember, I told you when you got here that another fellow had called to ask for permission to conduct research on a topic very similar to yours. When he arrived on Friday, he told me he was working with you—and I believed him at the time! We set him up to spend the day going through the same materials that you reviewed earlier in the week."

"The exact same boxes?" asked Sean, trying to clarify the issue.

"Yes," said the archivist. "The exact same boxes. He asked Brian, our assistant, to show him the papers that you had copied, and after that he focused almost entirely on those documents. It was as though he no longer felt the need to leaf through the contents of the other containers."

"That doesn't sound good," said Sean, murmuring his sentiments.

"Yes, I realize that now," said Penney. "As a matter of fact, if I had been keeping closer tabs on him, I probably would have become suspicious at that point. As it was, Brian was working with him, but this guy kept finding excuses to get him out of the room for periods of time throughout the day. We didn't find out why until this afternoon."

Sean was silent for a moment, considering the situation. "I take it that he removed some materials from your collection?" he ventured.

"Yes, it does appear that way," said Penney, her tone amped up a couple of notches.

"What's missing?" asked Sean.

"Well, Brian showed me an old folder that had been given to Frank Stewart by a descendant of Robert Patterson back in the late 1850s. His request was that Stewart return it to the appropriate government office, since it contained official Treasury Department documents. However, Frank Stewart—for whatever reason—never did that, because they ended up in his permanent collection."

"Yes, of course," said Sean, recalling the instructions on the cover. "I came across that folder not long before I left your library. It had a number of fascinating papers inside, including an encrypted cipher message that was probably written by Robert M. Patterson himself."

"You are correct on one account," sighed Penney. "That folder *had* a number of interesting papers inside…"

"You mean, this guy walked off with the papers from the Patterson folder?" asked Sean, staring in disbelief. "How could he have gotten away with that? Even if Brian wasn't with him one hundred percent of the time, he'd still notice him stealing anything that looked that old and that aged. I mean, he couldn't have just stuck it inside his notepad and pretended it was fresh out of the copy machine."

"I don't know, Sean. I just don't know," replied Penney, the despair apparent in her voice. "I can't prove that he stole anything. All I know is that those documents were in that folder on Friday afternoon, but they're not there now. It's possible that Garvin just misplaced the papers and inserted them into a different box. But somehow, I doubt it. Brian found the original folder, and it still had a few pages left in it. But he quickly noticed that the large page with that matrix was missing, along with a few other documents that he'd shown Garvin throughout the afternoon."

"Garvin?" asked Sean. "Who is Garvin?"

"Leon Garvin. That's the name of the fellow who was here on Friday. The one who I think may have walked off with those papers."

"Penney, are you standing anywhere near your registration book?" asked Sean.

"Yes, it's sitting here on my desk. Why?"

"Could you please tell me where this fellow was from?" In his mind, Sean was recalling the address listed on the front of Ben Grainger's driver's license. He remembered it was a listing in Binghamton, New York, although he couldn't think of the street address.

"Let's see now, Garvin, Garvin," repeated the librarian as she ran her finger down the register list. "Yes, here it is.' He had a Pennsylvania license, and it shows an address out in Erie. Does that sound right?"

"No, it's not what I was expecting," admitted Sean. "But let me ask you another question. What did he look like?"

"He was a big strapping fellow, I'd guess in his late twenties or early thirties," recited Penney. "He had a slight bit of a belly, but he wasn't really overweight. Oh, and he had the brightest red hair you've ever seen! I would have expected him to have a face full of freckles with that hair, but he didn't have any."

Sean silently nodded his head as Penney provided the description, mentally comparing the visitor to the photo on the front of Chris' report. It all fit, and Sean needed no further evidence to convince him that they were discussing the same person, regardless of the different names. However, just to confirm his suspicions, he came up with an idea.

"Penney, I'm going to ask you to do something else for me, if you don't mind."

"Anything; you name it," she replied.

"I'm going to head outside and get a photograph of our prime suspect from my car. I'm going to scan that photo and send it to you. All I want is for you to tell me whether you recognize the guy's face in the picture. It'll only take me a few minutes."

"Of course," said Penney. "I'm here for another two hours anyway. I'll be looking for your email."

"Great," said Sean. "I'll call you back in a bit."

Sean quickly trotted out to his car and pulled out the copy of the report from Chris' folder. He then returned to the building and scanned the image of Grainger's driver's license. Next, he opened a graphics editing tool and cropped out everything but the photo, careful not to include Grainger's name or address, and emailed it to Penney at Rowan University.

Sean had planned to wait for at least ten minutes before calling Penney back, in case their computer system was running slowly, or she was away from her desk. However, within three minutes of sending his email, Sean's phone rang, and Penney's phone number re-appeared on the display. Sean answered on the first ring.

"It's him! It's him!" shouted Penney, without waiting to her Sean's greeting. "That's Leon Garvin!"

"I'm glad you recognize him, but his name isn't Leon Garvin," said Sean, matter-of-factly. "And he doesn't live in Erie, PA, as he said. As a matter of fact, I don't think he told you a single genuine fact about himself the whole time he was there."

"If he isn't Leon, then who is he?" asked Penney.

"If it's OK with you, Penney, I'd rather not disclose his real identity. I will promise you though, we will be working with the authorities to get this guy, if he did in fact steal anything from your library. Chances are pretty good that he's involved in some other shady business as well."

"I sure do hope he's caught," said Penney wistfully. "I feel a strong sense of ownership of the material in our collection, and I can't escape a feeling of guilt over having lost some parts of it."

"If it's any consolation to you, I made copies of every document in that folder," said Sean. "I know it's not as good as having the original paper, but I'd be happy to provide you with photocopies of the missing records."

"Thank you," said Penney, "but I won't rest until I get my hands on the stolen version of those pages."

"I understand," said Sean. "Is there anything else I can do for you right now?"

"I don't think so, but there are two more things I wanted to tell you," offered Penney.

"OK, go ahead," said Sean.

"The first is a piece of good news. While searching through the bottom of that box, I came across an interesting letter that looks like it came from inside that same folder. It has some information about the 1804 coins you were researching, although I can't be certain that it's talking about silver dollars. It's a bit hard to read, because it's very old, and the ink appears to have smudged a bit."

"OK, that sounds right up our alley," said Sean. "My schedule will probably have me passing through Philadelphia again sometime in the next two weeks. Why don't you set that document aside and I'll take a look at it then."

"OK, Sean, I'd be happy to do that for you."

"What's the other thing you wanted to tell me?" asked Sean, with his pen at the ready to take notes.

"I just wanted to give you a warning, that's all," said Penney, her voice dropping noticeably in volume. "This man was very interested in getting your name and email address. He said that you were part of the same team, working on the same project. At the time, I didn't give it a second thought because I had no reason to doubt him. But now, in hindsight, I realize that I never should have allowed him to look at that registration book. My God, he probably copied down your address and phone number, too."

Sean cringed inwardly, knowing that Grainger would certainly have copied everything he could get his hands on. No matter what, it was now too late. Sean decided to try to reassure Penney, as allowing her to fret over things would accomplish nothing.

"Please don't worry about it," said Sean soothingly. "He won't bother with us."

"I hope you're right," replied Penney. "I'd feel terrible if anything happened."

"It's OK," said Sean again. "And remember, I'll see you in another week or two. In the meantime, maybe you'd better lock that new document you found in a secure drawer somewhere."

"OK, Sean, I'll do that," promised Penney. "And remember to give me a call a couple of days before your visit. I'll bring the donuts."

True to his word, Chris turned the corner into his next work week at flank speed, maintaining a breakneck pace with new clients and business contacts. Even though he had intentionally scheduled a full week of local appointments, he still hadn't seen much of his house, outside of the hours between nine PM and six AM.

By coincidence, at the same time that Sean was talking with Penney about Grainger, Chris was taking a phone call from Wes Hawkins, the local coin dealer he'd befriended. Chris enjoyed Wes' company because the spark of youth often escaped from his elderly façade, giving Chris hope that it was possible to maintain that spirited attitude into old age.

Chris answered the phone immediately once he recognized the number. "Hey there, Wes! How's my favorite entrepreneur doing?"

"Hello, Chris," came the friendly reply. "I'm doing fine. How's life treating you?"

"Wonderful, busy, tiring, hectic, confusing, rewarding, and often impossible," summarized Chris.

"Welcome to the world of the working stiffs!" laughed Wes, his voice cackling over the lines of his old dial telephone. Wes was the only person Chris had ever met who still retained his original, rotary-dial phone. Most kids who came into his shop had never seen one and hadn't a clue how to use it.

"So tell me, how was your visit to Boston, and how did you make out with the dollar? Were you able to learn anything about its origin?" asked Chris.

"Well, yes and no," said Wes, sounding very noncommittal.

"Hmm, OK," said Chris, knowing there had to be additional information. "Were you at least able to determine when it was made, and how it was altered to look like an 1804 dollar?"

"Well, yes and no, Chris," answered Wes, repeating his previous answer without expression.

"Come on, old pal," said Chris, feeling slightly frustrated by the lack of cooperation. "Isn't there anything you can tell me yet? I thought you were taking this to Boston because your friend 'The Expert' was there."

"He was," Wes replied. "Could you come down to my shop sometime today? I'd like to talk to you in person, if possible."

Although Chris was surprised by the request, he decided to stop trying to extract information from the old dealer over the phone.

"OK Wes," he said. "I'll tell you what. My last meeting should end by a little after five o'clock, and I have a stop or two to make after that. Will you still be open at about five forty-five? I should be able to make it by then."

"That sounds OK, Chris. I'll be here. See you then."

Chris' day went about as planned, with some meetings running longer than expected and others ending earlier. By day's end, he was pretty much right on schedule and even had enough time to call Kristi for ten minutes of chitchat as he drove back across town. His new Jeep had a Bluetooth system that allowed him to talk while driving, a feature he used often while commuting between client locations.

Chris ended his call at the precise moment he pulled up in front of the coin shop. He recognized Wes' old Buick sitting in front of the store, alongside one other vehicle, a Cadillac, with Connecticut license plates that were imprinted with 'GR8 COINS.' Chris smiled to himself. He was always amused by the creativity some individuals employed while coming up with their own vanity plates. The car obviously belonged to either another dealer or an avid collector.

Before heading into the shop, Chris removed his jacket and loosened his tie, trying to relax from the rigors of the work day. He figured that this little stop with Wes wouldn't take long, after which he'd stop for some Chinese take-out and enjoy a rare evening with nothing to do.

Upon entering the store, Chris noticed that Wes was alone in the room, sitting on a stool behind the counter. However, he appeared to be listening to a conversation that was taking place in the narrow back room that led from the service area behind the cash register. The sound of voices drifted out, although Chris couldn't immediately determine how many people were speaking.

Wes looked up and smiled briefly at Chris, waving his hand but not saying anything for a few moments before turning his attention to Chris.

"Hello, Chris, and thanks for coming down. I'm sorry I couldn't tell you too much over the phone this afternoon, but I had a few things that I needed to show you in person. I think you'll find it worth your while."

"Sure, no problem," said Chris. "You got my attention, that's for sure. I take it you've found something interesting on the fake dollar?"

"Uh, yeah, you could say that," replied Wes. "But before we go any further, I'd like to introduce you to a couple of old friends."

The conversation from the back room ceased instantly, and two men appeared as if on cue.

"Chris, this is Ed Barton, vice president of the American Numismatic Association, and also the organization's head of the Standards and Grading Committee." Chris shook hands with the gentleman, who was short and thin and looked to be in his early seventies.

"Very nice to meet you," Chris mumbled.

"And this is Bill Sturges, who not only owns Atlantic Numismatic Antiquities, the largest internet-based coin shop in the country, but also writes columns on rare coins and currency in almost every numismatic magazine and newsletter in the country," continued Wes.

"Nice to meet you," Chris said again, shaking hands with the second gentleman. "I take it that you're not from around these parts?"

"No, we're not," said Bill, a large man with an extended beer belly and black, slicked-back hair. He looked about fifteen years younger than the other two men, although probably less fit in other ways. "I'm from New Paltz, and my colleague here is from Springfield, Connecticut. We're just passing through, but we thought we'd stick around to talk to you as long as you had the time."

"Sure," said Chris. "My time is your time. I take it that you've found something unusual in the specimen I brought in to Wes last week?"

The three men looked at each other, as if trying to figure out who should speak first. In the end, it was Ed Barton who decided to take the lead. He looked back at Chris and smiled, then placed his hand on Chris' shoulder.

"Chris, from what Wes has told us, you're an unusual young man," said Ed. "I gather you were personally responsible for tracking down and locating the Gordon treasure we heard about last year."

"The credit isn't all mine," said Chris, "but yes, I was involved in the find."

"It seems you have a penchant for doing unusual, noteworthy things," said Ed, winking as he spoke. "But first, in order for me to tell you about your coin, I'd like to give you some background on the early production processes of United States coins, as well as the telltale signs of fakes and 're-strikes.' How much do you know about these topics already?"

"Not much," admitted Chris, recalling his earlier days as a collector. "But I did read about several attempts to create fraudulent strikes of the 1804 dollar. As I recall, it involved scraping off the '3' in an 1803 dollar, and replacing it with a '4,' or some combination of substitution using a coin from a year that was close enough to that date to resemble the 1804 pattern."

"That's correct," nodded Ed. "That's one way that a skilled and knowledgeable craftsman could re-create a viable copy of the original 1804 coin."

"I checked that dollar, and I couldn't detect any scrape or burnish marks," said Sean. "Plus, the '4' didn't look as though it was added later. It looked like part of the original press."

"Correct again," said Ed, looking at Wes as he concurred with the response. "There are no signs of tampering whatsoever on the date of this coin."

"My friend, Sean, whom Wes has met, also told me that there were several 1804 dollars coined at the mint many years later, for a variety of different purposes," continued Chris. "But I'm certainly not expert enough to tell you whether this coin fits the description of any of those."

"Actually, all the 1804 dollars currently in the museums and collections in the U.S. were struck after the fact. Their genuine dates, if correctly stamped, would read anywhere from 1834 through 1858, and possibly even later," explained Ed. "To be precise, the eight 'Type I' 1804 dollars were minted as gifts to leaders of foreign governments in 1834. The remaining seven coins, which include one 'Type 2' and six 'Type 3' dollars, were created much later by mint employees without the approval of the facility's officers. However, they are as valuable today nonetheless."

"Are you saying that this coin is one of those originals, or re-creations, or whatever you call them?" asked Chris.

"No, your coin doesn't fit that mold either, no pun intended."

"OK, then you're saying it's a complete counterfeit?" asked Chris.

"Let me wait to answer that, if you don't mind, and I'll show you a few other things you need to know," said Ed. As he spoke, Wes walked into the back room and opened a large vault. He removed a small box, which he placed on the counter under his examination and magnification lamp.

"The truth of the matter is that, because none of the 'original' 1804 dollars we have today were struck until at least thirty years later, all of them display some certain characteristics that identify them as being atypical of the indicated mint year," said Ed. "For example, coins that were struck after 1828 had a raised flat rim around the outside of the coin, which was caused by the kind of press that was employed at that time. Naturally, since the 1804 dollars were actually struck in 1834 and later, they all had that same flat raised rim. Here, I can show you a picture," said Ed, opening a book and placing it in front of Chris.

"OK," said Chris, studying the photograph. "But if the later coins had this raised rim, how did the earlier coins appear?"

"They simply had a series of tiny lines called radials, extending from the outer surface of the coin inwards, towards the center. Also, they lacked these small semicircular patterns that we call dentils, which circled the outside of the coin in later years."

"Wow. It sounds almost as unique as a fingerprint," exclaimed Chris, looking closely at the page.

"In a way, that's *exactly* what it is," agreed Ed. "Now, I want to show you something else. If you look at the picture on the next page, you'll see it shows another part of the 'fingerprint' of the 1804 re-strikes, the ones that were created by the mint in 1834. Notice that the number 4 in the 1804 date has a serif base on the bottom; that's the horizontal line that squares off the bottom of the number. And yet, the serif on the horizontal line of the number 4 is missing. Instead, the line just ends without any serif. Now, look at these photos of large coins of other denominations minted in 1794, 1804, and 1814. Notice that all of them have the crosslet in the numeral 4 of the date, because that's just the way they made 4s in those years. But, because the 1804 dollars we know of weren't struck until 1834, they were given the later style, with no crosslet."

"So where are you going with all this?" asked Chris, who was starting to feel even more confused.

"That's a good question," said Ed as he opened the small box placed on the counter by Wes. "I want to show you a few details about your coin that make it unique from anything we've seen before."

Chris noticed that the silver dollar he'd given to Wes for identification had been placed inside a rectangular plastic container, with white plastic prongs holding it securely in place inside the housing.

"Based on what I've just told you, what observations can you make about your coin?" asked Ed.

Chris took the holder from Wes and held it under the lamp. He slowly turned the coin over, looking at the front and back sides under the magnifying glass as he recalled the fine points of the lecture he'd just received. Finally, after examining the coin for several minutes, he placed the coin holder gently on the flat countertop and looked back at the three experts.

"Well, first of all, there are no dentils and no raised flat rim around the outside of the coin. Instead, all I can see is a series of radials surrounding the exterior rim."

"Which means…?" led Ed, allowing his voice to trail off into silence.

"According to what you just told me, it means that this coin was pressed some time before 1828."

"That is correct," confirmed Ed. "What else do you see?"

"I also see that there is the serif you mentioned on the number 4, which also indicates that is was struck in an earlier era than the other Type 1 coins. Correct?"

"Correct again," said Ed. "Your conclusion, that this silver dollar was struck in the first years of the 1800s, is valid. And there's more, if you want to hear it."

"Sure," said Chris, who by now had forgotten all about his free evening. "This is incredible stuff."

"You have no idea," said Bill Sturges, who had remained silent up to this point. He was sweating slightly, despite the fact that the air conditioning was running full blast.

"The next item to consider is the lettering on the edge of the coin, which is extremely telling," continued Ed. As he spoke, he removed a pair of thin white linen gloves from his pocket. He then pried open the coin holder, making sure to do so over the soft mat to protect the coin. "Do you see the pattern of letters along the edge of your coin?" he asked, holding it up for Chris to view.

"Yes, I can see the words 'HUNDRED CENTS' imprinted into the outside of the coin, along with some other patterned shapes. It that unusual?"

Ed looked back and shrugged his shoulders. "Unusual, no. Those letters appear on every dollar of that era," he replied. "However, there was a significant change in the way that the mint pressed coins in the early 1830s. Prior to that time, when the power was supplied manually, using a screw press, the edges of the coins weren't compressed against the outside of the die, because the die was bigger than the coin. But later, when the press went to steam power, they switched to a collar die, which squeezed the edges of the coin together. If you look at any of the Type 1 or Type 3 1804 dollars, you'll notice that the letters in the words 'HUNDRED CENTS' are crushed, or else completely sealed up. But here, look at the lettering on your coin..."

Chris gazed carefully at the lettering along the edge, looking for signs of compression. "I can't see any evidence of crushed lettering, none at all," he said finally. "And, if I'm understanding you correctly, this is another sign that this coin was produced at an earlier date than all those re-strikes minted in 1834, right?"

"You're catching on," said Wes, who had been watching avidly from behind the counter. "Everything you've seen on this coin indicates an actual strike date that was sometime in the first few years of the nineteenth century, perhaps even 1804."

"Wow, that's pretty amazing," said Chris, the possibilities blossoming before his very eyes. "Is there anything else that backs up your theory?"

Ed smiled in a way that bordered on being smug. "Son, *everything* backs up my theory. From the "curl tip" on the top of Liberty's head on the coin's obverse to the lack of die breaks and absence of residual signs of die rust pitting on the rest of the coin, what you are holding in your hands right now is authentic and unique."

"Authentic and unique," repeated Chris, the color draining from his face. "You mean this is an actual, honest-to-God 1804 silver dollar?"

Ed moved closer to Chris and spoke in a hushed tone. "Chris, what I'm telling you is this. Not only am I one hundred percent sure of the authenticity of this coin, but I also believe that it is the first-ever example of an 1804 silver dollar that was actually struck in 1804. Do you understand what I am saying?"

"Yes, I think so," said Chris, leaning against the counter. "But then..."

"But what?" asked Ed.

"If this is a real 1804 silver dollar, pressed in that year, wouldn't that decrease the value of the other fifteen examples that are currently considered to be authentic?"

"This is a tough question to answer," replied Ed, "and I'm not really the best person to ask. Bill, would you feel comfortable answering that one?"

"Sure," replied Bill, who was almost drooling over the coin in Chris' hand. "No matter what, I don't think the value of the existing Type 1, 2, or 3 coins will ever decrease. They have too storied a history, passed down as they were through generations of families, or sold to wealthy American collectors and investors."

"So where would this coin fit in?" asked Chris, gazing at the uncirculated piece housed in plastic. "It has no history at all, none."

"But don't you see?" said Bill, spreading his hands out in amazement. "You have the only genuine 1804 silver dollar ever found. So, if you were asking for a price, I couldn't give you one."

"In other words, Chris, you have the Holy Grail of American coin collecting right there in your hands," explained Wes, putting an exclamation point on the discussion.

"Well, let's not forget a couple of fine points here," said Chris, looking to bring the conversation back to earth."

"And what might those be?" asked Bill.

"First, this coin doesn't belong to me. It never has and it never will."

"That's right," said Ed. "As I recall, Wes said that it came from the collection of the Adirondack Museum in Blue Lake, right?"

"Blue Mountain Lake," corrected Chris, amused at the error.

"Whatever," said Ed. "Just out of curiosity, what do they know about this coin that you borrowed from their collection? Do they know that it's worth millions?"

"Hardly," laughed Chris. "And please, let's not go there. They're still a bit suspicious of me for absconding with a couple gold pieces from the Gordon treasure that had ended up in their museum without their knowledge. I returned them, of course, because I'm an honest man, and I only needed them to help us solve the mystery of Robert Gordon's lost stash of gold. But you might say that I'm still on probation with that organization."

"Well, I'm sure you'll more than make up for it when you tell them what you've learned about this dollar," replied Ed.

"There is one more thing to ask you, and it's perhaps more important than anything we've discussed so far," said Chris.

"And I think I know where you're leading," said Ed.

"Really?" asked Chris, amazed they might be sharing the same thoughts.

"Yes," said Ed. "So please allow me to venture a guess, OK?"

"You're on," agreed Chris.

"You're probably wondering that, if one example of this original coin exists, what's to say that the full complement of 19,570 of the 1804 dollars listed in the treasury record weren't actually struck and then stashed somewhere like the one you've uncovered here. Am I close?"

"No, you're not close," confided Chris. "You're right on the money."

"Well, my good lad, if that was the case, we'd not only have a mystery of epic proportions, but if word got out, we'd also witness a full-scale panicked treasure hunt, the likes of which the world has never seen," concluded Ed.

"That doesn't sound like a very wise idea," said Chris.

"No, it doesn't," agreed Ed. Both Bill and Wes nodded their heads silently in concurrence. "Is there any way that you can fabricate a story for the museum, at least for the moment, to keep them from learning the truth? Tell them that the authorities are still looking at the coin. Tell them your dog ate it. Tell them anything that might buy us some time to sort this thing out amongst a few very select experts and figure out how this came to be."

Chris laughed at the suggestion, and then thoughtfully weighed the options. "Well, I don't have a dog, so I guess that alibi is out of the question," he said. "However, they're not calling me yet for the return of the dollar, which isn't surprising since I assured them it was a fake. I think I can hang on to it for another several weeks, at least."

"That's great," said Bill. "In the meantime, would you mind if we kept this beautiful specimen in our possession? It will, of course, be kept under heavy security, in a strongbox inside a vault."

"That's fine," said Chris. "But perhaps the best protection is its anonymity, because the world doesn't know of its existence."

"Very true," said Ed.

"I'll keep this to myself and my partner, who is working this story with me," said Chris.

"We appreciate your trust," said Ed.

Chris' face then assumed a suspicious expression. Looking back and forth between Bill and Ed, he said, "You came from New Paltz and Springfield, Connecticut, huh? My guess is that you two weren't really just passing through, were you?"

Ed laughed. "No, Chris, we were not. This was not a random drive over here. Once Wes showed us your specimen in Boston, we both wanted to examine it further, as well as talk to you about retaining it for further study."

"I figured," said Chris, getting set to depart. "OK then, I'll leave this here with you, assuming that you will assume all accountability for its safekeeping."

"We will," assured Ed.

"And maybe, just maybe, we'll be able to track down another twenty thousand of these things for you," said Chris, winking at the trio of men.

"That's OK," said Bill. "Even if this is the only surviving example, you've already turned the numismatic world on its ear."

"By the way, there is one other thing you should know," said Ed, his voice turning somber. "If the news of this does get out, you may need to watch your step. The value of your quarry is so great that some people would stop at nothing to acquire it for their own personal gain." Bill and Wes both nodded in agreement.

"I understand, and thanks for the warning," said Chris. It was an ominous ending to an otherwise incredible conference, but he appreciated their concern.

As Chris strolled empty-handed across the parking lot to his Jeep, he noticed there were significant hunger pangs rumbling from his gut. Remembering that he had skipped lunch, he decided to head immediately to grab some take-out. The small, family-owned Chinese restaurant he frequented was only a half mile down the road, and he was there in less than a minute.

The Jade Dragon Restaurant was well known for its ability to assemble wonderful meals at lightning speed, so it was no surprise that Chris was out the door within five minutes. In a large bag, he carried cardboard cartons containing Kung Pao shrimp, Chinese vegetables, fresh spring rolls, and a fortune cookie. The scents wafting from the boxes were tantalizing, and Chris quickly found himself salivating in anticipation of the meal. These sensations became even more overpowering in the confined interior of the Jeep.

As he pulled out of the parking lot, Chris decided to take the edge off his appetite by munching on the fortune cookie. Stopping briefly to tear open the wrapper, he snapped the cookie in half, devouring the first section in a single bite. Then, before finishing the remainder, he pulled the fortune strip from the crease and glanced at its message. It was written in bold letters in a plain red font. The words that jumped off the paper stole Chris' attention.

The fortune read: AS YOU EMBARK ON A NEW ADVENTURE, BEWARE. DANGER AWAITS YOUR ARRIVAL.

CHAPTER 12

Wednesday night, still August 20, 2015

The town of Westmoreland, New York, is very small, even by the standards of the largely rural Mohawk Valley. The entire community is comprised of about six thousand people, and the fields that are farmed by the locals extend almost to the middle of the hamlet. It is a quiet, peaceful place that is just far-enough removed from the Thruway to avoid the noise of the trucks and cars streaking by on their east-west passage.

Westmoreland has one more geographic feature that was of little consequence to anyone other than Chris and Sean. For them, it represented the halfway point between their two homes; the geographic midpoint at which they could meet in the event of a crisis or other important event. Over the years, the two friends seldom had to take advantage of this emergency rendezvous spot, but each knew that the other would be there within forty-five minutes if the situation warranted. Tonight, they had both decided independently to initiate that call, each with their own agendas. However, it was Chris who dialed first, and they set up an impromptu meeting for later that evening.

Close to the Thruway exit in Westmoreland sat a small, red brick restaurant called Wendy's International Café. It wasn't fancy, and some people unfamiliar with the establishment probably classified it as a "greasy spoon" while driving through the town. But it served an impressive menu of designer sandwiches and lunches, gourmet desserts, and specialty coffees to the local population. The owner, Wendy Culligan, had trained as a chef at a top culinary arts school, and she kept the menu updated with her latest creations.

Chris and Sean staked their claim to a booth situated in the rear corner of the restaurant. It was already nine thirty PM, and both had eaten substantial dinners, so they settled for a couple cups of coffee and a sampling of the upscale desserts for which Wendy had acquired her reputation. Chris ordered the warm chocolate puddle cake, with chocolate sauce oozing out the middle underneath a layer of thick whipped cream. Sean tried the cinnamon apple sponge cake that had once been served at a previous presidential inauguration feast. The sweets helped revive their thought processes, as both men had experienced long and tiresome afternoons. Chris started the conversation by bringing up the subject of the 1804 dollar.

"First things first," Chris began, as he pulled a photograph of the dollar piece from his pocket. The page held images of the front and back of the coin. "This is the dollar from the museum. I tried to find some traces of alteration that would explain the 1804 date, but I couldn't. But I'm not a trained numismatic expert. Why don't you have a look and tell me what you see?" He pushed the paper in front of Sean and sat back to observe.

"Hey, if you're looking for an expert in this field, you've asked the wrong man," said Sean, looking carefully at the photo nonetheless. "I can't seem to see any sign of alteration on the date. But wait – I might know another way it could have been altered," he said as he focused instead on the photo of the reverse side.

"What are you looking for?" asked Chris, puzzled at his actions.

"I'm looking for a mint mark, like the letter 'D' for Denver, to see if it might have been removed to make the dollar look like a plain 1804 mintage," Sean replied.

"No, that's not possible, because Philadelphia was the only mint in operation in 1804," said Chris. "As a matter of fact, you just flunked your first test in Coin Collecting 101, because Denver didn't start minting coins until 1906. So congratulations, you only missed it by 102 years!"

"You're such a geek," said Sean, ignoring the ridicule. Then, after studying the photographs for another minute, he finally gave up and returned the page to Chris. "OK, I give up, so tell me. Where is the hidden clue that screams 'FAKE!'?"

"There isn't one."

"There isn't one?" echoed Sean.

"Nope," replied Chris, his face registering only a deadpan seriousness that Sean couldn't interpret.

"OK, then, how can you tell it's a fake?" asked Sean, looking confused.

"It isn't," came the two-word reply.

"It isn't? What?" said Sean, acting perturbed. "Chris, you're playing games with me and I'm too tired for that. Would you please just explain, in plain English, what you're saying?"

Chris slowly put down his fork and napkin, then lowered his voice and spoke in a conspiratorial tone. "The experts' examination of the coin proved that it is a genuine 1804 silver dollar, as real and as pretty as the day it came off the press in Philadelphia in 1804."

Sean didn't say a word. He just sat and stared, with a forkful of sponge cake frozen in mid-air, resembling a mechanical device that had been turned off for the night.

"Not only that, but it's the only 1804 dollar ever found that was actually coined in that year, instead of the 'real' re-strikes from 1834 or 1858. The significance of this, of course, is that it proves that they did make silver dollars, or at least *a* silver dollar, that carried the 1804 mint year."

"And that means," said Sean, following the logical progression of things, "that there could be more."

"Or not," suggested Chris. "After all, this is the only 1804 dollar ever found in the 211 years since it was minted. If there were more, at least some would have surfaced somewhere."

"One would think so," agreed Sean, whose hand finally resumed transporting the sponge cake to his mouth.

"How is that cake, anyway?" asked Chris, as he devoured his own dessert.

"To die for," murmured Sean. "And yours?"

"Same," said Chris, soaking up the liquid chocolate with the cake.

After taking another few minutes to polish off the rest of their desserts, Chris moved his dish to the side and returned to business. "So what is it that you want to share with me, now that I've dropped my bombshell on you?"

"I want to talk about your buddy, this Grainger fellow," said Sean.

"What about him?" asked Chris. "It's too bad that he's out there, probably looking for the exact same thing as we are. But he's not breaking the law, is he?"

"Yes, as a matter of fact, he is," said Sean.

"He is?"

"I'd say that theft of priceless historical documents falls into the category of a crime in our penal system," replied Sean.

"So, now it's your turn to be cryptic," said Chris, smiling for the first time that evening. "It's OK; I guess I deserve it. Allow me to reword my question: PLEASE, Mr. Riggins, tell me what Ben Grainger stole, and from whom, that classifies him as a crook?"

"Penney, the archivist from the Frank Stewart Room, called me this afternoon. She said a man matching Grainger's description stole several documents that I had found in their collection. They had all been inside one old folder that Frank Stewart had acquired in the 1850s. Included in that folder was the missing page 154 of the treasury records your man noted from the Archives, as well as the cipher page that had been encoded by Robert M. Patterson."

"Hmm, that could be bad news," agreed Chris. "Did you have copies of those documents?"

"Yes, and so do you," reminded Sean. "I gave you copies of all that material last weekend at my house."

"OK," said Chris. "I remember. So we still have the material to work from."

"Yes, but so does Grainger," said Sean. "And, as you pointed out last week, he also has access to his ancestor's record books from inside the mint, and we have no clue what leads those provide."

"True, but we have the edge over him in a few areas as well," said Chris.

"Such as…?" asked Sean.

"First, Grainger may not know for a fact that the 1804 dollars really do exist. The journal from the 1804 mint, assuming that's what it is, may hint that there were dollars pressed in 1804 with that mint year stamped on the coin, but given the fact that none of the coins have ever surfaced, he can't be sure. So far, you and I, along with Wes and the two other numismatists who were at his shop, are the only ones who know that with certainty."

"OK, that's helpful," said Sean. "But we know that he suspects their existence or he wouldn't be in this crazy search in the first place."

"True," said Chris. "Second, and this is a big one, he is now a wanted man, and he probably knows it. He committed theft of historical documents from a state library, assuming that they can prove that. That will affect his ability to travel and conduct research at other facilities."

"Uh huh, sure it will," said Sean, sarcastically. "But can you tell me how the other facilities will find out about his pilferage, assuming that it can be proven? Also, what happens if he shows up posing as Leon Garvin again instead of Ben Grainger? How would they even know to keep him away from their collections, or better yet, to call the police and have him arrested?"

"I guess it's up to the 'A' Team to spread the word, isn't it?" replied Chris, a sly smile on his face.

"Us?" asked Sean, shocked at the suggestion. "That means that we'd have to be down there, in that area around Philly and Glassboro, New Jersey, and visit those locations in person. Is that what you're suggesting?"

"My friend, after the week that you and I have had, I think it's about time that we took a road trip together. May I suggest the sunny climes of central Philadelphia? I've heard it's very nice around there at this time of year."

"It would be a pleasure," said Sean. "The next couple days are booked pretty tight, but I think I could clear my schedule by the weekend in time to spend part of next week down there. How about you?"

"I'm in the same boat," said Chris, recalling his schedule for the next few days. "I was going to try to work on a couple of new pieces of business early next week, but none of them are carved in stone yet, so I can probably clear most of next week as well. At this point, I honestly think it would be time well spent. Heck, it might even be a blast. If we have a little extra time, maybe we could take in a Phillies game."

"Sounds like fun," agreed Sean. "Do you have a plan of attack for the trip, assuming that we'll be down there for the good part of the week?"

"Yes, I do," said Chris, laying out a mental schedule as he spoke. "I think we need to scout out the two places where Robert Patterson and his son left the bulk of their papers and writings. That would be the University of Pennsylvania Library, and the American Philosophical Society. Between the two of those, I think we could come up with some nice insights on the thought processes of Robert M. Patterson in the years leading up to his death. I don't know what that will lead to, but I think it's the most logical place to start."

"Anything else?" asked Sean.

"Yes, I think you need to return to the Frank Stewart Room at Glassboro and look at the rest of that material," replied Chris. "It might also be a good idea to see what new documents your archivist friend, Penney, was able to find since your last visit."

"That's been on my to do list since the moment I left there last week," said Sean. "Her phone call this afternoon only strengthened my resolve to get back there."

"How about your other old friend, Rosemary Stewart? Do you think she'd be useful to talk to again? Perhaps she might have remembered additional details since your last visit," suggested Chris.

"No, I really don't think so," said Sean. "The only assistance I'd expect from that family right now is her niece, Tracey. Remember, she's the one who is the student at the University of Pennsylvania, and she agreed to help us out in their library."

"How could I forget?" sighed Chris, thinking back to the photo she'd attached to her email the previous weekend. "All I can say is, you're a brave man, asking your girlfriend to open an email from a beauty queen like that. What was going through your head, old man?"

Sean laughed in response, hanging his head above his empty plate and coffee mug. "I guess I wasn't thinking at all," he agreed, recalling the episode vividly. "But you know, Tracey is a smart, ambitious young woman. Why not take advantage of a ready helper when they're already living where you need them?"

"Hey, I'm agreeing with you," said Chris, still grinning. "But still, you've got to admit, she's a pretty stunning-looking girl. Maggie was bound to be jealous."

"Yeah, I know," said Sean. "I guess next time I'll have to hire a male assistant named Hugo, or something like that."

"OK, so we've decided to take the show on the road," said Chris, returning to the original conversation. "We'll probably need at least three days in Philly, including the time that we spend at the Frank Stewart Room."

"That will take us through Wednesday or Thursday of next week," said Sean, jotting out a rough schedule on the back of his papers. "Is there any place else you'd like to visit?"

"Yes, there is. I can't help it, but I keep getting this gut feeling that there is something to be found in that mining town that Patterson visited in the early 1850s. Patterson seemed pre-occupied by the place. It's also the connection to the VanderBrooke character who was in charge of building the blast furnace up there. Remember, it was inside his parcel of letters that I found the 1804 dollar. Somehow, I can't shake the feeling that that dollar came from Patterson himself, and that the story we're investigating runs right though that little ghost town."

"Sounds plausible," agreed Sean. "Too bad that the village of Adirondac, or Tahawus, or McIntyre, or whatever you want to call it, is in the exact opposite direction from the route we're taking to Philly."

"I tell you what," said Chris, his eyes brightening. "Why don't we spend a few hours this weekend driving up there just to hike around and look at things? From what I've heard, they've restored a few of the buildings, and they've cleared the vegetation away from the blast furnace too.

We could make a day trip of it and still be home in time for an early departure for Philadelphia on Sunday."

"Wow, once you make up your mind to jump into a project, you don't mess around, do you?" said Sean.

"No one ever won a race by jogging at half speed," replied Chris.

Sean nodded his agreement with Chris' statement. He realized it not only addressed the plans for the weekend, but also summarized the way Chris lived his life. It was either full speed ahead, which was ninety percent of the time, or complete rest. For as long as he had been friends with Chris, he had never known him to have a second gear.

As they prepared to pay the bill and part ways, Chris noticed that something seemed to be bothering Sean. He mentioned this to his friend, who paused for a moment and then responded.

"I'm afraid you know me a little too well, my friend," Sean said, his face shrouded in thought.

"What's wrong? Is there something we haven't covered?" asked Chris.

"Yes, there is one detail that bothers me, and I haven't yet told you," admitted Sean.

"Tell me," urged Chris.

"When Grainger was inside the Frank Stewart Room, he somehow convinced Penney that he and I were both working on the same research project. He told her that he had lost my email address, and she allowed him to copy it from the registration book."

"Ouch," said Chris. "That's more than a trifling detail, isn't it?"

"Yes, it is," agreed Sean, "particularly since my full name, street address, phone number, and email address were also in the book. Heck – he's got everything but my Social Security number, and he could probably find that if he wanted to."

"Well, the advantage we have is that he doesn't know that we're on to him," said Chris, trying to comfort his friend. "So we can keep tabs from afar, while he doesn't have a clue that anyone even knows his name."

"I guess that's some consolation," agreed Sean, clearly uneasy about the situation. "Still, I'm thinking of having an alarm system added to the house, even if just to make a ruckus if someone breaks a window or something."

"Might not be a bad idea," agreed Chris. "But for now, here's my plan for the next week, if you're really committed to doing this."

"I am, so let's hear it," said Sean.

"OK. On Saturday morning, I'll try to make it to your house by seven o'clock. From there, we head north, through Old Forge and Long Lake en route to the ghost village in Adirondac. We can spend the day there, and even toss up a tent if the spirits move us, or we can return all the way home on Saturday night. But Sunday, we're on the road to Philly, where we start turning pages first thing on Monday morning. I'm bringing enough clothes to last through the end of next week."

"Cool," agreed Sean. "I'll send an email to Penney letting her know that we'll be stopping by on Monday. I'll also send one to Tracey to tell her we'll be down, and ask her to get us set up at the University library."

"Great," said Chris. "I guess I'll get going now so I can get started on my packing."

"I'll have breakfast waiting when you get there on Saturday," promised Sean.

The two friends paid the bill, leaving a healthy tip to the waitress for her hospitality during their extended snack. Then they parted ways to start preparations for their trip.

For the most part, Chris had the easy part of the preparations detail. He returned home and grabbed his "extended weekend" bag, which he filled with two pairs of pants, a half-dozen polo shirts, and a corresponding number of underwear and socks. He also grabbed a day pack, which he filled with his hiking boots, canteen, and the basic essentials he'd need for an afternoon in the woods. As an afterthought, he tossed his tent and sleeping bag into the back of the Jeep and called it a night. It was already closing in on midnight as he turned off the lights and climbed into the loft that housed his bed.

Sean, on the other hand, drew the short straw. In addition to packing his things for the trip, he had emails to send out to various people, arranging the library visits to Rowan University as well as the stop at the American Philosophical Society. He also had to contact Tracey to let her know that they'd be down the following Monday.

Prior to emailing Penney, he put together a sort of "wanted" poster on Ben Grainger. The full-page document carried a large blow-up of the photo from his driver's license, followed by his name and a list of his suspected transgressions. Sean also decided to include Grainger's alias, Leon Garvin, in case he decided to reuse that name. He did not include his own name. The only purpose for the document would be to serve as a warning, shared between librarians, to keep an eye out for the suspicious stranger with the bright red hair.

Finally satisfied with his work, Sean attached the poster to his email to Penney, along with the suggestion that she forward it to her counterparts at the American Philosophical Society and the University of Pennsylvania. Unsure of just how much he should say, he decided to be diplomatically low key. His email to Penney was simple and direct:

Penney – I'll be down to your library on Monday or Tuesday of next week. I was sorry to hear about the theft of your documents last week. In view of the illegal activity of Ben Grainger (a.k.a. Leon Garvin), it might be advisable to warn your counterparts in other facilities who also possess related materials. These other libraries include the University of Pennsylvania as well as the collection held by the American Philosophical Society. I have prepared a write-up about Grainger (attached) that you can send them. I believe that this warning would be heeded with more seriousness if it came directly from your Rowan University account than from me. – Sean

After sending his message, Sean decided to follow up with a phone call. Even though he knew he'd only get Penney's answering machine at this time of night, he wanted to give her a heads-up about his email. Spreading the word about Grainger was high on Sean's list of priorities, and he didn't feel guilty at all about making unsubstantiated accusations.

The next two days seemed to fly by, with Chris and Sean both tending to their businesses in advance of their upcoming trip. Chris remained close to home, nurturing the Syracuse market, while Sean's business took him north into Vermont on a special consulting gig. However, both men were able to wrap up early on Friday to take care of any last minute preparations for their trip.

As promised, Chris pulled into Sean's driveway shortly before seven AM on Saturday, having left his house in relative darkness at five forty-five. Rather than take the direct route through his back door, which Sean seldom locked, Chris instead chose to press the buzzer next to the front door. This action was followed immediately by the sound of footsteps approaching, and then the door swung open.

Sean was standing in the entranceway wearing a T-shirt and shorts, grinning from ear to ear. "All packed up and ready to go," he said. "And your ham, egg, and cheese croissant is waiting on your plate."

"Wow! With service like that, who needs McDonalds?" replied Chris, sidling up to the table.

The two consumed their breakfasts quickly and then got Sean's bags and other things loaded into the back of Chris' Jeep. Rather than steer the most direct course leading towards the north woods, Sean made a quick side trip in the direction of the closest coffee shop, since Chris wouldn't touch the coffee that came from his ancient machine. Within twenty minutes, they were northbound, coffee in hand, on the road to the heart of the Adirondacks.

According to Sean's GPS, the distance to the town of Newcomb was 114 miles. They followed Route 8 up through the picturesque town of Speculator, and then turned onto Route 30 to Indian Lake and points north, stopping only to pick up sandwiches in Long Lake. They then turned east, following Route 28 north into the tiny village of Newcomb, where the road continued until they diverted north onto Route 84. From there, they were able to find the small County Road 25, which would lead them to the "Upper Works" road. It was a long trip, and the distance they traveled on the small, narrow winding county road amazed Sean.

"This feels like we're driving right up into the High Peaks," he said, referring to the area surrounding Mount Marcy and the other towering giants of the state's highest mountains.

"We are," said Chris. "We can climb Marcy and any other of a dozen or so peaks from right here. There's a trailhead at the end of this road, with a sign-in booth for the hikers. We're going to park right next to it."

As they approached the final quarter mile of the road, Sean glanced out the passenger side window and got his first glimpse of the giant McIntyre blast furnace. Since the trees and other vegetation had been cut away from the massive stone walls, the behemoth remnant of the bygone era stood out even more than in previous decades, dominating the landscape with its sheer, naked mass.

"Oh my God," he said, entranced by the spectacle.

"Yeah, pretty amazing, isn't it?" replied Chris, observing the same sight. "It's hard to believe that beast has been sitting there like that for over one hundred fifty years, untouched, forgotten, and left to become buried in the overgrowth the way it was. From what I heard, they only cut back the trees and shrubs within the last few years."

"You know, I've seen pictures of this thing online, and drawings, and stuff like that. But until you get up close and personal like this, it's impossible to really imagine just how huge it is."

"Tell you what," suggested Chris. "We've got a lot of ground to cover today. Let's just head up and park, and then we can backtrack down and have a closer look at the furnace and some of the other buildings."

Sean nodded his approval, and Chris pulled the Jeep forward until the road ended in a dirt parking area. About a dozen cars were spaced across the lot under the trees, their owners already departed into the woods beyond the sign-in register. Another two hiking parties were completing their final preparations, checking their packs and tightening their boot laces. Chris pulled into a spot next to another large SUV, and the pair got out of the Jeep.

"Two hours," said Sean, looking at this watch. "Pretty good time for a city driver."

"It's a good thing the radar traps weren't out yet on Route 30," laughed Chris. "I was flying low along some of those straightaways south of Indian Lake."

"Let's start off by doubling back to the furnace and having a look around," said Sean. "I'd like to see what it looks like from the inside, looking up the stack."

"That's not a very good idea," said Chris, pausing to reflect on the condition of the structure. "When I was here last week, en route to my meeting in Plattsburgh, I had a peek into the interior of the smelting chamber, and I didn't like the looks of it. There were loose refractory bricks hanging out all over the place. I wasn't comfortable without a hardhat. I think that anyone who goes into the middle without proper safety attire is a bit foolish."

"OK, then, I'll yield to your better judgment," said Sean. "We can just walk around the exterior and do the usual visitor's tour of the site."

"There's actually a lot more to see down by the river," said Sean, as they clambered down the embankment and around the back side of the furnace. "All the machinery for generating the air blast is located down there."

As the two walked around the front of the furnace, Sean stopped once again, gaping in awe at the massive proportions of the structure. He could not comprehend the amount of sheer force that was required to move the stones that formed the side walls. Some of them were the size of a small automobile and must have weighed between ten and twenty tons.

"It really makes you appreciate what the early settlers could do with mechanical advantage and a few simple tools, doesn't it?" asked Chris, amused at his friend's reaction.

"You can say that again. Look at all those pieces of metal interspersed throughout the rock," observed Sean. "Were those used in the smelting and refining process, or are those structurally needed for the furnace itself?"

"Those are entirely structural," replied Chris. "The pieces you see on the outside, which are either square on rectangular, are called anchor plates. They serve to hold the ends of the long metal tie rods that extend from one outer wall of the furnace to the other."

"I saw those in use when I took a tour of the colonial houses around Fredericksburg," exclaimed Sean. "The Colonists used the tie rods to anchor the brick walls of their homes together."

"It's the same principle," agreed Chris. "Only this is magnified on a much greater scale due to the mass of the stones and the fact that they would be expanding and contracting with the heat of the fires inside the furnace."

"Wow, look at the size of those gear wheels," said Sean, looking back down towards the river. The massive rust-encased waterwheels lay piled in a heap, jumbled and warped with time and use.

"Those were used to harness the direct force of the river's current, providing the energy to operate several sets of massive bellows," lectured Chris. "The forced air is what stoked the charcoal-fueled flames to such high temperatures, creating the optimal heat for the refining process."

"Good grief," said Sean, surveying the land between the river and the furnace. "Could you imagine what would happen if we ever wanted to use the metal detector up here?" As he spoke, he motioned to the general area around the furnace, including the land extending down toward the massive waterwheels. It was strewn with countless bits and pieces of rusted metal, most of which had been part of the furnace operations at one time.

"I thought the detector could discriminate between precious metals and the rest of the iron-steel junk?" asked Chris.

"It can," said Sean. "But it's tough when *everything* on the ground is metallic, which is what you see here. And I'd be willing to bet there's a lot more buried right below the surface. Getting any kind of a signal through that kind of armored plating would be a challenge."

"That's OK," said Chris. "I still think that Alexander Graham Bell would be proud of how far his invention has come," referencing Sean's metal detector.

"Alexander Graham Bell... I thought he just invented the telephone," exclaimed Sean.

"Nope, he was a lot more versatile that that," replied Chris as he motioned for Sean to follow him back to the road. "Bell first came up with the concept in a frenzied race against time to save the life of President Garfield, when he'd been shot in 1881. The detector, which Bell called the 'electromagnetic induction balance,' was designed to find the bullet slug inside Garfield's body."

"You ought to go on one of those television game shows," laughed Sean.

"Ha!" roared Chris. "That would be interesting! Maybe I could cash in on my large store of useless knowledge."

As the two strolled back up the road, Chris removed a few folded pages from his back pocket and began studying the landscape. He was comparing the derelict houses, many of which had collapsed on their foundations, with an old map that he'd copied at the Adirondack Museum. By looking at the locations of the few recognizable structures and establishing their placement along the road, he was able to figure out the approximate sites of several other demolished buildings that had been scattered about the woods. One by one, they visited a number of these wrecks, some of which were little more than piles of decayed lumber.

"What is it you're looking for?" asked Sean. "It seems that most of these smaller dwellings down by the river are carbon copies of the others. Are you interested in something specific?"

"Yes, I am," replied Chris, sounding pre-occupied with the task. "I'm trying to find the spot where McIntyre's house would have been, even though there's no chance that anything but a foundation remains today."

"Not unless the Tahawus Club preserved that building as a lodge for its club members," added Sean. "They did rebuild quite a few of the original houses into cabins for use during the busy months."

"Yes, that is possible," said Chris. "Also, I'm interested in finding the location of the guest house where Patterson stayed when he visited here in the 1850s."

"Do you honestly believe there is any chance of finding it?" asked Sean, looking at the map over Chris' shoulder.

"Maybe, although it might take a stroke of luck," admitted Chris. "There is one other thing that I'd like to find, but I can't say that it was ever here in the first place, which would tend to complicate the search process."

"Yes, just a little bit," chuckled Sean. "Would you mind telling me what that is? Maybe I'll pick up on something around here that you'll miss."

"OK," said Chris. "I'm looking for a cave, or a mine shaft, that might be located underneath one of these buildings. Have you seen any of those in the past hour?"

"A cave or a mine shaft underneath a non-existent building that probably collapsed fifty years ago? Sure! And I've seen a pink elephant, and a band of monkeys playing harmonicas, and…"

"STOP!" shouted Chris, trying to look stern. "You asked me, so I told you. In case you're wondering, I read that bit about the cave in a letter up in Blue Mountain Lake. I thought it might be linked to Henderson's original search for silver in the area, so I figured it might have really existed. However, when I asked Kristi about the possibility of silver ore being present in the ground here, she said it was highly improbable."

"OK, buddy, just checking your sanity," said Sean.

After completing their tour of the Upper Works site, the duo decided to eat their sandwiches and then hit the trail for Calamity Pond. After reading about Patterson's interest in the monument for David Henderson and the ceremony in which it was dedicated, Chris wanted to view the memorial for himself.

"Are you up for a short nine mile stroll in the woods?" Chris asked his companion. "It's fairly level, and we should catch some great views of the peaks as we go."

"It sounds OK, but from what I've heard we can expect some pretty muddy trails on the way in there," warned Sean.

"Not to worry, my friend," chided Chris. "It's been a fairly dry month, so a lot of the standing water should be gone. Anyway, do you really expect to keep your feet dry walking through the wilderness?"

Sean laughed, because he had heard Chris use that line several times in the past. He was often critical of hikers who wanted to remain squeaky clean while enjoying their "wilderness experience."

As Sean pulled on his hiking boots, Chris removed a large red cooler from behind the rear seats. The cooler had been filled with ice, which they used to keep the sandwiches and sodas cold. "It's not as convenient as Maggie's snackmobile, but it'll do in a pinch," quipped Chris. As he spoke, he passed Sean his chicken salad sandwich and beverage.

"How long do you think it'll take us to get in and out?" asked Sean as he unwrapped the parcel.

"Maybe about four hours, perhaps a little longer if it's really wet," said Chris. "It's a bit under four and a half miles each way, with a total elevation gain of about nine hundred feet. But most of it is relatively level, except for a few moderate climbs in the second half of the hike in. By my estimate, we should be able to make at least two miles per hour on the way in, and a bit faster coming out. If we hit the trail by one o'clock, we should be out before six, even if we stop and take photos."

"I've got my camera with me," said Sean. "I already took a couple shots of the blast furnace, and I'll get a few more of the Henderson memorial when we reach Calamity Pond."

"Don't forget to shoot the monument from all four sides, if we can get around the back, and then maybe get one or two of the base it's set on," said Chris.

"Any reasons why Patterson was so interested in the monument?" asked Sean. "You don't think that maybe he helped build something into the stone, do you?"

"I doubt it, but then again, we really don't know much of anything about it," said Chris. "Even the best photos in the guide books only show the inscription on the front. I just want to be sure that we cover all our bases and photograph the entire memorial so that we don't have to make a return trip."

"Yes, sir, I'm on it," said Sean, throwing a fake salute in Chris' direction.

After finishing their lunch, Sean and Chris finished loading a few provisions into their backpacks. Then, as the hour hand touched the "1" on Chris' old analog watch, they signed the register and headed off down the trail toward Calamity Pond.

True to Chris' word, the first mile was almost completely flat, with a slight, gentle uphill trend as they followed the path of Calamity Brook over its tumbling path. The ground had dried sufficiently for the pair to avoid the major sink holes that are the source of so many complaints in the spring and early summer months, and they were able to make good time as they marched along. As the trail tilted uphill at a steeper grade in miles two and three, Sean complained that Chris' longer stride helped to propel him along at greater speeds. However, all the jibes were good natured, and the miles flew past as they traded thoughts about the upcoming week.

Taking only one rest break of less than ten minutes, they reached the clearing next to Calamity Pond, where the monument to David Henderson appeared as if out of nowhere. In the middle of such a vast expanse of wilderness, the ornately-carved stone stood alone, silent and starkly out of place. Placed on the north shore of the small body of water, the memorial was a somber reminder that carelessness in the woods can wreak merciless consequences.

"This is a horrible place to die," said Chris, pensively looking around the forlorn clearing.

"Excuse me?" said Sean, looking back at Chris as he screwed the top off his canteen.

"This is a horrible place to die," repeated Chris. "Those were the words uttered by David Henderson just before he passed away that afternoon in September of 1845."

Chris gazed upon the words carved into the front of the stone and read out loud: "This monument, erected by filial affection to the memory of our dear father, David Henderson, who accidentally lost his life on this spot 3rd September, 1845."

After a few moments of silence, Sean spoke again. "I wonder if this place looked any different back then than it does today."

"Tough to say," said Chris. "Henderson himself tried changing the landscape back here by combining the flows of the Opalescent and Hudson Rivers, you know. Maybe he tried his hand at altering the rest of the landscape as well."

"Yeah, I guess it would be impossible to judge that today, over one hundred fifty years later," agreed Sean.

"He was a very popular fellow, you know," said Chris, recalling his readings about the gentleman who served as one of the original partners in the venture. "He was also quite accomplished in music and the arts. According to the stories written about Henderson, he used to play the violin for his workers many nights after dinner. He was a beloved man, which is why the entire village joined in his family's grief following his death."

"I wonder why Patterson was so interested in the memorial?" asked Sean.

"I do not know," said Chris, still gazing speculatively at the obelisk. "But let's go ahead and get those photos now, if you don't mind, and then start thinking about hitting the trail again. We've got a long day ahead of us."

As Sean retrieved his camera, Chris navigated a circle around the monument, making careful observations about the stone from a distance of less than a foot. He diligently examined each of the four sides, tracing the corner edges from top to bottom looking for a seam. He then studied the area around the inscription, noting that the entire monument appeared to be one solid piece, with the carvings engraved into the core of the stone itself. After ten minutes of viewing the memorial in excruciating detail, he finally felt satisfied that there was nothing else to find. Sean, meanwhile, had photographed the entire piece from top to bottom, and from all four sides. At this point, there was very little else for the two to see. For the second time in three hours, Chris and Sean saddled up their packs and hit the trail, this time heading downhill.

"This is pretty amazing," observed Sean, taking his first steps on the return trip. "We've been in the woods for over three hours now and we haven't seen a soul."

"We had people right next to us," replied Chris, staring back at him in surprise. "Didn't you hear the group up at the lean-to?"

"Lean-to?" repeated Sean. "Where did you see a lean-to?"

"The Calamity Brook lean-to was about a quarter of a mile up the stream from us. I could hear voices of two men talking when we first arrived. I thought you must have heard it."

Sean gave Chris an incredulous stare, but made no reply.

"Hey, I can't help it if you set the volume on your headset too loud," joked Chris. "See that? You're not even thirty years old and you're going deaf already."

"Watch out or I'll tell Kristi that you asked me for Tracey's phone number," countered Sean.

"That won't work, pal," snickered Chris. "You're the one getting the emails saying how much she loved meeting you."

"Don't remind me," groaned Sean.

With Sean in the lead, the pair made a gravity-assisted descent to the parking lot in less than two hours, arriving by five thirty. Since they had made better time than expected, they decided to forego spending the night in a tent. Instead, they hopped back into the Jeep and headed south towards Sean's house in Little Falls. Their revised plan called for spending the night there, then getting an early start on Sunday morning for Philadelphia and points south.

"Riggins Inn and Suites is open for business, vacancies available for immediate occupancy," declared Sean proudly.

"The price is definitely right," agreed Chris. "But I'm not sure that all of me will fit on that lumpy couch of yours."

"Heck, that didn't stop you from passing out during the Super Bowl last February," laughed Sean. "You slept through the entire second half and the post game show. Kristi almost had to pour a pitcher of water over your head to get you up for dinner."

"That's only because my team was losing," said Chris, inventing a transparent excuse.

The traffic on the return trip to Little Falls was almost non-existent, and Chris was able to have them back at Sean's course-side home by eight o'clock that evening. Sean immediately went for the phone to order a pizza, while Chris sat down at the desk in front of Sean's computer. A stack of papers was loosely arranged on the corner of the desk, and Chris scrutinized the top page closely. It was a copy of the cipher that Sean had brought back from the Frank Stewart room, reduced in size to fit on the standard-sized paper. The page was filled with rows of evenly-spaced letters, apparently random in distribution. The rows were numbered sequentially in a column of digits that ran down the left-side of the matrix.

"Have you taken a shot at deciphering this code yet?" Chris called into the kitchen.

"I've looked at it," replied Sean as he completed their pizza order. "Even with the explanation, though, it isn't an easy task."

"Explanation?" said Chris. "Where did you find that?"

"It's online; anyone can access it," replied Sean. "The guy who cracked that code first is down near Princeton, New Jersey. I think he accomplished that back in 2007, although he used some pretty heavy-duty computer programs to help. If you want to read about it, I printed the whole story. It's sitting on the back of the desk in my in-basket."

Chris shifted his gaze to the series of black wire-meshed trays behind the computer. In the middle tray was a reprint of an article, titled: "Mathematician Solves 220 Year-Old Code." The page had a sticky-note attached to the front, which was annotated with some of Sean's handwriting. Chris took the article, along with the copy of the cipher itself, over to an easy chair and plopped himself in a semi reclined position.

After studying the article for a few minutes, he looked up at Sean in amazement. "This thing is ingenious," he remarked. "It's so elementary, and yet it is almost unbreakable unless you know the key numbers and the technique."

"Thomas Jefferson himself wasn't able to crack it," said Sean, nodding in agreement. And I'll tell you, I looked at this one with the assistance of the information in the magazine article, and I still couldn't make heads or tails out of it."

"And what makes it so frustrating is that you found this page right next to the missing treasury ledger from 1804. It was almost as though Patterson himself wanted to say something about that sheet in the record, but was afraid to do so in plain English."

"I know, and I agree," said Sean, looking down at the encoded document.

"What is this name and number on the sticky note?" asked Chris, pulling it off the page.

"That's the name of the guy who successfully deciphered the code eight years ago," said Sean. "I was able to find a phone number online, although I haven't tried it to see if he's the right person."

"Dr. Michael Tomlinson," read Chris. He looked down at the phone number, noting the 609 area code. "It's not even eight thirty yet. Do you think Dr. Tomlinson would mind if we gave him a call?"

"It can't do any harm, unless he's an early-to-bed type," said Sean. "Go ahead, you've got my vote."

Chris pulled out his cell phone and entered the New Jersey number. A voice on the other end answered on the third ring.

"Hello, I'm trying to find Dr. Tomlinson, the cipher specialist I read about in the *American Scientist* article."

"That would be me," replied the man on the other end of the line. "To whom am I speaking, please?"

"My name is Chris Carey, and I'm involved in a rather fascinating study involving Robert M. Patterson and one of his codes. From what I see, you were the genius behind the deciphering effort that first broke his code."

"Thank you, Mr. Carey, but you are too kind with your credits," laughed the doctor. "I conceived of the idea and helped piece together the final blocks. But the computers and my many assistants performed most of the groundwork."

Chris was too observant to be fooled by the scientist's modesty. He had recognized this as a common trait in people with uncommon skills; they were often too embarrassed by their own superior intellect to claim their due credit.

"Regardless, Dr. Tomlinson, my hat is off to you. I'm sitting here with a newly discovered matrix of Patterson's code, and even with the aid of your excellent written explanation, I still can't make heads or tails out of it."

"You have a new cipher from Robert Patterson?" gasped Dr. Tomlinson, sounding extremely surprised. "Where did you find it, and who owns the document?"

Chris paused for a moment, unsure of how much to divulge. Then he decided that he'd have to trust the scientist's discretion anyway, if he was going to have a hand in translating the document. He decided to share part of the truth with the code breaker.

"We found it in the library at Rowan University, where a man named Frank Stewart donated his entire private collection of historical documents. We're using it in our research into the early days of the United States Mint in Philadelphia," explained Chris, omitting any mention of the hunt for the silver dollars.

"Sounds fascinating," said Dr. Tomlinson. "I'm only surprised because there aren't very many of Patterson's codes in existence. Personally, I love seeing them to try to break them myself. It's become sort of a pastime for me, almost like Sudoku, or a crossword puzzle. Would you mind if I had a look at it?"

"Of course not. To tell you the truth, that was my main reason for calling you tonight, to find out if you'd be willing to take a look and see if you could come up with a quick translation of the document," admitted Chris.

"I'd be happy to," said the doctor. "Since the time we first broke this code, we've developed high-speed software tailored for this very purpose. Once the characters of the matrix are entered into the application, it can usually develop the key to the code as well as the deciphered text in less than an hour."

"Amazing," said Chris, shaking his head.

After asking for Dr. Tomlinson's email address, he promised to scan the document and send it to him that evening. The mathematician answered by promising to have someone take a look at it the next day, if possible, and email to Chris the translated text.

"You don't know how much this means to us," said Chris as he concluded the call. "You've done us a greater favor than we could possibly repay."

"Please, think nothing of it," said Dr. Tomlinson. "I honestly enjoy these little riddles of Patterson's. They're one of the few bits of enjoyment I get in my ho-hum workday."

"Well, thanks anyway. I'll get that email off to you post haste," promised Chris.

"Very well, I'll look for it tonight. Good evening, Mr. Carey."

Chris stared wide-eyed at Sean, a gleeful grin creasing his face. "Well that certainly was easy!" he crowed. "By the time we log into our email tomorrow night, we just might have an answer."

CHAPTER 13

Sunday, August 24, 2015

With little to do on Sunday, Chris and Sean felt no need to be on the road by an early hour. Instead, they relaxed for a few hours, enjoying the omelets that Maggie made while stopping by on her break. Chris courteously stepped outside to observe the weather while Sean spent a few private moments alone with his girlfriend.

Once she departed, the two friends removed the pitching wedge from Sean's golf bag and headed out the back door. Since Sean's house was on the eleventh fairway of the community golf course, they often challenged each other to friendly chipping contests when no one was playing that hole. Although Chris was a decent golfer, he was no match for Sean, who carried an eight handicap, and often shot rounds in the high seventies. Today was no exception, as Sean managed to win eight of ten balls before the next foursome appeared at the tee.

By the time they reloaded the Jeep and hit the road, it was after noon. Sean once again brought the GPS system from his own car and entered the street address of the hotel they planned to stay at on the north side of Philadelphia. As they drove south, cruising along the county roads that would take them to Interstate 88 east of Binghamton, Chris reflected on their good fortune to date.

"You know, if you think about it, we could actually do quite well in this business," he said enthusiastically.

"What do you mean?" asked Sean, looking at him across the front seat.

"Well, just think about it," continued Chris. "We've already found one silver dollar that, by all accounts, should bring in at least five million dollars at auction, and possibly a lot more. So, if we decide to pay ourselves $100,000 a year, we could make that money last at least thirty years, even more with interest."

"I think you're forgetting the fact that the silver dollar doesn't belong to us," reminded Sean, laughing at his friend's backward logic.

"Petty details," scoffed Chris, laughing. "Besides, by the time we're done, we'll have discovered the entire cache of lost 1804 dollars, and we'll each be billionaires and live in huge mansions with full staffs of paid servants."

"Is that what you want?" asked Sean, looking at his friend questioningly.

"I'd rather live in a cave," replied Chris.

After checking in at the hotel and eating supper in the restaurant off the lobby, Chris and Sean had a few drinks in the lounge, taking in part of a ball game and chatting with the other patrons. They called it an early night in order to be up by seven o'clock the following morning. Their plan was to drive to the American Philosophical Society building, which is directly across the narrow road from Independence Hall. Chris was hoping to conduct research inside the APS library for most of the day, while Sean backtracked to Rowan University to follow up on some of the materials he had missed on the first go-round. However, since Sean had never seen the Liberty Bell, he decided to make the trip over to Independence Hall and do the "tourist thing" before heading out of town and over the bridge into New Jersey. They planned a rendezvous later on, back at the hotel, in time for dinner.

Monday morning, they left the hotel by eight fifteen, planning a nine o'clock arrival at the APS building. It took them longer than expected to crawl toward Independence Hall on Chestnut Street, where they were informed by a uniformed park ranger that the closest parking would probably be a parking garage on Third Street, near the Merchant Exchange Building.

Chris slowly navigated his Jeep between the stanchions of the parking garage and up the steep ramp of the multi-story building, taking advantage of his vehicle's tight turning radius to maneuver around the rows of parked cars. He had already ascended to the third floor and was about to hit the ramp for the fourth when Sean's hand grabbed his right arm.

"Hold it!" barked Sean, his face suddenly a mask of intense concentration.

"What's up?" replied Chris. "Did you see an open spot that I missed?"

"Back up a few spots," said Sean, half whispering his request.

Chris was about to make light of his demand, but when he looked at Sean again and saw a seriousness in his expression that he seldom witnessed in their twenty years of friendship, he decided against doing so. Without another word, Chris threw the SUV into reverse and backed down the ramp.

"There!" said Sean, pointing to a car that was angled into a narrow spot in the middle of a row. It was a red Mini Cooper with a white roof and New York license plates. "I think that's Grainger's car."

The vehicle was empty, and no one was in sight along the lengthy sloped incline of the parking ramp.

"Quick, hand me that folder of papers in the back seat," said Chris, motioning to the rear of the Jeep.

Sean turned around and leaned over the middle console, thrusting his entire torso into the gap between the seats. When he returned to his former position, he had both the folder with Chris' copies as well as a small black satchel. He handed the papers to Chris, and then quickly unzipped the bag, rummaging through the contents.

Chris, meanwhile, was rifling through the papers at top speed, searching for the investigative documents his father's firm had provided. His efforts were quickly rewarded, and he scanned the front page until he found his mark.

"Red Mini Cooper with New York plates, license ENP 3982," he read. He glanced at the car in the space ahead of them, immediately noting the match. "You have good eyes, my man."

Unfortunately, Sean was too busy to hear much of anything outside of the matching license plates, as he was still fumbling, trying to perform two acts of manual dexterity simultaneously. In one hand, he had the GPS tracking device that Maggie had given him, which he was trying to activate, while with the other hand he was attempting to don the headset for his cell phone. It would have appeared comical if not for the urgency of the activity.

"He's here," hissed Sean, his eyes on fire. "I'm getting out."

"You're WHAT?" replied Chris, his volume increasing by twenty decibels.

"Listen; here's the plan," said Sean. "I'm getting out here, and I'm going to attach the GPS tracker to the bottom of Grainger's car. Meanwhile, I want you to go to the top of this ramp and keep a lookout for Grainger. He doesn't know what you look like, so he shouldn't be suspicious. Do you have your phone fully charged?"

"Yes," answered Chris, looking down at his screen.

"Do you have reception in here? The concrete is pretty thick."

"Five bars," replied Chris, confirming that his signal was loud and clear.

"OK, I want you to dial my phone NOW. I'm going to put on my headset, and I want you to touch base with me every sixty seconds for as long as it takes me to get this thing installed, and then get out of there, OK?"

"I've got it," said Chris, who had already called up Sean's number. "Are you sure you want to do this?"

"All right, let's go," called Sean, completely ignoring Chris' question. He dived out the passenger side door in a crouched position and slithered between the Mini Cooper and the huge Chevy Suburban that was parked next to it. "Don't forget, go to the top of the ramp," said Sean as he pushed shut the Jeep door.

Once Sean disappeared from view, Chris immediately pulled the Jeep to the top of the ramp and backed into a no-parking zone.

"OK, Sean, how do I sound?" asked Chris, testing the phone from his new position.

"Loud and clear. Now just stay with me," came back Sean's voice.

Inside the library, Kimberly Kline was organizing the visitor slips behind the registration desk when the man pulled open the door from Library Street, which ran along the south side of the building. The door was quite close to the desk, so the receptionist had very little time to study his face before he stepped up to her station.

"Good morning," she greeted the stranger. "Welcome to the American Philosophical Society headquarters. How may I help you?" she asked in a friendly voice.

The stranger stared at her from beneath a brow of bright red hair, doing his best to force a smile.

"Good morning. I have an appointment to use your library today. I called ahead last Friday and spoke with Ken Gardner," he said. "My name is Leon Garvin."

"Welcome, Mr. Garvin. We're glad you're here," said Kimberly. "I'm going to give you a few forms to sign, and I'll need your identification, which can be a driver's license or other government photo ID."

The redhead took out his license and handed it across the counter to the APS receptionist, who in turn handed him a small stack of forms to sign. "Please read them and initial wherever you see a short space, then sign the bottom of each form above your printed name," she recited by rote.

The visitor took the forms over to a corner desk, where a chair afforded him the opportunity to sit in comfort while filling out the requisite paperwork. Meanwhile, Kimberly took his driver's license and began filling out the computerized form for his visitor's badge. As she glanced at the name on the ID, she suddenly noticed the photograph, which was in close proximity to the "wanted" poster created by Sean the previous week. The head archivist had printed it and taped it to both the register book and the computer monitor.

Kimberly's heart skipped a beat as she compared the photo on the ID to the image on the poster. They were identical. Next, she looked at the name on the license—Leon Garvin, from Binghamton, New York. It matched the alias on the poster, which was all she needed to see.

"Please finish filling out those forms, and I'll be right back," she said, still smiling sweetly at the man she now knew was not Leon Garvin. Then she pushed open the door into the staff area and disappeared.

Matthew "Matt" Brownell had been at the APS headquarters building longer than any of his employees. He was a no-nonsense administrator with a reputation for running a tight ship. He didn't care whom he offended, whether employee or "customer," if they were pushing the limit on the rules. "Fair but firm" was his maxim, and he lived it on a daily basis. He would also back his employees to the hilt, as long as they were upholding the regulations and mission of the facility. However, heaven help them if they were neglecting part of their official duties.

"Mr. Brownell, I could use your assistance," said Kimberly, a concerned look on her face.

"Yes, Miss Kline, how may I help you?" Brownell always spoke to his employees using their last names. His very manner of speech exuded the formal politeness with which he had been raised.

"Sir, there's a man here who wants to use our library," said Kimberly, still registering a worried expression. "He says he spoke with Ken to set up the appointment. But we have a warning about him from the librarian down at Rowan University, who says that he stole some historic documents from their library. He's evidently not a model citizen. Also, he's using a fake ID. His real name is Ben Grainger, although he has a state-issued ID listing the name Leon Garvin."

Matt looked at Kimberly for a few moments with a grim look on his face, plotting his course of action. Finally, his expression eased, giving way to a gentle smile which he flashed at the younger employee, if nothing more than to put her mind at ease.

"I'll handle this, Miss Kline," he said, rising from his seat. "Thank you for your vigilance and dedication to your post. Because of you, this scoundrel will not penetrate our facility. Well done."

Kimberly blushed as she accepted the compliment, and then retreated through the door to her desk. In a moment, she was followed by the imposing figure of Matthew Brownell.

Brownell marched straight to the receptionist desk, where he came face-to-face with the redheaded visitor.

"I'm sorry to inform you, Mr. Garvin, that your request for admission to our facility has been declined," he said without preamble.

"Declined?" repeated Grainger, clearly confused.

"Yes, that is what I said; declined," repeated the chief administrator.

"But I don't understand," said Grainger. "I am a law-abiding, tax-paying citizen of this country, and I followed all of your rules to arrange this session. Why am I being denied the use of a simple library facility for no apparent reason?"

Whatever trace of a smile that was left on Matthew Brownell's face disappeared as he leaned over the counter toward his quarry.

"Please allow me to explain," he said, enunciating every syllable to the max. "Your presence here is considered a hostile intrusion. You have been identified as a threat, *Mr. Grainger*, or whatever your real name might be." As he spoke, he emphasized Grainger's last name, drawing it out with increased volume and clarity. "We do not wish to allow you inside our facility. And so, I will offer you a choice," he continued, holding the driver's license over the counter. "You can either leave here, with your fake ID, on your own accord, or we will call the authorities immediately. Because of their close proximity to our facility, I can guarantee that they will be here within two minutes of my call. The choice is yours, Mr. Grainger. You have sixty seconds, starting now."

Grainger looked impassively across the desk for about ten seconds, then snatched the ID card from Brownell's hand in a rapid, impatient motion and exited the hallway for the side entrance.

"Thanks," said Kimberly, smiling up at her boss. "I couldn't have handled him the way you just did."

"Not a problem, Miss Kline," said Matthew. "You performed admirably. Congratulations on a job well done." He then turned on his heel and returned to his office.

Back in the garage, Sean was struggling beneath the underside of the Mini Cooper. The directions showed at least six or eight methods for affixing the GPS tracker to the undercarriage of a vehicle, and yet Sean was achieving little or no success. Try as he might, the magnetic attachment points would not remain permanently attached to the metal of the frame, and none of the screw mounts worked either. As he continued to labor, he heard a voice come through his headset.

"Sean, can you hear me?" came Chris' voice, sounding worried.

"Yeah, I gotcha," Sean replied, turning a screwdriver against an errant screw. "Whatcha see, buddy?"

"I'm looking out the side entrance of the building, facing 4th Street, and I'm afraid I've got some bad news for you. I think your buddy Grainger is coming back to the garage."

"Are you sure?" said Sean, looking at his watch. "It's barely quarter after nine. What would he be doing back here already?"

"I don't know," said Sean. "But if my powers of observation are any indication, he's your man, and he's heading your way. I'd estimate you've got about three to four minutes before he's right on top of you."

"Thanks," said Sean, sounding more frantic than before. "I've got to find a way to get this thing attached to his car, no matter what. Keep me apprised of his location. I might end up stuck under here until he starts the engine."

"You got it, buddy. But please, be safe," pleaded Chris. "I don't want to have to tell Maggie that you were flattened by anything as wimpy as a Mini Cooper."

"Ha ha, Chris," joked Sean, sounding nervous through the humor. "Thanks for the confidence builder. Now just stay with me until this guy is out of here, hopefully with Maggie's GPS tracker attached to the bottom of his car. Talk to you later."

Chris didn't bother answering. He was too busy watching Grainger's advance as he proceeded up the sidewalk until reaching the stairwell. He had desperately hoped that Grainger would bypass the stairs and take the long route, down to the elevator on the other side of the building. However, he was evidently not of that mindset, deciding instead to take the stairs two at a time.

"Sean, listen to me," pleaded Chris, hissing into his transmitter piece. "Grainger is less than two minutes away. Finish what you're doing and GET OUT OF THERE." He received no response.

Chris began to panic, looking around for something that could double as a weapon. The only thing he found resembling that description was a fire extinguisher. He felt helpless in the event of a physical confrontation.

"Sean, he's coming up the stairwell. I can hear him. If you can still get out of there, GO NOW!!!"

Nothing. The silence was as deafening as the loudest roar that Chris had ever heard.

As Chris watched, horrified at the lack of movement, Grainger emerged from the confines of the stairwell and strolled, unconcerned, towards his car in the garage. Knowing that Grainger would not recognize him, Chris decided to walk towards the Mini Cooper, perhaps pretending to own one of the cars parked beyond the red compact. He figured that, should a brawl break out, he could be of assistance in subduing the suspect. However, as he approached the small vehicle, he observed only the solitary figure of the owner, who was piling into the driver's seat. Within a matter of seconds, he turned the ignition key and began backing out of his space.

Chris paused casually near Grainger's car, as though he was waiting for the occupant to vacate his space before moving on. However, in the side window of the vehicle, he saw the face of the red-haired man, who simply waved him across. "Go on," he mouthed silently, allowing Chris to walk through before continuing on his way.

"Thank you," signaled Chris, accepting the pass as he continued down the row of cars.

Within twenty seconds, the Mini Cooper had completed its exit maneuver and departed the garage. Chris looked around, confounded as to the plight of his friend, who was nowhere to be seen. He stood there, perplexed, until he heard a muffled voice emerge from beneath the Chevy Suburban that was adjacent to the now-vacant parking spot.

"Where the heck have you been?" came Sean's annoyed remark. "I thought I was going to have to walk back to New York by myself!"

Chris literally leaped off the ground as Sean wriggled out from underneath the massive SUV.

"My God, I thought you'd been run over," said Chris, pounding his friend on the back.

"No such luck, pal," he said. "But I must admit, that tracking device needs a better attachment system. It took me right up to the last second to get it hooked onto the frame. And even then, I had to use some brute force instead of the last couple screws. I just hope it stays in place, because I had to force it underneath the shock absorber mounts to get it to stay," he said.

"Sounds like it should be OK," said Chris, happy to see his friend escape unscathed. "Even if it isn't, so what? We'll still be fine as long as we can stay one step ahead of the competition."

"Yeah, well, I think I got him," said Sean. "We'll know as soon as I activate the software on my laptop. Heck, we should be able to follow him anywhere he goes with the simple touch of a button. Ain't technology wonderful?"

"It sure is," said Chris, as he brushed the dirt and dust off of Sean's back. "That's why I hang around with a techno geek like you. Things like this can come in handy at times."

"Thanks, I think," said Sean.

The two friends exited the garage and then walked down Chestnut until they arrived at Independence Hall.

"OK, I guess this is where we split," said Chris, tossing Sean the keys to the Jeep.

"Yupper," agreed Sean, snatching the key ring in midair and stuffing it into a front pocket. "You sure you don't want me to pick you up later this afternoon? I can be back here before the building closes."

"No thanks, no need," said Chris. "The bus takes off from just over the other side of the square there," he said, nodding to the stop about three hundred yards away. "It should drop me off right in front of the hotel, so why bother? It would cost you at least an extra half hour to battle the traffic getting back here at rush hour."

"OK, it's your call. But I think you just don't appreciate my company anymore," argued Sean.

"Get out of here," said Chris, punching his friend on the arm. "Enjoy your sightseeing tour, and don't run into anything with the Jeep. Dad would have you drawn and quartered." The vehicle had been a present when Chris had finished his MBA a year earlier.

"I'll be careful. Catch you later," said Sean. Then, he turned away from Chris and continued across 5th Street, towards the Liberty Bell Center, whereupon he was instantly lost in the crowd.

Chris watched his friend for a moment, and then turned left to face the red brick edifice of the American Philosophical Society. The headquarters of the organization founded by Benjamin Franklin had, in fact, been built in the twentieth century, but had been cleverly engineered with materials that matched the brick and stone of colonial times. Chris walked past the front entrance of the building, which was not in use, and turned left onto Library Street. He opened the tall side door and approached the same registration booth where Grainger had stood only twenty minutes earlier.

Kimberly Kline was multitasking behind her computer, answering phone calls at the same time as she sent out replies to email inquiries. Chris waited patiently for her to finish a phone call before saying hello.

"Welcome to the American Philosophical Society headquarters. How may I help you?" she repeated her standard greeting.

"Hello, my name is Christopher Carey, Jr., and I have an appointment to conduct research here today."

"Welcome, Mr. Carey," said Kimberly, as she spotted his name on the daily access list. "I have some forms here for you to sign, and I'll need an official photo ID, such as a driver's license or passport."

Chris already had his license in his hand and was passing it to her as she finished her request.

"Unlike your previous visitor, this one is *not* a fake," he said, winking at the receptionist.

Chris' statement caught Kimberly completely off guard, causing her to fumble with her words. "I…but how…I…did you know…?" she stuttered.

"It's OK," said Chris, smiling in a disarming manner. "Yes, I do know who Benjamin Grainger is, and yes, I did assume that he was coming from your building when I saw him on the street a few minutes ago."

Kimberly's face clouded with doubt as she tried to judge whether the new visitor standing before her was friend or foe. Chris correctly read her indecisive expression and decided to show all his cards up front.

"Please don't be worried, Kimberly," he said, reading the name on her badge. "Not only am I one of the 'good guys,' but I'm also the one who had Penney McPherson from Rowan University send you that warning."

Kimberly looked down at Grainger's photo on the page, which was completely concealed from Chris' view. A light appeared to go on inside her head, and the edges of her mouth turned upward in a smile.

"That was you?" she asked.

"Uh huh. Not only did we ensure that you were forewarned, but my friend Sean actually put that poster together last week for that very purpose," said Chris.

"Well, you'll have to thank him for us," said Kimberly, finally deciding to trust Chris as an ally. "He probably saved us a lot of trouble, given what we read on that warning."

"I can do that, but you might want to thank him yourself. He'll probably be in here with me sometime this week."

After filling out the standard forms, Chris was assigned a locker, in which he was required to stash all of his personal items, such as his camera and notepads. He was provided with sheets of note paper and pencils by the library staff, but was allowed to carry nothing else into the reading room.

Chris entered the main room through a huge, floor-to-ceiling glass door. Inside, the library itself was classically designed and decorated, with ornate bookcases that extended all the way to the ceiling. Wood-grained catwalks wrapped around the upper reaches of the room, maximizing the amount of shelf space for the extensive collection. Three heavy wooden tables were supported by massive, hand-carved, pillar-style legs, while marble busts of the organization's founders gazed down from above.

As Chris stood in the entranceway to the room, he was approached by one of the establishment's archivists, who introduced himself as Vic. He then asked him about the topic of his research.

"Robert Patterson," replied Chris, simply. "Also, I'm looking for information on his son, Robert M. Patterson. Both of these men were officers in your organization in the early days of the nineteenth century."

Vic nodded enthusiastically as he recalled the names. "Yes, I know about them," he stated. "I believe we have quite a few papers here from both men. Let's go look in the card catalog."

Chris was surprised as Vic led him back out of the reading room and into an ante-chamber with bank after bank of old-fashioned card drawers. Each document was represented by its own file card, which was filled with many lines of highly organized information. Most of the cards appeared to have been typed on old-model typewriters, as the font was uneven and sometimes oddly spaced across the surface.

"I didn't know any libraries still used cards like this," said Chris, hoping that he wasn't offending his host. "Do you also have computer-based listings of your holdings, so that we might be able to fine-tune the search?"

"Of course we do," said Vic, as he eyed the labels on the front of a nearby cabinet of card drawers. "Most of our library is cataloged into our new inventory control system, which can be accessed from any computer inside this building, as well as remotely. However, some of the older letters and other handwritten documents are only listed inside these trays, which is why I always start here. Also, I love seeing the reaction of people such as yourself, who are amazed that this system is still in use *anywhere*. Believe it or not, kids coming through college degree programs in library science don't even learn about card catalogs anymore."

"That doesn't surprise me at all," said Chris, as he watched Vic home in on one particular card drawer and pull it completely out of its case.

"Here you go: Patterson, Robert, as well as Robert M. It looks as though you've got quite a bit of searching to do, Chris. There's at least a half a tray on these two gentlemen. They must have been very prolific writers in their day."

Vic set the tray down on a small table in front of a comfortable padded armchair and gave him instructions on how to develop a list for later viewing.

"We'll need a lot of information from that card, so make sure you write down the name, the catalog system number, the full date, or 'no date at all,' which can also be important," Vic explained. He continued to detail the information needed to locate the actual documents inside the reading room, and Chris quickly realized that it would be better to make a copy of the entire card, as most of the information was important in their search.

After receiving his instructions, Chris was left alone to scan through each of the many hundreds of cards, which was a tedious and time-consuming business. The card tray was over two feet long, and over half of it was filled with cards listing references involving the two Pattersons. He quickly realized that he would need at least one or possibly two days just to identify the documents he wanted to see, even without actually viewing the documents themselves. It would be a long week.

Working diligently and without a break, Chris moved slowly but steadily through the card catalog, making notes as he found references of potential interest. He was amazed at the incredible variety of topics addressed by Robert Patterson, the father, in his correspondence and writings to other scholars around the fledgling country. Had he the time, Chris felt as though he could have spent a month reading some of the more interesting-sounding titles, many of which had nothing to do with his current search topic. However, time was of the essence, and he tried to remain focused to make use of every possible minute.

He had been hard at work for a little over two hours when the sound of the noontime bells pealed from high above Independence Hall across the street. Listening to the historic bells slowly intoning their message of liberty, Chris felt goose bumps rising on his skin as he looked around the library. Surrounded by carved busts of historic founders and the labors of their lives, Chris experienced an overpowering feeling of connection to America's past. He reflected on this emotion for a moment before continuing with his work.

It was shortly after two o'clock when Chris came upon a series of items that made him sit bolt upright in his chair. It was a sequence of cards that identified a number of binders of Patterson's personal diary, organized by year from the late 1820s on. Each book appeared to represent several years of the director's life, and they continued sequentially until shortly before his death in 1854. According to the cards, each volume was several hundred pages long and available only in paper copy. He carefully recorded the information from each card onto his request, and then moved on in his search.

By late that afternoon, Chris had finished reviewing the cards attributed to Robert M. Patterson's papers, although he came across little else of consequence. He had hoped to find more correspondence between Patterson and the founders of the McIntyre Iron Company, but that never happened. He did locate some notes regarding the state geologist and his estimation of the iron ore potential, but most of that was already known to the public.

Rather than try to read significant chunks of Patterson's journal before the library closed, Chris decided to use the remaining hour to start searching the papers of Robert Patterson, the father of Robert M. It was difficult for him to maintain his attention, which had worn thin over the past seven hours of turning cards in the file tray. However, his perseverance was rewarded when he came across a number of letters between Patterson and President Thomas Jefferson, several of which dated from late 1803 and early 1804. This was prime material for Chris, who had prioritized his search goals into a few major categories. The first few months of 1804, and three years following Robert M. Patterson's retirement in 1851, were at the top of his list.

Satisfied with his day's work, Chris assembled his papers and exited the main reading room to retrieve his camera and other belongings from the locker room. He then turned his badge in at the front desk and headed outside, bound for the bus station on the other side of Independence National Historic Park. The bus was already waiting at the stop, and Chris was back at the hotel in less than thirty minutes.

Sean had not yet returned from Rowan University when Chris entered their hotel room. Rather than turn on the television and waste time, Chris decided to take a quick shower, and then head down to the hotel's business center to check his email. Although he was in the shower less than ten minutes, he was surprised to find Sean back in the room when he emerged from the steamy bathroom. Sean had his laptop open, and was simultaneously loading software from a CD-ROM.

"You don't waste time, do you?" said Chris, toweling off the rest of the water from his back.

"I'm just loading the software that came with Maggie's GPS device," said Sean, preoccupied with the screens on his monitor. "If this thing works the way it's advertised, we should be able to accurately determine the location of Grainger's car within about thirty feet."

"That's pretty slick stuff," said Chris. "It's a good thing you didn't let Maggie slip that underneath the seat in your car. She'd be able to tell every time you went down to visit that college student at the University of Pennsylvania."

"Are you done yet?" asked Sean, without looking away from the screen.

"I could be," said Chris, already abandoning the line of attack for some more constructive conversation. "Actually, I had a pretty useful day today. I didn't get into any of the library documents themselves, but I did make it through their entire card catalog files on everything they've got on

Robert Patterson and his son. They must have over a thousand letters, manuscripts, and other articles represented in the files. It took me all day, but I narrowed it down to about a dozen pieces that I want to start reading tomorrow. Some look pretty promising."

"Sounds like a gold mine of everything Patterson," said Sean, still jockeying around with the keyboard. "I had a decent day, too, although I never got to see the new stuff that Penney found after my last visit. I did make it through two more boxes, though. I've only got two left, but they keep getting bigger as I go, and the last two are positively crammed with letters and other documents. I'll tell you the truth; I'm a bit worried about wrapping up down there before Thursday, which means I won't have time to help you in the APS archives, and I also won't have a chance to see what Tracey uncovers from the Patterson collection at the University library."

"Why don't I come down to the Frank Stewart Room with you tomorrow?" suggested Chris. "We could work in tandem, and knock the rest of their collection out of the way in one fell swoop. Then, you won't have to waste any more time commuting back and forth over the river, and we can concentrate on the manuscripts at the American Philosophical Society."

"We could do that," said Sean, who had finally succeeded in launching the GPS tracking application on his computer. "I'd welcome the company." As he spoke, he pumped his fist in the air in a triumphant display.

"Find anything?" asked Chris, peering across the room at the laptop screen.

"Sure did," said Sean. "This thing is neat as all get-out. I can see exactly where Grainger's car is located, right down to the street address. Oh man, when he's in his car driving, I can even get a reading on his direction and speed. Good grief...I love this thing!"

"OK then, where is our elusive Mr. Grainger right now?" asked Chris, pulling a shirt on over his head.

"He's still in the area," said Sean, "although no longer in downtown Philadelphia. There's evidently a small town called West Conshohocken that's about twelve miles northwest of here. It's located off Exit 332 on

Route 76. If you wanted to find Grainger, you'd get off the expressway there, and then follow Front Street to Bullock Avenue, where you'd make a left turn. His car is parked near the corner of Bullock Avenue and Pleasant Street."

"What's he having for dinner?" asked Chris, sarcastically.

"Just wait another few years and the software might tell you that, too," quipped Sean, playing with more of the settings on the locator program. "I tell you, with stuff like this, who needs a private detective? This is straight out of a spy movie."

"Oh, would you do me a favor?" asked Chris, opening his wallet and removing a business card.

"Sure, ask away," replied Sean.

"Would you please go into your email and forward a copy of your now-famous "wanted poster" on Grainger up to the Adirondack Museum? You can send it straight to Debbie Santori's email account, and ask her to pass it around to the staff."

"No problem," sad Sean, copying Debbie's email address off the card. "You obviously think Grainger might eventually follow the leads up into the Adirondacks?"

"I don't know where he'll follow anything," admitted Chris, running a comb quickly through his hair. "I don't know what he knows, or what evidence he has. All I know is that I don't want him to steal anything from anyone else. He's already resorted to that once, so he might try it again."

"Good thought," said Sean, who had already attached a copy of the poster to an email and sent it. "Done," he exclaimed triumphantly.

"You do nice work, my friend," said Chris approvingly.

Unlike the previous evening, Chris and Sean decided to venture back into the city for dinner. Chris parked his Jeep in a lot off of Walnut Street, and they meandered into Alma de Cuba for a taste of Latin cuisine. Because they hadn't bothered to make a reservation, they were informed that there would be about a thirty-minute wait, which they decided to pass in the bar.

"Care for a look at the menu?" asked Sean, handing a menu over the table.

Chris looked at the list of tempting yet pricey entrees and winced. "I see this is going to set me back a bit more than my normal take-out Chinese," he said.

"You're a bean-counter," argued Sean, referring to Chris' accounting background. "Just deduct it as a business expense."

Once they were seated, the two could easily understand how the restaurant had gained its outstanding reputation. The staff was attentive and friendly, and the aromas of the various dishes that passed by from the kitchen just oozed with the seductive scents of fresh seafood, vegetables, and spices, perfectly blended and prepared.

After perusing the menu for another five minutes, the waiter appeared to take their orders. Sean had the rum-cured duck breast with fried rice, black currants, pine nuts and scallions. Chris ordered the Cuban shrimp enchilada with verde clam rice, and a spicy tomato and pepper stew. They asked for a basket of sweet fried plantains to share between them.

"You know, I could see us doing this a little more often," said Sean, holding up a glass of Chardonnay in a toast.

"So could I, if I could afford it," laughed Chris. "But I'm afraid I'd go bankrupt if I hung around with you for very long."

"Nonsense," scoffed Sean. "By the time the Adirondack Museum sells their 1804 dollar and pays you the finder's fee, you'll have all the money you need for the next few years."

"Yeah, fat chance of that happening," said Chris, breaking off a warm piece of freshly-baked whole grain bread from a basket on the table. "We'll probably have our names stuck onto another exhibit in their main hall, but that's about the extent of it."

"It'll be interesting to see if Debbie answers my email," said Sean. "And if she does, do you think she'll ask about their silver dollar? I'm not sure I'd want to lie to her about its authenticity."

"No need to lie about anything," commented Chris. "Let's wait to see what she says, and then go from there."

Sean was about to reply when he felt his cell phone vibrating. He looked at the display, which glowed vividly in the dim light of the restaurant. Recognizing the number, he decided to take the call. It was a brief conversation, and Sean appeared deep in thought throughout the duration. Chris could only hear one half of the dialogue, which lasted about two minutes, and ended with Sean arranging a meeting for the following evening.

"What was that all about?" asked Chris, looking quizzically at his friend.

"That was Tracey, who just spent the entire day at the University's Van Pelt-Dietrich Library, which is the home of their rare books and manuscripts collection. She said that most of their material on the Pattersons appears to be directly related to their stints as professors and administrators, including the father's tenure as vice-provost of the university from 1810–1813. But she didn't find anything in their library that was directly related to the mint, because most of those documents had already been assimilated into the materials that went to the Archives early on, or were later collected by Frank Stewart and then donated to Rowan University."

"You sounded pretty interested in something she had to say," stated Chris. "Why else would you want to set up a meeting with her?"

"She said she found one paper, written by Robert M. Patterson near the end of his life. It was on the topic of slavery and the tension between the northern and southern states. In it, he mentioned meeting a group of Africans whom he believed to be runaway slaves, up in a cave in the North Country," explained Sean. "I was wondering whether we could find out where that took place, or whether there were any clues inside that same document that might put us in the ballpark of the Adirondack Park."

"Might be worth a try," agreed Chris. "But I don't think it'll buy us anything in the search for a potential load of silver dollars. Unless, that is, there's more to this than meets the eye."

"What do you mean?" asked Sean, looking puzzled.

"Oh, I don't know," said Chris, a twinkle showing in his eye. "There must be *some* reason why you want to meet with Tracey tomorrow night."

"That does it," cried Sean, launching a section of bread crust over the table at Chris' face.

"OK, OK, I'm sorry," laughed Chris. "But you gotta admit, it sure looks suspicious from this side of the table."

After enjoying a leisurely meal at the Cuban restaurant, Chris and Sean returned to the hotel, where Sean powered on his laptop and opened the GPS tracker application.

"Looks like he's heading home," said Sean, following Grainger's track. "He's on Route 81, heading north towards Binghamton."

"Good—I hope he stays there," said Chris. "Maybe he'll be out of our hair for a few days."

"At least he's abiding by the law of the highway," observed Sean, reading the data displayed on the screen. "He's doing sixty-eight miles per hour in a sixty-five zone; that's not too bad."

"That's a lot better than me," conceded Chris.

"Oh, wow!" exclaimed Sean, opening his email. "Guess who got back to us while we were out at dinner?"

"Dr. Tomlinson?" guessed Chris.

"What are you, psychic or something? You take all the fun out of everything," cried Sean. "Yes, Dr. Tomlinson. Let's see what he's got for us."

Sean selected the email from the prominent mathematician and scientist. Chris, who was just as eager for good news on the cipher, looked over his shoulder and read the text simultaneously. The email left them slightly impatient and bewildered. Instead of a translation from Patterson's code from the 1700s, it offered an apology, which read:

> Sean,
>
> I am sending you this email to report that, as of this evening, our automated software has yet to decipher the encrypted text you sent me on Saturday. Unfortunately, I have been unable to dedicate my own time to this effort, and have relied upon a couple of associates, both of whom have significant experience with

this code. Additionally, the software for decoding this particular cipher is capable of functioning in autonomous mode, since we perfected it over seven years ago.

The problem appears to be in either the line, or "chunk" intervals, or the number of random numbers sequenced into the beginning of each row. Despite the fact that Robert M. Patterson became predictable at this phase of his life (1850 and later), he appears to have abandoned his normal sequencing patterns for this particular cipher. We tried using all of the standard keys that he used and re-used in the last years of his life, and still came up short.

My schedule appears to be easing in a few weeks, after which I will be able to personally spend some time working this code. However, until that time, all I can do is to send you copies of the attempts we made using Patterson's standard keys. They are copied into the attachment to this email, so please feel free to look for yourself. Please be advised, however, that our program automatically detects single words and sentences, and recognizes every word in the English language, so I don't believe you will discover anything new.

Good luck, and I'll be back in touch by sometime in September or early October.

Regards,

Michael Tomlinson, Ph.D.

"Well, that's something we hadn't expected," said Sean, leaning back in his chair. "I thought his guy was supposed to be the Albert Einstein of cryptology."

"He didn't say he was giving up," said Chris, reminding his friend to remain patient. "He just said that he can't give it his personal time until next month. Let's cut him some slack, OK?"

Chris and Sean were able to avoid much of the rush hour traffic the following morning by waiting until nine o'clock to hit the highway. Sections of Routes 76 and 676 that had been moving at a snail's pace an hour earlier were now tolerable, and they made decent time making it across the bridge into New Jersey and down Route 55.

Sean looked at his watch as they pulled past the guard shack on campus. "A few minutes past ten," he said, nodding his head approvingly. "I'm glad I asked permission to start early this morning. Usually, they don't have anyone in the Frank Stewart Room much before noon."

"Good job," concurred Chris. "Maybe we'll even be able to get out of here at a decent hour today."

The pair walked inside and signed the guest register at the downstairs desk, just as Sean had done the previous day. The only difference was that Sean and Chris were now permitted to take the elevator up to the third floor without an escort.

When the doors opened, Chris and Sean stepped out and were greeted by one of the student volunteers. The last two boxes that Sean had yet to search were already positioned on the table at the far end of the room. For the second time in as many days, Sean signed the visitor's register and received his badge. Chris followed suit, and the two of them were allowed to commence work.

In order to boost their efficiency, Chris and Sean decided to spread out over two tables, with each man taking one box. Penney passed through the room briefly, stopping to introduce herself to Chris. She then assigned a student volunteer to help the two men search for documents, make copies, or assist in any way possible. She also put a second worker on notice, too, in case additional aid was required.

"I'll be in the document preservation and repair room, in case you fellows need anything," Penney said. She then waved and disappeared, leaving the two alone with the massive cartons of materials.

Chris looked with some degree of trepidation at the box sitting in front of him. "There's got to be over ten thousand pages inside this thing," he said, shaking his head in wonder.

"I've got at least as much as you," countered Sean. "Well, there's no point in feeling sorry for ourselves. We might as well dig in."

The two got started at about the same time, and they quickly got into the rhythm of picking up documents, visually scanning them for valuable information, then replacing them in their original order. It was a boring task, repeated hundreds upon hundreds of times, with little or no conversation between them. Shortly before noon, their volunteer assistant was afforded a lunch break by another student, who introduced herself as Alexa. Chris and Sean, however, decided to stick to their task without a stop.

Finally, a little before one o'clock, Penney strolled into the room and addressed the pair. She was carrying a long black folder that was devoid of writing or labeling on the outside. She pulled out an old-looking document and held it up for Sean to see, since it had been the topic of conversation after his first visit almost two weeks earlier.

"This is the document I mentioned to you when I called you about the theft last week," she said. "We found this in the bottom of the box where you first saw that folder of letters that the Patterson family had tried to forward to the National Archives. I can't tell who wrote it, because it isn't signed. But it is dated, see," she said, pointing to a date in the upper left margin, above the rest of the text. The date on the paper read May 11, 1804.

Sean accepted the worn and faded document from the librarian and confirmed the date written along the top margin of the page. Then he carefully placed the page on the table, and read the small cursive words side-by-side with Chris. The document didn't appear to be part of a larger book, nor did it look to be an official record. Yet, the words written on the dark parchment-like paper jumped off the page and struck both men like a kick in the gut. It read:

> May 11, 1804
> This morning we removed 19,570 dollar coins from the
> Mint storeroom, plus seven assay samples from the Mint

assay cabinet, per direction of Mr. Boudinot. All coins were returned to the smelting building and converted into bullion as of this date. The assays on said dollar coins averaged 416 grains, fineness averaged 892.4. Silver reclaimed from dollars is hereby re-allocated to inventory for purposes of striking smaller denomination coins. Specific totals for coins struck of half-dollar, quarter, and dime, will be reported in the figures provided in the annual Treasury Department report at the end of the first quarter of next calendar year.

The initial reaction from both Chris and Sean was grim silence. In their hands they held a document that chronicled the melting of all the 1804 silver dollars that were the purpose of their search. It removed the reason for their entire activity and doused their flames of enthusiasm with a cold, wet dose of reality.

After a brief few moments of solemn inactivity, Chris pushed back his chair and made a rather odd declaration. "You know something? I could *really* go for a cup of coffee," he stated firmly.

"Oh my God, so could I!" exclaimed Sean. "I was just sitting here looking at this paper, and I suddenly just felt the need for a cup of espresso."

"Hmm, great minds must think alike," said Chris. "Let's step out and find a coffee shop somewhere. I have some thoughts on this whole matter that I'd like to discuss with you."

As Chris spoke, Alexa, their student assistant, raised a hand to speak as though in a lecture hall. Chris smiled and gently chided her. "It's OK, Alexa, we don't bite. What can we do for you?"

The college girl blushed a bit and cleared her throat before speaking. "I just wanted to tell you that it's not only great minds that think alike. Just about the time the two of you mentioned the word coffee, I got hit by the same craving. It's so weird, but all of a sudden I'm dying for a hazelnut coffee. By any chance, are you two going to the coffee shop in the student union?"

"That depends," answered Sean. "Where is it?"

"It's in the building right next to us. It only takes a minute to get there from here," she said.

"Then I guess that's the best place for us to go," replied Sean. "Would you like us to pick up something for you?"

"PLEASE," cried Alexa. "Get me a medium-sized hazelnut coffee with two sugars and two creams." As she spoke, she lifted her purse off an end table and took out two dollar bills.

"Nope, this is on me," said Chris, putting up his hand. "As long as we're the ones who started this coffee stampede, I'm not going to take your money just for signing on."

"Thanks so much," said Alexa. "It's almost like I can already smell it. I guess I must be addicted to the stuff."

As the two friends exited the building to head next door, Chris voiced his thoughts in a detached manner. It was as though he was randomly generating arguments both for and against the message conveyed by the document they had just discovered.

"I'm really not sure what to think about this letter, which doesn't have a name or signature and isn't attached to any other official record. I mean, who would record that in such a manner? If the supervisor of the assay office or the smelting operations had written that as a letter, it would have been signed, right?" he asked.

"Makes sense to me," said Sean, "unless it was part of a larger record, which could have been the case, because it did have a date listed above the entry, as in some log books. But then, why is it the only entry on the page, with no page number at the top or bottom?"

"There are a couple other things that don't make sense to me," said Chris, as he pulled open the door to the student union building. "If all the 1804 dollars were melted back into bullion—and that's what this letter says—then how do you explain the coin I found at the Adirondack Museum?"

"You can't," agreed Sean. "That dollar shouldn't exist. Even the seven coins that were reserved for assay were mentioned in the letter back there. It doesn't make any sense."

Chris and Sean walked down a hallway to an area where several take-out stands were arranged around a central seating area. The food court was home to a small, franchised coffee shop that had become popular with the students. Since the campus was fairly empty over the summer months, they walked right up to the counter without a wait. While placing their orders, they continued their discussion.

"I just thought of something else that is completely illogical," said Sean.

"What's that?" asked Chris, as he grasped his own coffee as well as Alexa's for the walk back to the library.

"If this paper had been in Frank Stewart's collection all along, why would he have wondered about the possibility of the 1804 dollar's existence?" explained Sean. "He would have known they had been minted and then melted. But according to his writings, Stewart spent a lot of time investigating this issue and even tried chasing down some of the rumors about the coin. He wouldn't have done any of that if he had read and believed this letter."

"That's another good point. But I wonder if there's any chance that Frank Stewart might have acquired this paper and then never read it?" questioned Chris. "No, that's probably not logical either, given that he was an avid historian who read and collected everything he could get his hands on."

"It is a conundrum," agreed Sean, as they entered the elevator and returned to the library. Alexa took her cup to the staff lounge, while Sean and Chris stood outside the reading room for a few minutes and finished their drinks.

"Regardless, I'm not ready to give up on this yet," said Sean, thinking back on the activity of the past two weeks. "I don't know why, but it just feels like we're on the verge of finding something big, if only we could pull together the last couple pieces of the puzzle."

"I know what you mean," agreed Chris. "I have that same feeling. I also believe that someone out there is toying with us, although I can't explain why. Just a gut feeling, I guess."

"OK, I'm ready to wrap this up whenever you are," said Sean, tipping back the last of his cup.

"Let's do it," said Chris, following suit.

The remainder of the afternoon seemed to drag on forever, as Chris and Sean sifted through thousands of additional pages of letters, pamphlets, manuscripts, and other documents. However, none of them appeared to have much relevance to their hunt. By five o'clock, they were both happy to see the staff making preparations to close the doors. Wordlessly, they packed up their notes and personal belongings, along with the copy of the unsigned letter about the melted coins.

"I'm sorry you boys didn't seem to find much else of interest today," said Penney, returning to bid them farewell. "I hope it's been a productive week for you, though."

"It has, Penney," said Sean, shaking her hand. "Even the minor finds we've made here have been interesting, and of great benefit to us."

"We can't thank you enough for all your help and direction," added Chris, also taking her hand.

"I only wish I hadn't blindly assisted that red-headed fellow, the guy who walked off with our stuff," said Penney. "It's bad enough that I cost our collection some valuable historical documents that we'll probably never see again. But I also made trouble for you, Sean. I hope he doesn't bother you now that he has your name, address, and other information. I feel very badly about that."

"It's OK, Penney, really," reassured Sean. "We'll take care of it."

After the librarian took back their badges and returned their driver's licenses, Chris and Sean left the facility and took the Jeep back to the hotel. Although they didn't talk about it, they were thinking about the same thing: Ben Grainger. What did he know, and what were his plans? They now had a way to track his vehicle. If only they could do the same with his thoughts. He was one of the two great unknowns left in the puzzle.

By the time Chris and Sean made it back to their hotel, it was already five forty-five. They had arranged to meet Tracey in the lobby downstairs at six o'clock, so they didn't have much time to spare.

"As long as you're the one who invited her to join us for dinner, will you also be picking up her restaurant tab?" Chris teased.

"You just don't give up, do you?" retorted Sean. "Yes, I'll get it; I wouldn't want you to have to tell Kristi that you paid for another woman's meal. Especially since she was working for us to help crack this case."

"Lighten up," said Chris, as he held the door open for his friend. "I'm just pulling your leg. Let's get out of here. I'm hungry."

When Chris and Sean emerged from the elevator in the lobby, Tracey was already waiting for them, browsing through the small gift shop next to the front desk. She looked radiant in a flowing flower-pattern white dress, and the lights from the overhead display seemed to dance off the highlights in her long hair. Two male customers in the shop were directing covert glances in her direction at every chance.

Sean walked up directly behind Tracey and looked over her shoulder.

"May I interest you in the Liberty Bell refrigerator magnet or the fake reprint of the Constitution?" he said.

Tracey whipped her head around in surprise. "Oh, I never saw you coming," she said, giggling in response. "No thanks, I can live without the fake constitution." Then, holding up a copy of the replica document, she observed, "But you know, they do make these things to look pretty authentic, don't they?"

"I guess," replied Sean. "Anyway, Tracey, I'd like to introduce you to my very good friend, Chris."

"Very nice to meet you," said Chris, smiling into the pair of luminescent blue eyes.

"You too," said Tracey. "Sean told me all about you the last time we met."

"None of it is true," quipped Chris. "I plead the Fifth Amendment."

"Hmm, the Fifth Amendment. Come to think of it, I think that's in here too," laughed Tracey, as she quickly sorted through the basket of replica documents until her search was rewarded. "Yes, here it is!" she cried, brandishing yet another of the replicas. "The Bill of Rights. And it's only $12.99, on sale today. Gosh, this thing even looks and feels real."

"It's printed on specially-treated paper," explained Sean. "The process discolors it and also gives it that wrinkled appearance. But that document was probably printed within the last few months, on a high-speed digital printer. Anyone who has any real knowledge about antique paper and inks of previous centuries would pick out the difference in a heartbeat."

"Speaking of papers, I brought along a copy of that article I was telling you about last night," said Tracey. "It's the one written by Robert M. Patterson about his thoughts on slavery. It was written early in 1854, the same year that he died."

"That's great," said Chris. "We're looking forward to reading it. But why don't we plan on doing that after we get to the restaurant? You are still going to join us, correct?"

"Yes, Sean asked me last night, and I'd love to. I get kind of tired with the same old salad every night," she replied. "But..." her voice faltered.

"What's the problem?" asked Sean.

"It's nothing, except, you see, I'm a vegetarian, and I don't want to cramp your style," she explained.

"That's not a problem at all," Chris reassured her. "We'll make sure to find a restaurant that has something you'd enjoy."

"Thank you so much," said Tracey, flashing her beautiful white smile. "In that case, I'd love to join you."

After consulting a directory at the concierge's counter, the three of them decided to try out an Indian restaurant located on Chestnut Street inside the city. The New Delhi restaurant, with its modern glass façade, had earned a reputation over the past two decades for its sumptuous cuisine. Chris had guessed that it would present a wide range of choices, including vegetarian, to please each of their tastes.

Unlike most of the large steakhouses, the Indian restaurant offered immediate seating, even in the middle of the dinner hour. They were shown to a nicely situated table and immediately presented with menus.

"Wow, this doesn't happen very often in Philadelphia," said Tracey, pulling her chair closer to the table.

"I imagine you must get asked out to dinner on a fairly regular basis," said Chris, making reference to the college social scene.

"No, not really," said Tracey. "Most of the guys I know want to spend their time and money in bars. I'm not twenty one yet, and even if I was, I've never really seen the point of living inside a bottle."

"Smart girl," nodded Sean, as he unfolded a menu.

"By the way, I'm sorry I didn't come up with more for you about Robert Patterson or his son," said Tracey. "But like I said, most of the material at the university is in reference to their roles at the university. It was pretty frustrating, because I spent a lot of time there this week."

"That's fine," said Chris. "Your work saved us from having to spend a lot of time there doing the exact same thing. As a matter of fact, because of you, we were able to spend more time at the other libraries, where we did make some real finds. So please, Tracey, accept our thanks for everything you've done."

"Not to mention your unofficial paycheck, which I'll be happy to give you tonight," added Sean.

"Thanks," said Tracey. "That makes me feel a lot better about accepting anything for this work."

A waiter appeared and poured their water, then asked for their orders. After he departed, Tracey lifted her handbag off the floor and removed a set of folded papers from inside. "This is what I wanted to show you," she said, flattening the pages and passing them across the table to Sean. "It's about the only mention of the North Country I could find in either of the Pattersons' papers. It was written by Robert M. Patterson the same year that he died. But it's really interesting, if only from the viewpoint of his ideology. He speaks of slavery and his general distaste for the entire concept. He was a very intellectual man, and his writing reflects his advanced thinking on many subjects. I was really impressed by his superior mastery on such a wide variety of disciplines."

Chris and Sean looked carefully at the papers Tracey set before them. As she had originally said, it appeared to be an article that he had written, perhaps for a journal, or to add to a larger collection of works. In it, Patterson expressed his beliefs that a country could not develop morally, financially, or spiritually as long as a portion of the economy was based upon the total subservience of one ethnic population to another. He developed this belief carefully and logically through the paragraphs of the essay, while managing to refrain from introducing an abundance of emotionally induced verbiage into the text.

About two-thirds of the way through the exposé, Chris and Sean saw a section that Tracey had decided to highlight with a yellow marker. They focused in on the brief paragraph, which described a personal experience in Patterson's life. In an instant, they were glued to the page, engrossed in the words which applied to the very core of their own search. In Patterson's characteristic, compact script letters, appeared the following:

The fact that the plight of the common slave in this country is a miserable subsistence cannot be denied. That they would risk everything in life, including food, shelter, and indeed the very cohesiveness of their own families, in exchange for a small chance of permanent freedom speaks volumes of their intense desire for personal liberty. My own experience provides ample proof of this theory. I once happened upon a group of slaves, who were traveling north in the direction of Canada. It was in a cave, in a remote mining village of the North Country. And yet, even though their plight and conditions were the very definition of misery and destitution, there was not a soul among them who would be convinced to return to relative comfort in exchange for their freedom.

"What do you think of that?" asked Tracey, once the two men had finished reading and set down the paper.

"Wow!" said Sean, his single-word reply packed with emotion and compassion.

"Yeah, wow," agreed Chris, but with a different mindset. "But Tracey, you know, this paper is even more important that you realize, because, in addition to expressing Patterson's thoughts on slavery, it also confirms something that I've seen recorded elsewhere."

Sean nodded knowingly. "The cave?" he asked, looking at Chris.

"The cave," repeated his friend.

"Based on what I've heard from Sean, I thought that might be important," said Tracey.

"It might be very important," agreed Chris, "although we'll have to consider this information along with the other references we've found, and then try to place it in context with what we already know about the village of Adirondac."

"Would you two do me a favor, please, and let me know how all this turns out?" asked Tracey. "I'd really love to know."

"By all means," said Sean. "And no matter how it ends, we'd both like to thank you for everything you've done."

After the meal, Chris and Sean drove with Tracey back to their hotel, where they dropped her off next to her vehicle. Sean got out and handed her a check as she prepared to unlock her car door, and she glanced at it briefly.

"Oh my God!" she exclaimed, noticing the amount of the payment. "I only worked for about seven hours. Surely I don't deserve this much."

"I'm afraid you're thinking in student minimum wage terms," countered Sean. "When you're working as a highly skilled consultant for Riggins & Carey Enterprises, you're paid on a different wage scale entirely."

"Riggins & Carey," repeated Chris, his voice registering mock indignation. "I thought that was 'Carey & Riggins'?"

"Whatever," said Sean.

"Thank you so much," said Tracey, her voice rising up another half-octave. In her joy, she leaned over and hugged Sean, then gave him a big kiss on the cheek.

"Hey, what about me? Don't I get one of those?" asked Chris playfully. Tracey ran around the front of the Jeep and hugged Chris though the driver's door window.

"Please let me know if you ever need library help again," she pleaded. "I'll work for the two of you anytime."

Once Chris and Sean watched Tracey drive off, Chris pulled into her vacated parking spot, and the two men stopped into the lounge off the lobby of the hotel. They ordered a round of draft beers and sat down to discuss the information Tracey brought to light.

"You know, this really brings up something of interest," said Chris, studying the foamy head on the side of his mug. "When I was reading in the Adirondack Museum, I found several references to a cave or mine, where Henderson supposedly believed that silver ore could be extracted."

"Yes, you told me about that," said Sean, trying a sample from his own glass of lager. "But didn't you also tell me that Kristi said that there probably wouldn't be any appreciable amount of silver in the ore around the McIntyre Mine?"

"Yes, but they wouldn't have known that in the 1800s, when it was pretty much a guessing game," replied Chris.

"So you think that this cave was actually a mine shaft of some sort?" asked Sean.

"There are several possibilities," speculated Chris. "But I think there's a greater chance of it being a man-made shaft than a naturally occurring cave. The area just didn't seem right for a cave, although I'm going to ask Kristi to take a trip up there with me to check it out."

"Sounds like a good idea," agreed Sean.

"Something else sounds like a good idea to me," said Chris, looking at Sean with an apologetic expression. "I received a couple phone messages today from some clients back in New York. I really think that I'd like to be back home late Thursday to see to some business on Friday. Is that OK with you?"

"Sure, I can do that," said Sean. "That still gives us two days to work together at the American Philosophical Society. We're pretty much through down at the Frank Stewart Room, and I don't think anything else is going to come out of the University of Pennsylvania, either."

"OK then, let's wrap it up these next two days, and then try to leave for home at a decent hour on Thursday."

The following morning, the two men were up again in time to have a substantial breakfast at the hotel restaurant before departing for the APS building. Chris carried with him the listing of references he had identified while perusing through the card catalog two days earlier.

They parked their car at the same garage on Third Street, which represented some of the only open parking in the entire area around Independence Hall. Sean shuddered as they walked past the same space where Grainger's car had sat just forty-eight hours earlier.

"Remind me never to try a stunt like that again," said Sean, shaking his head violently at the memory.

"I thought you did a great James Bond impersonation," said Chris, making light of his friend's risky adventure.

"No way," replied Sean, as they descended the steps toward the street. "I don't have the character to be a secret agent. I have an aversion to having guns aimed anywhere in my vicinity."

Within another five minutes, Chris and Sean were stepping inside the APS building, where they found Kimberly Kline back in residence behind her desk. "Hello again, Chris," she said, smiling from her chair. "Back again, but brought the cavalry along to help?" she asked jokingly.

"We're going to work in tandem today," nodded Chris. "Kimberly, I'd like you to meet my good friend and partner-in-crime, Sean Riggins."

"How do you do, Mr. Riggins?" said Kimberly, accepting Sean's proffered handshake. "It's very nice to meet you. And I understand that you were the man who put together that warning poster that helped us stop that thief on Monday."

"Yes, that was mine," admitted Sean, shifting his feet awkwardly. "But it was Chris' idea to draft it and send it out to you, so the credit should go to him."

"Kimberly, I need a favor from you," said Chris, interrupting the conversation. "I never requested advance permission for Sean to conduct research here with me for these next two days. Is it OK if he accesses your collection with me, even without the advance notice?"

"Sean, for everything you've done for us this week, I would be honored to bypass the official rules to give you a day pass," beamed Kimberly. "I'd ask my boss, but I know he'd say the same thing."

"Thank you so much," said both Chris and Sean at the exact same time.

"Not a problem," said Kimberly. "Now, you know the routine, Chris. I'll need an official photo ID from each of you, and you'll both need to fill out one of these forms." As she spoke, she passed the now-familiar package over the counter to Chris.

"Thank you, Kimberly," said Chris. "We'll have these back to you in a few minutes."

Within five minutes, Chris and Sean were entering the reading room, where Chris was approached by Vic, his accomplice from earlier that week.

"Hello again, Mr. Carey," said Vic, extending a handshake. "How very nice to see you again. Are you back to conduct more searches in the catalog stacks?"

"No, I wrapped that up on Monday," said Chris. "My friend and I are here these next two days to read through the various documents I found on Monday. Here's the list, organized as you requested."

The archivist took the printed page from Chris, who had taken all the data from the cards and entered it into an Excel spreadsheet, which he had printed at the hotel business center.

"Wow!" he exclaimed. "I wish all our library users were as organized as you. It certainly would make my day easier."

Vic excused himself with the list of references. While he was gone, Chris provided Sean with a guided tour of the impressive facility. The main room, complete with the ornate balconies, statues, and wood-carved shelving, was enough to impress just about anyone. He then led Sean into the microfiche storage room, where a series of short, six-inch shelves housed literally tens of thousands of tiny boxes, each containing a roll of several hundred frames. It was a massive collection.

Sean marveled at the extent of the microfiche library, which was organized by year and topic. He read, in awe, the titles printed on the outer edges of the boxes, star-struck at their content. "Washington: early years." "Adams: correspondence with Jefferson." "Jefferson: letters to Monroe."

"And there's lots more where those came from," said a voice from in back of the two. Sean and Chris both turned to see the figure of Vic, standing in the doorway with folders in hand.

"Here, these are a few of the first items on your list," said Vic, handing Chris a stack of the white manila folders. "I'm still looking for the remainder of your requests, but these should keep you occupied for a little while."

"Thanks," said Chris, accepting the pile from Vic. "We'll get going on this right now."

"I should be able to find the rest of the documents within the next hour," said Vic. "But there is one item you requested that appears to be a multi-volume journal, or diary, of some sort. That might take a bit longer, because I think that's maintained in our rare books and manuscripts collection."

"That's fine," said Chris. "I'm really interested in those volumes, so I hope you can locate them."

"I'll do my best," said Vic, who immediately departed for the archives.

Chris looked down at the stack of folders in his hand and grinned. "Looks like we've both got some reading to do," he said, nodding at Sean. "I hope you've got your schoolboy beanie on today."

"I'm ready," stated Sean, moving to a chair at the nearest reading table. "Let's divide and conquer."

The pile of folders was about eight inches thick. Chris took the top four inches of paper and placed it in front of his friend, then seated himself in a chair opposite from Sean with the rest of the stack. "Ok, buddy, let's see what you've got," he said, prodding his friend on.

"I got an A+ in Speed Reading 101," replied Sean, opening the first folder in his stack. "Eat my dust, pal."

For the next two hours, there wasn't a sound from either of the pair as they plowed through the files at lightning speed. There were no breaks for the weary, only a continuous procession of papers that flowed past their eyes, like barcodes being read by a scanning device, as they each raced to find the one critical clue that might unravel the mystery.

The first big break came around eleven thirty, as they were each about halfway through their respective piles. Chris' stomach had begun its characteristic rumblings, reminding him of the approaching lunch hour.

"I'm a bit on the hungry side," he exclaimed, glancing across the table at Sean. "Let's go check out that salad bar in the front entrance of the Bourse. It's only a block away, and we can be in and out of there in less than a half hour."

Sean did not respond. Instead, he just sat, immobile, his hand clutching a single page.

"What's the matter?" Chris asked.

Again, there was no reply. Chris looked more carefully at his friend, scrutinizing the look of concentration and wonder in his eyes. He knew, from experience, that Sean was not someone who was easily excited or overly expressive, which tweaked his curiosity to the breaking point. Rising from his seat, he moved around the table until he was standing behind Sean's chair.

"Find something of interest?" he asked, looking over Sean's shoulder.

"Yeah, I think I did," muttered Sean, still focusing on the document. "This is evidently a letter penned by Robert Patterson, and it's dated Tuesday, September 22, 1807."

Chris began to read the text of the letter and was instantly as excited as his partner. It read:

Tuesday, September 22, 1807

To my President, and to my Executor,

The contents of this parcel are the result of an error committed by the United States Mint. These coins exist only through a lack of commitment to accuracy and direction by myself, your humble servant. Had I to conduct these matters of the U.S. Mint coinage anew, I would have served in this capacity with stronger oversight and increased devotion to detail of task. For this, I profess my extraordinary sorrow. May it please you to be advised that I have made personal compensation for this silver from my own personal assets, and that the United States Government has suffered no loss from my poor judgment. I remain your loyal and obedient servant.

Robert Patterson

Director, United States Mint

Sean finished the letter a minute before Chris, who parsed through the text twice, in order to check his own comprehension. Once they had completely studied the document, Chris silently took the page and set it on the table in front of him. He placed a clean sheet of the blue note paper next to the letter, and hand-copied it, word for word, onto the page. Then, he replaced the letter inside its folder and moved the folder to the bottom of Sean's pile.

"What was that all about?" asked Sean, observing Chris' actions from across the table.

"Let's get some lunch," said Chris, his face devoid of emotion. "I could do with a break about now."

Sean hesitated a moment, not certain what was behind Chris' change in demeanor. Then, he simply shrugged his shoulders and stood up to leave. Chris, meanwhile, combined the two stacks of folders, his own and Sean's, and walked them over to Vic's desk.

"Vic, we're going to go out for a little fresh air and a bite to eat," he said. "I'm beginning to fall asleep in here."

"Yes, I know what you mean," laughed Vic, looking up through his thick, black-framed eyeglasses. "That can happen pretty easily in here. I've seen some folks come pretty close to falling right off their chairs."

"Would you mind if we left these papers here with you while we stepped out for a sandwich?" asked Chris. "We're not done with them, and I'd hate to have to go through the trouble of tracking them down again."

"Certainly," agreed Vic. "And by the way, I located that series of journals recorded by Robert M. Patterson. Would you believe they're spread out over six volumes? And it doesn't appear as though anyone has ever checked them out before. That's a funny thing, too, because I know for a fact that at least one short biography was written on the story of his life."

"That sounds great," said Chris, encouraged by the find. "We'll probably start looking at those within the next hour or so."

Chris placed the folders on Vic's desk, then immediately headed for the side door. Sean followed without saying a word. Their silence persisted as they strolled a few hundred feet to the corner of 5th Street and Chestnut, where a hot dog vendor was doling out red and white "hots," complete with all the toppings.

"What's your pleasure?" asked Chris, reaching into his back pocket for his wallet. "Would you prefer a red fat pill or a white one?"

"Whatever happened to the salad bar inside the Bourse?" asked Sean, amused at the change in venue.

"I changed my mind," said Chris. "Besides, when was the last time you ever heard of putting chili on a salad?"

Sean decided not to argue the point, and instead followed Chris' lead by ordering a white hot with sauerkraut and chili. "I'll have to remember to take an antacid before we get back to the library," he said, looking at the concoction as it was served.

The two also asked for a couple bottles of soda, then headed for a bench in nearby Washington Park. Sean was the first to speak, as he was puzzled by some of his friend's actions.

"Chris, I know why you wanted to talk out here instead of inside," he started. "That's really a startling document we just found, depending upon how we interpret it. But why didn't you just make a copy to bring along with us? Don't you think copying it by hand was just a tad bit over-cautious?"

"You think?" asked Chris, looking at Sean while removing the foil from his lunch. "And tell me, what happened to the last documents you photocopied, the ones in the Frank Stewart Room? Do you have any idea where those are today?"

"No, I don't," admitted Sean. "But we've also prevented Grainger from gaining access to the APS Library, much less checking out their collection. I don't see what you're worried about."

"What I'm worried about, Sean, is that we have now uncovered some very interesting pieces of evidence which may never have been seen before. And even if this letter has been reviewed by scholars interested in Robert Patterson, I can almost assure you that it wasn't read in the context of the search for the 1804 silver dollars. This is unique, and *it's dated in September of 1807*. That means it supports every thought we've had about the coins existing beyond the date of May 11, 1804. I don't even want some innocent scholar looking into the photocopy records for the month and seeing that we've copied this document. I want to return it to the library's collection as quietly and unnoticed as possible."

"Sounds fair to me," agreed Sean. "But what's this about May 11, 1804? I don't get what's so significant about that date?"

"That's the date on the unsigned letter we found at the Frank Stewart Room yesterday," explained Chris. "Remember? The document that talked about melting each and every 1804 silver dollar back into bullion?"

"OK, so if I'm following you correctly, you're saying that the letter from the Stewart Room is an intentionally misleading text?" asked Sean.

"I think that's a strong possibility," said Chris, chewing his food thoughtfully. "The only other possibility is that the erroneous silver coins

Patterson mentions in this letter are something other than dollar coins, or they're from another year. But I've been through the mint production record every year from 1792 through 1824, and I can't think of another possibility. I'd bet a grand on it right now."

"Patterson also wrote that he 'made personal compensation for this silver' using his own assets," quoted Sean. "That might mean that he assumed ownership of the coins once the mistake was discovered. Heck, for all we know, this letter might have been placed inside the same box as the 1804 dollars."

"The same thought occurred to me," said Chris, anxiously tapping the heel of his shoe against the sidewalk. "In which case, Patterson could have followed one of three paths: he could have melted the coins himself, hidden them, or passed them to someone, most likely his son."

"Two of those three options might mean that they are still out there today, somewhere," added Sean.

"I've changed my overall outlook on this entire event," said Chris, speaking in a low voice. "From everything I've read about Patterson, he wouldn't have melted those coins. He could have had that done at the mint as soon as they were pressed. Also, if he meant to destroy the coins by melting or any other method, he wouldn't have addressed the letter to his executor, because there would have been nothing left to explain. My guess is that he passed them on to his son, who then disposed of them in some undisclosed manner. They're still out there, somewhere. I can feel it in my bones."

"I've got goose bumps on my back," chuckled Sean, thinking of the possibilities. "And that's saying something, considering the fact that it's probably ninety-two degrees out here."

"Well then, let's finish up this fine culinary feast and get back to work," said Chris, gulping down the rest of his diet cola. "It's quiet and air conditioned in there."

The two friends walked quickly back to the library and retrieved their documents from Vic's desk. Rejuvenated by the meal and the sunshine, they threw themselves into their work and were able to finish the review of the folders within the next hour.

Chris looked up at the clock on the wall at the precise moment the bells began to chime from Independence Hall across the street. "Two o'clock," he said, gathering up the collection of folders to return to the archivist. "We might as well ask for those Patterson journals and get through as much of them today as possible. We've only got another eight hours to work tomorrow, and we've still got a lot of reading ahead of us."

"Don't remind me," said Sean, stretching his arms over his head to fend off the fatigue. "This reminds me of cramming for midterms back in college."

Vic looked up as Chris piled the folders onto a corner of his desk. "Did you find anything interesting?" he asked.

"No, not really," replied Chris, hoping his eyes didn't give away his deception. "Just about everything in there is stuff we've seen before, although some of it made interesting reading. I think we're ready to start on those journals now, if you could bring them out."

"I can allow you access to them; however, we can't do that in here," said Vic. "Those books must remain in our climate-controlled handling room, which is in a different part of the building. Please follow me."

Chris and Sean followed Vic through the tall doors of the main reading room, then down the main corridor to another section of the building. They walked through an area containing administrative offices and computer rooms, ending up in front of a glass door on a vault-like enclosure.

"This is our specially controlled rare documents room, where we keep several thousand of our older and deteriorating volumes," explained Vic. "Many of the books inside this chamber were left to fall apart, lost, or abandoned in conditions of high temperatures and humidity. The paper on which most of these were printed was not conducive to surviving such extremes, resulting in extremely fragile documents that, in some cases, cannot be opened without incurring significant damage."

"What is the condition of the Patterson journals?" asked Sean. "Can we open them for reading if we promise to use extreme care in their handling?"

"As a matter of fact, the Patterson books are in relatively nice shape," answered Vic, smiling to relieve their angst. "It appears that whoever owned these books between 1854 and the 1950s took excellent care of them, and never exposed them to the elements. As a result, they are all available for your perusal, although I must insist that each of you wear a pair of special, white linen gloves while handling the books."

After settling Chris and Sean into seats at the only table in the room, Vic reviewed the rules that no documents could be photographed or photocopied without permission, and that every book and paper must be handled with the utmost care to prevent additional wear. Chris noticed that a closed-loop television camera was monitoring them from a mounting shelf overhead to prevent theft or other abuse of the resources.

Once the door closed behind Vic, Chris looked over the table at Sean and proposed a strategy. "From what I read of the relationship between Robert M. Patterson and the principals of the McIntyre Mining Company, most of the journal entries that would concern us would have taken place between 1850 and 1853. Additionally, I'd be tempted to look at the year that Robert Patterson, the father, died, in 1824. Lastly, there might be clues to be found in the years immediately preceding and following Robert M. Patterson's selection as director of the mint, which was in 1835."

"You seem pretty fixated on the younger Patterson's connection to the mining operation in Adirondac," stated Sean. "Do you think there is a chance that he used that location as a hiding place for the cache of silver dollars, assuming as we now do that they did exist?"

Chris didn't answer, instead shifting his gaze quickly towards the overhead camera. Sean instantly understood the meaning of his stare. "Oh, sorry, I forgot. We'll talk later."

Chris simply winked in return, and the two friends divided the pile of journals between the two of them. They found the particular volumes that Chris had suggested as launch points for their search and began to read. Sean started in the year 1824 and then jumped ahead a decade to 1835. Chris picked up the volume that contained the years from 1848 to 1852.

Within a few minutes, Chris and Sean decided independently that they had never "met" a more literary person than Robert M. Patterson. His journal was a daily pursuit, and it was as diverse in content as any they had ever seen. The entries discussed topics from the weather and politics to science and medicine. Apparently, whatever was on his mind that day was instantly recorded and incorporated into the written story of his everyday life. The only reason there weren't many more physical books in the collection was the diminutive size of his handwritten lines. They were both amazed at how many words fit on each line, and the number of days crammed onto each page. The extreme compression of his written thoughts enabled each volume to contain several years of his life.

Something else that impressed Chris was the very personal nature of many entries. Patterson not only recorded the events of the day, but also his inner feelings and emotions as he described the events of his life. At times, it seemed as though the journal itself had assumed human characteristics, and Patterson was speaking directly to it, as he would to a close friend or confidant. Some of these essays were very touching, leaving Chris and Sean deeply moved.

Sean finished scanning the first two volumes quite rapidly without finding much of interest. He then reached for the edition that started at the end of 1852 and extended until the end of Patterson's life in 1854.

Chris, meanwhile, was moving much more deliberately through the years 1848 and 1849. There was much that interested him, because many of the journal entries included mention of his correspondence with Archibald McIntyre, as well as his plans to visit the mining town of Adirondac. He spent several hours reading the daily records leading up to Patterson's visit in 1850.

It was after four o'clock when Chris stumbled upon a passage that quickened his heartbeat. It was written under the header "Thursday, July 11, 1850," and described Patterson's first day in Adirondac following a four-day transit to that remote location. The paragraph that grabbed Chris' attention contained the following text:

Thursday, July 11, 1850: During the night, I was awakened as if in a dream, by the sound of a child whimpering in the darkness. Upon investigating, I found my way through the exterior darkness to a cave-like excavation that extended beneath the very building in which I was berthed. My probe into the depths of this concealed enclosure revealed a great many humans, of all age, and apparent African descent, hiding in and under every conceivable obstruction. In their eyes, I detected the look of abject fear as they considered my intentions, and I considered theirs. I cannot say that I was without fear myself, although they remained passive throughout my intrusion into their realm. I will not allow myself the diversion of speculating on the nature of their presence, although my suspicions have been naturally stimulated. Suffice it to say, however, that although our co-mingling lasted for only a few short minutes, I shall remember this event for the rest of my life.

After finishing the passage, Chris looked up and summoned his friend. "Sean, I think I just found the front end of the article that Tracey copied for us," he said.

"What do you mean?" asked Sean, moving around in back of Chris.

"The article she found that was written by Patterson on the topic of slavery. If you remember, it talked about how he had come upon a group of slaves in a North Country mining town," explained Chris. "I was fairly certain that he was talking about Adirondac, and I think that this proves it."

Chris showed Sean the journal entry for that date, which he quickly read.

"I'd have to agree with you there," said Sean, nodding his head. "So that pretty much proves that somewhere, there is or was a cave or tunnel of some sort beneath the mining town. And it also means that the cave was located near or under the house where Patterson stayed when visiting in 1850."

"It sure does," agreed Chris. "I'm not sure whether this has anything to do with our hunt for the 1804 dollars, but it certainly is an interesting side story."

"I wonder…" said Sean, failing to finish his sentence.

"What's that?" asked Chris.

"Think about it," continued Sean. "Upstate New York was the last stretch of ground that runaway slaves had to traverse in their trek for freedom to Canada. We know that the Underground Railroad had quite a few stations in the region, and we also know that John Brown's Tract was almost due north of Adirondac, on the outskirts of present day Lake Placid. Could it be that the cave, or mine shaft, or whatever it was in Adirondac, could have been the last stop prior to John Brown's Tract on the way to freedom?"

Chris paused, plotting a mental image of northern New York in his mind. "You know, you might have something there," he said, looking at Sean with renewed respect. "That's an angle I just hadn't considered, although it is an overwhelming possibility."

"Of course it is," said Sean, warming up to the idea. "When you think of it, the iron ore would have been mined from the surface. But if David Henderson had originally believed in the existence of a silver vein, he may have ordered the excavation of a couple shafts into areas with the most promising mineral profiles. Those shafts would have served as perfect hideouts for escaping slaves."

"It's too bad that we couldn't locate any of those shafts today," said Chris. "Or maybe there is a way."

"Sounds fascinating; let's talk about it on the drive home," said Sean. Then, remembering the camera overhead, he frowned and pointed upward. "I guess we kind of blew the 'silence policy,' didn't we?"

"No matter," said Chris. "As far as I'm concerned, anyone who wants to investigate the Underground Railroad is free to do so. Far be it from me to withhold information."

Sean just rolled his eyes at the change of attitude. Meanwhile, Chris once again hand-copied the text of Patterson's journal from July 11, 1850, onto a growing stack of notebook paper. It was a slow process, and he was just transcribing the last words when the door to the private reading room opened. An attractive young woman with short blond hair leaned into the room to give them notice.

"Vic wanted me to tell you that we'll be closing in less than fifteen minutes, so you've got to return all your materials to the reshelve bin," she said, nodding at the gray metal letter box at the end of the table. "Also, he'll be by to inspect your belongings before you depart the rare books vault."

"Thanks for the warning," smiled Chris. "We'll be sure to return all our stolen merchandise before he arrives."

The young woman's face registered a momentary look of confusion, as she didn't know whether to smile or sound the alarm. She finally decided that Chris was kidding, and excused herself from the room.

"You'd better watch yourself, or you're going to land both of us in the slammer," said Sean.

"What's life without a little humor?" asked Chris, leaning back in his seat. "Besides, I feel brain dead. Let's grab a bite to eat and call it a night."

Rather than waste the time and money on another expensive meal, Chris and Sean decided to forego the restaurant scene on Wednesday, instead settling for a couple of submarine sandwiches and a bag of chips. They carried the bags of food up to their room and spread the contents across the large round table next to the window. As Sean unwrapped the food and drinks, Chris laid out the various papers they'd found that appeared to be part of their search. The path through the clues started out winding and convoluted. Yet, the more they searched, the more they found, and the clearer the road became. Both men were astounded at the progress they'd made in the period of a few short weeks.

"Let's lay this out as a giant timeline, OK?" asked Chris, mouthing the words around a bite of roast beef sub.

"Sounds logical to me," agreed Sean.

"We're now positive that at least some 1804 dollars were struck in the year 1804," Chris began. "We have proof of that from the museum coin, plus we have the missing page from the treasury department's mint report that showed the die crack on March 26, 1804, with an additional 2,620 coins reportedly produced after that date."

"Yes, but we can't be sure that they didn't have another 1803 die, so that doesn't mean anything positive yet," countered Sean.

"OK, point taken," said Chris, yielding to Sean's logic. "But we also have to consider Patterson's own letter of September 1807. Assuming that he was talking about the silver dollars, that letter would have proved that there were a considerable number actually produced, and that he still had possession of them as late as 1807."

"And that he probably never destroyed them," continued Sean.

"Correct," observed Chris. "As a matter of fact, the only evidence we have of any of the coins being melted is the rather dubious unsigned letter we found in the Frank Stewart Room, and I'm not about to put my faith behind that document. It's just too self-contradicting."

"I agree on that point as well," said Sean. "But what's next?"

"Next, we fast-forward about seventeen years, to the year of Patterson's death," Chris surmised. "At which time, if we assume that Patterson still held the contraband coins, they would have passed to someone else in the family whom he could trust."

"Let me guess," said Sean, knowing that Chris was leading him along. "It would have been someone close, like a son or daughter. It probably was someone who most likely shared his love of scholarly pursuits, and who might also have even been a college professor. And maybe someone who also was a member of the American Philosophical Society."

"Robert M. Patterson," agreed Chris. "I really don't see any other logical alternative. My guess is that his father passed the coins along to him when he died in 1824. But from there on, we've got a vacuum."

"Yeah, I know," conceded Sean. "The clues do tend to get rather sparse after that."

Both men paused for a few minutes to polish off the rest of their subs.

"Do you know what the wildcard is in all this?" asked Chris, wiping his mouth with a napkin.

"What's that?"

"The missing records from the mint that Grainger holds," said Chris. "Remember, the researcher from my dad's firm who went into the National Archives here in Philly said that Grainger had an unofficial day log from the mint's coining press room from 1804. I'd love to know what's inside that book."

"You've got his email address and phone number," said Sean, smiling at his friend. "Why don't you just call him and ask?"

"Why certainly, that's a splendid idea!" laughed Chris. "I'm sure he'd be happy to share with us, especially since he probably knows it was you who raised the red flag about him to the folks at the APS library."

"You really think so?" asked Sean, concern showing on his face.

"Yes, I think it's a pretty safe bet," said Chris, turning serious again. "I wouldn't trust him as far as I could throw him, but I do think he's probably intelligent enough to have figured that out by now."

"It's a shame we couldn't have him arrested, and then get a look at that mint record," said Sean. "That might be the missing piece that we need."

"True, but you can't have someone arrested without proof of the crime, and we don't have that. For all we know, Penney could have misplaced that file somewhere inside the Frank Stewart Room. Then you'd be dealing with someone crying slander and false arrest."

"So, if we assume for the time being that we'll never see that record book, we're left with the last thirty years of Robert M. Patterson's life," Chris observed. "Of that time, he spent from 1835 through 1851 as the sixth director of the mint. Nowhere in that interval have we found a single mention of the mint ever melting those coins."

"Not only that," said Sean, "but it was during those years that the mint was asked to produce a few samples of the 1804 dollar to give away as gifts to the foreign dignitaries. If the younger Patterson still had physical custody of the original coins, I wonder why he didn't just grab a half dozen from his personal supply and add them to the gift sets?"

Chris thought for a moment before replying. "That's a good point, and I hadn't considered that yet. But when you stop to think about it, Patterson couldn't do that, because he'd be admitting that he had them in the first place. By 1834, he'd presumably already owned them for a decade. He wasn't about to break his silence and expose the existence of the entire cache."

"No, I suppose you're right," conceded Sean. "So what do you think he did with them?"

"Well, from 1835 through 1851, he was filling the role of mint director, which by that time had become a full-time job," said Chris. "It's true that he probably had time to do some traveling, and we know that he got out of Philadelphia occasionally. But most likely, his days were spent at the mint building on Seventh Street. My guess is that he didn't do anything with them until he left his job at the mint."

"Which brings us to 1851," said Sean. "We already know from his journal that Patterson had visited Adirondac once, in 1850. You also found references in the Adirondack Museum that he made several other trips to the mining community in 1851 and 1852, possibly later. Now what we need to know is, why? Did those trips, and possibly even the mine shaft, have anything to do with the silver dollars? How else could the foreman of the construction crew have obtained one?"

"I don't know," admitted Chris. "But I'm hoping that we can find something tomorrow, because we're running out of places to look down here."

"I've got to finish the journal from 1852 through 1854," said Sean, "which shouldn't take long because he started missing a lot of entries as he neared his death in September of 1854. Still, he was a pretty prolific writer up until the last few months of his life."

"I still have the period from July of 1850 until the middle of 1852, where the end of my volume meets the beginning of yours," said Chris. "And then, if we don't find anything in there, we can either browse through some of the other volumes, or else put our tails between our legs and crawl home."

"I wouldn't sound quite so sorrowful," said Sean, looking bright-eyed at his companion. "We've made some huge strides in the last three days. Better things are on the horizon. It's just like you told me over lunch hour today—we're so close I can 'feel it in my bones.'"

By Thursday morning, Chris and Sean were on autopilot. They'd developed the same routine of eating breakfast, followed by a stop at Starbucks, after which they'd drive to the garage on Third Street. The final walk to the APS had become so familiar that they felt as though they worked there.

"OK, let's try to get through this before noon," suggested Chris.

Vic appeared from an inside office and set them up for their final day in the rare books room, where they returned to work on the last two volumes of Patterson's journal. With something akin to dread, Sean opened his book to the beginning of 1852 and commenced reading. Chris did the same in his own journal, starting with July 12, 1850, and working forward.

Chris and Sean were both dealing with conflicting emotions by this point. Chris had suggested that they move ahead rapidly in order to hit the road for home by noon. They both wanted to achieve that goal because they'd been away since Sunday and had each read many thousands of pages in that time. The strain was beginning to show, and their attention spans were dropping by the hour. Yet, as they moved through the journals, turning page after page, they realized that their chances of finding *the clue* were decreasing proportionately. There were other volumes left to read, but they considered those to have less promise than the documents they currently held in their hands. Accordingly, they found themselves actually slowing somewhat, reading the last few sections of the journal more deliberately, hoping against hope to find the answer.

Chris was turning a page, about to start the last month of his volume, when he heard a one-word call from Sean.

"Chris," was all Sean said, more of a murmur than salutation.

"You called, young grasshopper," said Chris, imitating the old martial arts television show.

"I found it," said Sean, once again in the same quiet, subdued tone.

"You found it?" mimicked Chris. "What did you find?"

"I found it," said Chris, again. "I found our smoking gun. The clue we've been searching for."

In an instant, Chris sprang from his chair and flew around to the other side of the table.

"Here, in this entry, dated September 8, 1853," said Sean. "Read it for yourself, but keep your voice and your emotions down."

Chris sat down in the chair next to Sean and accepted the open book from Sean. The words were electrifying, sending shock waves through the very core of his body. He felt unable to move as he absorbed the meaning of the words penned on the stained page before him:

> Thursday, September 8, 1853
>
> In the silence of the night, Henry and I moved the chest, which tested his superior physical brawn to the utmost, to its final resting place. Although my body has lost all of its vitality and vigor, my mind is now at ease, secure in the knowledge that I have preserved the family honor, and kept my promise to my dearly departed father, may God rest his soul. Tomorrow, we shall commence our voyage home. I have already bid my dear friends, Archibald McIntyre and Peter VanderBrooke, a fond farewell.

After finishing the passage, Chris pushed himself back from the table and stared into space for a few moments, his eyes misting with emotion. He then turned his head slowly until he faced Sean, who stared back with a similar expression.

"Sean, old buddy, you've found it," said Chris, his voice quavering a bit in the stillness of the quiet vault. "I'm now ninety nine percent convinced that Robert M. Patterson, for whatever reason, selected the mining community at Adirondac as a final resting place for the objects of our search, and that those objects are still there today."

Sean realized that Chris was substituting "the objects" for the 1804 silver dollars, in case anyone was monitoring the room via the closed-circuit television microphone that was mounted overhead. He played along, just to be safe, and used the same term in his response.

"That must have been the deal," Sean said solemnly. "Robert M. Patterson must have promised his father to dispose of the objects. They were never again to see the light of day."

"My guess is that the father passed them on to his son very close to the end of his life," guessed Chris. "But what I'd like to know is just how many objects there were, and how many are left. I'd also like to know whether that letter you found from Patterson, dated September 22, 1807, was originally stored with the objects, which is my guess, and how it ended up in this library."

"I don't know," said Sean. "I don't think we'll ever figure that out."

"Never say never, my friend," said Chris.

"So what comes next?" asked Sean. "To head up to Adirondac and start looking for any objects seems a hundred times harder than finding a needle in a haystack. Do you have anything in mind that might narrow the search?"

"I do," said Chris, "and I'd be happy to share it with you. But let's hit the road for home first, if you don't mind. Just give me a couple minutes to copy this text into my notepad, and then we can be on our way."

Chris spent the next few minutes scanning the pages that covered a few weeks before and after the critical journal entry, just to make certain that they weren't leaving any vital information behind. Not finding anything else of interest, Chris transcribed the entry of September 8, 1853, onto his note page, and then stacked the rest of the journals into the reshelve bin.

As he completed his work, Sean signaled the same young librarian who had spoken with them the previous day, who in turn used the intercom to call Vic. Within a minute, Vic appeared to debrief the two, and to conduct the mandatory search of their materials.

"So, did you fellows find anything of interest?" he asked, more as a courtesy than anything.

"Oh, we found a lot of fascinating ideas and notes from Patterson's years as a journal keeper," said Sean. "But we really didn't come across anything that will help us in our current study. Still, it's been an interesting week, and we really appreciate your assistance with all the books and articles."

"My pleasure, boys. I always enjoy seeing kids as young as you taking an interest in our nation's history." As he said this, Sean smiled to himself. At twenty-six years of age, he hardly considered himself to be a "kid." However, Vic appeared to be in his early to mid sixties, so it was all a matter of perspective. Anyway, Sean felt a certain affinity for the man, who always looked as though he was ready with a joke, if only they were outside the library in another setting.

Chris and Sean shook hands with Vic, then turned in their badges and headed off to the garage. They had already checked out of the hotel earlier that morning, so all that remained was six hours of highway that would lead them back to the Mohawk Valley and their respective homes.

The entire trip would be on interstate highways, the kind that Chris normally avoided in favor of the scenic local roads. However, on trips of this length, that was impossible, so he pointed his Jeep towards Route 476, which would eventually lead him to Route 81 in Scranton, and then up the long concrete corridor to Syracuse. It would be a long, boring ride, although they had a lot to discuss, and Sean offered to share the driving.

As they followed Commerce Street toward their route home, Chris suggested stopping for a last cup of coffee before hitting the expressway.

"Sure, I could go for some caffeine," said Sean, already weary after staring at printed pages all morning.

"I see a Starbucks sign up ahead," said Chris. "I don't need a GPS for this one; I'm locked on and going in!"

As they approached the store, Sean brought up the missing treasury ledger, page 154, that they'd found in the Frank Stewart Room.

"You know, what I'd love to know is exactly how many of the 1804 dollars actually rolled off the press," Sean said. "Once the die cracked on March 26, there was one more entry for dollar coins that appeared in that log. It was on March 28, when they recorded 2,860 dollars from the press. Could it be that all of those were 1804s?"

"It's possible," said Chris, nodding his head thoughtfully. "As a matter of fact, I'd even say it's probable. If all depends on whether any of those 2,860 coins were struck before the die broke. But regardless, I'd guess that a majority of them were 1804s."

"I think so too," agreed Sean gleefully. "I really do!"

Chris pulled across traffic into the parking lot of the coffee shop. As he did, Sean turned and glanced into the back seat.

"Hey, are we going to be inside for a few minutes?" he asked.

"We could be," replied Chris. "Why?"

"I'd like to quickly check my business email, if we could spare a few minutes. Also, I'm curious as to whether Dr. Tomlinson had anything else to say about the cipher."

"Sure, bring the laptop in," suggested Chris. "They have wireless inside, and I can get one of their almond chocolate cookies while you work."

"Thanks," said Sean, walking around to the back of the Jeep to fetch his computer case.

As they walked inside, Chris headed into the bathroom for a minute while Sean unzipped his laptop from its case. He opened his email and quickly perused the inbox, disappointed that there was nothing in the past few days from Dr. Tomlinson. As Chris emerged from the men's room, Sean gave him a "thumbs down" signal. "Not a thing on the code yet," he intoned.

"We didn't expect there to be anything for a few weeks, remember?" said Chris, stepping up to the counter. "He said maybe in a month, but he's tied up until then. But nice try."

"Hang on, I'll be right with you," said Sean, closing his email and opening another application. "As long as we're looking, we might as well see where our buddy Grainger is right now. My guess is he's probably at home licking his wounds."

"Sure, I'd be interested in seeing where he is as well," said Chris, considering Grainger's next move.

Sean stood over the display waiting for a moment, before deciding to order his coffee while the application came to life. "I do wish this thing came up a little faster," he said, stepping away from the machine. "Still, it's a pretty neat piece of software. It's kind of fun keeping track of someone who doesn't know they're being watched."

Sean stepped up to the counter and ordered a large coffee, and then added a little cream. As he pulled out his wallet, Chris moved back to their table and set his cup down next to the computer.

"OK, you're up and running," said Chris, moving closer to the monitor.

"Cool. Be there in a minute," said Sean, counting change from his pocket.

Chris looked again at the computer screen, doing a double take. His eyes narrowed, and the corners of his mouth turned downward in a deep scowl.

"Sean, what should you be looking at right now on the screen?" he asked intently.

"The GPS application," replied Sean. "I just started it up."

"I know," said Chris, impatiently. "But what should you be seeing in the display right now, at this very minute?"

"I should be looking at the precise location of Grainger's car," said Sean. "If he's on the road, I should be looking at his route, including direction and speed. If he's parked, I should be seeing his current street address. Why do you ask?"

"Any chance you might have programmed this thing wrong?" asked Chris, his look of concern deepening even further.

"Not a chance," replied Sean, carrying his coffee back to the table. "Why? What the heck's going on?"

"The address showing up in the locator field," said Chris, hesitating with doubt. "It's 487 Reservoir Creek Road, Little Falls, New York."

"You're kidding me, right?" said Sean, dashing behind the monitor to gain a glimpse of the screen.

"I'm afraid I'm not," said Chris, looking at his friend. "It appears as though Ben Grainger's car is currently parked outside your house."

CHAPTER 14

Thursday, August 28, 2015

Thursday mornings were among the least busy times of the week at the community golf course in Little Falls. The first tee saw very little action, as most people were at work, and even the retired local golfers usually waited until the early afternoon to strike their first shots.

After touring the entire course with the drink cart four times, Maggie decided it was time for a well-earned break. She pulled the cart off the asphalt path along the right side of the eleventh fairway and detoured into the back yard of Sean's small white cottage. Sean always left her the keys to his house while out of town, and she used his refrigerator and kitchen to take her lunch breaks.

Maggie maneuvered the specially modified cart alongside the patio, and climbed out onto the flagstone surface. It was a sunny day, so she couldn't see anything looking into the darkened windows of the cottage. Everything appeared as it should, with the chairs arranged around the table next to the barbecue grill, and the wind chimes playing pretty tunes into the late summer air.

It took only a moment to slip the key into the doorknob of the back door and push it open into the gap between the kitchen and the tiny eating area. It was a small house, without much open space beyond the main living room where Sean had arranged his chairs and couch around a big-screen television set.

Maggie never looked beyond the kitchen as she turned left, facing the refrigerator, to get her brown-bagged lunch. She always enjoyed her simple noon meal of strawberry yogurt and "something else," which could be anything from a half sandwich to a small container of noodles.

After retrieving her bag from the refrigerator, she stepped over to turn on the television for a few minutes, or as long as it took to consume her meal, but what she saw next stopped her in her tracks. The file drawer that fit into the right side of Sean's desk was pulled completely out, and the contents were dumped in a heap on the floor. An open tray containing letters and other papers on top of Sean's desk had been turned upside down, and the contents were spread across the floor near the front door of the house. Likewise, a plastic, portable file case of organized folders had been emptied on a chair, with each folder emptied in another stack, the papers randomly tossed about the floor.

Unsure of what to do, Maggie peered around a corner, noticing that Sean's bedroom was a complete mess, with clothes strewn everywhere. She knew all of this was out of character for her boyfriend, who was hardly compulsive about neatness, but yet managed to maintain a fairly orderly house.

Maggie walked quietly over to the window and peeked out into the driveway. Sean's Mercedes was still sitting idle in the driveway, as it had been all week. Everything else looked normal as well, although she noticed that there was a red Mini Cooper with a white roof parked in the street in front of the house. Maggie had never seen that vehicle in the area before, and shrugged it off as a visitor to another house. She turned back into the living room and continued her tour of the house.

"Sean?" she called out, moving towards the bedroom. "Sean, are you home?" Receiving no answer, she hesitated for a moment, registering the first tingling sensation of fear. Still, she inched forward, thinking that perhaps Sean had returned early, and dumped out the paper while hastily searching for some business forms.

"Sean? Honey?" she called out. Reaching the door of the bedroom, she leaned into the interior of the room. More of Sean's belongings were spread across the floor, and the contents of his closet shelves were pulled off the racks.

"Sean, are you in here?" That was the last thing that Maggie remembered. In a moment of blinding speed and motion, the bedroom door slammed shut, smashing its outward edge into the right side of Maggie's face. Her body was thrown sideways, and the left side of her skull crashed into the side of the doorframe. She lost consciousness as she fell to the floor between the bedroom and the short hallway to the bathroom.

As soon as she hit the floor, a shadowy figure appeared from behind the door and nudged a foot under Maggie's shoulder. He rolled her body, first in one direction, then the other, checking to see whether she was indeed beyond the realm of consciousness. Then, he pulled the quilt off Sean's bed and wrapped it around the inert form. Finally, he dragged Maggie away from the doorway, where she might have been seen by someone looking in the front window, and deposited her on the other side of Sean's bed.

The entire scene had taken less than five minutes. Yet, to Maggie, it might have been an hour, a day, or a week. She was far beyond the point of remembering anything about her attacker, or even the events leading up to the assault. All that remained visible of her physical being was a pair of feet, clad in leather sandals, which protruded from the end of a bundled roll of bedding. Everything else in her mind and her memory would be just an empty book.

Back in the Philadelphia coffee shop, Sean was stunned into immobility at the revelation that Grainger's car was parked outside his house. For a good ten seconds, he stood in a statue-like pose, his face a contorted mask revealing elements of confusion, anger, and fear.

"But, but, th-th-that's my house!" stammered Sean. "He can't be there."

"He can, and he is," said Chris, looking at the display with Sean. "We need to call the police, and NOW."

As Chris spoke, he was already dialing 911 on his own cell phone. He realized that Sean's mind was probably shrouded with emotion right now, and Chris assumed responsibility for calling for assistance. An emergency response operator answered on the first ring.

"This is an emergency call," Chris began. "There is an emergency at an address in Little Falls, New York. That's near Utica. We have a report that there is a break-in at a residence at 487 Reservoir Creek Road."

Sean listened anxiously as Chris relayed the details, along with the best way to summon help.

"It's critical that they send someone out to that residence at once," he continued. "A friend on the golf course nearby saw a man breaking in through the rear window."

As Chris spoke, Sean was once again amazed at his friend's ability to think clearly through complex problems in times of duress. His fabricated story, while technically against the law, was the only way that they could call for police assistance without admitting that they had illegally tampered with Grainger's vehicle. It was a fast bit of thinking that might save them from an embarrassing explanation later on.

Once the 911 operator relayed the call to the Little Falls Police Department, which called in the State Police from Herkimer as backup, she turned her attention to Chris for more details. Sean could tell that she desired additional information, such as the owner's name, present location, and identity of other occupants. That last question spurred Sean into action, and he quickly opened his own phone and pressed a speed-dial button that was keyed to Maggie's cell phone.

Maggie and Sean had been dating for about eighteen months, and in that time, he had never known her to ignore a phone call. Maggie always had her ringer set at full volume, which sometimes landed her in trouble on the golf course when its piercing notes sounded as a golfer was lining up a difficult putt. As a result, she usually answered her phone on the first ring, and certainly no later than the second. However, on this day, there was no response. Sean listened desperately to the unanswered rings, one after another, as they sounded in his ear. Each unheeded wave of sound heightened his feeling of terror. Finally, after eight rings, the phone forwarded the call to an automated message system.

Not bothering to leave a message, Sean hung up his phone and looked at his watch. It was almost noon; time for Maggie's lunch hour. She should be at his house right now. The panic deepened.

Chris had only been off the phone for a matter of minutes when it sounded a melodic tune, signaling an incoming call. He answered it immediately, finding himself on the line with a member of the New York State Troopers. After explaining again the circumstances by which they had learned of the break-in, he handed the phone to Sean.

"Sir, this is Trooper Anthony Gianello, of the New York State Troop D Station in Herkimer, New York," the deep voice sounded. "Are you the owner of the residence at 487 Reservoir Creek Road?"

"Yes, I am," replied Sean.

"Sir, we can confirm at this time that there appears to have been a break-in at your residence. The window on the back left side of your house is broken, and the window frame has been pushed inward. Are you within a short distance of home right now?"

"No, I'm not," replied Sean, the stress evident in his voice. "Is there anyone inside the house right now?"

"We're just entering the house now," said the trooper, "but the perpetrator does not appear to be inside. He or she was apparently looking for something, because there are a lot of things that are tipped over and dumped out, as though someone rummaged through the place pretty thoroughly."

"Sir, I need you to do me a favor, RIGHT NOW," Sean pleaded.

"What's that?"

"I need you to look out in back of the house, near or on the patio. I need you to tell me whether there is a golf cart parked back there."

After just a few moments, he replied, "Yes, there's something back there, but it's not really a golf cart. It's sort of a modified snack cart on wheels. But it looks like it might have once been a golf cart. Is that what you're looking for?"

"Oh my God, she's inside the house," cried Sean.

"Sir, who is inside the house?" asked the trooper. "It doesn't appear as though anyone is inside."

"My girlfriend, Maggie," yelled Sean. "She works at the golf course behind the house, and she eats lunch there every day. That's her cart parked back there now. You've got to find her!"

"We're looking now," said the officer, "but so far the house appears to be empty. And I have some other good news; you have what appears to be several hundred dollars in cash sitting on a bookshelf in your living room. Whoever broke in here apparently missed it, because it's still there, untouched. You know, you really shouldn't leave that kind of cash sitting out in plain sight. That alone could motivate a thief to force their way in here."

Sean was in the process of mentally walking them from the bathroom to the bedroom when he heard another male voice in the background exclaim, "Oh, it's a girl!"

"What's going on there?" demanded Sean, who had walked out the front of the coffee shop and into the side parking lot. As he spoke, he paced back and forth across the pavement of the lot, followed by Chris. "Did you find Maggie?"

"I can confirm that we have found a girl," confirmed the officer.

"Can I speak with her?" asked Sean, impatiently.

"No, I don't think she's in any shape to speak right now," said the trooper. "Please bear with us, and we'll give you a status as soon as we can."

"Is she OK?"

"Sir, please bear with us right now. I can't tell you anything for the time being, but I will let you know as soon as I find out," Gianello reported.

"Is she OK?" whispered Chris, looking at Sean's terrified expression.

"I think she's hurt," cried Sean. "For all I know, she may be dead." As he spoke, the emotional dam gave way, and tears flooded down Sean's face. Chris reached out and gently motioned for the phone, which Sean passed to him while turning the other way.

Chris stepped away from his distraught friend and spoke quietly into the phone. "Officer, this is Chris Carey, Sean Riggins' friend. Sean's quite upset right now, so if it's OK with you, I'd like to ask a couple questions on his behalf."

"Yes, Mr. Carey, what can I do for you?" asked the official.

"Could you please let me know whether the girl you found is alive. I think you could do that much, just to put our minds at ease a bit," Chris asked, trying to sound as calm as possible given the circumstances.

There was another pause on the other end of the line, and then Trooper Gianello sounded off again. "Yes, sir, she is breathing, and another officer is tending to her. That's all I can say right now, Mr. Carey. I'll be happy to remain on the line with you, but I simply can't tell you any more than that. Please understand. We've already called for medical assistance, and they're on their way now."

In the background, Chris could hear more voices. He could also detect the faint sounds of additional sirens, which were growing louder by the second. He turned back toward Sean, who was simply wandering around the back of the lot, looking up at the sky and talking to himself.

"Sean! Let's go back inside and pack up our things, then let's hit the road. It sounds like Maggie's OK, but they're calling on the medics just to check her out. She should be able to talk to you before too long." Chris knew that not everything he said was completely true. But he also knew that Maggie was, at the very least, alive, and that they had to get back to Little Falls as quickly as possible to learn the whole story.

Chris held the door open for Sean, who rushed inside the shop and straight over to his laptop, which had gone into its screensaver mode. With one rapid movement on the touchpad, he refreshed the view of the GPS application, and glared at the updated display.

"He's on Route 90, headed west," said Sean, still choked up from the news. "Think he might be headed for your house?"

Chris considered the matter for a moment before responding. "No, he doesn't have anything that would lead him to me. He's probably heading back to Binghamton, possibly even to his house."

"But if he knows from our poster, that his name is already associated with a crime, why would he return to his official address, where he might risk being arrested?" asked Sean.

"My guess is that he's not thinking that far ahead; he has no idea we're following him from state to state," said Chris. "However, all that might change now that he's broken into a home and injured the occupant. He's got to know that the police will be following him soon."

Sean packed up his computer and zipped it into its case. Both men took their coffee, which was now lukewarm, and headed back into the parking lot.

"You just take it easy, buddy. I'll drive," said Chris, knowing that Sean had volunteered to drive the first shift of the trip.

Chris pulled the Jeep onto the city road, then into a gas station to fill up before starting the trip north. As he pulled onto Route 76, he stole a glance at Sean, who was sitting in the passenger seat, leaning against the passenger side door with his eyes closed. Clutched in his hand was his cell phone.

"Feel like talking, or are you planning on dozing off?" asked Chris, trying to divert Sean's attention from his misery.

"I'm OK," said Sean, swiveling back towards Chris. "At least I know Maggie's not dead. But I'll feel a whole lot better once I can talk to her."

"I'm sure they'll call back shortly," said Chris, speaking as softly and reassuringly as possible. "They'll take her to a doctor to have her checked out, and then probably bring her right back to her house."

"I wish this Jeep had the optional warp-speed motor installed," said Sean, with some degree of his sense of humor returning.

"I can't help you with that, but I do have the next best thing," replied Chris. "Do me a favor and open the glove compartment. Hand me the small black leather case on the left side."

"Ah, I know what that is," said Sean, his eyes brightening. "I see that you are intending to break the law a bit yourself this afternoon."

"Just a bit," said Chris, as he removed the radar detector from its pouch and plugged it into the cigarette lighter. He placed the detector in a mount on the dashboard and switched it on. Once that was done, and they had cleared the city limits, Chris depressed the accelerator and the SUV surged forward, its powerful engine taking them to speeds far in excess of the posted limit.

"Wow," exclaimed Sean, leaning over and peeking at the speedometer, which was topping eighty miles per hour. "I guess this trip will take less time than advertised."

"Unless this thing fails to detect a radar trap somewhere along the way," noted Chris. "In which case, you may have to finish the driving, because I'll probably be 'sans' license."

"I wonder what Grainger found inside my house," said Sean, his mind still on the break-in. "You know, not only did I have copies of all the documents I'd made from my first visit to the Frank Stewart Room, but I also had a set of the copies you'd brought back from the Adirondack Museum."

"Ugh, I hadn't thought about that," said Chris. "The stuff from the Stewart Collection wouldn't have mattered, because he stole most of those originals when he was down at Rowan himself. But the documents from Blue Mountain Lake, that's an entirely different proposition. If he found those papers, that means he'll know the same things we do about Adirondac. At least, he'll know what we knew prior to our trip this past week."

"He's really getting me angry," said Sean. "I'd like nothing more than to give that guy an express pass into the state penitentiary."

"He'll get there," said Chris. "But we've just got to be careful how we go about doing it, because remember, we broke the law ourselves by tampering with his car. I'm not quite sure what law that was, but I know it's not OK to attach monitoring devices to other people's vehicles unless it's ordered as part of a law-enforcement investigation, and we certainly don't qualify in that category."

The two friends talked back and forth for most of the next hour, before Sean's phone loudly buzzed against the palm of his hand. He had been holding it so tightly that his fingers cramped as he tried to press the "Talk" button. The display screen was indicating a 315 area code phone number from his home county, although his phone didn't match the number to anyone in his programmed list of contacts.

"Hello," Sean blurted into the phone. Chris could hear a female voice coming through the ear speaker of Sean's phone, causing Sean's hand to tremble as he listened.

"MAGGIE, honey, thank God you're all right," he cheered into the phone, unable to contain his relief. Then he listened for about two minutes, hearing about the incident first-hand.

Turning toward Chris, he relayed some of her comments. "They're taking her to Saint Elizabeth's hospital in Utica to have her checked out. It sounds like she got banged up pretty good. She said they're going to do some x-rays and other tests."

Sean then turned his attention back to Maggie. "Honey, how did this happen? Were you already inside the house when he came in?" Once again, Chris couldn't hear the answer, but watched as Sean listened attentively to the voice on the phone.

About that time, Chris noticed that they were about to drive past a rest stop off an exit on Route 81, just south of Scranton. "Hey," he said. "You go ahead and talk to Maggie. I need to go inside and use the rest room. I'll be back in a few minutes." Sean nodded.

Chris climbed out of the Jeep, cell phone in hand, and moved around to the back of the vehicle. He opened up the rear door and removed a single paper. It contained Grainger's photo, email address, and cell phone number. With the paper in hand, he strode purposefully toward the rest stop, rehearsing his speech, right down to the tone of voice. It would go something like this:

"Good afternoon, Ben. No, this isn't Sean, but don't worry about who I am. I just want you to listen for a minute, OK? I want to tell you that you made a very bad decision today. You broke into a house, and you hurt someone very dear to me. And in case you didn't realize it, the police are on your trail right now. As a matter of fact, if I was in your shoes, I wouldn't go anywhere near Curryton Road, because there's a police officer sitting outside your house just waiting to slap a pair of cuffs on your wrists."

Chris wasn't sure where it would go after that, but he could feel the blood coursing through his veins as he walked inside, determined to find a pay phone with a number that couldn't be traced to his name. Chris stepped over to the bank of phones located in the front of the facility. His hand was paused at the top of the phone, when for some reason, he pulled it back.

"Calm down, count to one hundred," he told himself. "Maybe it would be better if Grainger didn't realize that he, himself, was being stalked. Play the role of the silent hunter."

Chris walked away from the phone bank and instead used the men's room, as he had originally indicated. Then he strolled, at a more leisurely pace, back to the car.

Revenge would come, but at the right time.

Three hours later, Chris pulled his Jeep into the small housing complex on the south side of Little Falls where Maggie rented her one-bedroom apartment. The vehicle had barely come to a stop when the passenger side door burst open. Sean's form flew from the interior like a bull crashing into the ring in search of the matador. Chris had a hard time trying to keep up with his friend, who was inside the door of Maggie's building in an instant.

Sean knocked rapidly on the door of the first-floor apartment, which was opened shortly by Maggie's mother. "Hello, Sean," she said through a rather strained smile. "You made it back quickly, based on where you started this morning."

"Hi, Jean," replied Sean, trying to see past the woman to get a glimpse of his girlfriend. "Yes, you can credit Chris for the rapid transit from Philly to here. He put wings on the car for most of the trip home. Is Maggie still awake?"

"Yes, she is, and doing OK," said Jean, motioning for the two of them to enter the apartment. "But she's not a pretty sight right now, and the doctor wants her to take it easy for a few days."

"I understand," said Sean, making his way into the living room.

Maggie was sitting on a couch, half reclined into the corner cushion when Sean came into view. Her face was swollen, and both sides were bruised and deeply discolored. She didn't really have a traditional black eye, although both her eyes appeared to be connected to vertical stripes of bruised tissue that extended over her cheek bones and down the sides of her face. She didn't get up from the couch, but simply waved a lazy hand in the air and murmured a quiet "hello."

"Oh my God," cried Sean, for the umpteenth time that day, as he rushed towards her. He was only halted by her hand, which was raised in a "stop" motion.

"Whoa," she said, signaling for him to slow down. "Come sit with me, but no touching, OK? My entire head feels like it's been stuck in a giant vise for hours. It hurts like hell, and I've got a ringing in my ear that won't go away."

Sean sat next to her and gently took her hand. "Did you get a look at whoever did this to you?" asked Sean, although he already knew the answer to his own question.

"No, I never saw him. Or her, depending on who it was," Maggie conceded. "The last thing I remember, I was heading into your bedroom, and I had just looked inside. After that, it was lights out."

"So whomever it was, was hiding inside my bedroom," said Sean.

"That's what the police said," answered Maggie, still sounding somewhat foggy. "They said that the burglar seemed to be looking for something specific inside your house, something other than money, given the cash that was untouched."

"Yes, that's my guess, too," agreed Sean. "What did the folks at the hospital say about your injuries?"

"Oh, I've got a moderate-grade concussion from being hit in the head by the door, which they said was further compounded by another collision with something else, most likely your doorframe," recited Maggie. "But they also said that it's a good thing you've got nice thick carpeting in your hallway and bedroom, or I might have sustained a greater injury when I hit the floor."

At that moment, Jean came back into the room and handed Maggie a fresh ice bag.

"Thanks, Mom," Maggie said, accepting the cold pack from her mother.

"She was actually quiet lucky, you know," said Jean. "The doctor said that she apparently was struck in two of the thicker parts of the skull, and that she could have sustained a fracture under other circumstances."

"See? You always said I was a bit thick-skulled," said Maggie, trying to cheer up Sean with a little humor. She knew that he felt responsible since it occurred inside his house.

"I've never said anything of the sort, and you know it," said Sean, taking a tighter grip on Maggie's hand. "That's why you're going to end up with a 4.0 grade point average when you start your degree next year. So I don't want to hear any of that talk, OK?"

After a few more minutes of small talk, it became obvious that Maggie was tired and needed some sleep. "The doctor said to expect that as another symptom of the concussion," said her mom.

Sean kissed Maggie ever so lightly on her cheek and promised to return later. He then left the room with Jean, who told him that she was planning on staying with Maggie for the next few days, until she felt better and was cleared by the doctor to return to work.

"I'll gladly take that duty for you, Jean," volunteered Sean. "Or maybe you can stay with her in the mornings, and I'll take the afternoons. Whatever it takes."

"OK, dear, we'll work it out next time we talk. But I'll be here until then," promised Jean.

Sean and Chris walked out of the building and drove back to Sean's house by the golf course. The police had nailed a plastic cover and some boards across the shattered back window, and some crime scene tape remained on the outside of the place. Besides that, it was quiet and deserted.

"I see someone from the golf course has been by and picked up the drink cart," said Chris, noticing its absence from the spot beside the patio.

"Yeah, the trooper asked me about that earlier today. I guess the course manager himself came over to see what was going on."

"You still seem pretty down," said Chris, observing his friend's demeanor.

"I know; I am," admitted Sean. "I'm just plain ticked off at myself for not having that alarm system installed before we left for Philly," said Sean.

"You couldn't have known," said Chris. "Grainger appears to be a hardened criminal who won't hesitate to use violent force when needed, even against a woman half his weight."

"From everything we've learned about him, I should have known that he'd never be nominated for a citizenship award," said Sean, still kicking himself for his oversight.

"So what comes next?" asked Chris, unsure of how to proceed with his friend. "We've got a lot of great leads to follow up in Adirondac, but I'm sure you'd like to stay local for a few days and see Maggie through her recovery."

Sean looked back up at his friend with a sad expression for a few moments before answering. "Chris, I'm sorry, but I'm going to take a little time off this adventure. It may be a few days, or it may be a week. It might even be longer. I just don't know right now, because I don't want to rush Maggie at all. I want to spend at least part of every day with her until she's back on her feet and completely better."

Chris looked at Sean with renewed respect, realizing once again that his friend was blessed with a generous and caring personality and a heart the size of Texas. However, there was one favor that he did still need from Sean, and even though he knew that now was not the best time to ask, he decided to go for it anyway.

"Before I leave for home, I'd like to know one thing," Chris began.

"Sure, what's that?"

"Would it be all right if I called you once during the coming week, just to take advantage of your GPS application?"

"Sure," said Sean. "I'd be happy to help." Then, after considering the matter again, his face broke out in a grin. "Am I permitted to ask you why? Or is this something that I don't want to know about?"

Chris just smiled back and winked as he shook his friend's hand. "I'll be in touch. You take good care of that lady of yours, OK?" Then, he was gone.

CHAPTER 15

Friday, August 29, 2015

Chris focused entirely on business the following day, getting caught up and working with a few of his local clients. His only concession to the ongoing search was to call Debbie Santori at the Adirondack Museum to follow up on the poster about Grainger. She said that she had already made copies of the document and posted them by the front security desk. Chris was pleased that she didn't inquire about the silver dollar he borrowed from the museum a few weeks earlier, but simply thanked him for the warning about the possible thief. He wasn't the most enthusiastic fibber in history, and he hadn't relished the thought of making up a story or tap dancing around the truth.

As the weekend approached, Chris categorized the various items on his list of things to do. He had a date with Kristi on Saturday night, so he'd have to leave for Ithaca by sometime mid-to-late afternoon. He also wanted to change the oil in his Jeep and clean out his garage in preparation for the upcoming winter. But even with those tasks in front of him, he still had part of Saturday and all of Sunday free.

While doing his chores, Chris found himself thinking about their case, and also about Sean and Maggie. He wanted to know how she was doing as she progressed through the weekend, yet he didn't want to bother them by constantly calling for updates. Thankfully, Sean seemed to realize his concern for her plight, and he called at least once a day with reports of her recovery. It appeared as though she had come through the ordeal with little or no lasting problems, and by Saturday evening, most of the pain had dissipated, along with much of the swelling and the ringing in her ears. "It would take a lot more than a door frame to wipe me out for long," she told Chris when Sean handed her the phone.

Before hanging up, Sean also informed Chris of the police department's findings from the break-in. They hadn't come up with much in the way of physical evidence, although there was a small bit of blood on the back widow frame where one of the panes had been shattered during the break-in. The blood appeared to be fresh, and the sheriff was able to collect enough to serve as evidence, if needed. The police were also able to lift quite a few fingerprints from inside the house, especially around those areas that had been disturbed, such as the files and desk. After eliminating Sean's prints, they had determined that the prints belonged to another individual, although they would have to wait to obtain samples from Maggie and Chris to ensure that they hadn't accidently handled the same items. It was good news, because if Ben Grainger was ever captured, this evidence could establish his link to the break-in. Chris thanked Sean for the update, feeling happy that they had at least one solid piece of evidence to use against their adversary.

As Chris drove down to Ithaca to meet Kristi on Saturday, he found that he was extremely preoccupied with an idea. It wasn't a particularly new thought; he had been considering it ever since foregoing the phone call to Grainger's cell phone immediately after the break-in. Still, the temptation to go forward with it was growing in his mind, like a freshly-germinated seed sending out its first leaves, until it blocked out most of his other thoughts.

Kristi noticed that Chris' mind was elsewhere while they were together that evening. They had been sharing a wonderful meal at the Moosewood, a vegetarian restaurant on North Cayuga Street in downtown Ithaca. Normally, Kristi had a hard time talking her boyfriend into a vegetarian meal of any kind. However, tonight, he seemed to be on autopilot, and agreed with everything she said. Although pleased that he had consented to the idea of dining without meat, she found his lack of comment on the subject to be most disconcerting.

"Hello," she waved across the table at her steady date. "Is anyone in there? This is a communications check from Lunar Rover 2."

"I'm sorry, love," replied Chris, embarrassed by his lack of attentiveness to his partner. "With everything that's going on with Maggie, and Sean feeling down the way he is, I'm afraid I'm just not myself tonight. My mind keeps going back to the trip to Philadelphia, and the thought that I'm partially to blame for Maggie ending up in the emergency room."

"You?" said Kristi, incredulous at the idea. "It was never your idea to go down there in the first place. This has all been Sean's brainchild from the beginning; you've just been a coerced accomplice. So please don't go down that path; it's faulty logic, and you'll beat yourself up forever."

"Yeah, maybe," said Chris. "Then again, I'm also having a hard time sitting around doing nothing after the guy just attacked a 105-pound girl."

Kristi looked across the table at Chris as she lifted a spoonful of potato and corn chowder to her lips. "You're not thinking of doing anything stupid, are you?" she asked.

"Stupid, no," he replied, his eyes averting hers. "Don't worry, honey, I won't get myself into trouble. But I would like to make sure that Grainger ends up in the hands of the law, even if I have to find the evidence myself."

"OK, but I've seen that look in your eyes before, and I know what it means," said Kristi, placing her hand on top of his. "Just call me when you're back from wherever it is that you're going to do whatever it is that you're doing, OK? I just want to know that you're safe and in one piece."

"I promise," said Chris, suddenly flashing his old smile back at Kristi. "And please don't worry about me. I'll be careful; you won't get rid of me that easily."

"Just see that I don't," said Kristi.

After dropping Kristi off at her place near the Cornell campus in Ithaca, Chris returned home and immediately logged on to his email account. He was extremely pleased to see that Sean was also logged on. Without delay, he tapped out a message.

chriscarey1986: Hey – are you there tonight?

Sean-Riggins-IT: You bet. I just got home from Maggie's place. What's up?

chriscarey1986: Do you remember I asked you for a favor about the GPS thing?

Sean-Riggins-IT: Of course.

chriscarey1986: Well, I might need that favor tomorrow. What time will you be home and able to access your laptop?

Sean-Riggins-IT: I'm at Maggie's from noon until 6 PM, but free after that.

chriscarey1986: What do you say that I call you sometime after dinner, around 7:45 PM, for a position on Grainger's car?

Sean-Riggins-IT: If you need it sooner, I can bring my laptop to Maggie's and give you the info from there.

chriscarey1986: No, it's OK. 7:45 PM is fine. Until then, your job is to take care of Maggie with your undivided attention.

Sean-Riggins-IT: OK then, 7:45 PM it is. Anything else I can do for you?

chriscarey1986: All I'll need when I call is the exact location of Grainger's car. I guess it would also be nice if you could spend about an hour online with me, monitoring where he is and how far his car is from home.

Sean-Riggins-IT: Sure, you got it. What do you have in mind?

chriscarey1986: Nothing. I just want to know where he is.

Sean-Riggins-IT: You don't fool me for a minute. Where will you be?

chriscarey1986: I forget.

Sean-Riggins-IT: OK, now I'm REALLY curious, although I'm about 98% sure of your evil intentions. I love it! Just make

sure you avoid the radar traps on Route 81 South, and give me
a call when you're ready to move in. I'll be standing by.
chriscarey1986: Thanks, buddy. I'm signing off now. Catch
you on the back side somewhere.

Chris smiled to himself as he logged off. Even though he never divulged
his actual intent, Sean was able to see through his thinly veiled request. It
was usually that way between the two friends, who had operated together
as a team since their first grade gym class. If one of them needed an assist,
the other was always there to step up, without thought of ego or sacrifice.
Chris knew that tomorrow would be no different. No matter what, Sean
would be standing by to serve as his silent partner in the mission.

Before the clock struck nine, Chris turned out the light and climbed
into bed. Tomorrow would be a busy day.

The next day started just like most in the small A-frame up on the hill. The
lights were on by five thirty, and Chris' running shoes were pounding the
pavement within thirty minutes. Most of the town was still asleep,
although Chris' mind and body were both hard at work. Running always
gave him a chance to think about things—his new career, his friends, his
family. Today was no exception, although it was different in that all his
attention was channeled in a single direction. It was as though he was
clearing his head for a mission with a very specific target, and he needed
the time to mentally rehearse the act.

After his run, Chris showered, then turned on his computer to check for
messages. One piece of unopened email was the one sent by Dr. Tomlinson
to Sean, on which Chris had been copied. He opened that email now, and
read the exact same text he'd seen on Sean's machine the previous
Monday. However, neither he nor Sean had bothered downloading or
opening the attachment, which Chris did now. It showed line after line of
meaningless characters, spewed out across six pages of matrices. The doctor had said that the computer had been unable to process anything from

the initial attempts, and this was the proof. Chris took the gibberish-laden papers and laid them on top of his recycle pile.

Next, he opened up an online mapping application and plugged in an address: 148 Curryton Road, Binghamton, New York. The screen instantly displayed a map with a series of parallel roads leading off of Route 11, or Front Street, on the north side of the city. Chris zoomed in on the site, first using the mapping tool, then switching over to the satellite view that permitted him to see actual houses. Increasing the magnification, he could generate a birds-eye view of the place, including the driveway that led up to the separate garage in the back yard.

Chris was happy to see that the house had a lot of first-floor windows, although it was very close to the dwelling on either side. Since the houses on the street were all much longer than they were wide, it made the driveways appear like narrow alleys between the buildings. The entire neighborhood had a rather run-down look to it, and a few of the houses even appeared to be abandoned. Many of the other homes were surrounded by a number of cars, which led Chris to guess that they had been subdivided into multiple apartments. Chris zoomed in and out several times, studying the routes in and around the structure, as well as the various roads leading away from the place. When he was satisfied that he had committed the scene to memory, he closed the mapping application and shut off the computer. He had what he needed, and he didn't plan on logging back on that afternoon.

Meanwhile, Sean was sitting at the kitchen table in his house, installing a new sound card into an old laptop, when his phone rang. He looked at the clock over the kitchen sink, which read seven forty-eight. Right on time, he thought to himself as he looked at the display and confirmed it was Chris.

"Hey, bud, what's up?" he said, holding the phone with his shoulder and chin while still fitting the card into the machine.

"Not much," said Chris, sounding nonchalant. "Just thought I'd call and find out how our mutual redheaded friend is doing tonight?"

"Well as long as you're asking, let me go over to my desk and check," replied Sean. He had already launched the GPS application in anticipation of his friend's call, so he was able to provide an answer almost immediately. "Oh, splendid," said Sean as he viewed the map online.

"What's wrong?" asked Chris.

"Don't worry, he's nowhere near you," replied Sean. "But he is on the road, heading south on Route 28 just below Raquette Lake."

"Hmm, that could mean he's been at any one of several places," said Chris, "Adirondac or Blue Mountain Lake being the two most likely."

"I'd go along with that," said Sean.

"Anyway, he's a long ways away from his home, and that's about all that matters to me," sighed Chris.

"Where are you right now?" asked Sean.

"In my Jeep," replied Chris, keeping it simple.

"OK, you don't have to tell me," said Sean. "I guess what I don't know can't get you in trouble, right?"

Chris ignored the question. "That's great news about his location. That means that unless he's in an Indy car doing two hundred miles per hour, he won't be home for close to four hours, assuming that he is bound for Binghamton. Can you confirm that?"

On the other end of the line, Chris could hear his friend quickly tapping keys to obtain the data requested by his friend. Sean was back on the line within fifteen seconds.

"Well, according to the mapping feature that gives driving directions, it's only about 163 miles, which he should be able to cover in about three and a half hours," said Sean. "But the good news is, he's currently doing 42 miles per hour in a 45 zone, so he doesn't appear to be in a hurry. Apparently, he observes the posted speed limit most of the time."

"Yeah, he's a real good sport, when he isn't stealing stuff or breaking people's heads open," replied Chris. "Anyway, if he's that far away, you can forget about my request that you stick around. I shouldn't need you for the rest of the night, OK?"

"Don't be crazy, man," said Sean. "I'm not going anywhere tonight anyway. I'll have my laptop on and my cell phone turned up the entire evening. Call me anytime you want, OK? And no matter what happens, call me when you're done and on the road home. I want to know that you're safe."

"Now you sound like Kristi," chuckled Chris, thinking of the previous evening.

"I'm serious, *call me*," urged Sean. "I'm signing off now, but I want to hear from you when you're headed home."

"It's a deal," agreed Chris. "Talk to you later." He hung up without waiting for a response. Before long, he was rolling off the Route 81 exit ramp down to Front Street. The remainder of the drive down the local thoroughfare took less than five minutes, and Chris was soon parking his car on the gravelly edge of Curryton Road. He intentionally parked down about three houses, to avoid raising suspicions if a neighbor noticed something out of place at Grainger's house. He walked towards the faded blue multiple-family dwelling at a normal pace, comforted by the fact that this didn't look like the kind of area that maintained a neighborhood watch group.

At 148 Curryton, he turned left and walked unconcernedly up the driveway and towards the dilapidated white garage in the back yard. So far everything was looking good. The house to the right of 148 was dark, with no one apparently home. In 148, there were two rooms that were lit, but both were on the left side of the second floor of the house. According to the numbering on the front door, the lights appeared to belong to apartment 2.

Chris' next discovery was rather unnerving. As he passed by the front of the house, he could see that there was only one other door, which was labeled as apartment 1. There was no number 3, which was the apartment listed on Grainger's driver's license. Could the investigator from the Chris' father's law firm who looked into this have gotten it wrong? Chris proceeded down the right side of the building, remaining in the shadows as much as possible. He noticed that there was a door about halfway down the side of the house, but it appeared to provide access to some sort of storage room rather than serve as an entryway to the main dwelling.

After rounding the rear corner of the house, Chris was surprised to see a porch that extended halfway across the back of the building, with a table and a few lawn chairs scattered about. The table was a messy collage of papers, beer cans, and other assorted bits of rubbish. A large glass ashtray served as a paperweight, holding down a number of the loose bits of paper. The receptacle was filled with at least fifty cigarette butts, which overflowed onto the surface of the table itself. On the door, which was located on the left side of the porch, was a wooden placard with the number 3 affixed below a large glass pane.

Before stepping up onto the porch, Chris looked about the area and took stock of the conditions. The last traces of daylight were ebbing from the sky, and very little of the lighting from the street was visible in the back yard. The back of the house was completely dark, and no one was in sight as far as his eyes could see. A dog was barking from another yard, but that lot was completely obscured from view by trees and shrubs. Chris had never been in this situation before, but he couldn't have imagined better circumstances for his intentions.

Dressed in a dark, long-sleeve shirt and dark jeans, Chris faded into the darkness without a problem. The only things he carried on his body were a small flashlight and a compact, high-resolution digital camera. He also had the foresight to slip a pair of thin rubber gloves into his pocket, so as to avoid leaving behind any telltale fingerprints. His intentions were not to take anything from the residence but rather to gather "intelligence," and also to try to locate the missing documents Grainger had stolen the previous week. However, even without taking a thing, Chris was under no illusions about his own activity. If he slipped up in any way and was caught, he would suddenly find the tables turned, and he would be the one facing criminal charges.

Before trying to find the best way to enter the apartment, Chris pulled on the rubber gloves until they fit like a second skin. Next, he took the obvious course of action and rang the doorbell next to the window. He

wanted to announce his presence, in case there was another person, or perhaps a dog, inside the house. When he received no feedback from the doorbell, he tried knocking on the windowpane, which achieved a similar result.

Satisfied that there was no one home, Chris attempted the easiest route
into the house, which was to turn the doorknob on the main entry. It was
locked, as he suspected, so he left the porch and headed further across the
back of the house, where a door with a window led into a short hallway
with several other doorways leading off it. The outer door was unlocked,
and Chris silently swung it open and went inside. The inside doors were
also numbered, with one door for each of the apartments, and a fourth
door for a common laundry room.

Chris reached for the doorknob on the door of apartment 3 and found
that to be locked as well. He desperately wanted to gain entry to
Grainger's place without breaking anything, as he strongly desired to
make his visit a covert affair, leaving behind no signs of his presence.
Rather than risk trying a side window, where he might be observed by a
passerby on the street, Chris decided to return to the porch, where a pair
of windows looked into the rear-facing kitchen. The first window was
right next to the door, and it offered a view up the hallway into the front
part of the house. He placed both hands under the upper lip of the bottom
window frame and pushed up with considerable force, only to feel the
inside lock hold the frame securely in place.

Next, Chris moved over to the other porch window, which was in back
of the table with the lawn chairs. Hoping that this window wasn't painted
shut, he repeated the procedure, pushing upward in a pressing motion as
he willed the window to move ever so little. His heart gave a leap as the
entire panel of six windows lifted about four inches. He used the gap to
place his hands underneath the frame and pull from the bottom. The window slid slowly and grudgingly upward, creaky from years of disuse.

Chris poked his head and upper body inside and noticed with some
degree of amusement that the window was situated directly above the
kitchen sink. He would literally have to crawl in through the window and

straddle the sink, then find some way to swivel his feet around onto the ground without breaking any of the dishes or glasses that were scattered about the counter. As he completed the acrobatic feat, he thanked himself for the long hours of exercises he performed to enhance his flexibility.

Once inside the house, Chris decided that his next step should be to make sure that all the window shades were pulled down before he used his flashlight. There was enough light coming through the windows that he could navigate around the place and pull down the old-style rollup shades without using his own light, which might have given him away from the outside of the house. Now that the shades were drawn, Chris took out his flashlight and camera, and began to look around the place. It wasn't too big, and thankfully Grainger wasn't as messy as his back porch indicated. Chris was grateful for this fact, because he wanted to be in and out of there in less than thirty minutes.

Starting in the front living room, Chris systematically worked his way around the room in a counter-clockwise pattern, looking on top of every piece of furniture, then working his way through any drawers or other internal compartments. There was a tall bookcase against the left side of the front door entryway which was filled with old books on various topics. However, he found nothing of interest in any of the volumes, and he moved to the back of the room, where there was a low, narrow table with more papers and maps.

Chris was surprised to see that Grainger had printed a stack of articles about the original mint building, which had been torn down in 1913 by Frank Stewart himself to build the headquarters for his electrical supply business. This didn't make much sense to Chris, as the site had been built over in a very big way. It was now home to the W.J. Green Federal Building, a massive ten-story glass-and-concrete structure that filled an entire city block. If Grainger had hoped to find anything at the original site, he was sadly mistaken.

Before continuing around the rest of the living room, Chris stuck his head into the bedroom and looked around for a moment. He didn't need any additional time in there, as Grainger apparently used the room only for sleeping. The floor was completely covered with dirty and crumpled clothing, and a few pieces of unopened mail. Chris was grimly amused to see that the only reading material on the nightstand was a *Soldier of Fortune* magazine, which seemed fitting for Grainger's character.

Returning to the living room, the next location of interest was a table on the right side of the room. It had been placed right next to an old and battered desk, giving it the look of a single, continuous work surface. It was a jumble of paper, reprints, and other documents. Chris' eyes lit up when he saw a couple of very old-looking papers sitting alone at the top of a metal bin. He lifted them gently and instantly recognized them as the stolen documents from the Frank Stewart Room. One was the missing ledger, page 154 from the treasury mint record. Another was the full-page cipher code, handwritten by Patterson over 160 years ago. Chris took pictures of both these documents, showing their location in context within Grainger's apartment. Then, he replaced then in the bin where he found them and moved on.

Next up was the desk itself, which had several stacks of papers that were loosely organized into about three or four piles, but covered with other documents that had been scattered over the top. The source of one of the piles was immediately obvious—it was a stack of copies stolen from Sean's house. Chris felt his throat tighten in anger as he noticed the margins of the pages filled with notes that he himself had recorded at the Adirondack Museum. Once again, he photographed the pages as they lay on Grainger's desk. It made him sick to his stomach to leave all these behind, especially the stolen historical papers. However, he kept reminding himself over and over, as he had the day of the break-in, that revenge would come at the appropriate time.

Sifting quickly through the remainder of the papers on the desk, Chris found very little else of interest, although he did find an entire stack of copies pertaining to the Erie Canal and an old rumor about the 1804 silver dollars being lost en route to a bank in the western part of New York State.

He ignored these and went back into scan mode, looking for anything else that might be of interest. He had almost completed his examination of the desk when his eyes settled upon a small cubbyhole on the top right side, where a single volume, about half an inch thick, lay by itself. He lifted the volume out of its resting place, noticing the very old, tan paper cover, which was completely devoid of title or inscription. About a half dozen slips of paper were inserted as bookmarks into the volume, apparently by Grainger himself.

Chris opened the book and immediately noticed that it was a handwritten journal, of sorts, with several different examples of penmanship scrawled throughout. Each entry in the book was preceded by a date and a time, followed by an accounting of an event. Chris caught his breath as he looked at the first entry in the journal, which was dated January 1, 1804. Reading the entry, which described the details of the shift work inside the coin press room of the U.S. Mint building, Chris felt transported back to that day and age, when the workers were actually operating the screw press and cutting the coins one by one.

Breaking out his camera, Chris found that his hands were trembling slightly as pressed the power button and fumbled with the settings to accommodate the low light in the apartment. He was about to start photographing the pages individually, but curiosity got the best of him. He turned the pages, advancing chronologically, until he found the entries listed under March 26, 1804. His search was quickly rewarded, as the third entry under that date showed the following words:

Monday, March 26, 1804: Last of 1803 dies is damaged beyond repair. Replacing with new cut die to complete production. Count 16,950. – Hiram Perry, Supervisor

Chris exhaled, not realizing that he had been holding his breath. So that was it: on March 26, 1804, the last of the 1803 dies had indeed cracked, and it was replaced by the only possible substitution, which was an 1804 version. Coin number 16,951 through the final specimen, which was 19,570, must have been stamped with the 1804 date. Chris allowed himself the luxury of closing his eyes for a few seconds to do the math. The figure he arrived at was 2,620 coins, all of which should have been 1804. The possibilities were mind-boggling.

After shaking himself back to reality, Chris began snapping a series of rapid-fire photographs of the historic record, starting on page one and working his way through the book. The entire volume was only about seventy-five pages, and Chris was able to open the book flat on the table and shoot two pages with each photo. After checking a sample snapshot on his view screen to ensure that he'd be able to read the text on his computer, he proceeded to photograph the entire book, including the notes written inside the back cover by the head foreman himself. Chris noticed the name, Nathaniel Grainger, as the person in charge of the work detail.

At the back of the book, Chris found two pieces of new copy paper, on which Grainger had jotted a series of notes and observations. Chris didn't have time to read through these, but he did take a moment to photograph them for later perusal. As he did so, he noticed something extremely familiar about the handwriting. However, not being able to recall anything specific, he simply finished the snapshots, and then reinserted the papers into the same place in the volume, which he replaced into the cubby hole on top of the desk.

Feeling immensely pleased that he had been able to capture the entire ledger book on his camera, Chris examined the contents of a few more shelves and drawers, finding nothing that related to the silver dollars. Likewise, he opened the door to a closet off the small interior space that served as a dining room, intent on quickly searching the contents. While he found no papers, he did discover something of interest. The entire right side of the closet was lined with a wall of boxes, each containing expensive new electronic components, including computer hard drives, sound cards, other computer peripherals. Other unopened boxes contained dozens of GPS devices, DVD viewing systems, and music storage devices. Some of the larger cases had labels on the sides that were addressed to Steele Corp Electronics, Philadelphia, PA.

Chris looked at the collective stash of electronics and quickly estimated that the combined value of the loot must have been over ten thousand dollars. He quickly photographed the pile, making certain to get ample shots of the items that were almost certainly stolen from his previous employer. Chris knew that this contraband had nothing to do with their current case. However, the rage that burned within him filled his very soul with a steely resolve. He pledged to himself that once they discovered the final resting place of the coins, the trap would spring shut on Grainger, and he would rot in a jail cell for many years.

After a final look around the place to satisfy himself that he had not missed anything, Chris prepared to make his getaway. He glanced quickly at his watch—he had been in the apartment for exactly twenty-eight minutes. Not bad, thought Chris, and right on schedule. With all the lights out, he visited each window in the apartment and raised the shades to their original positions. All papers and books were stacked as Chris had found them, and the place looked the same as when he had entered. Finally, he double-checked to ensure that he still had his camera and flashlight. The mission was complete, and now all he had to do was to get back to his car unnoticed.

Chris exited the living room and walked quietly back through the hallway to the kitchen. As he emerged into the back entrance of the apartment, his first thought was to make sure that the window over the sink was completely closed. However, something caught his attention, and he stopped to investigate. On the right was a set of old metal shelves, which held a collection of containers, jars, and paper cups. Among the items were a jar of instant coffee, a small box of tea bags, and, most curious of all, a crushed and thoroughly mutilated pomegranate. Several of the paper cups appeared to contain prepared portions of the coffee or tea, and an old glass jar held what looked like the remnants of the blood-red pomegranate juice. Finally, a mayonnaise jar held a dark fluid, which Chris surmised was a mixture of all the other ingredients. A small paint brush, about one inch wide, was resting in the jar, its bristles submerged in the brownish-red concoction. The top shelf of the rack held a flat package that looked like a very small box of printer paper, but when Chris picked it up, he noticed that it was actually parchment paper, which must have been left over from the old days of manual typewriters.

Chris looked at the jar, with the brush protruding from the upper rim, for about a minute, lost in thought. He knew that he had to get out of there, and that every minute spent inside Grainger's apartment increased the chance of being discovered by some unknown set of prying eyes. However, his mind was in overdrive, recalling an article he'd seen in a magazine a few years ago. Suddenly, a smile broke out on his face, which quickly widened until it creased his face from one side to the other.

"Gotcha," Chris said softly.

Then, he checked the window one last time, and exited through the back door.

Once outside the house, Chris made sure the back door was locked, and then peeked around the corner of the house toward the street. The neighbor next door was still out, so the driveway was almost entirely dark. However, Chris observed a woman walking a small dog out on the street. He ducked back behind the house, remaining in the shadows for another few minutes until he was sure she had gone. Then, he walked calmly back out to the sidewalk and across the street, returning to his Jeep without incident.

Chris had a difficult time restraining his joy as he reached the end of Curryton Road and turned onto Front Street. The past few hours had netted him some important clues about the background of the 1804 dollars, while also yielding a pile of condemning evidence about their adversary. The combination of the new breakthroughs, coupled with the adrenaline released from his successful covert mission, pushed his system into overdrive, and he found himself singing along with the music on the radio.

A creature of habit, Chris stopped at a coffee shop before getting back onto the expressway. On his way into the shop, he rolled up the rubber gloves that he'd worn in Grainger's apartment and threw them into a trash bin outside the store. With some alarm, he discovered that he operated rather well in "criminal mode," although he quickly justified his activity of the night as part of the payback owed to the man who had put Maggie in the hospital.

Once he steered his Jeep back onto Route 81 North, bound for Syracuse, he called Kristi to let her know that he was fine and on his way home. Then he called Sean to pass along an enhanced version of the same message. The speed dial function on his phone quickly rang Sean's cell phone, and his friend answered on the first ring.

"Hey, where are you?" Sean asked, anxious for information.

"It's OK. I'm on Route 81, homeward bound," said Chris. "And I've got one heckuva story to tell you."

"I can hardly wait," said Sean, anticipating the news from Chris' evening. "Lay it on me."

"I'd love to," said Chris, "but let's wait until we can get together again, OK? Suffice it to say that I found the record book that the investigator told me about from the national archives in Philadelphia. It turns out that Grainger's ancestor was really the head supervisor in the mint building where the coins were pressed, and somehow Ben Grainger obtained ownership of the record book with all the daily notes. There's a ton of good stuff in there, which I'll share with you as soon as we can get together."

"Anything else you'd care to pass along before we bid farewell for the night?" asked Sean.

"Yes, we've been duped," said Chris in a subdued tone. "But at least we didn't let that stop us."

"What are you talking about?" asked Sean.

"Do you remember the letter we found in the Frank Stewart Room on Tuesday? The one that told us that all the 1804 dollars had been melted into bullion?"

"Of course," replied Sean. "Why?"

"It's a fake," disclosed Chris. "A complete, five-and-dime store phony. We knew something was fishy there, but I should have seen through the ruse right up front."

"Would you care to explain?" asked Sean, obviously intrigued with Chris' findings.

"Not right now, if that's OK with you," said Chris. "Let's plan on getting together sometime in the middle of this week to compare notes and plan our next moves. Maybe we could even invite the girls to join us."

"That sounds like fun," said Sean. "But I've got to warn you, Maggie is still a bit leery of coming to my place. She took quite a thumping here this week, and the thought of returning to the scene of the crime still has her creeped out for now."

"Not a problem," replied Chris. "Let's get together at my house, maybe on Wednesday evening. We could either do something easy like pizza, or I could try my hand at cooking something more elaborate."

"I've sampled your cooking before. I think we'll go with the pizza," quipped Sean.

"OK, I'll set it up with Kristi, while you see if Maggie is up to the drive over to Syracuse."

"It's OK," said Sean. "She's feeling a lot better, and she should be back on the job within a few days. I'm sure she'd welcome the diversion right now. Let's put it on the schedule."

"Sounds great," replied Chris. "And I promise you that I won't try to cook, OK?"

"Sounds fair," agreed Sean. "As far as our plans to go to Adirondac, do you have anything in mind?"

"As a matter of fact, I do," said Chris. "But let's save that topic of discussion for Wednesday, OK?"

"You got it," said Sean, preparing to disconnect. "Thanks for the call, and I'll talk to you tomorrow, OK?"

"Sounds like a winner, buddy. Catch you later," said Chris as he hung up on the call.

In the darkness of his Jeep, Chris looked at the illuminated clock on the dashboard. He had an hour of driving ahead of him before reaching home, which he would occupy by listening to tunes and planning out his next moves. He likened his situation to a football game. In relative terms, it was late in the fourth quarter, and his team held a three-point lead. He and Sean needed to find a way to break through for one more first down, which he hoped would seal the victory—as long as the other team had no trick plays up their sleeves, and he could avoid fumbling the ball.

PART III

CRACKING THE CODE

CHAPTER 16

Wednesday, September 3, 2015

Theresa Carey never knew when her son might drop by for an unannounced visit, and today was no exception. She was outside in the back yard of their spacious Utica homestead when she heard someone approaching from behind. She was up on a short stepstool, reaching for a few clusters of apples on one of their several fruit trees, and in no position to turn around for a look.

"Mom, let me get those for you," said Chris, placing his arms up to help his mother off the stool.

"It's OK," said his mother, stepping down while clinging to a mesh bag containing a half dozen apples. "I've done this before, you know, and I've grown accustomed to being rather self-sufficient."

"I know, Mom, but as long as I'm here, I do like to help you whenever I can. I'm entitled to that simple pleasure, aren't I?"

"Of course you are," said Theresa, patting her son on the back of his head. "And now, why don't you afford me the simple pleasure of pouring you a cup of coffee?"

"Sounds great," agreed Chris, following his mother into the house.

They settled into the kitchen, where Theresa placed a pair of ceramic coffee mugs on the table, along with a small package of biscotti.

"So, tell me how your latest adventures with Sean have been going. I haven't heard anything since last week about Maggie. I assume that means she's OK?"

"Yes, Mom, she's fine," said Chris. "But we're going to make the guy who did this to her pay for his crime."

"Isn't that the job of the police?" asked Theresa, looking at her son with concern. "Why don't you just tell them what you know and have them pick this guy up?"

"It isn't as easy as that, Mom," explained Chris. "We know it was him, a guy by the name of Ben Grainger, who broke into Sean's house and knocked Maggie over the head. Actually, that wasn't his intent at all; he was there to steal some papers that Sean and I have been working with. Maggie just walked in and surprised him. Anyway, even though we know it was him, we can't come right out and give our evidence to the police. I know this all sounds rather mysterious, but I'll be able to explain it to you someday."

"Well, according to your father, Grainger's a pretty shady character, and I don't think you should be messing around with criminals like that," said his mother. "You're not trained for that kind of thing, and it's definitely not your job."

"Dad told you about Grainger?" asked Chris, surprised at the disclosure.

"Yes. He's keeping closer tabs on you than you think," said Theresa. "Ever since you asked him to run a background check on that criminal, he's been worried sick that you're getting yourself into deep water."

"I had no idea. Anyway, Mom, I've got to admit that I didn't believe much of Sean's original story about a trove of long-lost invaluable coins that could be worth hundreds of millions of dollars. But without going into detail, I really do think we're getting close to finding something soon, and Grainger is involved for the same reason. Except he operates on the other side of the law."

"We're not talking guns and such, are we?" asked Theresa, looking even more worried.

"No, I don't think so," replied Chris. "But we really don't know too much about him. He's never been arrested that we know of, although he won't have a clean record for long. We've got evidence that could put him in jail for a few years, when we decide to go to the authorities with it."

"I don't like it one bit," said his mother. "But then again, I don't suppose that will change anything, will it?"

"We'll be careful, Mom. We always are," said Chris, leaning over the table and giving his mother a kiss. "I promise."

"So are you in town to see Sean this morning?"

"No, just passing through on business. I hope you don't mind the visit?"

"Of course not, dear," said Theresa, looking at her son affectionately. "I always love seeing you; you know that. I just knew that you were out of town last week and figured maybe you had things to finish up with him."

"I do. He spent most of this past week taking care of Maggie," said Chris. "But the two of them are coming over for dinner tonight, and Kristi's driving up, too."

"Well that's a nice idea," said his mother. "Kristi is such a nice girl. Your father hasn't stopped talking about her since you first introduced her to us. You know, I think he fancies her someday as a daughter-in-law."

"Really?" replied Chris, surprise showing in his face. "We really haven't talked about that, you know. Kristi doesn't have any idea where she'll end up finding work. And most of the companies that hire geologists don't use them in this part of the country, especially if she gets into the oil and petroleum field."

"I know, dear," said Theresa. "She just seems like a very nice girl, and now that you're finished with school, and working..." Theresa let her voice trail off.

Chris laughed and quickly drained the rest of his coffee. "You've got me all married off, don't you?"

"I never went quite *that* far," said his mom.

"That's OK, Mom," said Chris. "I'm just glad you like her. And if we do decide to tie the knot someday, you'll be the first ones we tell."

Chris stayed for a few more minutes to catch up on the local news, and then departed to see another set of clients and pick up some accounting paperwork. He had fallen badly behind in his consulting work, but he felt the inescapable pull of excitement from the search for the coins competing for his attention with every client. It was tough to concentrate, and he wanted nothing more than to get back to the hunt.

By the time he wrapped up his meetings, it was after three o'clock, and time to return to Syracuse. Once on the road, his cell phone sounded, and he answered immediately through his hands-free speaker.

"Is this Chris Carey?" The voice sounded vaguely familiar.

"It is," confirmed Chris. "Who is this, please?"

"Chris, this is Ed Barton, from the American Numismatic Association. We met a couple weeks ago at Wes Hawkins' coin shop near your home in Syracuse."

"Of course, Ed," exclaimed Chris. "Sorry I didn't recognize your voice. How are things going?"

"Very well," replied Ed. "As a matter of fact, the reason for my call is that we have a request to make of you."

"How can I help you?" asked Chris.

"We'd like to place your 1804 silver dollar on display at our upcoming annual conference in November," said Ed. "We'd like to make it the cornerstone of our front-table display, along with the story of its discovery. And please don't worry about security, Mr. Carey. We are used to handling items of its value and rarity."

"Ed, I'm sorry to tell you this, but I can't give you permission to do that. Not yet, anyway," said Chris.

"What's the problem?" asked Ed, sounding disappointed.

"Well, for starters, this coin is part of an investigation that is still underway," explained Chris. He used the word "investigation" to make it sound like a law-enforcement issue. "We may be ready to grant you permission to do this within a month or two, but I can't guarantee that. Also, the final permission would have to come from the Adirondack Museum, because as you remember, the coin actually belongs to them."

"Yes, I know. I was going to call them next to ask for their permission."

"NO! DON'T DO THAT," replied Chris, his voice increasing greatly in volume. "Please don't contact them at all. Not yet. Without going into detail, Ed, they don't yet understand what they have, because I haven't gone back and explained it to them. It could jeopardize the entire rest of the search."

"Rest of the search?" repeated Ed.

"Yes, Ed. Please, just help us to keep this quiet for another couple of weeks. Then, if nothing else happens, by all means we'll work with you to display the new 1804 silver dollar. But until then, the silence is critical."

"OK, you've got my word," said Ed. "Per our original agreement, we haven't told anyone about this yet, so your secret is still intact. But once this is done, I'd love to hear the whole story, if you don't mind. It sounds as though you're working on uncovering history, and I would like to be in on it."

"You will, Ed," promised Chris. "Thanks again, and I'll be in touch as soon as possible."

As soon as Chris hung up the phone, he saved Ed's phone number into his contacts list and then continued his drive home. Life was becoming more complicated by the day, and he was having a tough time handling the juggling act. He did look forward to that evening, though, when he'd enjoy the company of his girlfriend, along with that of Sean and Maggie. He valued his time with Kristi more than anything, although he was immensely pleased that Maggie had recovered sufficiently to make it a foursome.

Chris had been looking forward to the get-together for several days now, and he had made dining arrangements that were sure to please the group. Since the consensus was to have pizza, he had found a wood-fired gourmet pizza shop that specialized in unique, trendy combinations. He ordered two pies, one of which was a "Greek style," with ground beef, onion, garlic, and crumbled feta cheese, topped with a cumin and tomato sauce. The other was a Moo Shu Pork pizza, with strips of grilled pork, shiitake mushrooms, thinly sliced oriental vegetables, and baby corns, with a vinegar and hoisin sauce spread over the top. To complement the meal, he picked up some desserts from a local pastry shop, and several bottles of wine to match the menu.

Sean and Maggie were due at his house around six thirty, which would allow Sean to work his normal hours before picking up Maggie and driving across the Thruway. Kristi, however, would be there by five o'clock, simply to afford them some time alone before the others arrived. Chris also wanted to talk to her about a few matters of current interest, including the silver mine they had discussed a few weeks earlier.

Chris had just climbed out of the shower and thrown on a T-shirt and pair of shorts when the doorbell sounded. He bounded down the stairs from the bedroom loft and was unlocking the door within a few seconds. As expected, Kristi was there, looking radiant in a Dave Matthews concert T-shirt and pair of shorts. Her hair was combed back over her shoulders, with a floral hair clip on one side. Chris could never remember her having the same hairstyle twice, which always amazed him.

"You look marvelous," said Chris, using a fake Billy Crystal accent.

"You are absolutely crazy, but thanks, honey," she said, wrapping her arms around him. "I always love your opinions."

"Are you saying you don't trust my personal unbiased opinions?" asked Chris, returning the embrace and engaging her in a prolonged kiss.

"Well, do I get invited inside, or are we just going to stand in the doorway until Sean and Maggie get here?" asked Kristi jokingly.

"Please do come into my humble abode," replied Chris. "If you don't, I won't be able to get your professional advice on these maps that have been puzzling me for the past month."

"Is that the only reason you invited me here?" asked Kristi, faking a pout. "To ask me about a bunch of old maps in your pursuit of riches?"

"Not at all, sweetheart," Chris replied, putting his arm around her shoulder. "But once you help me out with your splendid powers of observation, I promise you that I'll be all yours for the rest of the night."

"At least until Sean and Maggie get here, right?" giggled Kristi.

"Something like that," replied Chris, winking back at her. As he spoke,

Kristi had already seated herself on the couch and taken hold of a couple of reprinted maps from Adirondac.

"So tell me what I'm looking for," said Kristi, turning the maps to achieve the correct orientation. "Or do you want me to guess at that, too?"

"Do you remember a few weeks ago I asked you whether it was possible to find a vein of commercially valuable silver in the Adirondacks, and you said no?"

"Of course," replied Kristi, "and I'll stand by my answer."

"I know, and I believe what you said was correct," said Chris. "However, we're now certain that someone in the McIntyre mining company believed there was a profitable source of silver in the area of the iron mine and excavated for that reason. Either that, or there was a naturally occurring cave with an opening very close to one of the buildings in the village of Adirondac. It might even have been directly beneath a house or other structure. What we have to do is to find that cave or tunnel."

"You're kidding?" asked Kristi, looking up suddenly from the map. "If it was a cave, you could probably still find it if you spent enough time searching. But an excavated tunnel, that's a different proposition altogether. The chances are pretty good it would have caved in or been otherwise filled over the past 160 years."

"That's what I figured," said Chris. "But I wanted to know if you'd be willing to go up there with me for one day and help me look. I'm really only interested in the area in and around the old mining village, and only to the extent that you'd be able to search without any fancy equipment. This is a shot-in-the-dark to see if we can get lucky with a minimal amount of effort."

"When did you have in mind?" asked Kristi. "My schedule this next week is pretty full, including this coming weekend, with the new students starting to arrive on campus. But I think I could probably swing over some time the following Saturday."

"That might work well," said Chris. "I'm planning on going up to the Adirondac ghost village this next weekend to test a couple theories, but

I'd love to have you look with me any time after that, too. Your background gives you a whole different perspective on the land that I just don't have."

"Flattery will get you everywhere," said Kristi. Then, looking at the maps again, she began trying to match the landscape with the remains of the now-defunct village. "Are these the approximate locations of the buildings as they stood in the original town?"

"Yes and no," said Chris, sitting next to her with the maps between them. "The map you see on top shows the buildings as they are remembered by survivors today, which means that they are from the most current generation of buildings. Most of those that are standing and in decent shape were used by NL Industries from the 1940s right through the 1980s. Finally, the map on the bottom shows the location of some of the known buildings that were constructed within the original town, starting in the 1820s. Most of those are only estimated locations, while some are the result of ruins that were discovered and then excavated in the last century. There are also a number of buildings that were constructed on the foundations of the original structures, which makes it almost impossible to date them unless some unique artifacts are found that can fix a given year or period to that site."

"It sounds complicated," said Kristi. "But why don't you see what you can find next weekend and mark that on the maps. I can check out as many of your sites as time permits the following weekend."

"You're the best, baby," said Chris, giving Kristi another hug. "Is there anything I can do to pay you back?"

"Another trip to that seafood restaurant in Boston might be a nice start," said Kristi, giggling at her own suggestion. Chris looked at her with a cockeyed grin, which she tapped playfully with her finger. "Well, you did ask."

About an hour later, Sean and Maggie showed up at Chris' door. They didn't bother ringing the bell, but walked into the living room where Chris and Kristi were still sitting on the couch.

"I hope we're not disturbing anything too intimate," said Sean, looking across the room.

"Yeah, you are," replied Kristi. "Your friend here was just playing a new reality-show game called 'Stump the Geologist.' He's winning."

"Somehow I doubt that," said Sean.

Kristi got up off the couch and went over to give Maggie a big hug. "You look great, Maggie. I can't believe you're back on your feet already after what you went through. Chris told me all about it; you really are one tough lady."

"Thanks. I would have rather skipped the whole episode, but I guess I came through it fairly well, all things considered."

The girls fell into a prolonged conversation about the events of the previous week, leaving Sean and Chris to talk between themselves. Since Sean had spent most of the week nursing Maggie back to health, the dialog was mostly one way, leaving Sean to sit back and absorb Chris' latest findings.

"It's been a few days since we've talked now, buddy," said Sean. "Sorry I've been out of touch so much. But now that Maggie's feeling better, I think I'm ready to jump back on the case."

"No problem," said Chris. "I'd be disappointed in you if you hadn't spent the time with her. I'm just sorry I wasn't really in a position to help."

"Hey, that's OK," said Sean. "And Maggie really enjoyed the balloon bouquet and box of chocolates you sent over last weekend. That was really nice of you."

"Yeah, it was," said Maggie, who had been listening to their conversation out of one ear. "That was really sweet of you, no pun intended. But next time, could you ask Sean to keeps his paws off? As soon as I opened it, he ate most of the box."

"Hey, you said you couldn't eat the ones that contained nuts," countered Sean, as the other three laughed.

After the brief interlude, Sean and Chris returned to their conversation, with Chris describing his visit to Grainger's apartment in Binghamton.

"Thanks for the backup," said Chris. "Without knowing Grainger's exact location, there's no way I could have spent the time to find everything that I did. I felt like MacGyver."

"I wish I could have been there," said Sean. "Don't keep me in suspense; what happened?"

"Well, first of all, we can now prove for a fact that Grainger was the person who broke into your house. All your papers and copies are sitting on his desk as we speak."

"Why don't we just call the police and have him arrested right now?" asked Sean.

"We could, and there probably wouldn't be anything wrong with that," said Chris. "But we also have the opportunity to hand him even more rope with which to hang himself."

"What do you have in mind?" asked Sean.

"I'll explain in a bit," said Chris. "But for now, let me tell you a few of the rather neat tidbits I came across inside his apartment. The first was the stack of your copies, which we really don't need, but which do give him access to everything we knew from my trip to the Adirondack Museum."

"OK, that would appear to tie the score," said Sean.

"Yes, but I also discovered the only real new piece of information that he had in his arsenal, the log book from his ancestor," countered Chris.

"Was that the journal from the coin press room that the librarian from the national archives was talking about?" asked Sean.

"Yes, it was," replied Chris. "Apparently, Ben's great-great-great grandfather was the head supervisor in the press room, and he maintained the unofficial daily shift record that the employees used to pass down information from shift to shift. My guess is that he simply took these books home with him as they were filled up, and that those records remained in the Grainger family until Ben finally obtained them sometime within the last ten years or so."

"Don't tell me you took the entire journal with you when you left his house?" asked Sean.

"No, I tried to leave the place exactly as I found it," said Chris. "I didn't want him to know that I'd ever been there, so I was really careful to return everything to its original position. But I did take close-up photographs of every single page of that ledger book, and I already downloaded it to my computer at home. Let me tell you, that camera was worth every penny I spent on it."

"Tell me about the good parts," urged Sean. "What did it say about the 1804 silver dollars; or didn't it?"

"It said plenty," said Chris. "But the good stuff was all packed into one entry, on March 26, 1804."

"Well, don't just sit there keeping me in suspense," said Sean. "Let's hear it."

"Basically, the entry describes the fact that the last of the 1803 dies had cracked, and that they had to replace it with a new die in order to complete the rest of the allotment of 1804 dollars. The log book listed a coin count of 16,950 at the time of the break."

"And what was the total number of 1804 silver dollars listed on the record of the 1804 Mint report?" asked Sean.

"The total shown was 19,570," answered Chris from memory.

"So what you're saying, if I read you correctly, is that the last 2,620 coins were struck with the 1804 obverse die, and carried the 1804 date," ventured Sean.

"That is a correct assumption," said Chris. "At least it matches my own calculation, although I did fail fifth grade math."

"You did?" said Sean, incredulously. "How did you ever make it to high school with that kind of a background?"

"My dad bribed the principal to pass me," joked Chris.

"So what you're saying is that the entire stash could fit inside a nine inch cube," said Sean.

"Wow, you're fast," observed Chris. "It took me almost an hour to come up with that computation."

"That's why you're not an engineer," joked Sean.

"Want to know something else that was pretty interesting?" asked Chris.

"Go ahead," said Sean.

"Do you remember the document we found when we were in the Frank Stewart Room together?" asked Chris. "The one that said that all of the 1804 dollars had been melted back into bullion later in 1804?"

"Of course," said Sean.

"It was a fake," said Chris.

"A fake?"

"Yes. A completely manufactured fake," said Chris.

Sean waited for a few moments before responding, lost in thought. "Well, we did think that there were a lot of rather strange disparities in that document, didn't we?" asked Sean.

"Yes, but if I recall, you also told Tracey that 'anyone who has any real knowledge in antique paper and inks of previous centuries would pick out the difference in a heartbeat.' Looks like you kind of dropped the ball, didn't you?" chided Chris.

"OK, OK, so I'm not an expert in that field! That's great that you were able to pick out the fake. How were you able to make that determination?"

"To tell you the truth, it was dumb luck," admitted Chris. "I was leaving Grainger's apartment after wrapping up my little probe, when I saw a bunch of cups and saucers on a shelf. They contained a combination of tea, instant coffee, and a pomegranate, of all things. I remembered reading about a method for manufacturing antique-looking paper in a craft magazine not long ago, and those were the prime ingredients. Then, when I saw the paint brush and package of parchment paper, that was the clincher."

"So that was it?" asked Sean, somewhat underwhelmed. "You saw the shelf where he supposedly made the mixture that stained the document, along with an old box of 'onion skin,' huh?"

"Listen, Sean," argued Chris, not about to be denied. "I know what I saw, and I know what it was. And that stuff had only one purpose, which was to create a fake, old-looking document, which is exactly what I found. And you know something else that's kind of comical, in retrospect?"

"What's that?"

"Do you remember how we were sitting there reading that old letter in the Frank Stewart Room, and all of us suddenly felt an uncontrollable urge for a cup of coffee?" asked Chris.

"Of course I do," replied Sean. "Even the girl who was working with us suddenly wanted a cup."

"That was because we smelled the coffee in the stain of the letter, which is what put that thought in our minds," explained Chris. "So, you see, it was almost like the reaction you'd get when you walk into a coffee shop. Suddenly, you've got to have a cup."

"OK, OK, I believe you," said Sean, backing off. Then, after a moment of thought, he turned to Chris with a quizzical expression. "Did you say pomegranate juice? What's up with that?"

"I read about it in that article; I think it might have even been a kids' magazine," answered Chris. "The coffee and tea stain the overall paper a nice shade of brown, and age the pulp somewhat, whereas the pomegranate juice tends to give the edges and a few of the larger fibrous strands a darker tinge. You can really make new documents look pretty old, with the right ingredients and a little practice."

"But what would be the motive? I mean, we already know from the coin you found at Blue Mountain Lake that the 1804 silver dollars do exist. So why go through the elaborate ruse to prove that they'd all been melted?"

"Because Grainger never knew that we had found the authentic dollar in Blue Mountain Lake," replied Chris. "He was looking for a simple way to throw us off the trail, and for the price of a couple cups of coffee and a single pomegranate, that very well might have done it. That's another reason why we need to keep quiet about that discovery, at least until we're ready to blow the lid off the entire U.S. coin collecting market."

"Which might come at the same time we get Grainger thrown in the slammer," added Sean. "I can't wait to see that come to pass. I think I'll volunteer to testify against him in person."

"That has a much better chance of happening than you might imagine," said Chris, recalling the break-in.

"So you found the documents he stole from my house, and you photographed the shift record book from the mint. Then, you discovered how he created a completely fake record and planted it in the Frank Stewart Room," summarized Sean. "Overall, I'd say you had a pretty successful evening of it. Did you ever consider applying for a job with the FBI?"

"Oh my God, could you picture that?" asked Chris as he slapped his forehead. "I'd do really well inside of a bureaucracy like that, wouldn't I? I'd probably be fired in less than a week."

"Somehow I doubt that," said Sean.

"Oh, I found something else that will help provide a little more cannon fodder against Grainger when he goes to court," said Chris. "He's got thousands upon thousands of dollars of stolen electronics equipment hidden in the closet in his living room. It's from the store in Philadelphia where he used to work before moving to New York. I'm sure that the business would love to press charges against him if they knew he had the stuff."

"We can make that happen," said Sean.

"And we will," assured Chris. "Remember, we will exact our revenge, but at the right time."

While Chris and Sean were comparing notes, Maggie had been filling Kristi in on all the details of her ordeal from the previous week. Kristi had only heard the story through Chris' words, and hadn't realized the extent of the trauma Maggie had experienced coming almost face-to-face with the ruthless criminal.

The conversations continued unabated, with all four losing complete track of time, until the doorbell rang.

"Ah, that will be our dinner," said Chris, leaping to his feet.

"Good thing, too," said Sean. "I'm getting pretty darned hungry. I was even about to settle for some of your own personal cooking, and I'd have to be pretty starved to give that a go."

"Thanks again, buddy," said Chris, as he paid for the food and tipped the delivery man. In the background, he could hear the two girls laughing at Sean's remarks.

Chris brought the two pizzas into the kitchen and arranged the boxes on the table along with some paper plates and utensils. The bottles of wine were uncorked and placed next to a quartet of long-stemmed wine glasses.

"I didn't know you had this much class," said Sean, looking at the stemware as he poured Maggie a glass of Riesling. "These are nice."

"Compliments of my mom," said Chris. "I think they came from a great-aunt, or something like that."

The four took their food and drink and moved over to the sectional couch, which fit into an "L" shape around a glass coffee table. On most evenings, this was where Chris relaxed and watched the big-screen television, which was mounted at an angle from a bracket suspended from the upstairs loft.

Maggie looked at Kristi as she took her first bite of the pizza. "So you're going up there to the ghost village with Chris the weekend after next?" she asked.

"Yes, he bribed me," laughed Kristi. "Otherwise I'd let him fend for himself."

"I'd come with you, but I need to work that weekend," said Maggie. "I'm kind of broke, since I lost all my hours last week after getting bonked over the head."

"That's OK," said Sean. "You could probably do with another weekend of just resting up around here. You don't need to be traipsing all over the North Country with us."

As they spoke, Kristi suddenly fell silent. She continued to enjoy her food, but her attention and focus appeared to be elsewhere.

"What's up, honey?" asked Chris, noticing the change in her demeanor. "There's the Greek-style pizza if you don't like the Moo Shu pork one."

"Hmm?" mumbled Kristi, her mind still a thousand miles away. "What's that?"

"Nothing—it just looked as though you deserted us and daydreamed yourself into another dimension somewhere," said Chris.

"I'm sorry," said Kristi, her face flush with embarrassment. "It's just that I keep looking at those papers next to your map; what are they?" Chris followed her stare to a pile of papers he'd placed on the corner of the table, next to the map of the ghost town of Adirondac.

"Those are the attempted translations of the page of cipher we found in the Frank Stewart Room," said Chris, reaching for the papers. "We actually tracked down the Ph.D. genius dude who broke the code on Robert Patterson's first message to President Jefferson. He told us how it was accomplished, and how he had helped to write a program to decode most follow-on ciphers written using the same method. However, for some reason, it didn't work with the sample we found. This scientist, Dr. Tomlinson, said it probably had to do with the fact that Patterson changed his code chunking, or varied from the normal code patterns he had used repeatedly in the last few years of his life."

"Code chunking?" asked Kristi, turning her eyes back to Chris. "What is that?"

"When Patterson wrote a passage in this code, he'd start by recording his message on a page using columns instead of rows, with no breaks between words," explained Chris. "Then he would perform all kinds of funky operations, like break the page up into groupings of eight or nine rows, then add a certain number of random characters to the front of each row, which had to be ignored when reading the final message. Tomlinson evidently got it down to a science, where he could use his program to break most ciphers in a single day. But in this case, it apparently crashed and burned. What you're looking at is a pile of failed attempts, with his most commonly used code keys on top, and the lesser used code keys on the bottom."

"He promised us that he'd do his best to jump back on it when he finished off some other work next month," added Sean.

"Do you think you need the information from this cipher to locate the silver dollars?" asked Maggie.

"We're not even sure if the message is related to the coins," admitted Chris. "But we did find it with a folder of other papers that were all pretty closely related to that topic, so we're hoping that it yields some clues."

"It looks like a game of word jumble right now," said Maggie, looking at the matrix. "I can't see a thing that makes sense, except simple words that happen to be together. Here's the word 'is.' Oh, and here is the word 'car.' But I guess that doesn't count for anything?"

"No, not really," said Chris. "Those are pure coincidences. The computer that compiled these pages compared the various combinations to every word in the English language and came up with nothing. Also, I don't think Patterson would have been talking about his car in 1804."

"No, probably not," laughed Maggie.

Kristi remained silent, once again staring at the page while ignoring the conversation.

"Why do I get the feeling that you're seeing something that we're not?" asked Chris, leaning over to look into Kristi's eyes.

"I don't know," said Kristi. "Maybe this is a coincidence, just like you finding the word 'car,' but I don't think so."

In an instant, Chris and Sean were both on their feet, looking over her shoulder.

"What are you seeing?" asked Chris, unable to detect any pattern in the rows and columns of the page. "Even if you think it might be a random pattern, it may be significant."

Kristi picked up the paper and pointed. "Following along this line, right here, is a full sentence, but it's written in French. It says: 'En regardant vers l'ouest, côté droit, quatre sur cinq.'"

"What does that mean?" asked Sean, barely able to contain himself.

"Well, it's been two years since my last French class at Cornell, but this is pretty easy to translate. It says: 'Looking west, right side, four over five.'"

"Anything else?" asked Chris, hoping for a more extended text that might lead them directly to a specific location.

"Not that I can see," said Kristi, still gazing at the page. "Everything else is just a scramble of letters with no meaning, in French or English."

Chris returned to his seat and sat down, lost in thought. Then, he turned to his friends and looked at them wide-eyed. "Did you know that Robert M. Patterson traveled to France after his college years in America? He lived there for a couple of years before returning home, and he spoke French fluently."

"Do you think he might have used the foreign language as an extra layer of security, to protect a secret that was especially near to his heart?" asked Sean.

"That's certainly something to consider," said Chris, already trying to figure out the meaning of the seven-word sentence. "Looking west, right side, four over five…"

"It seems like the clue wouldn't tell you anything unless you had a reference point, you know—where you were standing," said Kristi.

"I know," said Chris, poring over the details of the ghost town in his mind. "So even though we may have found *the* critical piece of the puzzle, it might be totally useless unless we can find the starting point."

"By the way, do you think we should send an email back to Dr. Tomlinson telling him that we've solved the cipher issue, just so he doesn't waste a bunch of time working on finding an English solution which may not even exist?"

"Not yet," replied Chris, thinking out loud. "Dr. Tomlinson said he wouldn't have time to work on the cipher until the middle part of September. If and when that happens, that's great. But until it does, the fewer people who know about this, the better."

"So what's the next step?" asked Sean.

"The next step?" repeated Chris as he raised himself back off the couch. "The next step is to have another slice of this Greek pizza and wash it down with the last of the Riesling, all performed while saving room for a big hunk of tiramisu for dessert."

"Ooh, I second the motion to snag the hunk of tiramisu," giggled Kristi, ogling the desserts in the cake box.

"Seriously," said Sean, attempting to herd Chris back on topic. "What's our next step here? Don't you think we might want to head up to Adirondac this weeekend and have another look around, just to see what scenarios and locations might match the wording from the cipher page?"

"I'm going up with my other partner-in-crime the following weekend," replied Chris, reaching around Kristi's waist and pulling her closer. "But I'd be willing to commit to the next two weekends, as long as nothing else comes up."

"How about Saturday morning?" asked Sean. "Even if we just go up for the day and then come back the same night."

"I'm game for Saturday, if you are," said Chris. "We could spend our time with the maps, trying to find the location of as many original foundations as possible. And who knows? Maybe something will jump up and kick us in the face about this 'looking west,' business. Maybe it's something so obvious that we just overlooked it while poking around there on our last visit."

"I know," concurred Sean, the excitement shining in his eyes. "After all, we did spend a good part of our day hiking up to Calamity Pond."

"Anything is possible," agreed Chris, "including the fact that we might run into Grainger up there."

"You think so?" asked Sean, looking rueful.

"Not really," said Chris. "But I do believe that he'll stop up and have a look around, now that we know he has our papers from your house. For all we know, he may there right now."

"Right," agreed Sean. "But at least the good news is, he doesn't know about the cipher clue."

"And the bad news," continued Chris, "is that we don't have a clue what it means."

Saturday morning was a mixed bag of clouds and sunshine. Per the usual arrangement, Chris drove to Sean's house in Little Falls to pick up his friend, stopping in the cottage for a quick breakfast.

I hope you don't mind if I load the metal detector into the back of your Jeep, do you?" asked Sean.

"Of course not," said Chris. "But I can see we're getting a bit optimistic here, aren't we?" he said in a patronizing tone of voice.

"I don't know; I always thought it was a good idea to maintain a positive attitude," countered Sean, as he picked up a moderate-sized black case. "Is your back door open?"

"Sure is," said Chris. "Help yourself."

Sean grabbed the carrying handle on his metal detector, along with a smaller pack for his extra accessories, and loaded them into the cargo compartment of the SUV. "Who knows? We might even have fun just seeing what we can find amongst the ruins. If nothing else, we might come up with something interesting."

Chris mildly protested as Sean moved his GPS into the Jeep, insisting that he didn't need a device to go someplace he'd been before. Sean, however, ignored the comment and plugged the power cord into the cigarette lighter as they pulled out of the driveway.

"Speaking of electronic devices, have you had a chance to check out where Grainger's traveled since my little visit last weekend?" asked Chris.

"Only once or twice," recalled Sean, "although it didn't appear as though he had left Binghamton. I guess I sort of lost interest in his wanderings since then. Or maybe I just forgot to check."

"No worries," said Chris. "It's just that, since he has the same information as us on Adirondac, I would have thought that he'd make a trip up there to poke around."

"You're really worried about him, aren't you?" asked Sean. "That's the third time I've heard you mention his name this week."

"I'm not really worried about him from a perspective of him going after us anymore," replied Chris. "Although it's bad enough that he attacked Maggie inside your house. But I am concerned about him getting in the way of our own search for the place where the dollars might be hidden. It will be difficult enough as it is to find them under ideal conditions. Who knows what complications might arise if that punk starts sticking his nose into it."

The two passed the hours and the miles reviewing the clues and what they knew about the possible solutions.

"In summary," said Sean as they neared the ghost village, "we're pretty certain that Robert M. Patterson was given custody of up to 2,620 silver dollars dated 1804, and that he chose to hide those in or near the defunct mining community of Adirondac. We think he did this in the middle of 1853, with the help of someone named Henry.

"We also know that he corresponded extensively with the foreman who oversaw the construction of the blast furnace, although that structure wasn't completed until 1854, and that somehow that foreman ended up with one of the 1804 dollars," continued Sean. "Additionally, Patterson was very interested in the monument that was erected in the memory of David Henderson at Calamity Pond and we know he attended the ceremony to dedicate that memorial in 1850, even though he never met Henderson in person."

"We also know that Patterson wanted to tell someone to look west, on the right side, four over five, or something like that," said Chris. "I wonder what that's all about."

"That will be tough," admitted Sean. "It could refer to a permanent landmark, like a chain of mountains when viewed from a particular spot, and the peak of the fourth mountain is aligned to a marked spot in the ground, sort of like Stonehenge."

"Or worse yet, it could be giving a clue to something like a house or other building, which has been gone for many decades already," said Chris.

"On top of everything else, we also know that Patterson stumbled upon at least one cave, or underground mine, beneath the area where he was given lodging," added Sean. "We have no assurance whatsoever that this subterranean space, whatever it is, has any bearing on the rest of our mystery, but it's still something to keep in mind as we look around the area."

"True," agreed Chris, "but I'm going to have Kristi look into that next weekend. My guess is that if it's a cave, she'll be able to locate it no matter where it is, especially if she can explore it first and announce it to the world."

"She might end up gaining a reputation as a world-renowned discover-er of yet another northern U.S. cave system," said Sean. He was referring to the fact that Kristi had been accorded those same honors with another Adirondack cave that the three of them had located just a year earlier.

"Maybe," laughed Chris. "Lord knows she can use all the fame she can get as she starts looking for employment outside the university. I know I wouldn't want to have to go through that again."

"Speaking of Kristi, would you please tell her that she owes me one?" asked Sean.

"How's that?" said Chris, answering a question with another question. As he spoke, he pulled the Jeep past the blast furnace on the Upper Works Road and prepared to park the car in the dirt lot.

"She's getting a cash rebate because I bought the same cell phone that she got, and I mailed in the card with her name and phone number," explained Sean. "If I'm not mistaken, she gets fifty dollars back in cash, or something like that." As he spoke, he held out his new hi-tech phone for Chris to examine.

"Wow, that must have set you back a pretty penny," said Chris, turning the device over in his hand.

"Yeah, but it's worth it. I'm tired of losing my phone service whenever I get outside of cell tower range, or out in the mountains, or anything like that. With this bad boy, I can reach anyone, anywhere, anytime I please. It doesn't seem to matter whether I'm twenty miles out in the woods, or way down in the cellar of a client's concrete building. I'm loving it."

Chris handed the phone back to Sean as they both piled out of the vehicle. Sean didn't bother with the metal detector, figuring that they could come back for that once they got their bearings. Instead, they retrieved their maps and other reference documents from the back seat and prepared to lay out a strategy for covering the site. Sean was about to make a suggestion when his eyes froze, looking towards the other end of the parking lot in dismay.

"It appears that we have company," Sean said, sounding somewhat glum.

Chris followed his friend's stare and was rewarded with an unwelcome sight. There, sitting beneath some trees at the edge of the clearing, was a red Mini Cooper with the now-familiar license plate: ENP 3982.

"OK, so what do we do now?" asked Sean.

Chris leaned against the back of the Jeep and closed his eyes for a moment, contemplating their next move.

"I think we should divide and conquer," said Chris, smiling broadly.

"How's that?" asked Sean, seeking more information about the plan.

"I'll tell you what," said Chris. "Rather than listening to me shoot my mouth off, why don't you spend a little time getting set up with the maps of the original village and lay out your first search lines. I'll be back in about five minutes."

"Where are you going?" asked Sean.

"Why, I'm now playing the role of 'Joe the Tourist'," said Chris, as he threw the neck strap of his digital camera over his head.

"Please explain," said Sean, sounding impatient. "I hate it when you start talking in riddles like this."

"I'm sorry," said Chris. "But really, I think this is actually quite simple. If Grainger is here right now, as it would appear from the presence of his car, then I'd be willing to bet that he's right down the road, as we speak, at the blast furnace. After all, that's the direction he'd get from most of the papers he lifted from your house."

"Then why do you want to head down there by yourself?" asked Sean.

"Because there's no way he could possibly know who I am," explained Chris. "Even the papers that I copied for you from the Adirondack Museum didn't have my name on them, and he couldn't have gained any knowledge about my identity from the rest of the stuff in your house. However, *you*, my friend, are an entirely different proposition."

"You think he knows what I look like?" gasped Sean, incredulous at the idea. "We've never met face-to-face, even if he was an unwelcome guest in my house."

"Yes, and he has your name, and obviously your address, and your driver's license number from the Frank Stewart Room," said Chris. "We can't be sure, because he may not be the most intelligent character on the block. But he is apparently cunning and shrewd, and if he is the least bit interested in his prime adversary, he probably would have done the same thing as us, which is to spend a few dollars and obtain a background summary about you, including your photograph. I wouldn't wager a lot of money that he wouldn't recognize you, especially in this setting."

"I could pull on a baseball cap and a pair of shades," volunteered Sean.

"Just hang out here in the Jeep for about five minutes, OK?" implored Chris. "And don't start with any of the superspy stuff. I'll be right back."

Chris turned away and started walking briskly down the road toward the clearing on the left, where the massive furnace dominated the landscape. As he neared the pavement adjacent to the corner of the furnace's foundation, he slowed his pace, matching the slow, unhurried speed of a vacationing tourist. He turned his head slightly to the left in order to observe the massive bulk of the rock foundry. Pretending to focus his gaze upward, toward the higher reaches of the masonry, Chris used his peripheral vision to scan the sides and lower reaches of the furnace. Other people were in the clearing, also taking in the sights of the industrial behemoth.

Because more than one group appeared to be present, Chris felt comfortable in lowering his eyes and consciously scanning the area around the stonework. There was a father-son pair walking around the base of the furnace, apparently examining the plants and small trees that were growing directly out of the cracks between the massive boulders in the structure. Farther down the hill, toward the river, a lone woman was standing on top of the rock retaining wall where the blast air baffles had once resided. She appeared to be contemplating the ancient, rusted equipment that lay tangled in a heap in the pit below her feet.

Continuing his inspection of the area, Chris saw the back side of a figure that was bent over, moving bits of rubbish on the ground in front of the furnace. As he watched, the man stood up and removed a water bottle from a belt holder, taking a deep swig while turning back toward the furnace. He was a tall man, with broad shoulders and a muscular build, with a slight bit of a beer belly in front. His face was framed with a full head of bright red hair, which looked as though it hadn't been trimmed in quite a while. It flowed over his ears on both sides, while the locks in the front occasionally fell across his eyes. Chris recognized him at once as Benjamin Grainger.

Playing his role of the tourist to the hilt, Chris removed his camera from the case and snapped about a dozen photographs. He never aimed the camera directly at his prime target, which was the red-haired figure who now stood on the right side of the furnace, examining the stones. However, each of his pictures did manage to capture an image of the man who had invaded Sean's house and callously injured an innocent and unarmed girl. These photos would later be cropped, and then enlarged, to provide the police with a detailed 360-degree view of the suspect. Only when he was satisfied that he had obtained a complete and comprehensive photographic composition of Grainger, did Chris turn around and head back toward the parking lot.

"What the heck took you so long?" exclaimed Sean. "I thought you said five minutes?"

"Sorry for the delay," said Chris. "Grainger is down there at the furnace, as I expected, so I took a bunch of photos of him, in case we need something to give to the police later," said Chris.

"Another wanted poster, huh?" asked Sean.

"Yeah, I suppose," said Chris. "Anyway, let's get started. I'm going back down to look around the furnace, while you head out into the woods and look around. You might even want to start out by crossing the bridge and checking out the remains on the other side of the river."

"OK," agreed Sean, as he smoothed out the oversized copy of the original village map. "I'll try to focus on finding anything along the main row of houses, and then see if I can find anything that matches the location of Patterson's guest cottage."

"Sounds like plan," said Chris, arranging a stack of blank note pages on a clipboard.

"What happens if you get into trouble and need help with Grainger?" asked Sean.

"That shouldn't be a problem," said Chris, still preoccupied with setting up his disguise. "As far as Grainger is concerned, I'll look like any other tourist, so there's no reason to sweat it. Even if there was, we both have our phones on, so I can just call you if anything goes wrong."

"Uh, OK, Dr. Einstein," said Sean. "Would you like to tell me how you plan on using your antique cell phone in this area?"

"Oh, I forgot about that," said Chris. He glanced at his phone's display quickly and confirmed that he had no reception at all. "Maybe that satellite cell contraption of yours isn't such a bad idea after all."

"Well, at least I can talk to your girlfriend, even if *you* can't reach her," said Sean, sarcastically.

"OK, never mind the small stuff," replied Chris. "Let's just get going and see what we can come up with. I'll see you back here in an hour or two. If you're not back when I finish, I'll come looking for you. But please, take your time and see how much of this map you can correlate to the landscape as it exists today."

"Will do," said Sean. "I've even brought some surveying line tape, which I'll tie around some small trees near anything worth coming back to investigate. I'll try to do it in an unobtrusive manner so that I won't give anything away, in case Grainger wanders up this way after we're gone."

"Good idea," said Chris, nodding in agreement.

"OK then, catch you later," said Sean, turning towards the trail that would lead him into the woods. "And try to stay out of trouble until I get back."

Chris laughed and retraced his steps back down the rough road, bound for the blast furnace. However, this time, rather than stay on the road, he detoured inside the guardrail and stepped down the steep incline to the bottom of the wall that surrounded the lower part of the furnace. Chris could not help but feel dwarfed by the incredible bulk of the structure, which contained individual stones that were larger than he was and weighed many tons apiece.

As he descended into the bottom of the pit, which had been carved into the side of a hill, he passed the father and his son, who were apparently returning to their car. The single female Chris had seen earlier was still down near the river, looking over a set of old stone bridge stanchions that once spanned the flow. Grainger was still in residence as well, examining the bricks in the archway directly in front of the furnace.

Chris walked around the front of the furnace, examining the front façade from the same angle as Grainger, although about twenty feet farther back. After taking a couple of photographs of the archway, he returned the camera to its case and quickly jotted down a few notes on the yellow pad. He performed this act while appearing to be oblivious to the presence of the other visitor, who was still directly in front of him.

Grainger turned towards Chris, as if to speak, before deciding otherwise. Then, without further warning, he squatted down onto all fours, preparing to crawl through the small opening that led into the furnace itself. Chris noticed with alarm that he didn't have a hardhat.

"Excuse me, sir, but I wouldn't do that if I were you," said Chris, blurting out the warning before giving himself time to think.

"No?" asked the redhead, backing out of the tunnel-like entrance and standing up.

"The entire construction of the furnace is under repair, and there are tons of loose bricks that can come loose at any time," said Chris. "Even the archway is dangerous, as you can see. But the inside of the stack is much worse, with many of the bricks ready to peel off with the least bit of motion. Even with a hardhat, it's risky entering the stack. Without one, it's suicidal."

Even as he spoke, Chris was baffled about his own concern for this man who would steal, beat up defenseless women, and possibly kill. But for some reason, he felt the need to warn another human being of immediate danger. He found himself repeating the phrase "revenge will come at the right time."

"Are you with the organization that's trying to put this thing back together?" asked Grainger, looking at Chris through squinted eyes.

"No, I'm not," said Chris. "My name is Mark Preston, and I'm doing some work for the Adirondack Park Agency. We're trying to develop our land use plan, and this whole area is now the subject of a study." As he spoke, he extended his arm to shake hands with Grainger. He wondered if he was the first person ever to introduce himself to another individual after just breaking into their house.

"I'm Leon," said Grainger, reverting to his previous fake moniker. "I'm just trying to have a look around the place. I have a friend who climbed up the inside of the stack, and I thought I'd look around in there and see about trying my hand at it, too."

"Yeah, that's not a good idea," said Chris, repeating his thoughts of a minute ago. "It's a very, very dangerous place to be until the entire brick-work is stabilized." Chris also knew that he didn't want this person spending too much time getting an up-close and personal look at parts of the interior that no one else might have seen since the furnace was built.

"Is there anything illegal about it?" asked Grainger, looking somewhat rebellious. "I mean, there's a warning sign, but nothing that says it's against the law. You're not some kind of a park cop here to stop me, are you?"

"No, of course not," said Chris, laughing to dispel any notion that he was there to enforce the agency's policy. "I just hate seeing anyone hurt, that's all."

Grainger looked at Chris for a moment, as though attempting to size him up and determine whether there was an ulterior motive behind his warning. Then, without saying another word, he returned to his four-legged stance and crawled through the opening into the darkness of the stack.

Chris watched, half amused and half in awe of anyone who could ignore such an obviously unsafe condition without taking the most minimal safety precautions, then shrugged and went back to his work. He spent the next hour walking slowly around the perimeter of the furnace, noting the relative distances between the stones of the furnace itself and the retaining wall that was built into the side of the hill bordering on the roadway. He then referred to a map and compass, noting the cardinal points on the compass needle as they applied to the furnace, the river, and the waterwheel apparatus.

Another thought that kept Chris' mind busy was the height of the furnace tower, which appeared to be about sixty feet tall. He tried to imagine the construction as it was accomplished over the period of five years, from 1849 through 1854, and wondered how high it would have stood in October of 1853, when Patterson last visited the site. Would it have been about forty feet tall, since that year represented about two thirds of the construction time? Or would they have built the entire outside of the furnace up to its full height first, and then spent the last year or two adding the brickwork and final masonry? Unfortunately, there were too many questions that required a great deal of speculation, and none of the answers had been available at the Adirondack Museum.

Chris persisted in his examination of the site, pacing off distances between the major components of the blast furnace and the surrounding features of the site. He tried to imagine how the area would have looked in 1853, with the woods largely removed to provide charcoal fuel for the massive fires that burned throughout the day in the refinery's other furnaces. He also tried to picture from the maps where the workers must have stayed, and the routes they probably traveled in order to get to their work every morning. Chris became so engrossed in his work that he completely forgot about Grainger, who was now invisible inside the middle of the furnace. He also lost track of time, which he suddenly remembered after about two hours of detailed sketching. Looking at his watch, he noticed that it was almost two thirty, which meant that Sean would probably be back to the Jeep by now.

After a last peek around, Chris climbed back up the embankment and marched up the road to the parking lot. He was slightly amused to see his friend walking out of the woods from the opposite direction at the exact same time.

"Sorry I'm late," said Sean, wiping the sweat from his forehead with an old bandana. "I got caught up in things down there and lost track of time."

"You and me both," said Chris, smiling back at his accomplice. "I had such a nice time chatting with our buddy Grainger that we decided to become roommates."

"Uh huh," grunted Sean. "Seriously, did you say anything to the guy?"

"As a matter of fact, I did," replied Chris. "I introduced myself with my phony name, and he said hello with his phony name. Then, I pretty much told him that he was an idiot for wanting to climb around inside the stack without a hardhat, but he went ahead anyway."

"Hmm—not the brightest candle on the birthday cake, is he?"

"Apparently not," agreed Chris. "But that's his problem, not mine. By the way, I told him that I was Mark Preston, with the Adirondack Park Agency, in case the subject ever comes up again."

"How do you do, Mark?" said Sean, faking an introduction. "My name is George Washington, and I'm darned pleased to meet you."

"Knock it off, wise guy," said Chris, brushing aside his attempted humor. "What did you find on the other side of the river?"

"Lots!" said Sean, his eyes as wide as half dollars. "I think I found the site of the original mill and a few other working buildings. But even more importantly, I'm pretty sure that I located the site of a row of residential structures, although there is almost nothing left of the actual buildings. But I came back for the metal detector, and it picked up enough domestic artifacts to back my theory about the fact that they were the houses of the miners and other company workers."

"Wow! Great job," said Chris, putting out his hand to high five his friend. "How certain are you of your identification?"

"Well, I can't say for sure," said Sean. "The foundations seemed to line up with the map. But it's tough to say whether everything is in alignment with the original buildings as they appeared on the map, which was first drafted in the 1840s. It's not an exact science, you know."

"Of course," said Chris, patting Sean on the back. "By the way, you didn't happen to notice anything obvious regarding the clue from the cipher, did you?"

Larry Weill

"No, nothing at all," said Sean. "I had that in the back of my mind as I was trying to line up the ruins, but it's tough to see anything through all the leaves and trees down there. To tell you the truth, most of the time I couldn't see anything that was more than a hundred yards away."

"That's understandable," said Chris.

"It's also tough to sort out which buildings were used at different times, because many of the original structures were re-built for use by the Tahawus Club, and then again for the National Lead Company when they mined here in the twentieth century. So, while some of the ruins are little more than humps in the soil, others are still standing, although you wouldn't dare to enter them for fear of your life."

"It sounds as though you've done one heckuva job. We'll chase down your leads when we come back here next weekend."

"Where was Grainger when you last saw him?" asked Sean.

"He was inside the furnace stack, perhaps even climbing the inside," said Chris, laughing softly. "I think he believes the coins are hidden somewhere in the brick lining of the interior."

"Is that a possibility?" asked Sean.

"I don't see how it could be," said Chris. "I was thinking about that while I was surveying the site, and it just doesn't seem feasible. From what I was reading about the design of the blast furnace, the fires inside were capable of heating the interior to over 3500 degrees Fahrenheit. That's quite a bit higher than the melting point of iron, which is around 2800 degrees, which was the intended purpose of the furnace. However, the melting point of pure silver is around 1761 degrees, and the temperature needed to melt silver coins is even lower, around 1615."

"How the heck do you know all that?" gasped Sean, amazed at his friend's virtual storehouse of metallurgy facts.

"Don't be overly impressed," laughed Chris. "I looked up all those figures when I was reading about the furnace up in Blue Mountain Lake. But the important thing to take away from all this is that the interior of the furnace was too hot to store anything that was silver, unless they intended to

336

melt the coins into a bubbly mass of silver bullion."

"Which Patterson never intended, or he would have done that right inside the mint itself, correct?" surmised Sean.

"Correct," said Chris. "So I think we can rule out any place inside the furnace as a potential hiding spot."

"Darn it all," whined Sean, exaggerating his facial expression. "Just when I thought we were going to solve the case this afternoon and bask in the glory, you go and shoot us down."

"Just get in the car," Chris said, giving Sean a playful shove.

Chris started the engine of the Jeep, and they rolled slowly out of the parking lot. As they passed the red Mini Cooper, Sean gritted his teeth and nodded his head out the window. "I have half a mind to take my pocket knife and slash his tires."

"Revenge will come, but at the right time," said Chris, patiently.

"Yes, I know. I've heard that before," said Sean.

"The time is getting near," said Chris. "Just hang on, buddy. I want to see Grainger behind bars as much as you do. Give it another couple weeks, and you'll be able to send him a postcard in Attica," explained Chris, referring to the state penitentiary.

"Is that a promise?" asked Sean, staring at his friend across the front seat.

"It's a promise," reassured Chris, feeling his blood run cold at the thought of the criminal. "Grainger will go to jail for his crimes, particularly for what he did to Maggie. You and I will provide the evidence that keeps him locked away for a very long time."

CHAPTER 17

Tuesday, September 9, 2015

The following week was a frantic game of catch-up for both Chris and Sean, as each had allowed the distraction of the hunt for the coins to infringe on their business schedules. Chris had to take care of several clients in and around Syracuse, but he also had to travel to Erie, Pennsylvania, on Tuesday, which made for a very long day on the road. Sean, meanwhile, spent the entire night on Monday inside a new office building south of Albany, setting up close to thirty new networked computers. Although he didn't appreciate the tight deadline imposed on his schedule, he did enjoy the higher payment agreed upon by the customer for the accelerated installation. In any case, neither Chris nor Sean had time to think about anything else until the middle of the week.

It was Chris who broke the silence. He was driving home on the Thruway late on Tuesday night when he decided to call Sean to arrange a late-week get-together. Sean's phone buzzed four times before he answered.

"Yeah, yeah, what do you want?" asked Sean, not bothering with a standard salutation.

"Huh! I wouldn't have called you if I'd known that I was bothering you so much," said Chris.

"I'm kidding, although I must admit I am pretty beat," admitted Sean. "Too much work and not enough sleep. I had to pull an all-nighter on Monday, so I've had bags under my eyes since then."

"Yeah, but just think about all the bucks you're raking in," chided

Chris. "You're going to need your own bank soon just to hold it all."

"Don't I wish," said Sean. "So tell me, what's on your mind? Or are you just calling to check up on me?"

"Actually, I was wondering if we might do a repeat of last week's dinner," said Chris. "That was a lot of fun. Do you have time in your schedule to get together again this week?"

"I'm not sure I can do anything for the next couple days," said Sean, mentally reviewing his work schedule. "But I'm not working on Thursday night, that's for sure. Maggie's coming over, and we're just hanging out and watching a movie or something."

"Sounds like fun," said Chris. "I take it that she's OK with coming back inside your house again?"

"Yeah, she's OK with it, as long as I'm here," said Sean. "She stopped by for a while on Sunday night. She said it was a little eerie returning to the scene of the crime, although she doesn't remember too much about it."

"She's a strong girl," said Chris.

"I know," said Sean. "Hey, I've got an idea. Why don't you and Kristi stop by and join us on Thursday? We could all have dinner here, and then figure out something fun to do later."

"Sounds great," replied Chris. "Let me call Kristi and see if she has any plans. I'll call you back within the next half hour."

Chris was able to reach his girlfriend, who was at her apartment in Ithaca, writing lesson plans for a freshman geology class. "Of course I'll go," she said instantly. "I'm always looking for an excuse to get out of town. I'll be by your house around four o'clock on Thursday."

After hanging up with Kristi, Chris called Sean back to finalize the plans. "We should be able to make it over there by five thirty at the latest."

"Sounds good," said Sean. "Anything in particular you'd like to dine on, or should we surprise you?"

"Just about anything will work," said Chris. "Don't go out of your way though. Even sandwiches will be fine."

"You got it, buddy," said Sean. "We'll see you on Thursday."

Larry Weill

Chris made it back to his house earlier than usual after work on Thursday, intending to use the time to gather up all his papers and other documents to bring to Sean's place. In addition to the maps and photocopied papers, he also carried some diagrams that outlined potential places of interest within the ghost town for their upcoming weekend search. Some of these were meant for their own use, while others were intended to give Kristi a head start in her search for the cave.

By the time Kristi arrived at Chris' house, he was packed up and ready to head out. "Don't we even get a little time by ourselves?" she asked, looking up into Chris' eyes as they shared an embrace by the doorway.

"I'll tell you what," said Chris. "How about we make sure to leave Sean's house a little earlier than usual, and you can stay over my place tonight?"

"Now that sounds like a fair trade," said Kristi, giving Chris a final kiss before heading back out to the driveway. "I was beginning to think that you enjoyed Sean's company more than mine."

"Oh, please!" cried Chris, rolling his eyes as he took Kristi's hand. "Sean and I merely tolerate each other in limited doses."

The couple spent the entire trip to Little Falls talking over their plans for the coming weekend. Chris was disappointed that their paths would cross very little over those two days, as Kristi had to be home to do some prep work for the following Monday, while Chris could not make it out of Syracuse until Sunday morning.

"Great. So I spend all day Saturday looking for your cave, or tunnel, or whatever it is, while you relax at home. Then, after I've gotten myself all dirty, I get to wave at you as you drive up on Sunday. Is that the deal?" Even though Kristi was acting upset, Chris knew that it was all a front.

"I suppose so," replied Chris, kissing her hand as they drove along the road into Little Falls. "But I'll make it up to you after this is all over, OK?"

"How?" asked Kristi, her eyes sparkling. "Give me details, man!"

"How about I let you decide this time?" suggested Chris. "Except try to plan something we can reach in a single day and won't bankrupt me."

"You're on," said Kristi, flashing her biggest smile. "This will be fun!"

Chris turned the Jeep into Sean's driveway and shut off the engine. They both climbed out of the vehicle and walked around the back of the house, expecting to find Sean and Maggie sitting out in their familiar positions on the back porch. However, the outdoor dining area was bare as they rounded the corner of the cottage, so Chris knocked on the back door. As he did, he was pleasantly surprised to see that Sean's back window had been replaced, and a new sign advertising a security company was affixed to the door.

"So now you're asking permission to come inside?" asked Sean sarcastically as he opened the door. "You've never bothered doing that before, so why start now?"

"I figured you've had enough uninvited visitors this month without me pretending to be one more," said Chris, shaking Sean's hand. Sean followed by giving Kristi a big hug.

"No more worries about that," said Sean, pointing to a small device mounted near the ceiling in a corner of the kitchen. "I've had the entire place covered with motion detectors. Once this thing is armed, you couldn't chew gum in here without alerting the local police department."

"Pretty neat," said Chris, following Sean around the rooms to view the sensors. "Are the windows wired as well?"

"No, only the two doors are actually wired," explained Sean. "But the motion detectors will trip anytime they detect motion in the living room, kitchen, or bedroom. So theoretically, someone could break a window and it wouldn't set off the alarm. But as soon as the intruder sticks a limb inside the room, it'll go off with an ear-piercing screech that will awaken the dead, not to mention sound off in the security company's control center. Then, from there, they can call the police to respond within a matter of minutes."

"Sweet," said Chris. "That must make Maggie feel more comfortable."

"It sure does," said Maggie, who was sitting on the couch. "It's even got a mode that I can use if I'm inside the house by myself. It will sound an alarm if someone opens a door while I've got the system activated, even without the motion detector turned on."

"That's great," said Chris. "You know, when Sean's here by himself, he can have the whole thing turned on all the time. He works so slowly that he wouldn't even set off the motion detector."

"Ha ha, very funny," said Sean. "Ever think of starting your own standup comedy routine?"

"Well, it's true," said Chris, poking fun at his friend.

"You'd better be nice to me or I won't share my latest discovery with you," warned Sean.

"And what, pray tell, is that?" asked Chris.

"I think I may have found the meaning of the hidden message in Patterson's code."

"Are you serious?" shouted Chris. "How did you do that? And when? And why didn't you call me?"

"To tell you the truth, it just came to me this afternoon, as I was setting out our papers to discuss tonight. I must admit, it was a revelation that just sort of jumped out and smacked me between the eyes," said Sean. "You'll be amazed when I show you."

"I can hardly wait," said Chris. "I've been thinking about that all week, and somehow nothing seemed to fit."

"Well, I do want to caution you, my interpretation may not be correct because there are a couple of things that bother me about it. But it's better than anything else I could think of, and it's certainly an interesting coincidence, if nothing else."

"Interesting coincidences are good things," said Chris. "But before we start looking, I've got to ask you an extremely important question."

"What's that?" asked Sean.

"What's for dinner? I'm positively famished."

Sean and Maggie both laughed in response to Sean's query. "Yup, that's my pal!" said Sean. "The heck with the clue that might lead us to hundreds of millions of dollars in silver coins. Chris' tummy is rumbling."

"I guess I'll just have to raid the refrigerator myself," replied Chris, acting indignant. He started for the kitchen as Sean put up a hand.

"OK, OK, you win," said Sean. "You said you'd be fine with sandwiches, so I got us a whole bunch of ingredients to make our own subs. I'll get the stuff set up on the kitchen table now, since you're so intent on grazing early." As he spoke, he headed off into the kitchen, stopping only once to glance back at Maggie. "Moooooo!" he called out, doing a fairly decent imitation of a cow, earning a grin from Maggie in return.

Kristi and Chris were impressed as Sean arranged the fixings for the sandwiches on the table. Rather than the traditional tuna or roast beef fillings, Sean had prepared separate bowls of shrimp and crab salads, along with a plate loaded with gourmet chicken salad for anyone not happy with seafood. Another tray held a variety of condiments, including herbed mayonnaise, tomato and pickle slices, shredded lettuce, and Dijon mustard. A nice selection of crusty sub rolls completed the array, while a healthy-sized bowl of German potato salad stood by as a side dish.

"My friend, you do know how to feed a pair of hungry guests after all," said Chris, complimenting Sean on his choices.

The foursome loaded their plates with food and seated themselves around the kitchen table. Sean passed around plastic cups filled with ice and then poured them all soft drinks from a pair of two-liter bottles.

"On second thought, you lose three style points for the beverage," Chris added.

"There's beer and wine in the refrigerator," answered Sean, nodding at the corner of the room. "Help yourself."

"Actually, I'd rather hear about your discovery," said Chris, already digging into the first half of his sandwich.

"Fair enough," said Sean, enjoying the build-up in suspense. "Do you remember the exact wording of the message that Kristi picked out of the cipher page?"

"Of course," replied Chris. "It said: 'Looking west, right side, four over five.' How could I forget that?"

"OK, now think back to the hike that you and I took up to Calamity Pond. What did we see?"

343

"I give up, Sean," said Chris. "Heck, we saw stuff all day long, but nothing matches the words from the cipher."

Sean left the table for a moment and returned from the living room holding a paper. "Let me refresh your memory. We walked up to Calamity Pond, and we looked at the monument for quite a while before returning to the parking lot. Are you with me so far?"

"I guess so, although nothing rings a bell yet," replied Chris, trying to get his friend to speed up his delivery.

"We took lots of photos of the monument, including the inscription on the front, which carried a very interesting message."

"Go ahead," urged Chris.

"The words on the monument read: 'This monument, erected by filial affection, to the memory of our dear father, David Henderson, who accidentally lost his life on this spot 3rd September, 1845.'"

"I still don't get it," said Chris, frustrated at his lack of comprehension.

"Don't you see?" asked Sean. "During the last few miles of the hike, we were approaching from the west. The date of 1845 was on the right side of the inscription plate, and the numbers '4' and '5' appear next to each other. Basically, we had to look from the west, on the right side of the plaque, where we could see '4' and '5'. Don't you think that's a rather impressive coincidence?"

Chris fell silent for a few moments, chewing his food while considering Sean's interpretation of the code. It was a thought-provoking suggestion, although there were a few details that didn't add up.

"It might be an interesting idea to check out," said Chris, taking another gulp of soda. "But first of all, when you're looking at the monument, you're actually viewing it from a north-south perspective; you're certainly not looking west."

"OK, maybe Patterson was trying to direct someone to the side of the monument; maybe it's got a secret compartment that was sealed shut after the engraving was completed," countered Sean.

"There are other problems here as well," continued Chris. "I'll agree that the year 1845 has both a '4' and a '5' that are next to each other, but what could 'four over five' mean? After all, if you look at this photo of yours, you'll see that both numbers appear in the same horizontal line. That doesn't make sense either."

"I'll agree, that one had me puzzled as well," conceded Sean.

"One other detail is that we both looked over every inch of that monument, and nowhere was there a seam or joint," said Chris. "The entire monument appeared to be carved out of a single block of marble. So I don't see any place where the coins could have been concealed, unless the entire stone is hollow, which just isn't practical."

"Maybe we just didn't look hard enough for a crease, where two pieces of the stone may have come together," suggested Sean.

"It's possible," said Chris. "But I'd put that investigation low on our priority list. For now, I'd rather focus on finding Patterson's guest lodging, as well as doing some more work around the blast furnace. We can always make another trip back to the monument if that doesn't pan out."

Once everyone had finished their meals and the table had been cleared, the group decided to relax in the more comfortable environment of the living room. Unlike Chris' house, in which the couch easily seated six people, Sean's overstuffed version was better suited to a single couple. However, the extra-wide easy chair presented a comfortable alternative. Chris settled into the plush cushions, while Kristi sat on his lap.

"I hear that you're not going up there with Sean and Chris," said Maggie to Kristi.

"That's right," said Kristi. "I'm busy with stuff to do for the new school year on Sunday, so Saturday is my only chance to get up there."

"Aren't you worried about the guy who attacked me last week?" asked Maggie, incredulous that Kristi was making the trip by herself. "What happens if he goes after you?"

"No, I guess I'm not really worried," said Kristi. "After all, this Grainger guy wasn't planning on hurting you. You just happened to be in the wrong place at the wrong time. According to what Chris said, there was a lone woman wandering around near Grainger at the blast furnace last weekend, and Grainger couldn't have been bothered. I don't think he'd give me a second glance."

"You'll have your phone with you at all times, right?" asked Chris.

"Yes, I will. So the plan is that I get up there as early in the day as possible on Saturday, work until about dinner hour, and then head back home," said Kristi. "Meanwhile, you two will leave Utica at some absurd hour on Sunday morning, search the whole day with the metal detector, and then come home at another absurd hour."

"That about sums it up," nodded Chris. "Sorry we can't be up there with you, but please, keep us informed by sending a text every so often, or give me a call. I'll be worried sick if we don't hear from you during the day."

"Don't worry about me," said Kristi, brimming with self-confidence. "I'm a big girl; I can take care of myself."

Having finished their meal, the two couples turned their discussion to music and movies, passing the next couple of hours engaged in a lively version of impromptu trivia. By the time the clock struck nine o'clock, Chris had begun making signs that it was time to head back to Syracuse.

"OK, I'll be by around five thirty on Sunday morning," said Chris to Sean. "In the meantime, you'll be sure to have your super duper satellite phone on your body all day on Saturday, in case Kristi can't reach me."

"It's a promise," said Sean, winking at Kristi. "I'll make sure you've got a friendly voice to talk to, don't you worry."

"Thanks, Sean," said Kristi, giving him a hug. Chris exchanged embraces with Maggie, and then he and Kristi headed out into the night.

Their drive back to Syracuse was nothing short of a full briefing by Chris regarding the layout of the township of Adirondac as it stood from 1826 through 1853. Chris had fully researched every possible source of information, and obtained copies of every map of the long-defunct community. He had corroborated as much of Sean's exploration as possible with a series of annotations on the map to show the most likely locations for the underground chamber noted in Patterson's writings.

"Now remember, this doesn't have to be an actual cave," said Chris. "It could be a totally manmade excavation, possibly dating back to one of David Henderson's attempts to find silver in the ore around Adirondac. So don't get hung up on finding the exact perfect rock substrate, because it may not exist."

"Yes, I remember you telling me that before," replied Kristi. "Do you have any idea how big the underground space was?"

"It was pretty good sized, if I'm correctly visualizing it from the notes," estimated Chris. "Look for a potential opening or entrance near the building that Sean noted on his map. It might even be underneath a part of the ruins, in which case it may be impossible to locate. But whatever you do, be extra careful if you decide to walk underneath or inside of any structure that is still standing, OK? Anything left that is still upright has been abandoned since the National Lead Company ran the place, which would have been at least thirty years ago. You're just asking for trouble if you set foot inside anything that still supports a roof. Most of them would cave in if a good-sized bird landed on top. Do you understand what I'm saying?"

"I do, sweetheart, and thanks for the concern," replied Kristi, leaning against Chris in the darkness. "And now, let's set aside the hunt for the time being, OK? That's all we've talked about all night, and I'm completely prepared to do my part on Saturday. But now, you promised me the rest of the evening to spend together, and I intend to hold you to that promise."

"My dear, you won't have to work very hard to get your wish," laughed Chris. "I'm all yours until the sunshine awakens us in the morning. As of this moment, any further talk of the Great Silver Dollar Hunt is officially forbidden until this weekend."

Two days later, Chris played host to Kristi again, as she decided to spend Friday night at his Syracuse home in order to shorten her drive into the central Adirondacks the following morning. It would be a long enough drive on Saturday, heading up to the ghost village in the morning and home the same night. After a pre-dawn breakfast of pancakes and sausage,

Kristi kissed Chris one final time and headed out the door. Chris stood in the driveway and waved her goodbye as her red Chevy Cobalt disappeared down the hill and back into town.

Chris had misgivings about sending Kristi on her way by herself, as the incident with Maggie was still fresh on his mind. However, he agreed with Kristi's own assessment of Grainger. He was definitely a miscreant who couldn't be trusted with anything of value, yet he didn't seem like someone who would go after another individual for the sole purpose of injuring them. Maggie had simply gotten in the way of his pursuit of Sean's accumulated stack of clues, and she had inadvertently cut off his escape route inside the house. Perhaps he hadn't even intended to injure her; maybe she had just been hit against the doorframe as he bulled his way from the bedroom. Chris didn't honestly believe that was possible, but he used it to further justify Kristi's solo venture in search of the cave.

A mixture of business and family responsibilities kept Chris busy throughout the morning hours, and he tried to relegate any thoughts of Grainger until the following day. Yet, as he fulfilled his obligations, an idea crept into his brain, which quickly germinated and bloomed into a full-fledged plan in a matter of hours. By early afternoon, he was almost bursting at the seams to act on his scheme. Unable to contain himself any longer, he dialed Sean's phone to share his thoughts.

Sean answered on the first ring and sounded off with an automated tone of voice: "Yes, yes, everything is status normal as of noon," he reported.

"Huh?" asked Chris, bewildered at the message.

"Kristi," Sean replied. "You're calling about Kristi, right? I checked on her just before noon, and everything is fine. She's working her way along the row of residences I marked off last weekend, looking for any signs of a tunnel entrance. She said that we can forget about any naturally occurring caves in the ghost village; the terrain and rock stratum just isn't there to support it."

"Oh my God, I forgot about her calls," said Chris, slapping his forehead is dismay. "How could I have done that?"

"No problem," said Sean. "She and I set this up last weekend, and we're all set to talk to each other every two hours for as long as she's up there. It's working just fine, so don't give it another thought."

"Thanks. Now let me tell you the reason I did call," answered Chris.

"What's that?"

"You've said yourself that you'd like nothing better than to send Grainger to jail, right?" asked Chris.

"That's correct," replied Sean. "Nothing's changed in that regard."

"Well, I think I've come up with a way for us to expedite that event."

"How's that?" asked Sean.

"Let me ask you a question," said Chris. "But first I need you to take a look at the tracker and see where Grainger's car is at this very moment."

"You got it," said Sean. "I'm sitting at the computer right now, so I should be able to give you a location within about three minutes." Sean fell silent, and Chris could hear the sound of keys tapping in the background. After a short delay, Sean came back on the line with the requested information. "I'm seeing Grainger's car on Route 28, heading north, about halfway between the towns of Wevertown and North Creek, doing about forty-five miles per hour."

"Hmm, that's not good," said Chris, thinking out loud.

"Tell me what's going on in your mind, Chris," prodded Sean.

"I can't be sure, but my guess is that Grainger is headed for Adirondac as we speak," said Chris.

"I thought you weren't worried about Kristi up there, even if Grainger was wandering around the area," said Sean.

"Oh, I'm really not, but still I am," said Chris contradicting himself. "But anyway, the main reason I'm calling is that I'd like to know if you can leave for Adirondac tonight, instead of waiting for the morning."

"Of course I can," exclaimed Sean. "I could leave within about ten minutes, if you were already here. I've been looking forward to this trip since we left there last weekend."

"Unfortunately, I'll need several hours," replied Chris. "I may not make it to your place until late afternoon, if that's OK with you."

"That's fine. We can stay at the Adirondack Hotel in Long Lake, assuming that we can get a room. I'll call them as soon as I get off the phone with you," said Sean.

"There's just one other thing I need to ask of you," said Chris.

"What's that?"

"I need you to drive your own car up there," said Chris. "The way I'm planning this, we'll need two vehicles to make it work."

"Oh," sighed Sean. "You're serious?"

"I'm serious," confirmed Chris. He was fully aware that Sean's 1966 Mercedes-Benz 250S was almost like another lover to him. He pampered and coddled it until it looked like a new model, right off the showroom floor. The mere thought of taking the vintage automobile on a dusty dirt road was enough to send his spirits plummeting.

"OK," said Sean, in a resigned voice. "But nothing better happen to her, or you're going to pay half of the cleanup costs, OK?"

"OK," agreed Chris, while cringing to himself knowing that he would later ask Sean to leave the car intentionally unlocked in an unguarded public parking lot. "I'll try to be by your house by four o'clock, but it might be a little bit later, OK?"

"You got it. See you then."

As soon as their conversation ended, Chris jumped into his Jeep and sped off to a nearby office supply store, where he picked up some parchment paper, a fountain pen, and dark ink. Next, he returned home and quickly placed a few cups of water in a pot and heated it until it boiled. It took only a minute to dump in about a quarter cup of instant coffee and a half dozen tea bags, which he allowed to stew in the water until it turned the shade of burned motor oil.

Once the water had reached its desired darkness, Chris found a large baking pan and poured the water into the bottom, which created a layer about a half inch deep. He then removed a few sheets of the parchment paper from the box, and one-by-one soaked them until they had achieved a dark brown tinge. He repeated this process, dunking the papers over and over again, until the stain deepened and permeated the fibers of the pages. Once this was accomplished, he spread them out on some old towels on his kitchen table and applied a hair drier to the soaked surfaces. He only stopped to run his fingers along the sides to peel off small bits of paper, making the edges look old and worn. With the temperature set on high, and the appliance held at a minimal distance from the page, he was able to rid the paper of all moisture in a surprisingly short period of time.

"Not bad. Not bad at all," he said, holding the final product up in front of the light to examine.

Chris' next task was to take the fountain pen and draw a detailed, accurate-to-scale diagram of the Henderson memorial stone by Calamity Pond. He took his time with this, constantly comparing the photograph to his sketching. He didn't have to be perfect; all he was trying to do was to pen a recognizable representation of the monument. However, he worked meticulously to show every detail possible, even imitating the text font on the stone tablet in the front of the piece.

Once the artwork was done, Chris drew a series of very straight arrows, pointing to the right side of the monument, about halfway up. In his most ornate penmanship, he wrote the words "Patterson's compartment; ordered and sealed January, 1853."

Once this was accomplished, Chris took the slightly crinkled page and inspected it from multiple angles, admiring the effect. It wasn't perfect; anyone with an observant eye would probably recognize the new ink from the fountain pen. However, Chris wasn't concerned about this detail, since he was intending to use a copy of this document instead of the original.

Finally, Chris placed his masterpiece into a folder and hopped back into his Jeep for another high-speed transit to the office supply center. He made three copies of the document, using the extra-dark control on the store's copier. The final appearance was everything he'd hoped for and more. It looked like a new copy of a very old drawing, and Chris found himself filled with glee over his artistic prowess.

Once the authentic-looking fakes were completed, Chris used a new felt-tip pen with red ink to write a note in the margin of one of the copies. It read: "Sean—let's go for this on Tuesday night," with an arrow pointing toward the invented "Patterson's compartment." Chris wasn't certain that it would work, but it was a product that reflected his best effort, and he was very pleased with the result.

When Chris knocked on Sean's front door late that afternoon, he was pleasantly surprised to find that Sean's car was completely loaded and ready to go, and Sean himself was set to step out the door.

"I got us a room at the Adirondack Hotel, and I told them that we might not check in until after midnight," said Sean. "That way, if we decide to do something nasty tonight, we'll still have a place to sleep afterward."

"'Something nasty?' Now what would that be?" asked Chris.

"I don't know," said Sean. "But you said that you'd like to get Grainger arrested, and you changed our arrival to tonight. I was hoping that those two events were somehow related."

"They are, my friend. They are," chuckled Chris. "Are you ready to push off for Adirondac?"

"I've been ready since about twenty minutes after you called," said Sean, his voice full of anticipation. "By the way, Kristi called about ten minutes ago, and said she's still making good time and finding some interesting artifacts, but no cave or tunnel."

"Hmm, that's disappointing," said Chris. "But I guess expecting to locate something that may have collapsed over a hundred years ago was a long shot."

"Well, I must say, if nothing else, she is reliable," noted Sean. "She's called me every two hours, always within five minutes of the top of the hour. I could almost set my clock by it."

"Yeah, she's pretty organized," said Chris, conceding the accuracy of his friend's observation. "Sometimes it's almost bizarre; when she's over at my house, she'll suddenly start folding my socks. Have you ever heard of anyone who folds their socks?"

"I fold my socks," said Sean, looking back at Chris with an exaggerated serious expression.

"I'm worried about you," said Chris, trying hard not to laugh.

Chris pulled out of the driveway first, followed by Sean in his old Mercedes. They had agreed to stop up in Speculator to grab a cup of coffee before proceeding the rest of the way. It was about five forty-five when they pulled into a small restaurant right on Route 30 in the middle of town. Sean was just adding some cream to his coffee when the phone on his belt clip sounded off. He looked at the number and recognized it as Kristi's.

"She's a little bit early," he said, handing the phone to Chris. "Maybe you'd like to talk to her this time."

Chris put the phone up to his ear and did his best to disguise his voice. "Hello, this is Maxwell Smart, Agent 86 of CONTROL," he said, imitating the 1960s sitcom.

"Stop it," said Kristi, her voice coming in loud and clear over the satellite phone. "You're way too obvious, honey."

"Sorry," said Chris. "I was just trying to lighten the mood a bit. How are things going up there?"

"OK, I guess," she said. "I've found lots of good stuff, including some really nice iron ore, if that's what you're after. But no caves or tunnels or mine shafts. I've been through almost everything that looks like a ruin, although there are two more really dilapidated structures that I still have to check out. Like I said, though, I've found nothing that resembles an underground chamber of any kind."

"That's OK, honey, it really doesn't matter at this point," said Chris. "By the way, we left early, and we're only about two hours away from you right now. We should be there by eight o'clock at the latest."

"I'll be long gone by then," said Kristi. "As a matter of fact, once I stick my head inside these last two ruins, and then rummage around the grounds to make sure there's nothing there, I'm going to take off. Remember, I've got to drive all the way back to Ithaca tonight, and I've already had a long day."

"Sounds like a plan," said Chris. "Call when you get home, but please, take your time. Stop for coffee as often as you need, and pull off the road if you get tired. And look out for deer, too, because we've seen a ton of them grazing by the side of the road."

"Yes, Dad," recited Kristi, her voice heavy with sarcasm.

"Honey, I worry about you. That's all," said Chris.

"OK, I'm signing off now," said Kristi. "Talk to you tonight."

Kristi was justified in saying that she'd had a long day. After driving almost four hours from Chris' house early that morning, she had spent the next seven hours crisscrossing every square foot of the abandoned mining village. As she worked, she constantly came across ruins that were in various stages of decay, with many of the older sites now resembling little more than piles of organic material. Only those structures that had been later used by the Tahawus Club or the National Lead Company were still recognizable as buildings, and only a few of those had walls or roofs that remained upright.

Before checking out the building sites for signs of a cave or mine shaft entrance, Kristi opened a pouch with her topographic maps of the area and looked for some of the more likely locations of naturally occurring caves. However, upon closer inspection, none of them offered even a remote possibility for containing a subterranean chamber of any kind. Everything in the geography and geology of the area was wrong, which is what she expected in the first place.

By two o'clock, Kristi had shifted her entire focus over to the prospect of finding a manmade tunnel or mine shaft. She knew from Chris' research that there was nothing in the literature about the mine itself that mentioned a submerged shaft. However, she had also read the extract from Patterson's journal that spoke of the underground bunk room, and this became the target of her search.

After her four o'clock check-in call, Kristi made a pass along the remnant of the road that had passed by some of the original industrial buildings, including the mill and the blacksmith's shop. None of these were still identifiable, although she could tell from the maps and the linear positioning of the bumps in the earth that they had once been part of the thriving community. On two occasions, Kristi found herself on the edge of steep depressions in the earth, which were bordered by unusually straight excavation lines. However, in both cases she was able to attribute the unnatural symmetry to the basements of long-defunct buildings. If one of these had been the original mine shaft described in Patterson's journal, there would certainly be nothing left of it to see.

As the day dragged on, Kristi's search became slower and less energetic, her spirits sinking somewhat with the declining sun. It was getting cooler outside, and she was almost out of ideas. It was five forty-five when she decided to place her last call to Sean, which he had received in the town of Speculator. With only a couple of possibilities left, she was almost ready to start the long drive home.

After saying goodbye to Chris, she wandered rather unevenly between the last few wrecks on the east side of the river. These were some of the last buildings to have been used, although several of them had been built on the foundations of earlier structures. She was tired, and her mind was somewhat blank, certainly not focused as it had been earlier in the afternoon. Because her attention was directed down at the ground, she hadn't noticed that she was being observed.

About one hundreds yards away, slightly uphill from Kristi, stood a man who had been watching Kristi work for the past twenty minutes. At first, he hadn't been interested in her perambulations; he was merely walking the site to find any other buildings that were still standing. However, there was something about Kristi's movements that fascinated the man. He stood completely still, and he could have passed for a cardboard cutout if not for the locks of red hair that blew in the early autumn breeze. He watched as she looked between a stack of papers in her hand and the next recognizable manmade feature, often walking around the perimeter of each structure while probing beneath boards and other obstacles. Ben

Grainger's stance resembled that of a big cat, or other animal of prey, slightly crouched as if attempting to remain hidden before pouncing.

Down below, Kristi continued her work, following transect lines and completing grid inspections around each and every remaining irregular hump in the soil. It was time to go, and she was still on-site only because of her reluctance to leave a job without ensuring it was completed to the best of her ability. The building she was viewing was better preserved than most, although also considerably smaller. As she stood back and contemplated its size and shape, she thought that it looked too small to be a year-round house. However, since it was in close proximity to several other residences, she reasoned that perhaps it might have been a small cottage or guest house. The roof had caved in and the walls were slumping inward, but at least parts of the siding and most of the brickwork were intact.

Although she didn't dare set foot inside the interior of the rotting structure, she did make a complete circuit around the outer walls, noting the locations of the entryways and stairwells. She continued around the back of the heap, where she was temporarily shielded from view from the stranger above. However, as she rounded the left side of the building, she was once more discernable through the trees and brush.

It was only when Kristi rounded the front left corner of the small house that she realized that the first section of roofing was not part of the building at all, but rather a separate storage shed abutted against the original outside wall of the house. The shed was in better condition than the rest of the structure, with three of four walls in decent condition. The roof also appeared somewhat stable, although its peak displayed a distinct catenary shape, indicating that it could crumble if the walls were jostled in any way.

Fascinated with the dark interior of the shed, Kristi poked her head into the musty space to look around. The entire area covered by the roof was no more than one hundred square feet, and most of that was within a body-length of the door. Kristi took one tentative step inside the gloomy confines of the rickety overhang, then another. In doing so, she experienced a feeling she hadn't felt all day. It was a combination of excitement, exhilaration, and fear all rolled into one.

Kristi moved slowly and deliberately, with one delicate step following another, until she was almost at the far corner of the room. Immediately in front of her face, she saw an unidentifiable oblong sphere that hung from overhead. Unable to speculate on its origin, she reached out and touched its outer surface with her hand, feeling its papery exterior shell. Only after a few seconds of tactile exploration did she yank her hand back in abject fear, suddenly realizing that the object was actually a massive hornets' nest, which probably housed thousands of the stinging insects. She froze for a moment, paralyzed in terror until she realized that the nest was several years old, abandoned and empty. Silently she cursed herself for not taking out her flashlight before entering the place.

Kristi's heart was beating through her chest as she leaned forward, feeling slightly winded from the adrenalin rush of the perceived threat. Even though she was in incredible physical condition, she found herself breathing hard from the peril of the nest. She wanted to lean up against a wall or other fixed object, but she didn't dare risk applying pressure to anything that might have structurally supported the roof. It was small, but it was still heavy enough to break her skull if it collapsed on top of her.

Taking a step away from the suspended hive, Kristi thought she detected a spring-like sensation. It was as though her left foot had ventured forth onto a trampoline, which responded to her weight with an upward surge of its own. Afraid that she might fall through an unseen hole in the floor, she tested the surface beneath her other foot, which was solid, with no sign of give. It was only below her left foot, which she tried once again with the same result.

Intrigued by the cause of the bouncing movement, Kristi stepped away, removed her satchel, and pulled out her small flashlight. She directed its beam at the floor in the middle of the room, and found nothing but a layer of leaves and dirt, and an accumulation of broken tools and nails. She worked her way across the floor towards the corner where she'd noticed the movement, all the while fearing that the floorboards might give way after years of neglect and rot. Dropping to her hands and knees, her fingertips detected a low, flat edge of a large board or plate. It was cold and hard, with the feel of very aged metal. She tried to lift the object up, but found that it weighed too much for her to get off the ground. However, she was capable of sliding it from side to side, and was thus able to move it across the floor in the direction of the front door.

What was revealed by Kristi's efforts was enough to take her breath away. There, in the inky darkness of the ancient storage shed, was an opening that led into the ground. Where, or how far, she did not know. All she could observe was that a makeshift ladder, constructed from very old tree limbs, led downward into the pit and disappeared from view.

Kristi turned her light back on and shined it into the depths of the hole, determining that its floor was probably only about twelve feet below ground level. It extended in the same direction as the house, although she could not fathom its dimensions or structural integrity. One thing she did know, however, was that this was not a natural cave. It had been excavated long ago, through sheer sweat and raw muscle, digging out the rock in agonizingly slow progression. She leaned into the hole and shined her light on the side walls, noticing that the rock sides of the shaft still showed the telltale scars of the pickaxe and shovel.

Unsure of how to proceed, Kristi's natural curiosity got the best of her. She forgot all about the time, as the thrill of exploring a long-forgotten subterranean chamber subjugated her previous plans. The ladder had vertical spars that were over six inches in diameter, and horizontal rungs that were about half that size. Heavy iron spikes had been driven through each side of the crossbars to hold them solidly in place. At one time, this improvised stairway would have probably supported several hundred pounds. However, as Kristi examined it in the beam of the flashlight, she realized that the wood had deteriorated in the many decades since its construction, and she eyed it with some degree of trepidation.

Finally overcoming her fear, she swung her body around to the seated position with her feet hanging over the edge of the opening in the ground.

She extended one leg in the direction of the ladder and tested the top rung with a small amount of weight. The foothold felt rock solid under her sole, so she increased the load until she was placing almost her entire weight on the aged wood. Mustering the courage to take the plunge, she surrendered the security of her grip on the ground above and placed both hands on the sides of the ladder.

Given her initial trepidation, the descent to the floor of the chamber was anticlimactic. The ancient ladder served its purpose without a hitch, although there were two or three rungs that protested her weight by bowing slightly as she passed. One rung in particular gave her cause for concern; the second step down from the top felt loose on the right side, as though the spike that fastened the rung to the vertical pole had rotted out. She made a mental note to try to avoid placing any weight on that side when she returned to the surface.

As soon as Kristi reached the bottom, she turned around and panned her light across the space in front of her, amazed at the sight. It was much bigger than she had expected, and extended out from the entrance into a cavernous room that was at least sixty feet long and forty feet wide. Whoever had hacked this cave from the ground had left a number of vertical rock pillars in place, presumably to serve as a support for the overhead ceiling. Wood bracing had been added as an extra precaution, although Kristi could not tell whether that was required here or not. She guessed that the original structure above had been built right over this excavation, either before the chamber was dug or after.

The interior of the underground room had a great many signs of human habitation, including a number of wooden frames that looked to have been used as platforms for bedding at one time. A stack of blackened tin pots and pans were piled in one area, next to a collapsed table that now lay flat on the ground. Kristi guessed that there were a lot of details that she could not see, as the darkness of the space seemed to absorb the glow of her flashlight. She turned it off at one point, just to confirm the absolute blackness of the underground chamber. There was a small amount of light from above, but it was not enough to use for navigating around the wooden obstructions or rock columns inside the chamber. She could also now see that there was only one entrance to the room; the entrance from which she had just descended.

Having reached the farthest extremes of the chamber, Kristi began to backtrack toward the ladder and the opening. As she passed a heavy board on the side of a bed frame to her right, her flashlight briefly illuminated a few words at the end of a written sentence. She came to an immediate halt and held her light on the inscription, which had been burned into the wood with a hot pointed object. The penmanship was amazingly neat, considering the crude utensil that must have been used to engrave the words into the grain.

Kristi held her breath as she read the words that had been written so long ago: "There is not a man beneath the canopy of heaven who does not know that slavery is wrong for him."

Kristi was now fairly certain that she knew the nature behind this hidden underground hole, and her body tingled with excitement as she stood in the place, thinking of the events that had transpired one hundred fifty years earlier. As her mind wandered, she shifted her feet and inadvertently kicked the end of a metal rod, which clanged loudly to the floor next to a rock stanchion positioned nearby. She directed her light down at the pole, which was about two feet long and roughly the same diameter as a thin cigar. For such a small object, it had made a surprising amount of noise when toppled against the hard surface, and Kristi could feel her heartbeat accelerate once again.

By this time, Kristi had been underground for about twenty minutes, and Grainger had become curious as to her disappearance. He discarded any plans to remain concealed and walked overtly down the gradual decline to the shed where he'd last seen her standing. After a quick inspection of the area, he became puzzled, and stood outside the dilapidated shed scratching his head. The woman he'd been watching had been there just a short while ago, and he hadn't seen her leave the area. The woods were fairly full with brush and other undergrowth, but not dense enough to completely cloak an adult walking away from the scene.

Grainger stared into the darkness of the covered shed for a minute or two, and then decided to move forward, much in the same manner that Kristi had a short time earlier. However, since the plate that had covered the hole was still moved to one side, he could see that there was an opening into the ground, which he assumed was the explanation behind Kristi's vanishing trick.

After allowing his eyes to adjust to the reduced light, Grainger stepped onto the top rung of the ladder. However, he was not as careful as Kristi, and his weight more than doubled hers. As the sole of his boot stepped onto the second rung down, the end of the limb gave way, and the metal spike tore rapidly through the rotten end of the wood. It levered downward, and Grainger's boot slipped off and down the ladder. Had both his hands been holding onto the vertical side poles, he might have caught himself from falling. However, neither hand was actually gripping the ladder itself. His right hand was loosely resting on the very top extension of the right vertical spar. Worse yet, his left hand had a firm grip on a piece of wood that appeared to be firmly anchored to the floor, just beside the top of the ladder. What Grainger didn't realize in the darkness was that his left handhold was actually the bottom support of a partition that was still attached to the wall of the flimsy shed.

The chain reaction caused by Grainger's fall was something out of a comic strip, if not for the seriousness of the situation for both Grainger and Kristi. As Grainger slid through the entrance, his left hand maintained its death grip on the wooden divider, which in turn exerted an inward force on the left wall of the shed. The wall buckled in from the base, causing the rotted roof to pull loose from the top of the framework. After a moment of suspended animation, the flat boards that comprised the side of the shed tumbled to the ground, leaving a roof and two very weak vertical supports. If the construction had been new, the two remaining walls might have withstood the pressure. However, with the sudden movement from the now-downed wall, the roof began to torque in a clockwise direction, further stressing the collapsing frame. Within ten seconds, the entire remainder of the rotten shed came crashing down in a twisted heap.

Grainger, meanwhile, had fallen straight down the ladder, making contact with several rungs as he tumbled. He probably would have been flipped backwards and sustained serious injuries had he not been able to hook his arm inside one of the last available rungs, about five feet above the floor of the chamber. As a result, his entire body was swung, still upright, around the back of the ladder while his feet made contact with the floor. The force of the fall, combined with the pressure exerted on his arm by the rough bark of the tree branch on the ladder, opened a cut on his bicep, while simultaneously throwing him onto his back on the cave floor. Yet, even through the pain and confusion of the tumble and ensuing impact on the floor, Grainger remained silent, not uttering a word or other sound to express his pain and irritation.

At the time of the cave-in, Kristi had been examining the architecture of the left side of the excavation. She was amazed that the walls had been carved away with such precision as to form superbly vertical planes. Because of this accuracy, the timbers of the bed frames fitted neatly against the wall of the space, and each frame appeared to be aligned perfectly with the one before it. Her review of the construction was interrupted by Grainger's fall, followed first by the crash of the shed wall and then the collapse of the roof as it landed on top of the exit chute.

Kristi's knee-jerk reaction was to shut off her flashlight and listen, afraid that some part of her own surroundings would give way to the same collapse. She noticed almost immediately that the light emitting from the entrance hole had suddenly gone dark, and that the blackness was now absolute. From that observation alone, she was able to deduce the fact that it was the outside shed, and not the actual cave entrance, that had caved in. She exhaled a lengthy yet silent breath through her nose, relieved that she either would be able to pick her own way out of the rubble, or else call Sean on his satellite cell phone to ask for help.

Kristi was about to turn on her flashlight to regain her bearings when she heard another noise. At the bottom of the ladder, Ben Grainger had picked himself up off the floor and mopped off the blood that was seeping from the lengthy scrape on his arm. Feeling the pain of the fall and the inconvenience of being trapped, he forgot all about the woman he'd followed into this awful abyss. He was also furious at himself for not carrying a light of any kind, which would make his escape even more difficult. After taking a moment to mentally summarize his situation, he expressed his sentiments with a single word.

"Shit," he said, spitting out the word with self-disdain.

The single expletive, rasped by the coarse voice somewhere in close proximity, struck instant fear into Kristi's heart. It took her all of a second to quickly and accurately reassess her situation, although her appraisal was anything but comforting. She was trapped underground, in total darkness, and she wasn't alone.

CHAPTER 18

Saturday, September 13, 2015

Chris and Sean had made great time since departing Speculator. It wasn't that they were driving quickly, because Sean didn't like revving the engine on his beloved Mercedes beyond the midrange of its capabilities. This drove Chris to distraction on many occasions, at which times Sean would point to the vehicle's odometer, which had clocked over 325,000 miles since it rolled off the production line. However, the pair had only taken the short, five-minute break in Speculator, with no other stops since leaving Sean's house that afternoon.

It was ten after seven when the two turned off of County Road 84 and onto the Tahawus Road that would take them to Upper Works and the ghost town of Adirondac. Sean had insisted that Chris take the lead for the entire trip, in case a deer ran out into the road. "It's a lot easier to find parts for your Jeep than it is for my Mercedes," he reasoned. As much as he tried, Chris couldn't argue with the logic behind that statement.

They rolled up the hill in the declining daylight, still able to drive perfectly well without headlights, although most people they passed back on Route 84 had them turned on already. Chris turned to glance at the blast furnace as it slipped by the window on the right, a veritable ghost monster asleep amongst the trees of the road. No matter how many times he saw the gargantuan structure, he would always be amazed.

At the parking lot, Chris looked around. It was as he had hoped; Grainger's Mini Cooper was still there, parked beneath the trees, silent and empty. Even better, Chris noticed, was the empty parking space immediately next to Grainger's car. Chris stuck his arm out the driver's side window and waved Sean into the empty spot.

"Perfect," he called out the window, giving Sean the "thumbs up" sign once he had settled his car into the opening.

Before Sean could even get out the driver's seat, Chris was already reaching over his body and positioning a page on the front seat. "What's that?" he asked, watching Chris place the paper in the middle of the leather surface.

"It's all part of my plan," said Chris, choosing not to explain every detail of his idea to snare Grainger. "Once Grainger steals this document from your car tonight, or tomorrow, or whenever, it's all over but the handcuffs."

"Let me see that," said Sean, snatching the paper off the seat. He quickly scanned the content, appreciating the attention to detail that Chris had paid in creating the phony artifact. "Wow, you're pretty good," he said, complimenting the work. "But how is Grainger going to get into a locked vehicle to steal this, if that's the big idea?"

"That's *almost* the big idea," replied Chris, winking back at his friend.

"Almost? OK, I'll bite—what's the 'almost' part?" asked Sean.

"Your car is going to be left unlocked tonight," said Chris. "That way, Grainger won't even have to break in. All he'll have to do is open the door and remove the paper, and we'll be ready to move in."

"I don't like that plan very much," said Sean. "Why don't we leave the paper in your car, and drive mine back to the hotel?"

"Have you forgotten, oh Wise One, that Grainger knows *your* car, and *your* house, and *your* everything, from the information he got at the Frank Stewart Room? That's why he broke into your home and not mine," countered Chris.

Sean fell silent while considering this point, a resigned expression on his face.

"Anyway, since your car will be unlocked, Grainger won't have to break anything to gain entry," continued Chris, furthering his point.

"I guess you're right," said Sean, looking a bit downcast. "Grainger probably knows more about me by now than many of my friends."

"I wouldn't be surprised if he sends you a Christmas card this year," said Chris, laughing and patting Sean on the back. "Now come on—let's head back to Long Lake and get our stuff into the hotel room. Besides, their bar room is open until eleven o'clock, and they've got great Rueben sandwiches in that place. I feel like I could eat a horse."

Sean hopped into the passenger side of Chris' Jeep and they started pulling out of the lot. Chris planted his foot on the accelerator and spun his wheels once, just for fun, before they began the reverse trek back to Route 28N and the town of Long Lake. Chris was about to make a comment about the improved condition of the Tahawus road when he was interrupted by his friend.

"Uh, Chris?" Sean said tentatively.

"Yes?"

"Kristi drives a Chevy Cobalt, right?" asked Sean.

"Yeah, she does," replied Chris, adjusting his mirror for night driving. "She got it about three years ago. She really loves it. Why do you ask?"

"It's red, right?" continued Sean. "Sort of a deep red, like a cross between a stop sign and a black cherry?"

"Well, that's an unusual way of describing it, but basically you're right on," said Chris. "Why?"

"Because a car that fit that description was parked in the corner of the lot back there," said Sean, looking at Chris with narrowed eyes, "and it had a Cornell parking sticker on the back window. It just looked like Kristi's car."

"You're kidding?" said Chris, suddenly applying the breaks.

"I think we'd better turn around and have a look, as long as we're up here anyway," said Sean.

Chris hung a three-point turn in the middle of the narrow road and quickly accelerated back into the lot. He flipped on his high beams and pointed them into the end of the parking lot, where Sean had indicated the position of the compact car in question.

"Yup, that's her car alright," confirmed Chris, recognizing the plate number beneath the rear bumper. "I'm glad you noticed it."

"What are you thinking?" asked Sean, worried about Chris's mindset.

"Well, the first thing I want to do is to have a look inside," replied Chris, parking his own vehicle and climbing out the side. "She said she was pretty tired; maybe she climbed into the back seat to catch a couple hours of sleep before heading south."

Chris and Sean walked around opposite sides of the car, quickly establishing that it was empty. As Sean stood by, Chris strolled around to the front of the vehicle and placed his hand on the hood. "It hasn't been run within the last couple hours," he said. "The engine is cold. She must be somewhere nearby."

"Does she own a tent?" asked Sean, wracking his brain for alternate solutions.

"I think she has one that belongs to the Geology Department, but she only carries that when she takes students on overnight field trips," said Chris.

Sean pulled out his new satellite phone and looked at the display for incoming or missed calls. There were none since five forty-five, which was Kristi's last regular check-in call. It was now almost seven thirty.

"Would you like me to try calling her number?" asked Sean, holding up his cell phone for Chris to see. "No matter where she is, I should be able to get a call through to her."

"Sure," replied Chris. "We might as well give it a shot."

As Sean dialed the numbers, Chris looked across the parking lot at Grainger's car. It was only about a dozen spots away from Kristi's car. The sight of those two vehicles sitting that close to each other made Chris nervous. In the background, he heard the sound of a phone ringing a couple times before going to the message recording.

"That's odd," said Sean, a reflective look on his face.

"What's that?" asked Chris.

"I haven't dialed Kristi's number more than a couple times," said Sean, "but last week, when we spoke to test her new phone and set up the features, she had set the messaging system to come on after five rings, not two. Maybe she's just talking on the phone right now, and it's set up to ring twice if she's on another call."

"Or maybe she's someplace where she just can't speak," said Chris, alarm registering in his voice.

"Do you think it would be a wise idea to call the police?" asked Sean.

Chris thought for a moment before shaking his head. "No, I don't want to press the panic button quite yet," he answered. "Besides, if we did call the police, there's really not much that we could tell them now. She's only been out of touch for about ninety minutes, and for all we know she could have taken a stroll down a trail. Or maybe she decided to do a little more snooping amongst the relic buildings, but just didn't think to call us."

"Is that what you really think?" asked Sean.

"No, it's not," said Chris. "But for now, I'd rather not dwell on some of the other possibilities."

Down in the depths of the pitch-black chamber, Kristi had been doing her best to keep her emotions and nerves in check. It had been over an hour since the hulk of the shed had collapsed over the opening to the underground room, and since that time she had remained absolutely silent. Even her breathing gave her cause for concern, as she was sure that she could hear her own respiration over the cathedral silence of her surroundings. It helped when the man with whom she was trapped attempted to lift up the timbers from the fallen roof over the entrance hole, because the noise he created permitted her to breathe regularly without fear of being detected. During those periods of activity, she also attempted to creep closer to the place where she had encountered the first rock stanchion, which was located in the middle of the chamber about twenty feet from the ladder. She wanted to find that pillar because she knew the metal rod she'd noticed earlier could be used as a weapon if the need arose.

Kristi wasn't certain that the man in the cave with her was Grainger, but she strongly suspected that to be the case. She knew from Chris that he had been in the area, and that his wanderings would have taken him within close proximity of her own search for the underground room. Even the sound of his voice, gruff and crude, matched her mental image of how Ben Grainger might sound. She tried to calm her nerves by telling herself that she could reason with Grainger, given that they were both stuck in the same predicament. After all, it might take a team effort to clear the route to the surface, and there was no one else available to help. But the red flashing "WARNING" signs pulsed repeatedly inside her head, telling her that this was a very dangerous man. She reminded herself of this by recalling Maggie's injuries of just a few weeks earlier, which was the only stimulus needed to keep her quiet and concealed.

After many minutes of excruciatingly slow progress, Kristi finally laid her fingertips on the hard uneven surface of the rock stanchion in the middle of the room. She knew from the angle of her approach that she was on the back side of the pillar, opposite from the man she suspected to be Grainger. Her next move was to quietly creep on all fours, circling the post to her left, which was counterclockwise around the column. It was a slow, painful process as the sharp rock floor and cinders bit cruelly into her thinly-clad knees. At one point, a pointed object that felt like a nail attempted to pierce the palm of her hand, and she had to bite her lip to keep from yelping out in pain.

After an additional few minutes of tedious movement across the rough substrate, Kristi's search was finally rewarded. The tip of her middle finger on her right hand came in contact with the end of a round metal object that felt like a teacher's old-fashioned pointer, only many times heavier. She waited until the unseen person, who was now trying to use a lever to move the materials off one corner of the hole, was fully involved in his task before she dared to lift the weighty metal rod off the chamber floor.

Finally, improvised weapon in hand, Kristi stood up and breathed a small sigh of relief. Making certain to remain silent, she decided to soundlessly retreat into the deeper recesses of the subterranean room, hopefully to hide until someone might notice the newly collapsed shed. As she planned out her next moves, she visualized the course she would have to take through the debris to reach the back of the room. That was one advantage that she realized she had over her adversary; she knew that he had never seen the bottom of the chamber before the shed had erased the last light from the space. In other words, she knew her way around the place a little, while he was literally in the dark.

Kristi was about to take her first step, comforted in the knowledge that she just had to travel about thirty feet over a relatively easy path in order to reach her objective, which was a wooden bunk along the back wall of the excavation. At that point, she would slowly lower herself to a prone position, and then slide underneath the platform she'd seen earlier with her light. From that obscured location, she felt confident that she could remain hidden until Grainger fell asleep sometime during the night. Once that happened, she would be able to use her cell phone to text Sean and give him her exact position and situation. She had the entire plot planned out in her head. In fact, she had thought of almost everything.

Except for the possibility that someone might try to call her cell phone.

Kristi's nerves shot through the roof as her cell phone suddenly blasted out the first several lines of Aerosmith's hit song "Living on the Edge." Making matters worse was the fact that the luminous screen lit up her immediate surroundings with a bright blue glow that further pinpointed her position. Kristi panicked, fumbling with the phone until it slipped from her fingers and rattled around the invisible rock beneath her feet. The song had played almost a full chorus by the time she was able to grasp it in her hand and shut off the sound. However, the only way she could turn off the lit screen was to shut off the phone itself, which she did with an additional several seconds of scrambling.

Despite her frenetic attempts to quiet the device, she realized it was all for naught. There was simply no way that the electronic sounds generated by her phone could have been missed by someone standing within thirty feet of her spot. As if to confirm her fears, a disembodied voice sounded off, stabbing her emotional psyche with a spear that penetrated through to her heart.

"Don't shut it off, little lady. That's a good song you're playing over there. I was looking forward to hearing a little more." The request was followed by an evil-sounding laugh.

Kristi knew that nothing she said would have made a difference to the man she now knew was Grainger, so she remained silent. To speak, to make any noise would have only served to update him on her position as she moved through the void. She had thought that Grainger was up on the ladder, trying to free himself from the dungeon. However, the sounds she heard next were definitely footsteps coming in her direction.

"I knew you were down here, little lady," the voice from the darkness sneered again. "I was watching you from up the hill, and I was admiring your work. But I wanted to ask you, why are you here?"

Kristi sensed the footsteps coming closer, moving in a direct line to her location. He was moving faster than she had expected, given the complete absence of light. She knew that he couldn't see, but she had expected him to use tentative steps to move slowly across the floor; apparently he didn't feel the need for such caution.

"Are you, perhaps, friends with my pal, Sean Riggins?" Again, the voice was followed by the twisted laughter. He was enjoying the game.

Kristi estimated that Grainger was now only ten to fifteen feet away, and still walking a straight path. She tried stepping backwards and to her left, hoping to sidestep his blind movements. However, because she was forced to move faster than before, she was unable to remain in "stealth" mode, and her feet produced an audible sound as they stepped across the rock and dirt floor of the chamber.

"Please don't go away, little lady. I want to see the papers you were reading outside. You *will* give them to me."

Kristi slipped her phone inside the pocket of her jeans and took a tighter grip on the metal rod, which she clutched in her right hand.

"Yes, you will, little lady. You will give me those papers, so you might as well do it now," said Grainger, trying to strike fear into her heart. "Believe me, I will get them from you. Making me find you down here will only make me mad, and you really don't want to do that."

Grainger was now less than ten feet away. He was still coming at her, although somewhat more slowly. Kristi used her last few seconds to attempt a trick she'd seen used in a movie many years earlier. She bent down as silently as possible and swept a fistful of coarse sand and grit from the floor of the chamber. It filled her hand as she straightened her body and waited for the assault that was about to commence.

"I hear you breathing, little lady. You're scared, aren't you?" He was now too close to avoid contact; escape was out of the question.

Kristi abandoned her silence and spoke suddenly, using a loud, commanding voice. "Don't force me to pull the trigger. I don't want to hurt you, but I will if I have to." She knew that he probably wouldn't fall for the deception, but it was worth a try.

"Oh, you have a gun, do you, little lady?" The question was laden with sarcasm, punctuated with another outburst of laughter. "Somehow, I don't believe you. You just don't seem like the type."

Grainger was now close enough that Kristi could almost feel his breath on her face, two feet away, perhaps three at most. Talking her way past him was not an option, and she was within three seconds of coming within his grasp. It was now or never. She only hoped that he had his eyes open, trying to use any glimmer of light or shadow that might have existed in that hellhole.

Kristi thrust her left arm in Grainger's direction in a move of blinding speed, her hand opening fully as her arm reached full extension. She aimed high, at an angle slightly above her own head, to account for Grainger's greater height. Her aim was accurate and true. The fistful of gritty particulate matter hit Grainger's eyes and face, halting his progress immediately. She heard him grunt once, followed by a few moments of spitting as he rid his mouth of the sand.

Kristi was mad, scared, and in no position to assume that she had permanently disabled her attacker with a handful of dirt. However, she also didn't want to resort to her weapon, the metal rod, for fear of inflicting severe injury, or even death, upon the man. Not unless it was necessary to save herself from a similar fate. Instead, she used a technique from her aerobic kick boxing class, and brought her right foot around in a high roundhouse movement against Grainger's upper body. However, instead of inflicting damage, her foot bounced off his rock-hard shoulder as though she had kicked a tree trunk.

"Now that wasn't very nice, little lady," snarled the voice, now with a much harder, more sinister edge. "I told you not to make me mad, and you ignored me, didn't you? Perhaps you'd like to kick me again? I don't think so. I like my massages harder than that, so don't waste your time."

Kristi's mind was in overdrive, forming a mental image of the man behind the voice as he stood in front of her. Because she had taken a step backwards as he spit the grit from his mouth, she estimated his distance at five feet. However, the next sound she heard was that of a footstep, as he resumed his quest to find her in the darkness.

"Now you're going to pay for that, little lady," said Grainger's voice. It wasn't filled with rage, or even anger. It was now just a cold, hard statement from an evil mind that had reached a decision. Kristi knew that her options had just expired.

Kristi never thought about her next move. It came purely from instinct and her natural sense of self-preservation. Placing a second hand on the rod, she raised it over her head and brought it straight down, as though chopping a log in half for the fireplace. Unfortunately, she hadn't counted on the end of the rod coming in contact with the roof of the chamber, which was only a few feet above her head. The steel still found its mark, but with a reduced velocity due to the obstruction from above.

Kristi stepped back again and listened to the sound of Grainger's rage, which had exploded with the pain of the strike. The only sound that came from his mouth was a single syllable that sounded like "aack," although she was no longer trying to make sense of anything he might have said.

She sensed he had abandoned all caution and hesitation and was launching his full body weight and strength into an all-out frontal attack. She turned her body sideways, so that her left shoulder was facing him, and pulled the rod back into the position of a baseball batter, coiled for the pitch.

Kristi knew that Grainger was tall, about the same height as Chris. But she also figured that his head would be slightly lowered as he charged, so this is where she chose to target. There was no room for error, nor time for compassion. Grainger was right on top of her, and she would get but one last chance. She gritted her teeth and swung with everything she had.

Kristi would never forget the feel of the metal rod as it made contact with Grainger's skull. The force of the impact sent vibrations down the length of the steel shaft and into Kristi's arms. The sound associated with the collision was more of a slap, although it was followed by the audible noise one would expect from an oversized tuning fork. This time, the blow was accurate and delivered with full force. So it was with much surprise that Kristi found herself still under attack by the invisible figure.

Grainger didn't grab her, or throw his arms around her in a bear hug. He simply crashed into her and pushed her to the ground, where she sprawled across the large flat surface of the broken table. Then, he fell on top of her, pinning her to the rough grain of the untreated wood. Kristi immediately kicked upward and squirmed, trying to get out of his grasp, before she realized that he wasn't actually holding her. As a matter of fact, as she reached around to try to claw at his face, she sensed that he wasn't moving at all. His entire body was slumped over hers, limp and motionless. She placed both hands on one shoulder and pushed him over, rolling his inert form away from her torso and onto the chamber floor. He was down for the count, an unresponsive hulk.

Kristi jumped up and snatched the phone from out of her pocket. She pressed the button to turn it on and immediately checked out the time on the top of the screen. It was seven forty-two, only twelve minutes after Sean's attempted call though Kristi didn't know that. For all it seemed, it might have been an hour, or a day. Time had no meaning right now, no relevance in the absolute darkness of her surroundings. She wanted nothing more than to be able to see, to part the curtain of invisibility with just a single beam of light, enabling her to take stock of her situation. Gratefully, she was able to find her small satchel, which lay nearby on the floor next to the rock stanchion. It took her but a moment to find the flashlight, which she energized immediately.

The first thing that Kristi saw in the eye of the beam was Grainger's body, unconscious and laying face-up next to the table top. The locks of bright red hair seemed to glow in the darkness, and she recalled how Chris had described him when he warned her of his evil intent. She crept close to him and shone the light onto his face, hoping not to find him dead. Instead, he was breathing regularly, with his eyes closed and an ugly wound across the left side of his face. A stripe of darkening redness appeared beneath his eye, and extended across his cheek to a point below his left ear. The gash was beginning to ooze blood from the torn skin, although Kristi didn't think that the overall injury was too severe. In fact, as she watched, Grainger moaned and turned his head a small amount before slipping back into unconsciousness. It made her nervous, and she immediately stepped away from the sleeping form.

She stepped towards the blocked entrance of the room and dialed Sean's number on her phone. She had to get through to him and find out where he was. Chris and Sean represented her only way out. If Grainger came out of his stupor before they could clear the stairwell, he would most certainly make every attempt to find and kill her. If anything, the stakes had increased.

Kristi turned off her flashlight and quickly tapped the contact number for Sean's cell phone on her own keypad. She listened to the first ring, which seemed to last forever, praying that he'd be able to answer before another second passed. She got her wish, as the connection clicked on and Sean's voice came across loud and clear.

"Hey, where are you, Kristi?" came the welcome sound of Sean's voice. "You've had us both worried for a while. We're here but couldn't reach you. Are you still down in the woods looking around?"

Kristi had to make a conscious effort to slow down and speak clearly, without allowing her emotions to convert her speech into a torrent of babbled syllables. She took a deep breath before starting and then spoke as concisely as her mindset would permit.

"No, I'm in deep trouble and I need immediate help," she replied. "I'm stuck in an underground room with your friend Ben Grainger, who is temporarily unconscious."

"Hold on," interrupted Sean, who took a moment to activate the speaker option on his phone. He then held the device in a position where both he and Chris could listen and speak.

"OK, Kristi—you're stuck underground in a room of some sort, and Grainger is there, but unconscious, is that correct?" Sean repeated.

"Yes," confirmed Kristi. "We're in some sort of a large basement that was underneath a small dwelling in the row of houses you looked at last weekend. The one that we're in had an old shed that was covering an entrance to a shaft that led down about fifteen feet to the excavated room; I think it was an attempted mine shaft, but I can't be sure. You'll need to look for a square roof, about ten feet on each side, with dull reddish roofing tiles."

Sean nodded in recognition as he listened to Kristi's description. "Do you remember if you saw any survey tape tied to the trees near this shed?"

"Yes, I know I did," replied Kristi, sounding excited but still in control of herself. "There was some yellow tape tied to some trees both in back of the house and on the left side. Oh, and by the way, the shed was built onto the left side of the house, but the main part of the building looks like it collapsed several years ago."

"Keep talking to us," said Chris. "We're leaving the parking lot, and we're running down the road right now. We should be there in a few minutes at most."

"No," yelled Kristi. "You've got to come over the bridge, and then double back along the back on this side of the river to get here."

"The hell with the bridge," said Chris, speaking loudly enough to be heard over the speaker phone. "We've got good lights with us, and it's a lot quicker to just walk through the river. How is Grainger doing?"

Kristi turned her flashlight back on for a moment and illuminated the figure on the ground once again. "He's still out, and hopefully he'll stay that way for at least another half hour, or until you get there."

"How did you manage that?" asked Chris, impressed that someone the size of his girlfriend could knock out a man as large as Grainger.

"I'll tell you about that later," said Kristi, "hopefully over a strong drink."

"I think we're almost to you," said Sean, as he and Chris pushed through the high vegetation and underbrush of the deserted village. "About another two hundred yards and I think we'll be able to hand you a rum and coke."

"Make it a double, please," said Kristi, trying to sound calm through the stress.

Sean soon found his own tape markings that he'd used the previous weekend as he surveyed the site, and they both began to follow them down the row of rotted timber skeletons. The darkness made the search more difficult, and at one point Sean was convinced that they had wandered off the remains of the residential road. However, in another three minutes, Chris spied the peaked top of a small square red roof that sat on top of a pile of decayed lumber. Everything matched the description given to them by Kristi over the phone, and Chris felt his heart give a leap.

"Kristi, can you still hear me?" Chris asked.

"Loud and clear," replied Kristi.

"I want you to move next to the entranceway of the basement you're in, and then let me know if you hear anything, OK?"

"With pleasure," said Kristi, her voice sounding hopeful for the first time.

Chris and Sean waited for about a minute, and then both began yelling down into the pile of wood beneath the red roofing tiles. "Hello, hello!" they called, over and over again.

"Yes, yes, I hear you!" screamed Kristi over the cell phone. Chris was ecstatic that he could also hear her muffled voice coming though the wreckage as well.

"Honey, listen to me," said Chris. "Can you hear me clearly?"

"Yes, I can," said Kristi.

"I want you to back away from the entranceway now, in case anything falls while we're pulling the roof off the entrance," instructed Chris. "As a matter of fact, I'd rather you got as far away from there as possible, in case Grainger wakes up while we're working. Maybe you could find a place to hide. Hopefully he doesn't have a flashlight of his own, does he?"

"No, he doesn't, or I'd probably be dead," conceded Kristi.

"Then find a good spot to cover yourself in there and stay hidden until we break through. I'll yell for you as soon as we're inside."

Sean quickly tied their fixed lantern to a low tree branch near the collapsed roof, and Chris strapped on his head light. The two of them instinctively moved around to the same side of the roof and tried heaving it out of the way, only to find that it was more than they could lift in a single attempt. Instead, they began to break off chunks of the rotted timbers and sections of tile as fast as they could move, tossing the debris off to the side. Within about ten minutes, they had created a second pile of discarded material that was now removed from the equation, lightening the load of the remaining roof.

"Think we should give it another try yet?" asked Sean, looking at the stripped-down rooftop remaining over the hole.

"We might as well," said Chris. "It'll only take us a second, and we can always rip off more if we need to."

The two men once again moved to the uphill side of the wreckage and stood shoulder-to-shoulder, each one placing both hands underneath the decayed frame of the downed roof. This time they were able to lift the frame off the ground much more easily. They were about to reach the tipping point where the entire roof would have flipped backwards and off the entryway, when they were interrupted by the sound of splitting boards ripping themselves apart. At that moment, Chris' half of the roof rolled forward, while Sean's half dropped suddenly back over the hole. Sean jumped out of the way, and narrowly avoided being gored by a row of protruding rusty nails.

"Watch it!" shouted Chris, as his friend jumped away from the hazard.

Sean breathed a sigh of relief and prepared to give the rest of the structure another try. "You ready?" he asked Chris, looking over his shoulder for assistance.

With the two of them working against the last remaining section of roof, they were able to easily lift it out of the way and off the rest of the crushed remains of the shed. They took only a second to exchange a celebratory high-five, and then set to work removing the rest of the side panels and four-by-four supports. Some of these pieces were surprisingly heavy. However, with the two of them working together, only moving the material that rested directly over the hole itself, they were able to finish clearing the entry within the next ten minutes.

Chris crawled over the rest of the shed that still surrounded the opening and leaned into the darkness. "Anyone home?" he called into the depths of the excavation.

"Yes, I'm here. I'm coming," Kristi yelled from below. As Chris watched, her face came into view at the bottom of the ladder.

"How's your sleepy friend doing down there?" asked Chris, as he prepared to descend the ladder himself.

"He's still out," said Kristi, looking back at Grainger. "He hasn't moved much since he tripped and hit his head on the floor."

As she spoke, Chris stepped down the ladder, taking care to avoid the rotted rung that hung askew from the left vertical pole. He was followed immediately into the chamber by Sean, who joined the two of them in front of Grainger's unconscious form.

Chris noticed the linear bruise on his face that had deepened into a heavy shade of purplish-black. It was totally incongruous with the accidental fall described by Kristi. Chris turned his head and looked at her suspiciously. "So, he fell down and hit his head on the floor, huh?" he said, his voice sounding intentionally cynical.

Kristi held up the metal rod and displayed it to the two of them in the beam of their headlamps. "I'm bringing this home as a souvenir," she said proudly. "Maybe I'll give it to Maggie as a memento of the payback."

"Good idea," said Chris. He took a moment to put his arms around her and give her a long kiss. "Now, let's get the hell out of here before this guy wakes up."

"We're not going to call the police and have him arrested tonight?" gasped Sean in disbelief. "After what he just did to Kristi?"

"What did he do to Kristi?" asked Chris, looking at his uninjured girl-friend. "Did he intentionally get the two of them trapped underneath a collapsed roof, and then ask her to knock him unconscious with a steel pole? No, Sean, that just doesn't work. There's no evidence in any of this. But give me forty-eight hours, just forty-eight more hours, and I can guarantee you that he'll be behind bars. Trust me on that."

Sean looked at his friend's face, framed by the light of his headlamp, and saw the look of determination in his eyes. Chris was his best friend, and he had never let him down. He knew that Chris' word was good, no matter what the circumstances. When faced with adversity, Chris was always at his best, and this was no exception.

"I trust you, buddy," he said. "You know that."

"Thanks," said Chris, already moving toward the ladder. "OK now, ladies first," as he gave Kristi a boost up the first rungs of the improvised stairs.

Kristi followed Chris and Sean back to their hotel in Long Lake, where she announced that she was not going to drive home until the following morning. "I'm not going to start a four hour drive at eleven at night," she said. "Besides, I could really go for that rum and coke you were talking about earlier."

"That's probably a good idea," agreed Chris. "You could use a good night's sleep before starting your drive."

"Sure—the three of us can easily fit in one room, as long as you don't snore," added Sean.

"Girls don't snore," Kristi giggled as she looked back at Sean.

After a late night snack and a round of drinks, the three went up to their room on the second floor. The hotel had graciously wheeled in a fold-up bed to accommodate the unexpected guest, and they decided that they'd turn in as early as possible.

"I've got to head back out to your Jeep for a minute, if you don't mind," said Sean to Chris. "Do you have the keys handy?"

"Of course," replied Chris, tossing him his rather large key ring. "What's up?"

"I locked my laptop in your storage compartment once you told me that we were leaving my car in the parking lot up in Tahawus," said Sean. "Supposedly, I can get wireless connectivity from inside the hotel here, so I'd like to give it a shot."

Sean took off for the lot outside the hotel, giving Chris and Kristi a few minutes of time alone. When he returned, they were sitting together on the couch talking.

"What's so important that you've got to work on it tonight?" asked Kristi, observing Sean as he opened his laptop and then accessed the hotel's wireless network.

"Nothing's really critical," said Sean, "but I'd like to see whether Grainger is on the move tonight. I don't expect him to still be in the underground mine at Tahawus, but I'm curious whether he's still parked up at the lot up there."

"My guess is that he's gone," said Chris.

"You can't tell where Grainger's car is just by looking at your computer, can you?" asked Kristi, amazed at the suggestion.

"I can," said Sean, concentrating on the application.

"How can you do that?" she asked incredulously.

Sean ignored the question and remained focused on the laptop.

"Did you hear me? I'd really like to know how you can do that," Kristi asked again, persistently seeking an answer.

"Chris, could you handle that question?" asked Sean without looking up.

Chris smiled at Kristi and shrugged his shoulders. "I plead the Fifth Commandment," he said meekly.

"You mean the Fifth Amendment, right?" Kristi corrected him.

"Yeah, that too," laughed Chris.

While they were trading barbs, Sean had activated the GPS application and was tracking Ben Grainger's Mini Cooper. "Here you go," said Sean, pointing to a blip on a small-scale map of the area between Tahawus and Newcomb. "Grainger's car is on the road as we speak, heading northwest on Route 28A." Then, looking up at Kristi, he said "looks as though you didn't do any permanent damage."

"Yes, but I bet he's got one heck of a headache," said Chris.

The next morning, Kristi took off early enough so she could be back at the university by noon. Meanwhile, Chris and Sean checked the GPS application again, and found that Grainger had driven all the way back to Binghamton. "I'm glad to have him out of the way," said Sean. "From what Kristi had to say of her rendezvous with him in the cave, he'd stop at nothing to get what he wants."

"I wouldn't get too comfortable," said Chris. "He'll be back here by tomorrow afternoon at the latest."

"You're sure about that?" asked Sean.

"About as sure as I am about anything," replied Chris. "Assuming that he went into your car and took the drawing, he'll try to get back to the Henderson monument before we do. And if you remember, I wrote a note on that page saying that we'd give it a shot on Tuesday."

"So you're saying he'll be in the woods either tonight or Monday night?"

"There's no way he'll go back there tonight," predicted Chris. "He's kind of beat up right now, and I'm sure he'll just want to sleep for a day. He might even have a serious concussion." After thinking of the damage that Kristi had inflicted, he shook his head and laughed. "Remind me never to get my girlfriend ticked off at me!"

"So that narrows the range to sometime late on Monday afternoon or

Monday evening," concluded Sean.

"Yes it does," said Chris. "And I, for one, have half a mind to stay here and watch it happen."

"You want to watch Grainger try to find something that isn't there in the first place?" asked Sean, somewhat bewildered.

"No," answered Chris, his voice smug with satisfaction. "I want to watch the expression on his face as the police slap the handcuffs on him."

After discussing the events of the last day, Chris and Sean decided to extend their stay by another three days. The hotel had empty rooms since it was now past Labor Day, and neither of them had pressing business events back home.

"I'd really like to go back and take a look at that underground chamber," said Sean. "Some of the things that Kristi described in there make me think it really might be the place that Patterson described in his journal."

"I know," said Chris. "When you stop to think about it, it really kind of gives you the chills. We were standing at a place where escaped slaves risked their lives to achieve the freedom that we all take for granted today."

"Chris, if what she said is true, then I think we really ought to consider contacting the authorities who maintain and preserve the various stops on the Underground Railroad. After all, this is history we're talking about."

"I couldn't agree more," said Chris, nodding his head over a second cup of coffee. "But let's just wait until things calm down a bit. We've had enough excitement around here for a couple of days. That room has sat undisturbed for at least 145 years. What's another week between friends?"

After checking their email and making a few phone calls, Sean and Chris once again headed north toward the village of Tahawus. The views of the mountains and woodlands were phenomenal, and the time flew by as they cruised through the hills of the central Adirondacks, talking about the case as they moved along the two-lane highway.

"Based on how tough it was for Kristi to find that subterranean chamber, I wonder if it's been used by anyone since the place was originally dug out as a basement?" asked Sean.

"That's no basement," replied Chris, recalling the construction of the chamber, with its solid rock walls and heavy timber bracing. "There is no doubt in my mind that the place was excavated as a mine, back in the days when Henderson thought there was still a chance of finding silver in the ground there."

"Which means sometime prior to 1845. That's when he died, right?"

"That's correct," confirmed Chris. "But the place was obviously used later than that, if we go by the assumption that the Underground Railroad used it as a permanent station en route to Canada. It might have been employed as a hiding spot right up until 1860, although I read that this place was flooded pretty badly around 1856."

"I thought New York was a free state," said Sean, as they pulled up the final stretch of narrow road into the Tahawus parking lot. "Why would they still need to run farther north, toward the Canadian border?"

"There were still agreements between the states to return runaway slaves," explained Chris. "The Fugitive Slave Act of 1850 penalized officials and federal marshalls for not arresting and returning suspected slaves to the state from which they'd escaped. Even ordinary citizens were liable to five hundred dollar fines and six months in jail if they were caught aiding or giving safe harbor to an escaping slave. Do you have any idea how much money five hundred dollars was in 1850?"

"About a full year's pay," replied Sean after thinking for a moment.

"Just about," said Chris.

Chris pulled the Jeep into the lot about three parking spaces down from Sean's Mercedes. As expected, the red Mini Cooper was nowhere in sight. Sean quickly jumped out of the SUV and trotted over to the driver's side of his own vehicle. Peering inside for a moment, he looked back at Chris with a jubilant expression.

"He took the bait!" he cried out happily.

"As I expected," said Chris. "Now, all we have to do is sit back and wait to reel him into the boat."

"Let's head down to the chamber, or cave, or mine, or whatever you want to call it," said Sean. "I want to look around some more. But this time, let's bring along the heavy-duty lighting."

Chris helped Sean unload two hefty million-candlelight lanterns from the back of the Jeep, which they had brought along for this very purpose. Chris also threw on a pack with his video camera, water bottles, tape measure, and notepad. In his other hand, he carried Sean's metal detector.

Their plan was to map out the place as accurately as possible, including its dimensions, layout, furniture, and bed racks, and anything else of interest. Chris also wanted to make a complete video record of the interior, just to document its original appearance and condition as Kristi had first found it.

It took the two of them several trips up and down the aged ladder to move all their gear and equipment to the floor below. "I'm not really certain I feel like trusting wood and spikes that are over one hundred fifty years old," said Chris, treading as lightly as possible to avoid repeating Grainger's fall.

Once they were down below, Sean suggested that they slide the metal back over the entry hole in order to camouflage the location of their work.

"I don't think we have to do that," said Chris, looking back up at the opening. "We're pretty far removed from the road, so I doubt we'll have any visitors. But that might be a good idea for when we leave here today, just to keep the sight safe until the state historical people can come in and take a look. We can even replace a few of the boards and timbers to camouflage it. But let's leave it open as long as we're working down here, just for the extra daylight and fresh air circulation."

"You got it," said Sean, as he went to work setting up the two massive lanterns at both ends of the chamber. When fully energized and arranged to maximize their reflectors, the effect was amazing. Even the light-absorbing uneven rock walls of the excavation were brilliantly illuminated, making it look like daylight throughout the subterranean room.

Chris quickly got to work with the video camera, panning around the outside walls of the chamber to record the overall shape of the room and signs of the original excavation methods. He worked his way from the front of the chamber, starting at the entrance ladder, backward to the most extreme corners of the space. There was a lot of area to cover, and Chris made extensive use of the camera's zoom lens to capture the place in excruciating detail.

Sean, meanwhile, mapped out all the interior items and furnishings, using graph paper to sketch in the bed racks, tables, and built-in furnishings to scale. He had been at work for about thirty minutes when he called for Chris' attention.

"Hey, come over here. I found that inscription that Kristi told us about last night," he called.

Chris left the video recorder running as he backtracked across the chamber and joined his friend, who was standing in front of a thick timber frame of a bed rack. There, burned into the side of the wood, were the words quoted by Kristi the previous evening.

"There is not a man beneath the canopy of heaven who does not know that slavery is wrong for him."

"It kind of sends a shiver up your spine, doesn't it?" said Sean, staring at the words that had been written two centuries earlier.

"It sure does," said Chris. "I wonder where the quote came from?"

"Came from?" repeated Sean. "Do you mean, who first said it?"

"Yes," said Chris. "It sounds like part of a speech to me. I couldn't tell you whether it originated with a politician, an abolitionist, or someone else. But it sounds too polished and well written to come from your average citizen."

"Well, since most slaves couldn't read or write, I guess that rules out most of the inhabitants of this room, at least during that era," said Sean.

"I guess we'll probably never learn the identity of the person who recorded this here," conceded Chris. "But no matter; it's the history of this room that I'm interested in today."

"I thought we were here to try to find a couple thousand 1804 silver dollars?" chided Sean.

"We are, we are," replied Chris. "But we'll start that hunt again tomorrow. Let's take care of one thing at a time, OK?"

The two men continued their work, stopping only for an improvised lunch of granola bars and warm orange juice. Then it was back to work documenting the details of Kristi's discovery. "She would have been a lot happier if this had been a bona fide, naturally occurring cave," said Chris, looking around the place as they returned to their labors.

"She's already been credited with the discovery of one new cave system in the state," said Sean. "Isn't one cave find enough for a newly graduated geology student?"

"Then you don't really know Kristi," laughed Chris. "She's one ambitious lady."

"Tough, too," said Sean, as he pointed out a blood stain where Grainger had fallen the previous night from Kristi's onslaught. "Not many women could have done what she did, keeping her cool while fending off a man who was over twice her size."

After another half hour of measuring and videotaping, Chris announced that he was going to take a quick jaunt across the river and check out the area around the blast furnace again.

"Hey, you don't think that Grainger will be up here again today, do you?" asked Sean, the concern showing on his face. "If he shows up here, hell-bent on revenge, I'd rather not be trapped here by myself without a weapon."

"I don't think that's a problem," said Chris. "My guess is he'll probably stay in Binghamton for the rest of the day. But if it will make you feel any better, I'll take the long way back to the road and check the parking lot for his car. And even if he was to arrive while I'm gone, I'd see his car as it drives past on the road."

"Thanks, buddy," said Sean, reassured of his safety.

"Oh, and don't worry," said Chris as he was climbing back up the ladder. "If you get scared, I can always call Kristi to come back up here and protect you!"

Having tossed the last remark at Sean for the sole purpose of annoying him, Chris chuckled and pulled himself through the hole and back into the natural sunlight of the early afternoon. The sun was warm, and the sky was a gorgeous hue of deep blue. Chris inhaled deeply, savoring the smell of the great outdoors.

Remembering to keep his promise, Chris retraced his steps over the bridge and past the trail sign-in register by the hikers' parking lot. He quickly scanned the lot for a red Mini Cooper, and after satisfying himself that none was in the vicinity, he strolled slowly down the gravel shoulder of the road until he reached the clearing around the blast furnace. The top of the brick stacks towered above him, even though he still stood at least ten to fifteen feet above the base of the massive rock structure.

Chris clambered down the incline to the level ground at the bottom of the wall and walked around to the front of the furnace. Several small groups of people were strolling by the massive archways, admiring the handiwork that had withstood the ravages of time in the harsh North Country environment. Nearby, a group of about a dozen men and women stood and listened to the leader of an organized tour as he explained the history and construction of the blast furnace. He spoke of the contributions of David Henderson and Archibald McIntyre numerous times. However, Peter VanderBrooke was never mentioned in any part of the conversation, and Chris felt as though the main craftsman of the project had been shortchanged.

With the sun shining so brightly from above, warming his hair and face, Chris felt the sudden urge to lie down and take a nap. Everything about the day was so perfect, including the whisper of the wind through the trees and the babbling waters of the river in the background. He closed his eyes and felt his thoughts drifting about his head, swirling and dancing and beckoning him to drift off to sleep for the rest of the afternoon. It would have been wonderful.

The only thing that repeatedly pulled him back to reality was the continuous string of questions posed by the group to the tour guide. He fielded a rapid-fire barrage of inquiries about the history, dimensions, and construction of the blast furnace, and answered them with a depth of knowledge that impressed everyone in attendance. In his trancelike state, Chris recited the answer to each question subconsciously without waiting for the guide's response, having memorized almost every known reference about the landmark. Then, suddenly, there came a question from a woman that lassoed Chris' attention and snapped him back to total alertness.

"What direction is this furnace facing, and does that make any difference in the smelting and refining process?" asked an attractive blonde-haired woman dressed in jeans and a flannel shirt.

"No, the orientation of the furnace really doesn't make a difference in how the furnace is fed or operated," explained the guide. "However, to answer your question, we are presently facing west, looking at the front of the furnace."

"Facing west," said Chris, silently repeating the words to himself. "Facing west."

Chris felt his pulse begin to quicken as he tilted his head backwards. The tower of the blast furnace dominated the landscape in front of him, massive and overbearing in every respect. He stepped another twenty feet back, to give himself a better perspective on the overall scene. His eyes took in the rough symmetry of the design: the stones, the even square shapes, and the rows of anchor plates that had been fitted so perfectly into the outer walls of the furnace so many decades before.

"Facing west," Chris muttered again. There was a significance here that he just could not shake. The symmetry. The anchor plates. Facing west. Suddenly, as if drawn by a supernatural influence, Chris' eyes were pulled to the right side of the furnace tower. There were two columns of anchor plates on each of the furnace's four sides, and he was staring at the plates on the right side of the front wall. Facing west, right side. Chris' stare once again returned to the bottom of the furnace, this time at the anchor plate on the right side of the archway. That would have been one of the first plates installed in the furnace as they started building the walls upward. Perhaps they might even have installed this anchor plate in the first year of construction, connecting it via a tie rod to another anchor plate on the backside.

Next, Chris' gaze moved up to the second anchor plate, which was about ten to twelve feet above the first. Then, to the third, and then on to the fourth and fifth plates, with the fifth being the highest. Facing west, right side, four over five. Four over five.

Chris' heart was now pounding inside his chest, and he felt the hairs on the back of his neck standing on end. His mind was operating at warp speed, processing images, numbers, and words faster than he could imagine. His eyes dropped again, but only to a point about thirty feet above ground level. He found himself staring, wide-eyed, at a single anchor plate. It was on the right side of the furnace, facing west, the fourth plate of five on that side.

As Chris stood there, fixated on the hardware attached to the furnace, he rapidly traced the construction of the furnace over the five-year period of time from 1849 through 1854. For each year of construction, he raised the level of the structure another eight to ten feet, counting off the year as he achieved the appropriate height. The fourth anchor plate up would have corresponded with early 1853, the year of Patterson's short and mysterious one-day visit to Tahawus. The year before he died. The year of his last-ever trip to the North Country ghost village.

The coincidences were overwhelming, the evidence now seeming conclusive. Chris felt his hands trembling inside the pockets of his fleece jacket. Even though he wasn't hot, he felt himself sweating through his thin cotton T-shirt as he continued to stare at that fourth anchor plate.

"Sir, are you alright?" came a voice from nearby.

Chris shook himself and refocused his eyes on the people standing in front of him. "Yes, yes, I'm fine," he said, wondering what he'd done to elicit such a question. He also noticed that the rest of the tour group had gone silent and was watching him with concern.

"OK, I just wanted to make sure," said the tour guide, looking at Chris as though he was about to faint. "You looked as though you were having a heart attack. Either that, or you were expecting the front of the blast furnace to topple over and crush all of us."

"I'm very sorry," said Chris, feeling embarrassed by the attention. "I guess I was feeling overwhelmed by the sheer size of this thing. But I'm really feeling just fine, thanks."

"It is easy to become awed by this monster," said the guide, smiling back at Chris. "It's a one-of-a-kind masterpiece, and there are very few of them left in this country."

"Sir, could I ask you a question, even though I'm not part of your tour party?" Chris asked courteously.

"Please, be my guest."

"What would happen if someone removed one or more of the anchor plates from around the outside of the furnace?" Chris asked.

"Well, I probably wouldn't be answering your question from so close to the bottom of this stack," said the guide, which elicited a round of laughter from his group. "But in all seriousness, this blast furnace is built a lot more solidly than most. It's a documented fact that the design of this particular furnace includes more horizontal and diagonal tie rods than any other furnace built in the United States. Whether all of them are required or not is probably a matter of debate, but my guess is that the entire construction is probably over-engineered."

"So you think the overall structure would remain intact?" asked Chris.

The guide thought for a moment before speaking. "Yes, that's true; I think that it would remain intact, at least for the time being," he said finally. "However, I don't think that the furnace would have remained so beautifully preserved if not for all the extra reinforcements. After all, it's stood for 160 years without shifting an inch. I think you'd have to agree that's a pretty impressive feat."

"Do you have any idea why VanderBrooke would have used so many tie rods and anchor plates if he knew that they weren't all required?" asked Chris. It was only after he had finished asking the question that he realized he'd name-dropped the identity of the master builder.

The tour guide looked at Chris for a moment, his eyes registering a mixture of amazement and respect. "Sir, are you a historian?" he asked quietly. "There aren't many people around here, or anywhere, who know of VanderBrooke's role in the construction of this site."

"Yes, you might say I'm interested in history," replied Chris, smiling at the compliment.

"To answer your question, I'd have to say 'no,'" replied the guide. "I don't know why he built this furnace so much stronger than the others of its day. Perhaps it was the immense size, or maybe to protect it from the extremes of heat and cold, since we're so far north. I really couldn't venture a guess."

"I have one other question to ask, if you'd be so kind," said Chris.

"Please, ask away," said the tour director, who obviously enjoyed sharing his knowledge.

"Given the extreme heat that was generated on the interior surfaces of this furnace, do you believe that the exterior surfaces, or even the outside two-to-three feet of rock also became hot?" Chris asked.

"No, I don't," replied the guide without hesitation. "As I already mentioned, this entire furnace was over-engineered, including the dimensions. Even when the blast fires were going full bore, the outer few feet of rock should have remained fairly cool to the touch. At least, they certainly weren't excessively hot, if that's what you mean."

Chris nodded his understanding and thanked the guide for his time, and then bid the group farewell. He felt slightly remiss in his promise to Sean to keep an eye out for Grainger's car, as he had been so totally absorbed in his amazing discovery this past hour. To ensure that Grainger had not snuck past him in his distracted "moment of enlightenment," Chris returned to the other side of the river by walking past the same parking lot again. As he expected, there was no sign of the red Mini Cooper in the lot, and he returned to the site of the subterranean chamber feeling happy and reassured.

"Honey, I'm home," he called out as he dropped down the ladder. "Did you miss me?"

Sean didn't answer with a greeting. Instead, he just waved his salutation from the rear corner of the excavated space, where two walls met at a ninety degree angle. He was wearing the headset that was hooked up to his metal detector, and he listened intently as he swept the search coil of the instrument back and forth over the rocky substrate.

"Sorry," whispered Chris, not wanting to interrupt the progress of his friend as he searched the site for anything metal.

"It's OK," said Sean, ripping off the headset and setting the detector down on one of the bed racks. "I've been at this for about forty-five minutes now, and all I've found is a bunch of old nails and some scrap metal. I'm beginning to think that this might be a waste of time."

"Of course it's not a waste," said Chris. "This place is a national treasure, a historic location from the Underground Railroad. It's probably a missing station that links up with John Brown's Tract to the north somehow. So please, carry on. It looks like you're doing wonderfully well."

Sean gave Chris a sour look, as though his friend had gone slightly loopy. "Sure, rusty old nails are great, I suppose, if you're into collecting nails. But I'd rather find the hiding place for the entire cache of silver dollars, given my druthers."

"Oh, you won't come across that down here," said Chris. "I already found where they're hidden while I was out walking." Chris tried to sound nonchalant as he spoke, as though his discovery was equivalent to finding a good Italian restaurant. Inside, however, he was bubbling over in his desire to share his discovery.

"YOU WHAT?" shouted Sean, staring at Chris with amazement.

"What I mean is that I *think* I found the place where the 1804 silver dollars are hidden. All of them," said Chris in a calm, quiet voice. "And the amazing thing is that they are hidden right here in this ghost town, almost in Mt. Marcy's shadow. But let's just keep this quiet, in case anyone is nearby. We don't need to inadvertently spread the news on this."

"Would you care to share the details?" asked Sean, trying to follow suit with a subdued tone of voice.

"Sure, I'd be happy to," replied Chris. "But first, I have a suggestion. Let's get packed up and get everything into the car. We can cover up the site here and hide it so that no one but us and Grainger knows about it. But once we're able to get a wireless connection and can confirm Grainger's location, we'll need to make a quick trip back to Syracuse."

"A quick trip back to Syracuse?" repeated Sean, incredulous at the idea. "That's an eight hour round trip!"

"Well, we've got nothing to do for the next thirty hours," said Chris, looking at his watch. "So unless you want to put up the fifteen hundred dollars for the equipment we'll need to retrieve the silver dollars, most of which I already own back home, then I suggest you come along with me."

"Like I said, I've been looking forward to going back to Syracuse all day," quipped Sean.

"Great minds think alike," said Chris. "Pack up your metal detector and the lanterns while I get the video gear and other junk together. We should be able to hide the entrance to the chamber and be on the road before three o'clock."

Chris and Sean departed Tahawus with both their cars, heading south in the same direction. They stopped once for coffee in Old Forge before continuing on their way home. The coffee shop also offered wireless Internet, so Sean logged on and confirmed Ben Grainger's current location.

"Hmm, that's still good news, I guess..." said Sean, his voice trailing off as he worked.

"What's up?" asked Chris, taking a sip of his steaming drink. "Is our red-haired friend still at home in Binghamton?"

"Still in Binghamton, yes; still at home, no," replied Sean. "I'm showing him at an address on Chenango Street, which is also listed as Route 7. Let me do a reverse street check on this and see what I come up with." Sean entered the street address listed in the GPS tracker display window. The answer came back almost instantly.

"OK, that makes sense," said Sean, looking at the listing. "He's busy doing the same thing we are; he's at a hardware outlet store, probably picking up the stuff he thinks he needs to dig out the silver dollars from the Henderson monument."

"Oh," said Chris, his voice adding a lot of expression to the single word. "I guess I should have counted on that."

"Isn't that what you wanted?" asked Sean, sounding somewhat confused. "I thought your whole goal was to divert Grainger to a decoy hiding place so that the police could catch him in the act and arrest him. This should be great news for us."

"It is," said Chris. "But from here on out, we need to be extra careful to track Grainger's every move. If he is actually allowed to sneak up there and destroy a monument that's stood for almost 170 years, all because of my scheme and failure to stop him, I'd never live it down."

"I have a great idea," said Sean. "While you're in Syracuse gathering whatever we need, I can try programming my phone with an application that will let me tap into the same GPS information. If I'm not mistaken, I can probably follow Grainger's car from my phone the entire way back up to Tahawus."

Chris looked at his friend with respect as he drained the last gulp of his coffee. "I've always said that it pays to hang around with computer geeks."

"Be careful or you just might learn something," laughed Sean. "Now shut up and let's get going."

On the way out of the shop, they decided to disband their miniature caravan, with Chris accelerating ahead and leaving Sean to cruise along at a slower speed in his fifty-year-old car. They had already agreed to meet at ten o'clock the following morning to return to Tahawus to help out with Grainger's arrest on Monday night. In the meantime, they had much to do as they arranged their own activities of the next two days.

With the view of Sean's Mercedes receding in the rear view mirror, Chris began plotting out his next twelve hours of activity. He was going to have to make tracks if he was to accomplish everything he needed and still have time to grab a few hours of sleep. As he motored along into the southern reaches of the Adirondack Park, he checked his phone to ensure that he had at least some signal with which to place a call. It registered two bars out of five, which was enough to accomplish his goal. He quickly pressed the speed dial function for his parents' house in Utica and listened to the phone ring.

"Hello," said Chris' mom, answering the phone on the fifth ring. Chris knew there was never a rush inside his parents' home in Utica, so he always counted on waiting for a bit before hearing anyone come on the line.

"Hey Mom, it's me. I was wondering if you'd like some company tonight for a late dinner."

"My goodness, it's the voice of the wandering minstrel, from somewhere out in the wilderness," kidded Theresa. "How have you been, honey? I've been trying to reach you these past few days. I've left two or three messages on your home phone."

"Sorry, Mom, but I haven't been home," explained Chris. "My cell phone doesn't even have coverage in the Adirondacks, so I can't check my messages from up there. Is anything going on that I should know about?"

"Well, your father is stopping by for a day or two, and I thought you might like to come by and say hello," said Theresa. "He's got more business with that big case in Albany, so he's coming in late tonight, and he'll be here until Wednesday. What time do you think you'll be stopping by?"

"I should be in town by six thirty or seven. What time is dad getting in?" asked Chris.

"His flight doesn't land until almost seven o'clock, so I expect it'll be at least an hour later before he can make it home."

"Great, Mom. I'll stick around for a while after he gets there, just to talk and get caught up. Would you like me to stop and pick up something for us to eat along the way?"

"Honey, just because you eat all your meals out of a take-out box doesn't mean that the rest of the world does," laughed his mother. "I hope you like meat loaf and hash browns, because that's what's on tonight's menu."

"Sounds great, Mom. Thanks."

"Is there anything else you need before you stop by?" asked Theresa.

"Well, now that you mention it, there is," said Chris. "Do you remember that portable fire escape ladder that you used to keep up in the extra bedroom on the third floor?"

"Of course, honey," said his mom. "It's still there. Thank God we've never had to use it, although I can't see why anyone would need to. No one has slept in that room since the cousins came down to stay with us for part of the summer when you were in high school."

"Could I borrow it?" asked Chris.

"Borrow the fire escape ladder? Sure. Am I allowed to ask why you need it?"

"Uh, could I explain that to you next week?" asked Chris, smiling to himself as he spoke. "It's a long story, and we'll have plenty of time once I get back from my next trip north."

"OK, honey. But you'll have to get it down yourself. I don't do heavy objects anymore."

"Thanks, Mom. I'll see you in about an hour," said Chris before hanging up his phone.

Chris made it to his parents' house in time to help his mom move a pile of winter clothes out of a storage closet and into her bedroom armoire. She then walked with him upstairs to the top floor of the house, where Chris found the fire escape ladder rolled up and stored in its customary location in a case underneath the large window overlooking the side of the house.

"I'm glad to see someone's finally using this thing," said Theresa. "But I'd still love to know what it's all about."

"You will, Mom," said Chris, giving her a kiss on the cheek as he hoisted the ladder onto his shoulder. "By this time next week, you should know the entire story."

After Chris returned from stowing the ladder in his Jeep, he and his mom passed the next hour talking about their activities over the past few weeks. Chris described the progress they'd made in localizing the potential hiding place of their goal, the 1804 silver dollars, as his mom listened intently. She made her son promise to be careful when dealing with Ben

Grainger, although Chris prudently withheld the story of Kristi's recent encounter with the thug in Tahawus.

When Chris Carey, Sr., arrived from the airport, he was greeted with a hug from his son and an affectionate kiss from Theresa. They enjoyed a leisurely drink together in the library, which contained several thousand volumes of the father's legal and personal books, in addition to the accumulated collections of the other family members.

"Have you had any further contact with the fellow from Binghamton?" asked Chris' father, as they settled into the cushions of a comfortable sofa. "He seemed like a pretty unsavory character, even if he didn't have a record of any prior arrests."

"He will by the time we're done with him," said Chris, pensively.

"Anything you need help with?" asked his father, looking at Chris questioningly.

"Maybe, Dad. I'll let you know," replied Chris. "Right now, there is so much going on, and to tell you the truth, yes, Ben Grainger has been getting in the way. There's a lot more happening, too, that I'm just not able to talk about yet."

"You're not in any legal trouble, are you?" asked Chris, Senior, the concern showing in his face.

"No, Dad, although Grainger will be once we see him arrested tomorrow," replied Chris.

"Tomorrow!" exclaimed his father. "How in God's name did you arrange that?"

"We made up a fake document showing him where the cache of priceless coins is buried, and it's going to lead him to a monument that is owned and maintained by the state of New York," explained Chris.

"Why do I have a feeling that I don't want to know about the details of all this?" asked his father, shaking his head slowly at the revelation.

"Oh, and something else I didn't tell you about," said Chris. "I think we're going to end up submitting an application to have another historic site designated and entered into the official register."

"How's that?"

"It looks as though we've come across a new station on the Underground Railroad."

"Are you sure?" asked his father, looking impressed.

"Yes, as sure as we can be," said Chris. "The evidence is pretty overwhelming."

"Send me what you've got, and I'll have one of our people look into it as soon as I get back to Washington."

"Thanks, Dad. I appreciate your help," said Chris.

Chris' mother, who had been sitting with them without joining in the conversation, excused herself to get the food out of the oven. Chris Senior waited for her to leave, and then quietly turned to his son. "Just be careful with all the other stuff," he said softly. "I probably don't have to tell you this, but men will be driven to do some awfully bad things if they know that there are millions of dollars in loot up for grabs."

Chris looked towards the door of the kitchen, to confirm that his mother was out of earshot, then answered his father's warning in an equally hushed tone. "Dad, we can't be sure of this, but we might be on the verge of a discovery that is up into the billions."

Chris watched his father's face for a reaction. There was none, although he thought he detected that a bit of color drained from his normally tanned complexion.

"Son, are you sure that you wouldn't feel more comfortable with one or two of my men along with you and Sean, just in case things get rough?" he offered.

"That's OK, Dad," said Chris, standing up to head into the kitchen. "We'll call you if we need any help. In the meantime, Grainger is our only problem, and he should be out of the way by this time tomorrow night."

"I'll be waiting to hear from you," said his father. "Just keep yourself out of harm's way, and remember to call in the authorities if you have to."

The rest of the evening's conversation centered around family matters, although Chris did receive a text from Sean. He opened his phone as nonchalantly as possible and read that Sean had confirmed Grainger's car was still at his house in Binghamton. Chris felt confident, perhaps even a bit smug, knowing that he had been able orchestrate Grainger's movements over the past week. The only glitch had been the mess with Kristi in Tahawus, but even that had worked out to their advantage.

Chris stayed around for a short while after dinner, but left shortly after nine o'clock in order to collect the items he'd need from his own house for the following day. It had been a long day with a lot of driving, yet he felt incredibly alive and filled with energy. After all their hard work, discoveries, and near disasters, he believed that they were on the cusp of something great. All he needed was for their luck to hold out for two more days.

CHAPTER 19

Monday, September 15, 2015

Monday morning, Chris was up and out of bed by five thirty, despite having slept for only five hours. He squeezed in a quick four-mile run, then showered and packed another two-day bag with changes of underwear, socks, and other necessities. As he placed the items into the small parcel, he thought to himself that he was becoming much too accustomed to living out of a suitcase.

In addition to his personal things, the table in the living room served as a staging ground for an additional pile of tools and equipment they would need over the next two days. Countless pieces of climbing gear were loosely arranged in order of size and category, including a slew of nuts, hexes, camming devices, and carabiners. Three climbing ropes of varied thicknesses and colors were coiled nearby, along with a pair of slings and other attachment devices that Chris deemed important to the mission. He's also included a heavy mallet and a massive vise grip, which looked strong enough to compress almost anything that got in its way.

Once everything was loaded into the Jeep, Chris started the engine and rolled down the hill en route to Sean's house in Little Falls. His mind was preoccupied with the mental checklist of preparations for the activities of the next forty-eight hours. As he pulled into the driveway in front of the cottage, he found his friend already outside the house waiting.

"Everything all set to go?" asked Sean, as he prepared to move his own equipment into Chris' Jeep.

"Yeah, but you'll probably have to put your bags and metal detector in the back seat. Most of the cargo area is pretty full," Chris responded.

"What's in the black case?" asked Sean, pointing to the bag containing the portable fire escape.

"That's our own personal stairway to heaven," grinned Chris. "Hop in and I'll explain along the way."

"Sure," said Sean, as he finished stowing his gear and climbed into the passenger seat. "But first, I've got some news for you."

"OK, let's have it," said Chris.

"First, I need to do a little show-and-tell," said Sean, as he pulled out his phone. "Do you know what you're looking at right now?" He held the display screen up for Chris to view.

"Oh, nice," said Chris, as he studied the application on the miniature device. "I take it that this is current information?"

"Yes, sir!" exclaimed Sean. "Grainger is still in Binghamton, although he's done some driving around in the city this morning. I should be able to follow his travels with the press of a button."

"Very impressive," said Chris, nodding his approval.

"There is one other thing that I wanted to tell you about," continued Sean. "Do you remember that sentence that we found burned into one of the timbers on Saturday?"

"Of course," said Chris, "although I don't think I could recite it verbatim."

"'There is not a man beneath the canopy of heaven who does not know that slavery is wrong for him,'" recited Sean.

"Very good," said Chris. "I hope you didn't stay up late last night memorizing it."

"I wasn't memorizing it," said Sean. "But I did do a search online to try to learn its origin."

"Did you succeed?" asked Chris.

"As a matter of fact, I did," replied Sean. "It didn't take me long, either. It turns out that line is a direct extract from a speech given by Frederick Douglas in Rochester, New York, on July 4, 1852."

"Interesting," remarked Chris. "That means that the chamber underneath Tahawus was still in use at least until the second half of 1852 and possibly even until the mining operations shut down with the flood in 1856. Who knows whether they ever went back to it after that."

"You should read the entire Douglas speech from that event in Rochester," remarked Sean. "He really sounds like a fire-and-brimstone orator who could speak his mind and get people to listen."

"Thanks for checking that out for us," said Chris. "All this is great information for the application to get the chamber added to the register of historic sites. I spoke to my dad about that last night, and he's going to help us by getting some of his people to jump on the paperwork."

"Must be nice to have family members in places of influence," said Sean.

About two hours after leaving Little Falls, Chris asked Sean if he could take the wheel for a while.

"Sure," said Sean. "You feeling a little groggy this morning?"

"No, but I do have a few administrative matters to handle, as long as my phone appears to be hitting a cell tower somewhere."

The two switched places, and Sean pulled back onto the road as Chris looked for a phone listing on a sheet of paper. Then he tapped a number into the keypad and waited for the response.

"Hello, I'm looking for Lieutenant Ken Folsom of the New York State Police."

"This is Lieutenant Folsom speaking," replied the official-sounding voice. "Who is this please, and is this an emergency call?"

"No, it's not an emergency, although I would like to request your assistance," said Chris. "This is Chris Carey, and we met last year when you helped us move a rather large amount of gold out of the West Canada Lakes Wilderness Area."

"Chris!" the officer exclaimed, his enthusiasm bursting through the receiver. "It's great to hear from you again! You've become quite famous around our department since that little venture."

"Oh, uh…thanks," said Chris, embarrassed by the compliment.

"Anyway, I'm calling to alert you to a crime that's about to happen."

"What is it?" asked Folsom.

"Well, it's a long story, but we're involved in another search for something else that's pretty valuable," explained Chris. "But this time, we've got a real thug who is interested in the same objective. This guy is a real loser who has already broken the law and beat up a few people in the process. I happen to know he's about to destroy a nice piece of New York State history all because of his greed. I thought I'd let you know, rather than try to handle it myself."

"No, please don't do that," said the officer. "We don't want to have groups of vigilantes running around fighting private wars. Just tell me the details and we'll take it from there."

Chris spent the next ten minutes explaining to the lieutenant about the run-ins they'd had with Grainger, including the stolen historical documents from the Frank Stewart Room as well as the incident with Kristi at Tahawus. He also hinted that he'd spoken with co-workers who had known Grainger in Pennsylvania and they suspected him of possessing stolen electronics equipment from their store. Finally, he provided a description of Grainger, along with details of where and when he would most likely make his move to try and recover the hidden cache of coins.

"Wow, that's a lot of detail," said Officer Folsom, who had been recording all of Chris' remarks as he spoke. "I'll contact the local rangers up in the Tahawus region, and I'll also call in the sheriff's department to help out. If this guy follows through on his plans, I can assure you that we'll be there to nab him before he lays a finger on that monument."

"Thank you, Lieutenant," said Chris. "I knew I could count on you to handle this. I'll call you back later in the day to confirm that Ben Grainger is en route to conduct his little mission of destruction. If he isn't, there's no point wasting anyone's time looking for him."

Before ending the conversation, Lieutenant Folsom gave Chris a cell phone number where he could be reached twenty-four hours a day. "Call me as soon as you know," he said again.

As Chris hung up, Sean looked across at him and posed an interesting question. "What happens if, after all this speculation, Grainger never shows up?"

"I'd be willing to bet that he'll appear right on cue," said Chris, confidently. "He knows when we're going after the same prize, and you know that he's just not going to let us waltz in there and claim it for ourselves. And since tomorrow is our day according to everything we've fed him, he has no choice but to go in and try and get it for himself tonight."

As Chris explained his logic, Sean pulled the Jeep into the lot of a small restaurant in Long Lake, where they had agreed to stop for lunch. It was still a little before noon, and they had time to burn before heading the rest of the way up to the ghost town. They walked into the front of the luncheonette and found a table near the side window overlooking the lake.

"I guess we don't have to worry about getting a hotel reservation for tonight," said Sean, slapping his forehead.

"Why's that?" asked Chris. "Are you planning on sleeping out in the woods?"

"No, but we never cancelled our room reservation for last night, so we still have it reserved until Wednesday morning," said Sean. "I should know; I put it on my credit card. We paid for an empty room last night."

"Great," exclaimed Chris, using a radio announcer's voice. "You get two nights for the price of three!"

As they were seated and handed menus, Sean set his phone on the table and pressed a series of buttons. The screen came to life with a miniature GPS map, which Sean examined carefully.

"Hmm, it looks like you were right. At least, I think you were; Grainger's on the move as we speak."

"Where is he now?" asked Chris.

"He's on Interstate Route 88, passing through the town of Oneonta. He's heading northeast at 68 miles per hour."

"That sounds about right," said Chris, looking across the table at the same screen. "I imagine he'll probably take 88 all the way over to the

Thruway near Albany, and then take the Northway up to the Pottersville exit, where he'll wind his way across to Route 28N."

"So what do you figure for his estimated time of arrival in Tahawus?" asked Sean.

"It depends on his speed and any stops he makes, but no earlier than three o'clock, and probably a little later," guessed Chris. "We can keep an eye on him with your phone."

After finishing their lunch, Sean and Chris backtracked down the hill in the middle of Long Lake and unloaded their equipment into their room at the Adirondack Hotel. Then, they climbed back into the Jeep, bringing only their hiking gear and a camera, and headed north back to Tahawus.

"We might as well make good use of our time while waiting for the guest of honor to arrive," said Chris, referring to Ben Grainger. "I'll show you what I have planned for tomorrow night."

After parking the SUV in the Tahawus lot, Chris spent the next ninety minutes giving Sean a guided tour of the front façade of the blast furnace. In a quiet voice, he explained his theory about the anchor plate, stating his case over and over again using different references to the furnace construction. He also described his plans for getting up to the plate, which was over thirty feet off the ground, and his idea for gaining access to the coins, if they were hidden there.

"It sounds like a great plan," said Sean, "but let me ask you a question. What happens if, after all this work, it turns out that the coins aren't in there? Maybe they were *never* in there. What happens then?"

"I don't know," said Chris, looking as though the thought had never crossed his mind. "I guess we start following Plan B."

"What's Plan B?" asked Sean.

"I'm not sure yet," laughed Chris. "Let's stick with Plan A for a while."

After completing the walkthrough around the blast furnace, Sean checked the location of Grainger's car once again. Chris used the opportunity to contact Lieutenant Folsom, and then hung up to set the trap in motion. Chris felt exhilarated, knowing that Ben Grainger would soon pay the price for all his transgressions, including his attacks on both Maggie and Kristi. As much as he didn't want to dwell on it, this had become personal, and Chris was not going to allow Grainger to walk away without doing time behind bars.

After returning to the Jeep, Chris and Sean decided to go back to the Adirondack Hotel for the rest of the afternoon and evening. The weather was gorgeous, with the trees already turning their characteristic shades of red and orange. From his Adirondack rocking chair on the front porch of the hotel, Chris yawned and stretched his body out to full length, contemplating the few swimmers left on the public beach across the street. Meanwhile, Sean looked at his phone and noted that Grainger had stopped for a lengthy spell on the Northway, but was now once again heading north, towards the exit that would bring him into the Tahawus area by early evening.

"Don't you want to be up there when Grainger arrives, just so we can be sure that he's actually going into the woods?" asked Sean.

"No, not really," replied Chris lazily. "There's no need; we'd just be risking the possibility that he'd see us and get spooked off."

"Do you think he'd recognize us?" asked Sean.

"He wouldn't recognize me," said Chris. "But I think we'd be taking our chances with you. Maybe if you wore a ball cap and a dark pair of sunglasses, we could get away with it. But the way I see it, this is a little bit like a football game."

"How's that?" asked Sean.

"The view is a lot better on television," laughed Chris, "which is why I say we stay here until we watch Grainger's car arrive on your GPS tracker, and then maybe head up there after dark."

"Sounds like a good idea," agreed Sean. "I still say that part of you was meant to be a secret agent."

"Thanks," said Chris sarcastically, "but I think you'd better stick to your computers and leave the human resources work to the professionals."

By seven o'clock, Chris and Sean had finished dinner and checked on

Grainger's status. As expected, he had arrived at the trailhead in Tahawus, although they were unable to follow his progress once he left his car. Chris called Lieutenant Folsom one last time, and was assured the proper precautions had been taken and the monument was in no danger.

"I can't really tell you who is in charge of the detail in the woods," said Folsom. "I wouldn't get involved because Tahawus is way out of my area. But I can assure you that whoever they've assigned, they'll handle the business well. We're all on the same team, you know."

Chris thanked him for the news, and then hung up the phone. "Well, would you like to go and watch the fireworks, or would you rather hang out here and watch a ball game in the lounge?"

"The lounge sounds more comfortable," said Sean thoughtfully. "But there's one other detail I need to take care of tonight, so would you mind if we head back out there later on and join the party?"

"Sure," replied Chris. "I'd love to be there when they bring Grainger out in handcuffs."

"I wasn't even thinking of that," said Sean. "But never mind; we can accomplish both our goals with one trip."

Ben Grainger had pulled into the dirt parking lot at seven fifteen and immediately removed his boots and backpack from the back of the Mini Cooper. To most people, he probably looked like the average hiker who was heading into the woods for a three-day stay. However, if someone had taken the time to examine his gear, they would have noticed that some things were very different than that of the normal Adirondack backpacker. First and foremost, the large, sturdy backpack was almost completely empty, with the exception of a couple small water bottles, a supply of flashlight batteries, and a five-pound sledgehammer that was dropped straight into the top of the main cargo compartment. However, since only the handle was left exposed above the top of the pack, it gave the appearance of a camp axe, and thus would not have raised any suspicion.

Grainger waited for another hour, until the last vestiges of daylight had left the sky, before hitting the trail. By eight thirty he was hoofing along, making good time until he encountered stretches of mud and standing water. Unfortunately for Grainger, he didn't own a genuine pair of hiking boots and had instead selected a pair of well-worn work boots. As the water soaked into his inappropriate footwear, his rough socks quickly bunched up on the bottoms of his feet, which resulted in several painful blisters within the first few miles.

He also discovered that work boots often have a smooth sole, which is fine for the confines of a factory or warehouse, but totally out of place on a wilderness trail. After several near-misses, he completely lost his balance on a submerged tree root, and his feet both came flying out from underneath his body. Grainger landed hard on his buttocks, where a sharp rock tore painfully into his flesh. He let out a torrent of foul language as he massaged the injured skin, feeling a small patch of blood that was already seeping through a tear in his pants.

Grainger had expected that he would be able to cover the ground to the monument in about two hours, and be out of the woods in less than five. However, he hadn't counted on the low visibility at night, or the wet and slippery conditions. Also, being a smoker and out of shape, he found himself in need of frequent breaks as the trail steepened in the third mile. He was wet, tired, and his feet ached as he plodded along the sloppy path, sometimes wondering whether he had taken a wrong turn somewhere along the way. This doubt deepened into alarm as he glanced at the illuminated dial on his watch and saw that it was after eleven o'clock.

However, despite his uncomfortable condition, Grainger was motivated to move onward by the image of the invaluable silver dollars that were hidden inside the Henderson monument. For years, the greed had burned inside him, consuming him, driving him to ignore everything other than his search to find the treasure that was hinted at in his ancestor's records. Now that he was so close, he would stop at nothing to find the coins. He'd convinced himself the money was rightfully his, and he would not let anyone or anything stop him until he held the dollars in his hand.

About a half mile from the pond, Grainger stopped suddenly when he heard a noise in the path ahead. Panning the flashlight back and forth across the trail, he was stunned into immobility when a pair of large, reflective eyes met his from a distance of less than thirty feet. As he watched, the form of a black bear rose up on its hind legs to have a better look at the newcomer. Grainger was so surprised that he dropped his flashlight, which smashed bulb-end first onto a pointed rock. The sound of breaking glass notified Grainger that his main light source was now gone. He picked up the damaged flashlight and pressed the "On" button, but nothing happened; the bulb had shattered into a hundred pieces. To make matters worse, he was temporarily alone in the darkness with the nocturnal bear, which needed no light to navigate through the woods.

Grainger began fumbling frantically with his pack, which he flung off his back and onto the wet ground, where it landed in a deep and muddy pool. As he searched for his small backup light, he heard the sounds of the bear moving about in the darkness. Not knowing whether the bear was coming at him, he began to holler as loudly as he could while pulling the sledgehammer out of the pack. However, he found that he couldn't hold the heavy tool in a position to defend himself while simultaneously searching for his spare light. By the time he found the penlight in a side pocket, the bear had wandered away in its nightly scavenge for food.

Grainger loaded the sledgehammer into the backpack, which was now sopping wet and coated in a thick layer of quicksand-like goop. He began to curse the woods, curse the bear, and even curse the people who hiked through the area. His mood grew more angry and impatient as he went.

Finally, with less than thirty minutes to spare before midnight, Grainger emerged from the woods at the tiny body of water known as Calamity Pond. His pace had slowed to a crawl due to the extremely low beam cast by the tiny penlight. To make matters worse, his mood had further deteriorated, and he wanted nothing more than to get the job over with and get out of the woods with the loot.

Grainger moved slowly and deliberately around the edge of the pond, often bending over to gain a better view of the obstructions in the trail. His eyes didn't pick up the outline of the monument until he was within about twenty feet of its setting, as the dark night offered little in the way of additional illumination. He stopped and stared at the huge stone for a moment, recognizing its form from the photographs he'd stolen from Sean's house and automobile. For the first time that night, a smile creased his face, as he approached the memorial with slow, measured steps. He couldn't believe he had finally made it to his destination undetected.

Grainger stepped up to the front of the monument and shined his penlight on the inscription that had been carved into the stone, then pulled out the fake drawing that he'd removed from Sean's car and held it up to the light. It matched, and he could clearly see the meaning of the diagram. It was all there—the monument, the location, and hopefully, the dollars.

With trembling hands, he reached down and pulled the sledgehammer out of his pack, then planted his feet in a steady, balanced position. Before raising the sledgehammer to strike, he smiled again at the stone and addressed it as though it was human.

"Thank you, Mr. Patterson, for making me a very, very rich man." His proclamation was followed by an evil laugh as he hoisted the steel mallet over his head, and aimed it at the right side of the memorial stone.

"STOP RIGHT THERE, Mr. Grainger! Put down the sledgehammer and put up your hands, and you won't get hurt."

The sharp, penetrating voice seemed to come out of nowhere. Grainger whipped around, ready to defend himself for the second time in the last hour. In a single motion, he dropped the sledgehammer and whipped out a six-inch folding knife, which he snapped into position. He crouched into a fighting stance with the knife poised in front of his body, ready to go after the first person he saw.

Unfortunately for Grainger, the first person he saw was a deputy sheriff, who was quickly joined by two more men in uniform, all of whom were holding high-caliber handguns pointed at his face and body. From further to his left side, he heard the unmistakable sound of a shotgun's safety being clicked to the "off" position.

In addition to the impressive display of force, Grainger suddenly found himself shielding his eyes from the full blast of several powerful flood-lights, all of which were pointed directly into his face.

"Mister Grainger, you are surrounded by five members of the New York State Police and the county sheriff's department. If you want to walk out of here unharmed, I suggest you drop that knife immediately and place your hands over your head."

Grainger instantly realized that he was outnumbered and vastly out-armed. However, there was some part of his character that refused to give in without a display of aggression. Without dropping the knife, he snarled at the figures concealed behind the blinding torches.

"I suppose that if I don't, you're going to shoot me right here on the spot, is that it, you pig?" Grainger said, his contempt scarcely concealed.

That was all the officers needed to hear. None of the law enforcement professionals were in the mood to take abuse from a knife-wielding punk who was hell-bent on destroying a priceless piece of Adirondack folklore. The next sound that permeated the night air was that of two gas-propelled X-26 taser electrodes, as their barbed hooks launched from the hand-held device and penetrated Grainger's shirt and skin, their conductive wires delivering a debilitating electrical charge into his already fatigued body.

In an instant, Grainger was on the ground, his body flopping like a freshly landed game fish on the wet rocks next to the monument. "MAKE IT STOP! MAKE IT STOP!" he cried over and over again while the offi-cers watched from a few feet away. After kicking the knife away from his convulsing body, the trooper switched off the charge, allowing Grainger's body to go limp on the cold ground. He lay there for a while, gasping for breath, while a series of short sobs escaped his mouth. Gone was the bel-ligerence of a moment ago, and he meekly complied when he was asked to place his hands behind his back to be cuffed.

Meanwhile, Chris and Sean had arrived, hoping to get a glimpse of the officers returning with Grainger. When they reached the trailhead, there were no other people in sight, and the lot was about half full. Among the cars was Grainger's Mini Cooper, which was parked in almost the same spot as during his last visit. Chris pulled in two spaces away from the small red vehicle and immediately turned off the engine. A careful inspection of the other vehicles revealed unmarked law enforcement cars that easily could have passed for regular civilian street automobiles.

"They're not taking any chances that Grainger would recognize their vehicles," remarked Chris.

"So, now that we're here, and the posse isn't, what do you suppose has happened?" asked Sean.

"I wouldn't expect them to be back yet," said Chris. "As a matter of fact, I imagine that we'll be up here at least a couple of hours before we see anything exciting. But I thought that as long as we're here, we might make an advance scouting trip to get a preview of tomorrow night's climb."

"We'll be up here at least a couple of hours," mimicked Sean, throwing his hands in the air. "*Now* you tell me! How do you expect me to get my beauty sleep if you keep me up until all hours of the night?"

"You can sleep when we get back home on Wednesday," replied Chris. "In the meantime, we've got a job to do."

"OK, but before we stage the dress rehearsal, I've got a job of my own to handle," said Sean, strapping on a headlamp and removing a small screwdriver from his pocket.

"What's that?" asked Chris, puzzled by his friend's preparations.

"As long as we are here with nothing to do, I'm going to pull my tracking device off Grainger's car," explained Sean. "This will probably be my last chance to get it back before the police impound the vehicle."

"Good thinking," agreed Chris. "We don't want the authorities finding that thing attached to the car after Grainger is arrested. I'm not sure whether there is any way of tracking us down from the serial number, but I don't want to even present them with the opportunity."

"OK then, let's make sure that no one is around, and then I'll go for it," proposed Sean. "You stand by the vehicle and give me a warning if anyone comes from any direction. I can always crawl out and sneak into the woods without being seen."

"It is a little easier than being in a Philadelphia parking garage, isn't it?" chided Chris.

"Don't remind me," exclaimed Sean, slapping his forehead. "I *never* want to go through that experience again."

After adjusting his light for optimum use, Sean lay flat on his back and swiveled his torso beneath the front of Grainger's compact car. Chris took up station in back of his own SUV, leaning against the vehicle as though he was relaxing after a hike. Meanwhile, his eyes were constantly scanning the area from the trailhead to the road south, looking for car lights or other signs of activity.

It took Sean a surprisingly short time to remove the device, considering the problems he'd experienced installing it the month before. In less than sixty seconds, he bounced back up from under the car, holding the dusty piece of electronic spy gear up triumphantly.

"Mission accomplished," he said, with a wide grin on his face.

"Good job," said Chris, complimenting him on his expediency. "I don't know how we would have accomplished what we have without it. You can thank Maggie, when you see her, for her role in getting Grainger busted."

"Ah, yes, I'll do that," said Sean. Then he added with a chuckle, "Although I don't think it was Grainger's car that she wanted to watch."

"That's right," laughed Chris, returning to his original pursuit. "Why don't you toss that device into the glove compartment of the Jeep, and then we'll wander down to the furnace and see how it looks at night."

After locking the doors to the SUV, Chris and Sean strolled down the road towards the massive furnace. The calm of the evening had a soothing effect on them both, as they enjoyed the feel of the cool fresh air and the smells of the spruce and balsam trees.

Once they dropped down to the plateau in front of the furnace, Chris directed his light straight up at the fourth anchor plate on the right side of the structure.

"That doesn't look like too tough of a climb, does it?" asked Chris, keeping his eyes focused upward.

"No, not at all," replied Sean. "The cracks between those stones are so big that you could probably even get your entire foot into most of them. I doubt you'll even need your climbing shoes."

"I brought them along anyway, just to be safe," said Chris. "I'll probably wear them no matter what, just for the added traction."

"How is the plate held in place?" asked Sean, squinting into the darkness. "It looks like there's another plate, or something like that, running perpendicular to the square anchor plate."

"It's actually a tapered, flat cotter pin," explained Chris. "The tie rod that runs through the furnace from front to back was extended through the hole in the anchor plate. The ends of the tie rods were manufactured with slotted holes, through which they inserted the cotter pins. Once the pins were fitted in place, gravity performed the rest of the job. It's all a very nice, tightly secure method for maintaining the overall shape of the furnace without allowing the stones to slide."

"And your theory is that the fourth anchor plate is a fake, right?"

"I'd be willing to bet a month's pay on it," replied Chris.

"How do you plan on getting the cotter pin out to remove the anchor plate?" asked Sean.

"First, I'm going to use a mallet to try to loosen it from the bottom the easy way," said Chris. "If that doesn't work, I have some lubricant that I'll try, in case there's a problem with the friction from built-up rust deposits. Finally, if it still won't budge, I'll use a miniature block and tackle in combination with a vise grip, fastened to the top of the cotter pin."

"It sounds like you've given this a lot of thought," said Sean.

"I've had to," said Chris. "I only want to try this one time, so we've got to get it right."

"Don't you think that taking apart a portion of the blast furnace is an illegal activity?" said Sean, posing the sober question.

"Yes, I suppose that it is," said Chris, looking back at his friend with a serious face. "But we're not damaging anything, and after we're done, we'll replace each and every bit of hardware exactly as we found it. As a matter of fact, within two hours of our arrival time, no one will be able to tell that anyone was ever here."

"I hope you're right," remarked Sean. "I don't think I could ever get used to the meals they serve in the county lockup."

"Speaking of the lockup, maybe it's time we headed back up the road to the car," said Chris, glancing at his watch. "It's going on midnight now, so we might start looking for some activity within the next hour."

The two returned to the Jeep, where they sat and talked, sharing their thoughts about the past month's activities. As the time passed, their conversation gradually slowed, until Sean finally pulled out his cell phone to check the time.

"Did you know it's after one in the morning?" he exclaimed, looking at the figures on the display and then at the trail heading into the woods. "What do you think is going on in there?"

"I don't know, but I'm not worried," said Chris as he levered his seat back into a reclined position. "As a matter of fact, I'm thinking of taking a quick doze until they make it back out with Grainger."

"That sounds like a good idea," said Sean, tilting the passenger seat back as well. "I'm a pretty light sleeper, so I think I'll wake up when I hear their voices. If nothing else, the headlights should rouse me out of my sleep in time to see them go by."

Sean wasn't sure why Chris was pushing on his shoulder. All he knew was that he had been sound asleep, and suddenly his friend was pushing him firmly against the passenger side door.

"Hey, Sean, *wake up!*" he cried, repeating his words for the third time in fifteen seconds.

"Huh?" mumbled Sean, barely able to speak given his semiconscious state.

"I thought you wanted to watch Grainger's chauffeured ride to the slammer," said Chris, nodding out the right side of the Jeep. "You're missing the show."

In an instant, Sean was wide awake, adjusting his seat to better view the activity around the sheriff's cars. "When did they come out of the woods?" he asked Chris tensely.

"Just a minute ago. It's a good thing you're such a light sleeper or we would have missed it," Chris joked.

"I must have been more tired than I thought," replied Sean, rubbing his eyes and stretching his back.

"That's Grainger they're loading into the back seat of the patrol car," observed Chris. "It looks like they've got him in handcuffs."

"They do!" exclaimed Sean. "Woohoo! I can't wait to tell Maggie. I think I'll send her a text right now."

"I don't think she'll get it for a few hours," said Chris. "It's almost two thirty."

"Oh my God," groaned Sean. "I really was zonked out for a while. But now that we know Grainger is in custody, let's go back to the hotel and get a few hours of real sleep."

"I agree. But first, let's wait for these guys to clear out of the area," Chris suggested. "I don't want to raise any suspicions by pulling out directly in front of them at this time of the morning."

"Are you kidding me?" asked Sean. "After everything Grainger has done to Maggie and Kristi, not to mention his other deeds, I almost feel like getting out of the car and waving to him as the cop car goes by."

"There's no need for that," replied Chris. "The trap of revenge has already sprung shut, and we're going to enjoy feeding them even more evidence to make sure Grainger remains stuck in jail for a long time."

Chris and Sean sat as the sheriffs secured their prisoner in the back seat, flanked by a pair of deputies. Two men in different colored uniforms bid them farewell and got into another unmarked car.

"It looks like they had quite the welcome party set for him, didn't they?" said Sean, satisfied at the sight.

"Good riddance, I say," answered Chris.

The two sat and watched in silence as the police cars turned on their lights and pulled out of the lot. Chris didn't bother turning on his engine until the last sign of the taillights disappeared around a bend in the road and were lost from sight.

Revenge, Phase 1, had been a success.

CHAPTER 20

Tuesday, September 16, 2015

It was a very late night for Chris and Sean. They didn't make it back to Long Lake and the hotel until almost three thirty, and the entire town was asleep. Only a weary front desk clerk was awake as they stumbled in through the front door and mounted the stairs to their room.

"Let's just hang the 'Do Not Disturb' sign out and sleep as late as we can," suggested Sean.

"Right," agreed Chris. "No need to be up before noon tomorrow, since we have everything we need already."

In spite of their plan to sleep late, the smell of bacon, eggs, and pancakes awakened them both around nine o'clock, whereupon they dressed and proceeded downstairs to the dining room for breakfast. The hotel had always offered sumptuous food at each of the daily meals, and this was no exception.

"I wonder if these would have tasted this good if we hadn't seen Grainger arrested last night," asked Sean, his fork loaded with syrup-laden pancake.

"It certainly helps," replied Chris, as he helped himself to another cup of coffee. "By the way, would you mind if I called Lieutenant Folsom on your phone to ask how things went with the arrest last night?"

"Of course not," offered Sean, sliding his phone across the table.

Chris referred to the folded piece of paper in his pocket for the number, and then entered it into Sean's cell phone. After waiting for a moment, a voice came on the other end of the line.

Larry Weill

"Lieutenant Folsom, this is Chris Carey," Chris began. "I'm just calling to find out how everything went with Ben Grainger last night."

"Hi, Chris," replied the veteran officer. "It went as well as could be expected, although from what I hear, he tried to give them a hard time during the arrest. They had to use the taser to get him to cooperate. After that, he seemed much more willing to listen to reason."

"I bet," laughed Chris. "You wouldn't happen to know what the initial charges against him are, would you?"

"Yes, I've heard some news this morning, because my buddy up in Essex County, Trooper Judd DelMonico, was in on the arrest, and he phoned me when he saw that I was the one who called in the alarm. Judd said that the initial charges included intent to destroy public property, attempting to deface a historic monument, resisting arrest, and attempted assault with a deadly weapon. But it doesn't end there."

"What do you mean?" asked Chris.

"Well, Judd said that he's not sure how this has happened, but all of a sudden there's a whole flood of information coming in on this guy that might have him locked up for a good many years. Evidently, he assaulted a woman down in the town of Little Falls, New York, last month, and banged her up pretty good. We never would have known about it if the case hadn't been brought to our attention by a third party, so if the blood samples and fingerprints from that crime scene match with this Grainger fellow, he's in deeper trouble than we originally anticipated."

"That's great news," said Chris, who was shocked to hear that they had already linked Grainger to the break-in and assault on Maggie at Sean's house. "If I might ask, how did the police make the connection between Grainger and the break-in down in Little Falls?"

"From what I've heard, it's all coming out of some high-powered legal office down in Washington, D.C.," said Lieutenant Folsom. "They also told my buddy Judd that they have additional evidence coming that will link him to even more crimes. For some reason that I can't fathom, this law firm has taken a real interest in this case and is on it like a swarm of

420

angry hornets." After a brief pause, the officer laughed and then added, "Leave it to a bunch of lawyers!"

Chris thanked the officer and then hung up the phone. He looked across the table at Sean for a moment before simply saying, "Dad."

"What's up?" asked Sean. "And what's all this stuff about my house? I'm assuming that's what you meant by Little Falls."

"Yes," said Chris. "It sounds like my dad's gotten behind the cause and has assigned a flock of assassin attorneys to make sure that Grainger stays locked up until most of that red hair has turned gray."

"That sounds like a reason to celebrate," said Sean, beaming back over the breakfast dishes.

"It is," agreed Chris. "Now hopefully our own luck holds out and we don't meet any unexpected snags tonight. I'd hate to be calling my dad's office asking for help from the defense lawyer's side of the courtroom."

Considering the unspoken tension in the air about the upcoming evening, Chris and Sean enjoyed a fairly relaxed day. They both took advantage of Sean's email and satellite phone technology to answer some business calls and respond to clients' emails. Chris was pleased to see that he had been asked to conduct an efficiency study of a financial group near his parents' house in Utica. Sean was also happy that he had no major IT issues with any of his customers, and that his newly installed network was functioning up to speed.

With little to worry about except the approaching operation, they spent a leisurely day browsing the shops around Long Lake. Sean suggested driving down to the Adirondack Museum in Blue Mountain Lake.

"Thanks, but not yet," replied Chris. "I'd prefer to let sleeping dogs lie right now. The next time we see them will be to present them with their million-dollar coin."

"Oh yeah, I forgot; we have a bit of explaining to do to our friends at the museum," agreed Sean. "But I'm sure they'll be a little less shocked than last time."

In order to pass the time and to ensure that they were mentally awake later, Sean and Chris agreed to try to get a few hours of sleep in the early part of the evening.

"What time do you plan on conducting our little soirée this evening?" asked Sean, eying the clock in the room.

"I'd like to be climbing the front of the furnace by one thirty, and out of there no later than three o'clock," answered Chris. "That should give us more time than we'll need, and hopefully we'll avoid any late night arrivals in the parking lot."

"That means we'll need to leave here by a little past midnight," estimated Sean.

"I'd settle for twelve thirty," said Chris.

"Sounds like a plan," agreed Sean. "We should be able to get about three hours of sleep if we turn in now."

"Let's do it," said Chris, as he collapsed on his bed. "On your mark, get set, sleep!"

Sean's cell phone and the room clock alarm sounded at the exact same moment, signifying the end of their brief snooze. Neither man needed to be urged from his slumber, and they both shot from their beds as if fired from a cannon.

The time was almost midnight, and the hotel was shrouded in complete and total silence. They did their best to preserve the calm, and they dressed without saying a word. Chris had moved the ladder and climbing gear into the cargo compartment of the Jeep earlier in the day, so all they had to do was to grab the lights and head out to the parking lot. Sean brought along a box of granola bars and a couple bottles of water for the ride.

Somehow, despite the months of hard work and sacrifice leading up to this moment, there didn't seem to be much the two had to say to each other as they followed Route 28 out of town. They had driven this road countless times now, and they had mentally rehearsed their roles in painstaking detail. As the miles clicked on the odometer, Chris' mind was already in front of the blast furnace, picturing his moves step by step. He'd studied his photos so well that he could see each crack and crevice in the rock, and he knew where each piece of climbing protection would fit. Everything that he could predict was in place, and the plan was now in motion.

There were, of course, a couple uncontrollable variables: would the silver dollars be where they expected them to be, and would they be able to retrieve them? Chris knew that there was nothing he could do to affect that outcome, and he quickly banished the thought of failure from his mind.

The drive to Tahawus seemed to take a week, and yet it was over in a flash. Chris stopped the Jeep directly in front of the short path down to the furnace instead of pulling all the way up to the parking lot.

"Let's get the gear unloaded here," he suggested, "rather than carry it all down from the end of the road."

Everything in the back was packed into one of three containers. The fire escape ladder was in a large canvas bag of its own. Another duffel held the climbing equipment, ropes, harnesses, slings, and Chris' climbing shoes and helmet. Finally, a heavy-duty cardboard box contained lanterns, two flashlights, and a pair of headlamps. Chris and Sean shared the job of moving the gear from the back of the Jeep to a spot in front of the furnace. Chris then took off to park the vehicle in the parking lot while Sean remained behind with the equipment.

In less than five minutes, Sean spied Chris' lean frame striding around the massive base stones of the blast furnace.

"You should have called for valet parking," said Sean, attempting to rid himself of the tension that had been building inside his head.

"I didn't feel like tipping the parking attendant" replied Chris, following his friend's lead.

Sean watched as Chris turned on his headlamp and used the light to pull on his climbing shoes. Next, he donned his climbing harness, which held a wide variety of hexes, nuts, and camming devices that he would need to affix the rope to the side of the rock surface. Sean also slipped into a harness to enable him to belay Chris from below.

When Chris was completely loaded and ready to go, he wiped his fingers on a block of chalk for added grip, and then started up the side of the furnace. Sean was impressed at the speed with which his friend ascended the vertical wall. Even though he had spelunked with Chris in several large caves, he was not accustomed to seeing him rocket upward with such momentum. He attributed it to the exceptional quality and availability of the handholds and footholds between each rock along the way.

When Chris was about twelve feet off the ground, he stopped briefly to insert a few pieces of protection into a narrow crack, pulling on them with force to set them firmly in place. He then used a pair of locking carabiners to anchor the rope to the wall before continuing upward. As he climbed, Sean tended the line from below, ready to assist on command. Sean also volunteered to direct one of the fixed lanterns on Chris' intended path up the rock, which Chris rejected. "Let's keep the lighting as low as possible, in case anyone is in the area," he whispered.

Chris continued up the wall, passing the second anchor plate at sixteen feet, and the third at twenty-four feet. Every four to five feet, he stopped and placed another set of nuts and hexes into the rock, to which he again fixed the rope with more of the locking carabiners. Below, Sean maintained his hold on the line, controlling the slack and offering advice about the rock ahead. Once again, Chris returned to the assault on the furnace, moving nimbly as a spider on a wall. Then finally, with a giant last step and reach of his arm, he grasped the rock directly above the fourth anchor plate and pulled himself up to eye level with the massive square fixture.

Rather than rest on his laurels, Chris immediately went to work to establish a temporary work platform at his newly attained height of thirty-two feet above the ground. Using six more nuts and a heavy duty sling attached to a quadruple pulley system, he was able to create an anchoring system for moving equipment and heavy objects up and down the vertical face of the furnace.

Chris then securely tied a carabiner onto the end of the rope he'd attached and lowered it to the ground below. As soon as it was within reach, Sean lifted the handles of the bag containing the fire ladder and used the pulley to convey it up the rock surface to Chris.

"Good work," said Chris as he attached the ladder and let it unravel itself as it rolled down the front of the furnace. "Care to join me?" offered Chris, smiling down at his friend. "And bring the mallet along with you when you come up."

Sean grabbed the heavy steel hammer and scampered up to join him. Chris took the mallet from him and set it inside the sling beneath the anchor plate. They exchanged a celebratory high five before making their next moves.

"OK, the first part is done," said Chris, satisfied at their progress so far. "Now I want to see just how tough it will be to budge this cotter pin." Rather than start with the oversized mallet, Chris decided to lubricate the inside of the tie rod hole with an oil made for dissolving corroded metal. He applied a liberal amount of the slippery fluid along both sides of the cotter pin, watching it seep into the crevice of the tie rod.

"How quickly will that work?" asked Sean, watching the operation from the ladder.

"It should reduce the friction as soon as it soaks through the cracks," replied Chris. "Of course, if we waited here until morning, it would probably work even better."

"No thanks," said Sean. "I'd have a pair of pretty tired arms by then."

"Speaking of which, it would probably be easier for me to maneuver if you weren't on the ladder right now," said Chris. "Why don't you head back down and I'll call you as soon as I start making some progress."

"How come I never get to have any fun?" said Sean, faking his disappointment as he stepped back down to the ground below.

After waiting a few minutes for the oil to work, Chris took the mallet and prepared to tap the bottom part of the cotter pin blade that extended below the slot in the tie rod.

"I sure hope this does the trick," said Chris, praying to himself. "I'm not sure whether the vise grip will work, and I really don't feel like setting up a block and tackle up here. Please, please, please..." he repeated as he tentatively knocked on the sides of the cotter pin, first one side, then the other.

"Anything happening up there?" whispered Sean, still trying to maintain the silence. "Not much," said Chris, audibly amused from his perch above the base of the rock wall.

"What's so funny?" asked Sean.

"I just think it's funny as heck that we're whispering like choirboys while I bang the living daylights out of an iron plate with a steel hammer," replied Chris, still chuckling at the image.

Chris went back to his work, applying more of the lubricant as he alternated swings from the front and back as well as from both sides, all trying to break the grip that had been sealed shut by 160 years of rust, heat, cold, and age. He was just about to give up when a heavy-handed uppercut swing from below made solid contact on the sweet spot of the hammer. Chris couldn't be certain, but he thought he detected a slight elevation of the pin in the elongated hole. A close examination of the pin revealed that it had indeed moved, as the rust stain from the inside of the tie rod was now visible on the cotter pin above the slot.

Chris was energized by the progress. Each stroke of the mallet now pushed the pin up another fraction of an inch, until it stood almost entirely free above the tie rod. It looked as though the very next strike would send the tapered pin flying out the top of the hole and tumbling to the ground.

Chris called out to Sean. "OK, buddy, you wanted to come up and play? Now is your chance."

"I don't have to be asked twice," said Sean, climbing back up the ladder to the same height as Chris. He immediately attached himself to one of the fixed lines anchored to the rock. "What comes next?"

"We finish the job of removing the cotter pin from the tie rod, which should allow us to pull the anchor plate off the end of the rod," explained Chris. "But that's where it's going to get tricky, because I'd estimate that the anchor plate weighs around eighty to ninety pounds."

"Ah, and that's why you've placed the sling beneath it, right? To hold the plate after we remove it from the tie rod?" asked Sean.

"Good guess," said Chris. "I wouldn't like to have to carry that thing back up the ladder if it fell...or even hold it while it was off the tie rod."

"OK then, let's get this done," said Sean. "You go ahead and strike the final blow on the pin while I catch it from taking the plunge."

With everything in place, Chris applied the weight of the hefty tool to the front of the cotter pin blade, which levered it backwards and out of the slot. Sean immediately lifted it out of the way and dropped it into the netting of the sling. Without the pressure of the pin to hold the anchor plate against the rock, the heavy square piece of rusted metal moved freely on the end of the tie rod.

"OK, my friend, here it is; the moment of truth," said Chris solemnly. "Let's both pull the plate and make sure we've got it positioned to fall into the sling. Then, if our theory is correct, we should have a view of something very near and dear to us right inside the front wall."

"How big do you think it will be?" asked Sean as he maneuvered himself into position to help with the lift.

"I've done the math, and my calculations say that the coins alone will weigh in around 143 pounds, and take up a little less than a cubic foot," answered Chris. "But the wildcard in the equation will be the container, assuming that they are packed inside something that survived the years and the environment."

"What if someone already beat us to the punch?" asked Sean. "Or the silver in the coins has fused into a single mass of rusted metal?"

"Silver doesn't rust, you pessimist," replied Chris as he placed both hands on the anchor plate. "Tarnish, maybe, but not rust. Now, are you ready to stop worrying and start giving me a hand? I'm tired of hanging around up here."

"Sorry," replied Sean apologetically. "Let's go for it."

Without another word, Sean and Chris worked the massive anchor plate back and forth as they walked it to the very end of the tie rod. Sean pulled the open end of the thick mesh sling out from the wall and, with a final tug on the anchor plate, they watched it fall into the sling.

Chris looked at Sean in awe, and sean returned his stare with the same wide-eyed expression. Chris directed his beam into the hole in the wall and looked inside the exposed cavity.

"Well, that's something that's not supposed to be part of the original construction," said Sean, reaching out and touching the outside of a compact opaque container, measuring roughly fourteen inches on each side. Neither Sean nor Chris could determine the material from which it was constructed, although it looked very old and heavy. It sat on a flat surface that had been engineered behind the original anchor plate.

"Nice, neat construction," remarked Chris. As he inspected the back of the space, another object caught his eye. He stared at it for a few moments, lost in the depths of his concentration, before he turned to Sean with a smirk.

"You're not going to believe this," he said in amazement, "but there's another anchor plate about three feet in back of the one we just removed. I think I just figured out how this thing was built. If I'm correct, the first anchor plate was placed there for cosmetic purposes only and has nothing to do with holding this whole pile of rocks together."

"The heck with the anchor plates," said Sean, his voice full of urgency. "Let's get this box out of here and see what's inside!"

"My thoughts exactly," replied Chris.

Chris and Sean leaned into the hole and placed their hands on the sides of the heavy container. However, because of its great weight and the friction of the bottom of the box on the rock shelf, they were unable to budge it from its position.

"I know," said Sean, looking at the surplus equipment still attached to Chris' climbing harness. "Pass me that extra sling of yours, and we'll feed that around the back of the box. That will give us a lot more gripping power than we have on the smooth sides of the container. My hands keep slipping off before I'm really able to generate much force on this thing."

"Good idea" said Chris, as he quickly removed the nylon mesh and tossed the middle of it over the top of the container. Each of them got a good handhold on the sling and gave a heave. To their joy and amazement, it slid a few inches closer to them across the flat rock surface.

"Ready for some aerobic exercise?" asked Chris, taking a firmer grasp on the netting.

"It sure beats Jazzercise any day of the week," replied Sean.

With both of them pulling in a coordinated effort, the box was soon poised on the outside edge of the wall, ready to be lowered to the ground.

"Who wants the first look inside?" asked Sean, his fingers wrapped around the top cover of the container.

"No reason we shouldn't be able to share," suggested Chris, his eyes fixed on the lid. "Let's pop this baby open and have a peek inside."

Sean lifted up on the bottom of the lid, only to be met with resistance he could not overcome. Without asking, Chris joined him, adding his wiry strength to the effort. However, the outcome was the same, and the cover would not budge.

Chris looked at the container suspiciously, moving within a couple inches of the smooth outer surface before turning away in surprise. "Do you know what I think we have here?" he asked Sean.

"No, but please feel free to enlighten me," replied Sean.

"I think this is a specially designed glass box that was made with a ground glass seal around the top. My guess is that the rim where the top and bottom come together was rubbed with some form of oil or other waterproof substance to create a better seal that would protect it from the elements," ventured Chris. "I've seen one or two of these from the early days, but never one this big."

"Yes, but if it's made out of glass, why can't we see the contents right through the sides?" asked Chris.

"Because it's so old, and has been exposed to such temperature extremes, the entire thing is filled with thousands upon thousands of tiny stress fractures." As Chris spoke, he rapped on the side of the box with his knuckles. "Listen, there's no doubt that it's made of glass. I'd bet anything that I'm right about the top, too."

"Do you have a flathead screwdriver, or something equivalent that we could use to break the seal?" asked Sean.

"I do, but I wouldn't recommend doing that," said Chris. "It would be better to keep the top on until after we get it down to the ground. Also, the glass may be very thick, but it's also pretty brittle. Any force we use to pry off the lid may shatter this thing into a thousand pieces."

"Alright then, I'll help you move the whole box into the sling and lower it to the ground," suggested Sean. "We should be able to work with it better down there."

"Let's do it," agreed Chris. "But first, let's see if we can get the anchor plate out of the sling and tie it onto the rock somehow. I don't want the glass box to fall on top of that heavy plate. It might shatter, and it'll also make it tough to remove the anchor harness from the sling if it's stuck underneath all that weight."

After a few minutes of acrobatics, Chris and Sean were able hoist the anchor plate up and secure it to the wire links above.

"You do nice work," said Sean, admiring the suspended plate.

"Let's save the compliments for the post-game party," replied Chris. "Now let's get this box down to the ground."

It took another joint effort between Chris and Sean to pull the glass container over the edge and into the sling, where it sagged through the net like a ton of bricks. Chris quickly rigged the box into the sling while Sean dropped back down the ladder, ready to belay the heavy load of cargo to the ground below.

When everything was in position, Chris pushed the mesh sling away from the wall and called quietly down to Sean, "On belay?"

"Belay on," replied Sean, signaling his readiness to receive the box.

Using his full body weight, plus the friction created by the figure-eight descender piece, Sean carefully guided the container down to the ground. He had thoughtfully spread out another sling on the rocky surface to soften the impact of the glass when it touched down.

"Perfect," cried out Sean once the box was on the ground. He quickly disconnected the line from the sling, which Chris pulled back up the side of the furnace. "Not only that, but I think that the vibration of the glass impacting the ground has jarred the lid loose!"

"Say no more—I'm on my way," said Chris, who unclipped himself from the line as he moved over to the ladder. In a moment, he was on the ground next to Sean. Their headlamps cast a yellow glow on the top of the heavy glass lid as Chris removed the carabiners from the top of the sling and the mesh fell away from the container.

"Hold your breath," said Chris, as he bowed his head and pried the lid open. Underneath, exposed for the first time in over a century and a half, were row after row of large silver coins. Each carried the depiction of a female bust directly above the date 1804 centered on the lower rim.

For a moment, the two sat on their haunches and stared at the coins, almost unable to comprehend the sight before them. Then, as if on cue, Sean and Chris launched themselves skyward and met in a massive bear hug. They celebrated for a full minute, jumping for joy while still somehow preserving the silence. Neither of them could believe that their quest had finally reached a successful terminus, and their plans and assumptions had all been proven correct.

After taking time to enjoy the find, Chris checked his watch and discovered that it was already almost three fifteen. "We've got to make tracks and get out of here," he said, his mind recalling the original schedule. "We can probably expect company anytime after four thirty or five o'clock."

"Let's head up and replace the anchor plate on the furnace, then we'll pack up and hit the road," said Sean.

The two of them used the ladder to ascend back up to the opening in the furnace, where they manhandled the anchor plate back into position and replaced the cotter pin.

"Looks as good as new, doesn't it?" asked Sean, looking over their handiwork.

"It sure does," agreed Chris. "You couldn't tell that anything's been moved. Now, you head down and clean up the stuff on the ground and get as much of it packed up as possible. I'll lower the fire ladder down to you, and then I'll remove all the camming and protective devices from the rock up here. I'll let you know when I'm ready to come down."

"You got it," replied Sean, already gathering up their gear and packing it into the original three bags.

It took less than ten minutes for Chris to remove all signs of their work from the front of the furnace. Sean then belayed him safely to the ground, where they put everything, including the container with the silver dollars, into one pile.

"You stay here while I run up and get the Jeep," said Chris, as he took off at a trot. "We're certainly not going to carry a two-hundred-pound box all the way to the parking lot."

Once Chris returned with the vehicle, he opened the rear door and then backtracked to meet Sean for the grueling task of moving the box up the hill. The total distance they had to move was less than one hundred feet. Still the load was very heavy, and the nylon mesh bit into the flesh of their fingers. It didn't help that the last forty feet were steeply slanted against them. Finally, after close to fifteen minutes of heavy exertion, they lifted the box up and into the back of the SUV. Chris threw some old blankets over the top of the container before closing and locking the door.

"Now, let's get the rest of our stuff and blow out of here," said Chris.

It took only one more trip to bring everything else up the hill, and they were soon packed and ready to go.

"Chris, would you do me one favor before we head back?" asked Sean, looking at Chris questioningly.

"What is it?" said Chris, as he started the engine.

"Could we look at those silver dollars one more time?" implored Sean. "I just want to see them again before we head back to the hotel."

"Sure," said Chris. "But I have a better idea; let's not go back to the hotel. We can stop there to check out, but I think it would be much safer to head home this morning rather than leave the coins in the Jeep or try to bring them inside the hotel. Neither one is a very good option."

"You're right, of course," agreed Sean. "Still, I want to see these things in the light before we start the trip home."

Chris turned off the engine, and the two men walked around the back of the Jeep. Chris opened the door and pulled the blankets off the box.

"Wow, look at the luster on some of those dollars," exclaimed Sean. "A few of them have barely any tarnish on them at all. They look as though they've never been touched by human hands."

"Most of them were probably touched only twice," added Chris. "Once in 1804, after they were pressed, and the other time when they were loaded into this case by Robert M. Patterson, probably early in 1853."

"It's too bad these are discolored," commented Sean, pointing at some of the dollars on the outer edges of the stacks. "They've tarnished and turned a dark shade of blue or brown."

"That's OK," explained Chris. "In coin collecting terms, that's called a patina, and a lot of collectors actually prefer that over the pure silver color. It certainly doesn't detract from the value of the coin."

"Amazing," said Sean, shaking his head from side to side as he stared at the contents of the heavy glass chest. "Simply amazing."

"OK, let's get this stuff stored away so we can get going," said Chris. Once again, he replaced the lid on the ancient glass box and tossed the blankets over the top. He rearranged all the other gear neatly in the back of the Jeep, finishing with the large bag containing the climbing gear. He was preparing to lock everything in when a car approached and pulled into the lot behind their vehicle.

"Looks like we have company," said Sean, looking back at the large car which he identified as a Dodge Charger. Then, before he could say anything else, the entire back of the Jeep was lit up in the glaring beam of a police search light.

"How are you boys doing tonight?" asked the sheriff as he got out of his car.

"We're doing great, although we're pretty tired," replied Chris, waving back as though he'd just returned from an extended hike.

"You boys been doing some climbing?" queried the Sheriff as he looked at the climbing gear and harnesses.

"Yeah, but nothing big," answered Chris, trying to maintain an innocent expression. "We've just been practicing on some small rock walls; I've been trying to teach my friend here some technique."

"That's a good sport," nodded the officer. "I used to enjoy it a bit when I was younger, although it's been a few years since I've been on a rope myself."

Chris just nodded back in reply while Sean stood passively nearby.

"Well, you boys be careful, OK?" said the Sheriff. "We had a bit of an incident here last night."

"Yes sir, and thanks for the warning," replied Chris.

The officer nodded back to them and then pulled his unmarked cruiser out of the lot. Chris and Sean breathed a heavy sigh of relief and jumped into the front seat for the drive home.

Robert Patterson's secret had been uncovered at last.

CHAPTER 21

Wednesday, September 17, 2015

Considering the excitement of the past forty-eight hours, the transit back to Utica was anti climactic. Chris drove the entire distance, although Sean stayed up to make sure that his friend remained alert despite his fatigue. They stopped several times for coffee and to use the restroom, agreeing to keep one person in the car at all times and never leave the Jeep unattended.

Along the road, they discussed the best place to unload the cache of coins for temporary safekeeping. Sean's house had the benefit of an alarm system. Yet they also knew that Ben Grainger was fully aware of Sean's address, and he may have had an accomplice to whom he passed the information prior to his arrest. Instead, they decided on the anonymity of Chris' house in Syracuse, where they might hide the box until it was turned over to the authorities.

After pulling into the driveway in Little Falls, Sean ran into his house and grabbed a change of clothes. Meanwhile, Chris had been on the phone with his mom, who readily agreed to have the two of them over for breakfast and to open the overhead door so he could park his vehicle inside the detached two-car garage.

"Does she have any idea why we're stopping by?" asked Sean, enjoying the buildup.

"No, not at all," answered Chris. "For something of this magnitude, I'm not going to trust my cell phone. I want to call my dad's office and speak to him using the landline from my mom's house."

"Wasn't she suspicious that you asked if you could park your Jeep inside the garage?" asked Sean.

"No, she didn't ask any questions," replied Chris.

Thirty minutes later, the moss-green Jeep rolled into the extra-wide garage on the right side of the Careys' house. Theresa remained inside, but watched through a window as her son parked the vehicle, locked the doors, and closed the garage door. Her interest was further raised when she noticed a small red LED light suddenly flashing on top of the master alarm panel in the hallway.

As they entered the house, Theresa came into the front entryway and looked at her soon with a frown. "Honey, I see you activated the alarm system inside the garage. Why did you bother doing that?"

"I've got a fair amount of cash in the car, Mom, and I don't want to risk it being stolen," he replied, as he kissed her on the cheek.

Theresa was not only a very bright woman, but she also knew every trick in Chris' playbook because he reminded her so much of her husband. "'A fair amount of cash,' huh?" she replied, not falling for the line. "How much cash?"

"I'm not exactly sure, Mom," Chris replied honestly. "But if I was to count it, I can guarantee you that it would come up to less than three thousand dollars."

Sean maintained a straight face, even though he almost choked over his friend's deceptively true statement.

"Somehow I don't believe you," laughed Chris' mom. "But please come in and sit down anyway. I've got breakfast waiting."

While Chris and Sean feasted on a meal of eggs Benedict and fresh orange juice, Theresa persistently massaged the truth from her son. Once she heard the story, she urged him to call his father immediately.

The call lasted only about two minutes.

"Dad, I need your help," said Chris.

"You're not in any trouble, are you?" asked his father.

"No, not at all, although I could use a little help with the governor's office to explain how we found something," admitted Chris.

Following a short silence, Chris' father replied in a hushed tone. "You found them?" he murmured softly into the phone.

"Yup."

"How many were there?"

"I didn't count them, but if I had to take a guess, I'd say there were 2,619 of them, all stacked in neat piles," replied Chris.

"And where are they now?" asked his father.

"They're locked inside your garage," laughed Chris. "I hope you don't mind the intrusion. If you'd like, I could pay one day's rent for the space."

"Chris, stay right where you are," said his father's, suddenly sounding tense. "Ever since you told me about these coins, I've been reading about their value. I'm not sure that even you know what you've got there. So for the time being, I want you to stay at our house with the coins locked in the garage. I'm leaving Washington now and should be there within four hours."

"Are you sure that's necessary, Dad?" asked Chris. "I mean, we could use some help with the announcement and the public relations, but I don't want to ruin your whole day by having you travel all the way up here."

"Chris, I'm hanging up now, and I'll see you before noon," said his father. "One more thing; don't worry if you see a car sitting in the drive-way within the next hour. You may consider its occupants friendly."

"Thanks, Dad; I understand," replied Chris. "See you later."

True to his word, Chris Carey, Sr., arrived from his flight at eleven forty-five, driving a massive SUV with darkly tinted windows. He got out of the vehicle with two gentlemen who could have played offensive line on any team in the NFL. As he approached the front door of the large house, he waved at the pair of men who had been sitting in a Chevy Impala in the driveway for the past three hours. The one in the driver's seat saluted, then drove away.

Chris' father had arranged for a bank vault to store the silver dollars until the formal announcement would be made the following week. One of the jumbo-sized guards lifted the two hundred pound box as though it was a pair of shoes and loaded it into the SUV. Chris and Sean joined the crew inside the vehicle for the short ride to the bank, where the treasure was locked inside the largest security box available in the city.

After returning home, Chris, Sr., took his son and Sean aside for a confidential talk.

"Look, boys, I'm only going to be up here for a day or two, just to help you get things arranged," he said. "I have a phone conference with the lieutenant governor tomorrow afternoon, and I'll use that time to help smooth over any ruffled feathers over your little venture up the front of their treasured blast furnace. But after that, I'll back out of the picture; this is your accomplishment, and you're the ones who should get the credit."

"Thanks, Dad," said Chris, shaking his father's hand appreciatively. "We will also take you up on your offer to do the application to have the Underground Railroad station designated as a state historic site. Your people did such a great job on the paperwork for French Louie's site last year; it really made the process go a lot quicker."

"I'll have one of my assistants start the research this afternoon," said his father. "Just remember to send me a copy of all the photos you took so that we can add those to the application package."

"You got it," said Chris.

"Anything else I can help with, as long as I'm still here?"

"Well, actually, there is something that you might be able to handle for me, but only if you really want to become involved," said Chris, speaking hesitantly.

"Please, let me know now, as long as we're still together," urged his father. "As you know, I never was one for lengthy phone calls."

"You remember Ben Grainger, who is now in jail awaiting trial on multiple charges?" asked Chris.

"Of course; we helped to feed some additional information to the authorities to make sure he stayed behind bars for as long as possible."

"OK then, here's the deal," explained Chris. "In addition to the charges he's currently facing, he also stole some historical documents from Rowan University's Frank Stewart collection, and I'm sure they'd like them back. He's got the originals inside his Binghamton apartment, along with a bunch of stolen equipment from a previous employer. Could you find a way to get the police to obtain a search warrant for his place so the documents can be returned to the library where they belong?"

"That shouldn't be too difficult," said his father, who looked at his son with curiosity. "What kind of stolen equipment are we talking about here?"

"Small consumer electronics devices, such as GPS systems, music and video storage devices, voice recorders, and lots more. He's got cases of the stuff from a place called Steele Corp Electronics in Philadelphia, which was his last known employer. My guess is that he's got about ten- to fifteen-thousand dollars in stolen goods, if you use retail value."

"Son, exactly how is it that you happen to know what Grainger has stashed away inside his apartment?"

Chris hesitated before answering, a sheepish expression on his face. "Uh, would you believe it if I told you that I interviewed the lady who cleans his apartment?"

"No, I wouldn't," replied his father, trying to act stern. "Come to think of it, I don't want to know about it. As far as I'm concerned, that is now protected information. But I will take care of it and get the local police department to head in there with the search warrant."

"Thanks, Dad," said Chris. "Will I get to see you again soon?"

"I'll definitely try to make it up here when they introduce the two of you in Albany as the dynamic duo who solved the greatest mystery in U.S. coinage," replied his father.

"Albany?" exclaimed Chris. "How the heck is Albany connected with this story?"

"It's the New York State Museum," replied Chris Senior. "During my brief conversation with the Governor while I was on the flight up here, he mentioned that he'd like to use their facility to announce your discovery to the world. By the way, I'm sure that the Smithsonian in D.C. will be interested in getting in on the action as well. The two of you are going to be pretty busy for quite a while."

"Hopefully not for too long," said Chris, looking weary at the idea of spending time in the limelight. "If you remember, things quieted down after about a week when we announced finding the Gordon treasure, so hopefully this will be about the same."

"Son, the gold from the Gordon treasure amounted to what—about six million dollars? I'm sure you've done the math to figure out that this one is exponentially larger."

"I wonder how much larger," said Chris. "We won't really know how much the 1804 silver dollars are worth until they come to market, assuming they ever do."

"I think they will, once the legal haggling is worked out and ownership can be established," said Chris' father. "But you've got to figure that the fifteen examples that are currently known sell for about four to five million dollars each. Even at ten percent of that figure, you're still looking at well over one billion dollars."

"That's a nice round number," said Sean, who had been quiet throughout the father-son conversation.

"It is," agreed the lawyer, turning towards Sean. "Unfortunately, it will probably take several years to filter this through the court system, as I'm sure that quite a few federal and state entities will file motions to claim possession of the coins. I also wouldn't be surprised to see one or two citizens with links to the original owners try to file as well."

"What about us?" asked Sean. "Do you think we'll ever see a penny as a result of doing all the work to find and recover the coins?"

"It's possible," said Chris Senior. "You might be granted a finder's fee, too, by the state or federal government, if they end up with the final custody of the coins. You never can tell how these things will play out."

"OK, Dad, thanks for the help," said Chris. "I'll keep you in the loop and let you know as soon as I hear when they're doing the announcement.

Maybe I'll see you and mom there."

"Great," said his dad. "And remember to bring that wonderful little lady of yours along too, OK?"

"Kristi wouldn't miss it for the world," Chris assured him.

Then, after saying goodbye to Sean and Chris, the attorney tipped his hat and climbed back into the SUV for the return trip to Washington.

PART IV

PERSPECTIVES

CHAPTER 22

Thursday, September 25, 2015

Nine days later, Chris and Sean found themselves traveling together once again, this time en route to the press announcement in the state capital. Although Chris had expected to pick up his friend and transport them to Albany in his Jeep, Sean insisted on chauffeuring them in the comfort of his 1966 Mercedes.

"I just had the shocks replaced," he claimed, wiping a speck of dust from the roof lovingly. "It's a lot more comfortable than your four-wheel drive beast, as long as we're not on any more dirt roads for a while."

They arrived in Albany thirty minutes in advance of the ceremony, which was arranged in the palatial main exhibit hall on the first floor of the State Museum. Parking was difficult to find, even with the multitude of lots surrounding the Empire State Plaza, and the two men had to settle for a spot that was several blocks away.

"I thought we were supposed to be the guests of honor at this gig?" asked Sean, as he finally maneuvered his stately vehicle between a telephone company truck and a pizza delivery van.

"That and a couple bucks will get you a cup of coffee at any shop in town," quipped Chris. "Now let's get going; we don't want to be late for the party."

In spite of the size of the exhibition hall, it rapidly turned into a very crowded room as over a thousand people turned out for the event. Row after row of chairs had been arranged in front of an elevated table, which was furnished with about a dozen seats for the speakers and VIPs. Meanwhile, a projection screen was raised behind the head table for displaying images of the coins, the blast furnace, and other parts of the story leading up to the discovery. On one side of the room was a specially constructed glass exhibit case that held several of the newly recovered silver dollars, along with the heavy glass box which had housed the coins inside the furnace in Tahawus. A pair of armed guards stood watch over the exhibit to dissuade anyone from considering anything crazy.

As soon as Chris and Sean entered the foyer, they were greeted by Theresa, who kissed both her son and Sean and handed each of them blue slips of paper.

"What's this?" asked Sean, looking at the colorful ticket.

"That's so you can get inside for free," said Chris' mother indignantly. "Would you believe it—they were going to make all of us pay to get into the public announcement of the treasure that *you* discovered and turned over to them!"

Chris roared with laughter. "Yes, that would have been the ultimate irony, wouldn't it?"

Once inside the door, Chris Carey Senior pulled Sean and Chris into a small meeting room where he introduced them to the governor, who would be making the introductory remarks.

"You two fellows have made a real habit out of tracking down valuable parts of our state history," said the governor, as he shook hands with Chris and Sean. "I read everything about the Gordon treasure from Lake Champlain a year ago, and I found that to be amazingly interesting. But now, this; I've never heard anything like it. You boys should be awfully proud of your accomplishments."

Chris and Sean expressed their thanks and were then ushered out to the table in front of the crowded room. Less than ten minutes later, the lights dimmed slightly and the governor made a short speech to introduce the two high school friends and summarize their achievements. Then, Chris and Sean were called to the podium, where they shared the microphone and described their activities over the past two months. Sean had prepared a presentation with maps and photos, which they used to illustrate their adventure. Chris, meanwhile, expressed their thanks to everyone who had played a role in solving the 210 year-old mystery, including the many librarians and archivists who had helped them find and interpret the historical records that yielded the clues.

Once Chris and Sean had wrapped up their presentation, a member of the state Historical Preservation Office stepped up to the podium and announced the organization's intentions to work with the Adirondack Park Agency and the Open Space Institute to preserve and protect the entire area around the Tahawus furnace and ghost town. The possibility that a portion of the sale of the silver dollars, if ever authorized, would be diverted back to the preservation efforts was also raised. The director of the State Historical Society was also present, and announced that there would be a separate gathering the following week at the newly discovered Underground Railroad site. Neither Chris nor Sean had been aware of that event, although they both looked forward to participating in the dedication ceremony.

Finally, the radio and newspaper people were permitted fifteen minutes of time to pose questions, which Chris and Sean took turns answering until the members of the press were satisfied. The entire assembly took about an hour, although the reception that followed was expected to run through lunch hour.

As they filed off the stage and into the reception area, Chris saw Maggie and Kristi standing together next to the exhibit case. Sean and Chris wriggled their way through the crowd, stopping to shake hands with well-wishers and members of the press, until they were able to join their respective female companions.

Kristi looked into the case, admiring the tarnished yet still-lustrous silver dollars. "Any guess how much these things will be worth at auction?"

"I've heard a range of figures from $400,000 to $600,000 per coin," replied Sean. "It would have been much higher, just due to the mystique of the 1804 date. But the mere fact that there are over 2,600 of them is keeping the price from escalating over a million dollars. What I'm wondering is how much they will *decrease* the value of the fifteen 1804 silver dollars which have been in private collections for the last two hundred years. As you know, some of those have exceeded four million dollars a coin."

"Not much," said a man who was standing on the other side of the cabinet.

Chris looked up at the thin, elderly gentleman who was looking into the cabinet, gazing adoringly at the samples inside. "Ed Barton!" he cried out, stepping over to shake the man's hand. "It's nice to see you here! We haven't had a chance to speak since the meeting we had in Wes' coin shop last month."

"No, that's true," said Ed, nodding in agreement. "But I'm here because I have something to return to you, and I also couldn't wait to see the collection of new 1804 silver dollars, so here I am."

Chris introduced Sean to Ed, who wanted to know all about how they'd moved the coins from the ghost village down to the museum in Albany. While they talked, Chris recognized yet another familiar face approaching.

"Chris, I had to come and see this!" exclaimed Debbie Santori. "Is it true that some of the papers that we worked on together last month in Blue Mountain Lake helped you to discover this pile of million-dollar coins?"

"It is," confirmed Chris. "Debbie, we couldn't have done it without you, and I can't thank you enough. As a matter of fact..." his voice was cut off as Debbie interrupted his sentence.

"I hope you also brought along that counterfeit copy of the 1804 dollar that we found in the museum that day," chimed the effervescent curator. "Even though it's a fake, it's still an interesting side story to your big discovery. I told our director about it, and he suggested that we set up a display around it with an explanation of how it was found in our collection."

Chris smiled and turned to Ed, who had been standing by with his hand in his jacket pocket. "Ed, do you happen to have that coin with you?"

"As a matter of fact, I do," said Ed, grinning as he removed the plastic coin holder from his pocket and handed it to Chris.

"Here you go, Debbie," Chris said as he placed the coin in her hand.

"Thanks," she said, looking at the piece and then flipping it up in the air, catching it like a piece of change from the candy machine.

Sean's expression showed his dismay, and Ed looked as though he was about ready to faint. Chris simply leaned over and whispered something quietly into Debbie's ear, which caused her face to turn a fine shade of gray, and then white as the shock set in.

"You're kidding me," she said, looking at Chris through wide eyes.

"Nope, I'm not kidding," he said, smiling back at her.

Next, it was Debbie's knuckles that turned white as they clamped tightly around the plastic case in her hands. She shifted her gaze over to Ed and opened her mouth to speak. However, before she could utter a word, he pre-empted her with his own remark.

"Chris is right," the numismatist said. "He's not kidding."

"Oh my God," said Debbie, looking down in amazement at her clenched fist. "This still belongs to our museum?"

"It's all yours," said Chris, chuckling at her reaction.

"I...I...I've got to leave," stammered Debbie, "right now!" As she retreated towards the front door of the museum, she turned back and called over her shoulder, "I'll talk to both of you when I get back. I want you to come up to Blue Mountain Lake as soon as you can." And then she disappeared out the door.

"Wow, that was pretty touching!" said Kristi, watching the woman walk away. "At this rate, you guys will soon have a wing of the Adirondack Museum named after you."

"Oh yeah, the Carey-Riggins Building," said Chris, faking his interest in the idea.

"No, I think it should be the Riggins-Carey Building," Sean chimed in.

"If you two youngsters can't even agree on a name, how are you going to ever come to terms on how to divide this?" said Ed, stepping between the two friends with a folded check.

"What's this?" asked Chris, his eyes furrowed in confusion.

"Let me explain," said Ed, wiping off his glasses as he handed Sean the note. "One of our past ANA presidents was an *extremely* wealthy man, and he was an avid believer in the theory that the 1804 silver dollar had, indeed, been coined and then lost. He was so ardent in his belief that he put a fifty thousand dollar reward into a trust fund for anyone who could prove him right. And you, my two friends, have done just that."

Sean gasped as he opened the folded check and looked at the numbers inked on the "dollars" line.

"Oh my God," whispered Kristi, looking over his shoulder. "I don't think I've ever seen so many zeroes after the number '5.'

"That's a lot of money," agreed Ed, having discharged his duties as the disburser of the award. "What are your plans for it?"

Chris and Sean looked at each another with expressionless stares before turning their heads towards the girls.

"Your college loan is a little over $23,000, right?" Chris asked Kristi.

"And your first year," Sean told Maggie, "should cost you around $18,000 after applying financial aid."

"Looks like the math works out almost perfectly, with a small bit to spare," said Chris.

"Nothing like investing in the future," said Ed, nodding in agreement.

Meanwhile, Chris' father put his hand on Chris' shoulder and addressed him quietly. "By the way, son, your information about Grainger's apartment was entirely accurate. The Broome County Sheriff's Department and the Binghamton police went in on a joint search warrant yesterday afternoon, and they found over seventeen thousand dollars in stolen electronic gear from that outfit in Philadelphia. They will be able to return the equipment to the business, where it was suspected, but couldn't be proven, that he was behind the theft."

"Did they find the stolen documents from Rowan University's collection too?" asked Chris.

"Yes, along with other papers that Grainger had lifted from Sean's house," continued Chris Senior. "So now, they've got him on grand larceny and theft of museum property, too. Between all the different crimes, which he committed in three different states, it's almost certain he'll get at least ten to fifteen years behind bars."

"That's great news, Dad. Thanks for all your follow-up on that," said Chris. Then, looking at both Maggie and Kristi, he added "I know I'm not the only one here who feels safer with Grainger locked away for a while."

Within thirty minutes, the reception was winding down and the crowd was beginning to disperse. Chris, Sean, Kristi, and Maggie were standing in a knot, talking among themselves and with Chris' parents. As they conversed, a middle-aged man in a dark suit approached them and asked which one was Sean.

"That's me," said Sean, stepping away from the others. "What can I do for you?"

"You've already done more than you know," said the gentleman, who extended a handshake that also carried a business card. "My name is Bill Sexton, and I'm with the Smithsonian Institute in Washington."

"Oh, yes," said Sean. "We heard that your museum would receive at least one of the 1804 silver dollars. On behalf of myself and my partner-in-crime, I can only say that we are proud to have made that possible."

Sexton cleared his throat and looked at Sean with an embarrassed expression. "Thank you, Mr. Riggins, but that's not the reason why I'm here."

"It isn't?" asked Sean, now clearly confused.

"No, not really," continued Sexton. "You see, when you were down in Philadelphia doing your research work last month, you met a woman by the name of Rosemary Stewart. She contacted us to say that she had some interesting pieces of Americana for us to look at."

"Oh my God, she actually decided to call you!" exclaimed Sean.

"Yes, she did," said the museum representative. "She said that you had changed her life and helped her to become independently wealthy in the course of a half-hour conversation."

"Yes, she unknowingly possessed a few items of great worth, which I pointed out to her," explained Sean. "She was going to try to auction a couple of the rare coins that had been in her family for several generations and use the proceeds for living expenses. But she also had a few other objects that were of even greater historical value, and I encouraged her to donate those to your institution."

"That is exactly what she did," said Sexton. "You cannot imagine how thrilled we are to have them. They are some of the best preserved examples of George Washington's silver ever found. And they also corroborate the legend that Washington donated the silver to be used to make America's first coins, the half disme pieces. Thank you; thanks to *both* of you for your invaluable contributions."

Sexton then turned around and was about to walk away when he apparently had an afterthought. "Oh, I almost forgot; Tracey Stewart wanted me to say hello, too. She said you are a wonderful guy and that she really enjoyed working with you."

"Oh, uh...thanks," mumbled Sean as he watched the representative leave. As soon as he was outside of range, Sean felt simultaneous contact from both Chris and from Maggie. Chris had gently nudged his left side with his elbow, whereas Maggie swatted him on the seat of the pants.

"Hey!" he cried out. "Didn't I just fund your college education?" he said, looking at Maggie reproachfully.

"Yes dear," said Maggie, her face set in an exaggerated pout. Chris simply chuckled.

The next week, Sean and Chris attended the announcement and dedication of the Underground Railroad station in Tahawus. The event attracted a small but enthusiastic crowd of state officials, history buffs, and devotees of abolitionist lore. They both were impressed to find that the state had already built a permanent structure with a locking door to guard the entrance of the underground chamber, while the aged wooden ladder had been replaced by a temporary metal staircase.

As the ceremony progressed and the speakers discussed the significance of the site, both Chris and Sean were relieved to see that they would not be called upon to address the gathering. As a matter fact, Kristi's name was mentioned more than any other, which was justified because she was the first one to find the entryway and descend into the darkness below.

"I'm almost glad that she's not here today," whispered Chris to Sean. "I'm not sure how she would have reacted, having to think back to the place where she had to defend herself against Ben Grainger's onslaught."

"I told you this once before, but maybe you forgot," replied Sean in a muted voice. "That's one tough lady you've got there. And if you want a piece of unsolicited advice from a friend, I wouldn't let her get away."

Chris simply nodded in agreement before turning his attention back to the speaker.

The event extended until late in the afternoon, after which Chris and Sean remained to do an interview with a local newspaper. It was early evening by the time they hit the road for home.

With the formal events out of the way and the thrill of the hunt now gone, both Chris and Sean felt an overwhelming sense of relief that life would now return to normal, and they could get back in touch with their everyday lives. The tension and stress seemed to drain out of their bodies as they headed south, surrounded by all the beauty of the Adirondacks. As if to put a final exclamation point on the day, a gorgeous sunset appeared to the west, which lit up the sky with a vibrant array of reds and yellows, then deepened into purple as the sun descended below the horizon.

Suddenly, Sean turned towards Chris and looked at him with a slightly worried expression. "You don't suppose that Maggie is genuinely upset with me about Tracey, do you?" he asked.

"I don't know," replied Chris, shrugging his shoulders. "Should she be?"

"No, of course not," said Sean. "She's a nineteen year-old college student I hired to help us out, but our paths will never cross again."

"I know that, and you know that," laughed Chris. "But the question is does Maggie know that?"

"She should," said Sean.

"I don't know," chided Chris. "Now that you've got that GPS device back from Grainger's car, she might be able to put it to good use."

"Oh yeah, I forgot about that," said Sean, reaching forward to the glove compartment and pulling out the black box. "It sure was helpful, wasn't it?"

"Yes it was," said Chris as he steered the Jeep down a sandy stretch of road that passed along the waterline of Seventh Lake. "Do you mind if I stop for a moment?"

"No, of course not," said Sean, rolling down his window and breathing in the fresh air with pleasure. The remains of the spectacular sunset had dwindled to a few residual bands of crimson, which painted iridescent streaks across the hills on the far side of the lake.

"I'll miss being up here for a while," said Chris, observing the sights and sounds of the coming night. "I love everything about this land, from the views of the lakes and mountains to the calls of the owls and coyotes."

"And the sounds of the frogs," added Sean.

"Frogs?" repeated Chris, unable to discern the expression on Sean's face in the darkness of the Jeep.

"Yes, frogs," said Sean. "Just listen…"

Chris cocked an ear towards the open window, and within five seconds, he heard the distinct sound of something hitting the lake near the vehicle: "KERPLUNCK!"

"See? There goes one now," said Sean.

"Was that you?" Chris asked, looking at his friend suspiciously.

"Me?" said Sean with a fake indignant voice. "I'm sitting right here next to you!"

Chris looked down into Sean's lap, where he had held the GPS device only a moment ago. Both Sean's hands and his lap were empty.

In the darkness, a smile appeared on Chris' face that rapidly spread from ear to ear.

"You didn't?" asked Chris, looking out at the water.

"I did," answered Sean.

Within moments, the interior of the Jeep reverberated with the sounds of laughter, which reigned unabated until they rounded the next bend in the road and disappeared into the night.

ABOUT THE AUTHOR

Larry Weill has led a career that is as diverse and interesting as the subjects in his books. An avid outdoorsman, he has hiked and climbed extensively throughout the Adirondacks and the Northeast since his days as a Wilderness Park Ranger. He has also worked as a financial planner, a technical writer, a technical trainer for Xerox Corporation, and a career Naval officer.

A self-avowed "people watcher," Weill has a knack for observing and describing the many amusing habits and traits of the people he meets. He is the author of *Excuse Me, Sir...Your Socks are on Fire*, about his days as a Wilderness Park Ranger in the West Canada Lakes Wilderness of New York State. His later books, *Pardon Me, Sir...There's a Moose in Your Tent* and *Forgive Me, Ma'am...Bears Don't Wear Blue*, have entertained a new generation of Adirondack enthusiasts and generated a renewed interest in the concept of wilderness camping in New York's largest state park. *Adirondack Trail of Gold*, Weill's first venture into the genre of historical fiction, has also captivated the audience of Adirondack readers.

Weill lives in Rochester, New York, with his wife and two daughters. They vacation and hike in the Adirondacks annually.